By George R. R. Martin

A SONG OF ICE AND FIRE
Book One: A Game of Thrones
Book Two: A Clash of Kings
Book Three: A Storm of Swords
Book Four: A Feast for Crows
Book Five: A Dance with Dragons
Dying of the Light
Windhaven (with Lisa Tuttle)
Fevre Dream
The Armageddon Rag
Dead Man's Hand (with John J. Miller)
Old Mars (with Gardner Dozois)

SHORT STORY COLLECTIONS
Dreamsongs: Volume I
Dreamsongs: Volume II
A Song for Lya and Other Stories
Songs of Stars and Shadows
Sandkings
Songs the Dead Men Sing
Nightflyers
Tuf Voyaging
Portraits of His Children
Quartet

EDITED BY GEORGE R. R. MARTIN
*New Voices in Science Fiction,
    Volumes 1–4*
*The Science Fiction Weight-Loss Book
    (With Isaac Asimov and Martin
    Harry Greenberg)*
*The John W. Campbell Awards,
    Volume 5*
Night Visions 3
Wild Cards I–XXII

CO-EDITED WITH GARDNER
DOZOIS
Warrior I and II
Songs of the Dying Earth
Songs of Love and Death
Down These Strange Streets

By Gardner Dozois

NOVELS
Strangers
*Nightmare Blue (with George Alec
    Effinger)*
*Hunter's Run (with George R. R. Martin
    and Daniel Abraham)*

SHORT STORY COLLECTIONS
When the Great Days Come
*Strange Days: Fabulous Journeys with
    Gardner Dozois*
Geodesic Dreams
Morning Child and Other Stories
Slow Dancing Through Time
The Visible Man

EDITED BY GARDNER DOZOIS
The Year's Best Science Fiction #1–30
*The New Space Opera (with Jonathan
    Strahan)*
*The New Space Opera 2 (with Jonathan
    Strahan)*
Modern Classics of Science Fiction
Modern Classics of Fantasy
The Good Old Stuff
The Good New Stuff
*The "Magic Tales" series 1–37 (with Jack
    Dann)*
Wizards (with Jack Dann)
The Dragon Book (with Jack Dann)
A Day in the Life
Another World

Old Mars

Old Mars

Edited by GEORGE R. R. MARTIN
and GARDNER DOZOIS

Bantam Books
New York

Copyright © 2013 by George R. R. Martin and Gardner Dozois

Published in the United States of America by
Bantam Books, an imprint of
the Random House Publishing Group,
a division of Random House LLC, New York,
a Penguin Random House Company.

BANTAM BOOKS and the rooster colophon is a registered trademark of Random House LLC.

LIBRARY OF CONGRESS CATALOGING-IN-PUBLICATION DATA

Old Mars / edited by George R. R. Martin and
Gardner Dozois.
pages   cm
A new anthology of all original stories.
ISBN 978-0-345-53727-0
eBook ISBN 978-0-345-53859-8
1. Science fiction, American. 2. Short stories,
American. 3. Science fiction, English. 4. Short stories,
English. I. Martin, George R. R., editor of compilation.
II. Dozois, Gardner R., editor of compilation.
PS648.S3043 2013
813'.087620806—dc23   2013001349

Printed in the United States of America on
acid-free paper.

www.bantamdell.com

10 9 8 7 6 5 4 3 2 1

Book design by Donna Sinisgalli

For Edgar Rice Burroughs,

Leigh Brackett, Catherine Moore,

Ray Bradbury, and Roger Zelazny,

who inspired this book,

and Robert Silverberg,

who should have been in it.

Contents

Introduction
RED PLANET BLUES

BY GEORGE R. R. MARTIN

ONCE UPON A TIME THERE WAS A PLANET CALLED MARS, A world of red sands, canals, and endless adventure. I remember it well, for I went there often as a child.

Born and raised in Bayonne, New Jersey, I came from a blue-collar, working-class background. My family never had much money. We lived in a federal housing project, never owned a car, never went much of anywhere. The projects were on First Street, my school was on Fifth Street, a straight shot up Lord Avenue, and for most of my childhood those five blocks were my world.

It never mattered, though, for I had other worlds. A voracious reader, first of comic books (superheroes, mostly, but some *Classics Illustrated* and Disney stuff as well), then of paperbacks (science fiction, horror, and fantasy, with a seasoning of murder mysteries, adventure yarns, and historicals), I traveled far and wide while hunched down in my favorite chair, turning pages.

I soared among the skyscrapers of Metropolis with Superman, fought bad guys in Gotham City with Batman, swung between the water towers of Manhattan with Spider-Man. I sailed the South Seas with Long John Silver and Robert Louis Stevenson, and swam beneath them with Aquaman and Prince Namor the Submariner. Scrooge McDuck took me to Darkest Africa to search for King Solomon's Mines, and H. Rider Haggard returned me there. I swashed and buckled and fought the Cardinal's men with the Three Musketeers and Dumas Père, sang of the Green Hills of Earth with the blind singer Rhysling and Robert A. Heinlein, trekked across Big Planet with Jack Vance, sped through the Caves of Steel with Isaac

Asimov, and dared the terrors of the Mines of Moria with J. R. R. Tolkien. Books became my passport to Arrakis and Trantor, Minas Tirith and Gormenghast, Oz and Shangri-La, all the lands of myth and fable . . .

. . . and to the planets, moons, and asteroids of our solar system as well. Frozen Pluto (still a planet!), where the sun was just a bright star in the sky. Titan, with Saturn and its rings looming overhead. Mercury, one face turned eternally toward the sun, where life could only survive in the "twilight zone" between day and night. Mighty Jupiter, whose fearsome gravity made its inhabitants stronger than a hundred men. Venus, hidden beneath its shroud of cloud, where web-footed natives (Venusians or Venerians, take your pick) hunted dinosaurs through fetid, steaming swamps.

And Mars.

Growing up, I think I went to Mars more often than I went to New York City, though Manhattan was only forty-five minutes and fifteen cents away by bus. We usually made a Christmas trip to New York, saw the holiday show at Radio City Music Hall, ate in the Horn & Hardart automat in Times Square. That was pretty much all I knew of New York City (yes, I knew of the Empire State Building and the Statue of Liberty, but never visited either one until the seventies, long after I had moved away from New Jersey).

Mars, though . . . I knew Mars inside and out. A desert planet, dry and cold and red (of course), it had seen a thousand civilizations rise and fall. The Martians that remained were a dwindling race, old and wise and mysterious, sometimes malignant, sometimes benevolent, always unknowable. Mars was a land of strange and savage beasts (thoats! Tharks! sandmice!), whispering winds, towering mountains, vast seas of red sand crisscrossed by dry canals, and crumbling porcelain cities where mystery and adventure lurked around every corner.

Mars has always had a certain fascination for us Earthlings. It was one of the *original* planets, the Fab Five of antiquity (along with Mercury, Venus, Jupiter, and Saturn), the "wanderers" who refused to march in step with the stars, but made their own way through the heavens. And Mars was *red,* its color visible even to the naked eyes of the ancients; the color of blood and fire. Small wonder the Romans named it after their god of war. Galileo's observations of Mars through his telescope, Cassini's revelation of the polar ice caps in 1666, and Asaph Hall's discovery of the Martian moons Phobos and Deimos in 1877 only served to make the red planet even more appealing . . . but it was Italian astronomer Giovanni Schiaparelli's announcement that he had observed "canali" on Mars that cinched the deal.

The name Schiaparelli gave the dark lines he saw on the Martian surface actually means "channels," but when reported in English it was rendered as "canals." Channels can be natural; canals are artificial. And 1877 was part of an era when man-made canals were very much in the public consciousness. The Erie Canal, completed in 1825, had played a key role in the westward expansion of America. The Suez Canal had opened in 1869, connecting the Mediterranean to the Indian Ocean. The French would begin work on the Panama Canal just a few years later, in 1881; the Americans would finish it in 1914.

Each had been a massive undertaking, a wonder of modern engineering, and if there were canals on *Mars* . . . well, surely there must be canal builders as well. Surely there must be *Martians.*

Small wonder then that when Herbert George Wells sat down a few years later to write a "scientific romance" of alien invasion called *The War of the Worlds,* he looked to the red planet for his invaders. "Across the gulf of space," Wells wrote, "minds that are to our minds as ours are to those of the beasts that perish, intellects vast and cool and unsympathetic, regarded this earth with envious eyes, and slowly and surely drew their plans against us."

Schiaparelli's observations had awakened the interest of scientists as well as novelists. In particular, they had excited the interest of the American astronomer Percival Lowell. Lowell's new observatory in Flagstaff, Arizona, boasted larger telescopes than Schiaparelli's in Milan, and had less light pollution to contend with as well. Powell trained those telescopes on Mars . . . and saw, not "channels," but *canals*.

Mars became Lowell's passion. For the rest of his life he studied the red planet extensively, finding more every time he looked, drawing extensive, intricate, and detailed maps of the Martian surface, complete with canals, double canals, oases. He published his findings and theories in three enormously popular and influential books: *Mars* (1896), *Mars and Its Canals* (1906), and *Mars as the Abode of Life* (1908), promulgating the theory that the canals, long and straight and obviously artificial, had been built by a Martian race to carry water from the polar ice caps to the vast deserts of their arid planet.

Other astronomers turned their telescopes on Mars as well. Some of them saw Lowell's canals, confirming his findings at least in part. Others saw only Schiaparelli's channels, and put them down as natural features. Some saw nothing at all and insisted all these canals were optical illusions. By and large, the astronomical community remained skeptical of Lowell and his observations . . . but the idea of Martian canals, and the Martian civilization it suggested, had taken firm root in the public consciousness.

Especially in the minds of the storytellers.

H. G. Wells had given the world Martians, but he himself never took us to Mars. That task he left to a (much lesser) writer named Garrett P. Serviss, who published a sort of sequel to *War of the Worlds* called *Edison's Conquest of Mars* in 1898. Though largely (and deservedly) forgotten today, the Serviss novel was widely read and influential in its day, and was the first to carry the reader across the gulf of space to the red planet, with its two moons, windswept deserts, and Schiaparellian canals. But it was a later writer who truly brought that landscape to life, and established the template that would inspire generations of science-fiction writers to come, and thrill and delight thousands upon thousands of readers like myself.

"Normal Bean," he named himself when he sent his story off to the editors at *The All-Story* magazine in 1911. Someone thought that was a typo (it wasn't), and "Under the Moons of Mars" was bylined "Norman Bean" when it began its serial run in February 1912. The writer behind the pseudonym was Edgar Rice Burroughs. The serial would be retitled *A Princess of Mars* when its installments were collected together and republished in book form in 1917. Under that title, it would remain in print for the better part of a century, and give birth to numerous sequels, spin-offs, and imitations.

Barsoom was the name that ERB's Martians (green and red both) gave their dying desert planet. Burroughs took Lowell's notions and ran with them, filling up the red planet with Tharks and thoats and flying boats, with radium rifles and white apes and atmosphere plants, with daring swordsmen and egg-laying princesses clad only in jewels. Though never a great writer, ERB was a master storyteller, and in John Carter and Dejah Thoris he created two characters that generations of readers would come to love and cherish, their popularity eclipsed only by that of his other creation, the jungle lord called Tarzan. Ten more Barsoom novels would follow over the next half century, some featuring John Carter, some other characters . . . but the world that Burroughs had created, his Mars, with all its lands and peoples, would remain the true star of the series, from the first to the last.

Barsoom was his, and his alone. But Percival Lowell's books and theories were out there for all to read, and Otis Adelbert Kline, Stanley G. Weinbaum, C. S. Lewis, Jack Williamson, Edmond Hamilton, and myriad other writers soon joined in with their own takes on Mars and its inhabitants. Though E. E. "Doc" Smith had taken science fiction to the stars with *The Skylark of Space* in 1928, only a few of his fellow scribes ever followed him there. From the twenties to the sixties, most SF writers preferred to remain closer to home, in a solar system teeming with life, where every planet, moon, and asteroid was more exotic than the next.

How many tales were set on Mars during the heyday of the science-fiction pulps? Hundreds, surely. Thousands, probably. Tens of thousands? Maybe. More tales than I can possibly list? Certainly.

Most forgettable and forgotten, to be sure, but every tale, even the least and worst of them, helped to make the red planet a little more familiar, a little more real. The Mars of my childhood was not the invention of H. G. Wells or Percival Lowell or even Edgar Rice Burroughs, as important and influential as they were, but rather an amalgam created by many different writers, each adding their own touches and twists over the years and decades to create a kind of consensus setting, a world that belonged to everyone and no one.

That was my Mars. As it happens, I never read the Burroughs novels when I was a kid (I came to them much much later, when I was in my forties, about three decades too late), but I knew and loved the works that ERB's Barsoom had inspired. My first visits to Mars were in the company of Tom Corbett, Astro, and Roger Manning, the crew of the *Polaris* in the classic series of juvenile (today we would call them YA) space operas derived from Robert A. Heinlein's *Space Cadet* by way of the television series *Tom Corbett, Space Cadet*. Heinlein himself took me back to a somewhat different Mars in another of his Scribners' juveniles, *Red Planet*. I learned about ferocious Martian sandmice from Andre Norton and her doppelgänger Andrew North. In the drytowns, I faced "Shambleau" with C. L. Moore and Northwest Smith. Then came Leigh Brackett and Erik John Stark, another of the great space-opera heroes. Later, a little older, I encountered *The Martian Chronicles,* and a very different take on Old Mars from the pen of Ray Bradbury, elegiac rather than adventurous, but just as magical, just as memorable.

Roger Zelazny's haunting, poetic "A Rose for Ecclesiastes" was probably the last great story of The Mars That Was. First published in the November 1963 issue of *The Magazine of Fantasy & Science Fiction*, the Zelazny story became an instant classic. (Zelazny also wrote the last great story of Old Venus, the Nebula Award–winning "The Doors of His Face, the Lamps of His Mouth.")

By the time I encountered the works of Bradbury and Zelazny, I was already writing stories of my own. My first efforts were prose superhero stories for the comic-book fanzines of the sixties, but I soon moved on to sword-and-sorcery tales and mysteries and SF, and started dreaming about making a career as a writer. One day, I expected, I would be writing my own Mars stories.

It was not to be. For even as Zelazny was penning his tales of Old Mars and Old Venus, the space race was heating up. I watched every manned launch on our old black-and-white television in our apartment in the projects, certain that I was seeing the dawn of a new age, where all the dreams of science fiction would come true. First came Sputnik, Vanguard, Explorer. Then Mercury, Gemini, Apollo.

Yury Gagarin, Alan Shepard, John Glenn.

And Mariner . . . oh, Mariner . . .

It was Mariner that put an end to the glory days of Old Mars . . . and to its sister planet, Old Venus, wet and watery, with its drowned cities, endless swamps, and web-footed Venusians. Mariner 2 (launched August 1962) was the first successful planetary flyby, reaching Venus after three and a half months of spaceflight. Mariner 4 (November 1964) did the same honors for Mars. Mariner 5 (June 1967) was another Venus probe. Mariner 6 (launched February 1969) and Mariner 7 (launched March 1969) were a Martian double-team. Mariner 8 was lost, but its sister Mariner 9 (May 1971) entered Martian orbit in November of that year, joining Phobos and Deimos to become a third Martian moon, the first artificial satellite of the red planet. Mariner 10, the last of the series, cruised by not only Venus, but Mercury as well . . . demonstrating that the innermost planet did not, in fact, keep one face perpetually turned toward the sun, as had been previously believed.

And all of that would have been tremendously exciting, only . . .

The Mars that NASA discovered was not the Mars of Percival Lowell and Edgar Rice Burroughs, of Leigh Brackett and C. L. Moore. The Mariner probes found no trace of cities, living, dead, or dying. No Tharks, no thoats, no Martians of any hue or color. Lowell's network of artificial canals was not in evidence, and neither was Schiaparelli's "channels." Instead, there were craters; the real Mars resembled Luna much more than it did Barsoom. And Venus . . . beneath those clouds, instead of swamps and dinosaurs and web-footed Venerians, Venus was a toxic hell, volcanic, sulfuric, far too hot for humans to survive.

Mariner's findings thrilled scientists around the world and gave us a detailed and accurate picture of the nature of the inner planets, but for the readers and writers of science fiction like me, the excitement was mingled with disillusionment and dismay. This was not the Mars we wanted. This was not the Venus of our dreams.

I never wrote that Mars story. Nor any stories on Venus, or Mercury, or any of the worlds of the "lost" solar system of my youth, the worlds that had provided the setting for so many wonderful tales during the thirties, forties, and fifties. In that I was not alone. After Mariner, our genre moved to the stars in a big way, searching for the colorful exotic settings and alien races that could no longer be found here "at home."

Science fiction did not entirely abandon Mars as a subject after the Mariner probes. The occasional story and novel continued to be written. But these new tales were set upon the "new Mars," the real Mars, Mariner's Mars . . . where canals, dead cities, sandmice, and Martians were conspicuously absent. Kim Stanley Robinson's award-winning trilogy about the colonization and terraforming of the fourth planet—*Red Mars, Green Mars,* and *Blue Mars*—was the most ambitious and memorable of those, and a worthy effort it was.

Overall, though, the number of science-fiction stories set on Mars and its sister planets declined sharply after Mariner, for understandable reasons. The real Mars was simply not as *interesting* as its pulp predecessor. Airless, lifeless, dead, the planet the Mariner probes showed us could not plausibly support either the swashbuckling interplanetary romances of Burroughs, Brackett, and Moore, nor the evocative, elegiac fables of Bradbury and Zelazny. Post-Mariner, when we talked about the possibility of life on Mars, we were talking about microbes or maybe lichen (though even lichen seemed to be pushing it), not sandmice and thoats. And while the discovery of Martian life would no doubt be electrifying to biologists and space scientists around the world, there's never been a microbe with the appeal of Dejah Thoris.

And so the lichens triumphed. Dejah Thoris and all her fellow Martians were banished to the outer darkness and the backlist, never to be seen again . . . not even in the movies. When Steven Spielberg filmed his adaptation of *The War of the Worlds* in 2004, the invaders were no longer Martians, as they had been in the Wells novel and the Orson Welles radio broadcast and the *Classics Illustrated* comic book and the 1953 George Pal film, but rather aliens of undetermined origin. Spielberg's invaders came to Earth in lightning bolts (!), rather than cylinders fired across the gulfs of space by intelligences vast and cool and unsympathetic. I was not the only one who missed the Martians . . .

Which brings us, at long last, to *Old Mars,* the anthology you hold in your hands, a collection of fifteen brand-new stories about Old Mars, lost Mars, the Mars of the canals and the dead cities and the Martians. With a few very notable exceptions, the contributors to this volume began their careers after Mariner. Like me, they grew up reading about Old Mars but never had the chance to write about it. That Mars was a lost world, gone forever.

Or maybe not.

Yes, the Mars of Percival Lowell and Norman Bean and Leigh Brackett and C. L. Moore and Ray Bradbury does not exist, but why should that mean we cannot write about it? Science fiction is and always has been part of a great romantic tradition in literature, and romance has never been about realism.

Western writers still write stories about an Old West that never actually existed in the way it is depicted; "realistic Westerns" that focus on farmers instead of gunslingers don't sell nearly as well. Mystery writers continue to write tales of private eyes solving murders and catching serial killers, whereas real-life PIs spend most of their time investigating bogus insurance claims and photographing adulterers in sleazy motels for the benefit of divorce lawyers. Historical novelists produce stories set in ancient realms that no longer exist, about which we often know little and less, and fantasy writers publish stories set in lands that never did exist at all. And as no less an SF luminary than John W. Campbell Jr. himself observed, in the final analysis, science fiction is actually a subset of fantasy.

Purists and fans of "hard SF" and other people with sticks up their butts may howl that these stories are not "real science fiction." So be it. Call them "space opera," or "space fantasy," or "retro-sf," or "skiffy," any term you like. Me, I call them "stories," and like all stories, they are rooted in the imagination. When you come right down to it, I don't think "real" matters nearly as much as "cool."

Mariner could not find Old Mars. But you can.

Just turn the page.

—*George R. R. Martin*
August 2012

Old Mars

ALLEN M. STEELE

Allen Steele made his first sale to *Asimov's Science Fiction* magazine in 1988, soon following it up with a long string of other sales to *Asimov's,* as well as to markets such as *Analog, The Magazine of Fantasy & Science Fiction,* and *Science Fiction Age.* In 1990, he published his critically acclaimed first novel, *Orbital Decay,* which subsequently won the Locus Poll as Best First Novel of the year, and soon Steele was being compared to Golden Age Heinlein by no less an authority than Gregory Benford. His other books include the novels *Clarke County, Space; Lunar Descent; Labyrinth of Night; The Weight; The Tranquility Alternative; A King of Infinite Space; OceanSpace; ChronoSpace; Coyote; Coyote Rising; Coyote Frontier; Spindrift; Galaxy Blues; Coyote Horizon;* and *Coyote Destiny.* His short work has been gathered in five collections, *Rude Astronauts, All-American Alien Boy, Sex and Violence in Zero-G, American Beauty,* and *The Last Science Fiction Writer.* His most recent books are a new novel in the Coyote sequence, *Hex,* and a YA novel, *Apollo's Outcasts.* He won the Robert A. Heinlein Award in 2013, as well as three Hugo Awards, in 1996 for his novella "The Death of Captain Future," in 1998 for his novella "Where Angels Fear to Tread," and, most recently, in 2011 for his novelette "The Emperor of Mars." Born in Nashville, Tennessee, he has worked for a variety of newspapers and magazines, covering science and business assignments, and is now a full-time writer living in Whately, Massachusetts, with his wife, Linda.

Here he takes us to a Mars very different from the Mars of his Hugo-winning novelette, the Old Mars of ancient dreams, and deep into the Martian Badlands, on a mission that could plunge two races, and two worlds, into all-out war.

Martian Blood

ALLEN M. STEELE

THE MOST DANGEROUS MAN ON MARS WAS OMAR AL-BAZ, AND
the first time I saw him, he was throwing up at the Rio Zephyria
spaceport.

This happens more frequently than you might think. People
coming here for the first time often don't realize just how thin the
air really is. The cold surprises them, too, but I'm told the atmospheric pressure is about the same as you'd find in the Himalayas.
So they come trooping down the ramp of the shuttle that transported
them from Deimos Station, and if the ride down didn't make them
puke, then the shortness of breath, headaches, and nausea that
comes with altitude sickness will.

I didn't know for sure that the middle-aged gent who'd doubled
over and vomited was Dr. al-Baz, but I suspected that he was; I hadn't
seen any other Middle Eastern men on his flight. There was nothing
I could do for him, though, so I waited patiently on the other side of
the chain-link security fence while one of the flight attendants came
down the ramp to help him. Dr. al-Baz waved her away; he didn't
need any assistance, thank you. He straightened up, pulled a handkerchief from his overcoat pocket, and wiped his mouth, then picked
up the handle of the rolling bag he'd dropped when his stomach re-
volted. Nice to know that he wasn't entirely helpless.

He was one of the last passengers to step through the gate. He
paused on the other side of the fence, looked around, and spotted the
cardboard sign I was holding. A brief smile of relief, then he walked
over to me.

"I'm Omar al-Baz," he said, holding out his hand. "You must be
Mr. Ramsey."

"Yes, I'm your guide. Call me Jim." Not wanting to shake a hand that just wiped a mouth, which had just spilled yuck all over nice clean concrete, I reached forward to relieve him of his bag.

"I can carry this myself, thank you," he said, not letting me take his bag from him. "But if you could help me with the rest of my luggage, I'd appreciate it."

"Sure. No problem." He hadn't hired me to be his porter, and if he'd been the jerk variety of tourist some of my former clients had been, I would've made him carry his own stuff. But I was already beginning to like the guy: early fifties, skinny but with the beginnings of a potbelly, coarse black hair going grey at the temples. He wore round spectacles and had a bushy mustache beneath a hooked, aquiline nose, and looked a little like an Arab Groucho Marx. Omar al-Baz couldn't have been anything but what he was, an Egyptian-American professor from the University of Arizona.

I led him toward the terminal, stepping around the tourists and business travelers who had also disembarked from the 3 p.m. shuttle. "Are you by yourself, or did someone come with you?"

"Unfortunately, I come alone. The university provided grant money sufficient for only one fare, even though I requested that I bring a grad student as an assistant." He frowned. "This may hinder my work, but I hope that what I intend to do will be simple enough that I may accomplish it on my own."

I had only the vaguest idea of why he'd hired me to be his guide, but the noise and bustle of the terminal were too much for a conversation. Passenger bags were beginning to come down the conveyor belt, but Dr. al-Baz didn't join the crowd waiting to pick up suitcases and duffel bags. Instead, he went straight to the PanMars cargo window, where he presented a handful of receipts to the clerk. I began to regret my offer to help carry his bags when a cart was pushed through a side door. Stacked upon it were a half dozen aluminum cases; even in Martian gravity, none small enough to be carried two at a time.

"You gotta be kidding," I murmured.

"My apologies, but for the work I need to do, I had to bring specialized equipment." He signed a form, then turned to me again. "Now . . . do you have a means of taking all this to my hotel, or will I have to get a cab?"

I looked over the stack of cases and decided that there weren't so many that I couldn't fit them all in the back of my jeep. So we pushed the cart out to where I'd parked beside the front entrance and managed to get everything tied down with elastic cords I carried with me. Dr. al-Baz climbed into the passenger seat and put his suitcase on the floor between his feet.

"Hotel first?" I asked as I took my place behind the wheel.

"Yes, please . . . and then I wouldn't mind getting a drink." He caught the questioning look in my eye and gave me a knowing smile. "No, I am not a devout follower of the Prophet."

"Glad to hear it." I was liking him better all the time; I don't trust people who won't have a beer with me. I started up the jeep and pulled away from the curb. "So . . . you said in your e-mail you'd like to visit an aboriginal settlement. Is that still what you want to do?"

"Yes, I do." He hesitated. "But now that we've met, I think it's only fair to tell you that this is not all that I mean to do. The trip here involves more than just meeting the natives."

"How so? What else do you want?"

He peered at me over the top of his glasses. "The blood of a Martian."

When I was a kid, one of my favorite movies was *The War of the Worlds*—the 1953 version, made about twelve years before the first probes went to Mars. Even back then, people knew that Mars had an Earth-like environment; spectroscopes had revealed the presence of an oxygen-nitrogen atmosphere, and strong telescopes made visible the seas and canals. But no one knew for sure whether the planet was inhabited until Ares I landed there in 1977, so George Pal had a lot of latitude when he and his film crew tried to imagine what a Martian would look like.

Anyway, there's a scene in the movie where Gene Barry and Ann Robinson have made their way to L.A. after escaping the collapsed farmhouse where they'd been pinned down by the alien invaders. Barry meets with his fellow scientists at the Pacific Tech and presents them with a ruined camera-eye he managed to grab while fighting off the attackers. The camera-eye is wrapped in Ann Robinson's scarf, which was splattered with gore when Gene clobbered a little green monster with a broken pipe.

"And this"—he says melodramatically, showing the scarf to the other scientists—"blood of a Martian!"

I've always loved that part. So when Dr. al-Baz said much the same thing, I wondered if he was being clever, copping a line from a classic movie that he figured most colonists might have seen. But there was no wink, no ironic smile. So far as I could tell, he was as serious as he could be.

I decided to let it wait until we had that drink together, so I held my tongue as I drove him into Rio Zephyria. The professor's reservation was at the John Carter Casino Resort, located on the strip near the Mare Cimmerium beach. No surprise there: It's the most famous hotel in Rio, so most tourists try to book rooms there. Edgar Rice Burroughs was having a literary renaissance around the time it was built, so someone decided that *A Princess of Mars* and its sequels would be a great theme for a casino. Since then it's become the place most people think of when they daydream about taking a vacation trip to Mars.

Good for them, but I want to throw a rock through its gold-tinted windows every time I drive by. It's a ten-story monument to every stupid thing humans have done since coming here. And if I feel that way, as someone who was born and raised on Mars, then you can well imagine what the *shatan* think of it . . . when they come close enough to see it, that is.

It was hard to gauge Dr. al-Baz's reaction when we pulled up in front of the hotel lobby. I was beginning to learn that his normal expression was stoical. But as a bellhop was unloading his stuff and putting it on a cart, the professor spotted the casino entrance. The doorman was dark-skinned and a little more than two meters in height; he wore the burnoose robes of an aborigine, with a saber in the scabbard on his belt.

Dr. al-Baz stared at him. "That's not a Martian, is he?"

"Not unless he used to play center for the Blue Devils." Dr. al-Baz raised an eyebrow, and I smiled. "That's Tito Jones, star of the Duke basketball team . . . or at least until he came here." I shook my head. "Poor guy. He didn't know why the casino hired him to be their celebrity greeter until they put him in that outfit."

Dr. al-Baz had already lost interest. "I was hoping he might be a Martian," he said softly. "It would have made things easier."

"They wouldn't be caught dead here . . . or anywhere near the colonies, for that matter." I turned to follow the bellhop through the revolving door. "And by the way . . . we don't call them 'Martians.' 'Aborigines' is the preferred term."

"I'll keep that in mind. And what do the Mar . . . the aborigines call themselves?"

"They call themselves *shatan* . . . which means 'people' in their language." Before he could ask the obvious next question, I added, "Their word for us is *nashatan,* or 'not-people,' but that's only when they're being polite. They call us a lot of things, most of them pretty nasty."

The professor nodded and was quiet for a little while.

The University of Arizona might not have sprung for a grad student's marsliner ticket, but they made up for it by reserving a two-room suite. After the bellhop unloaded his cart and left, Dr. al-Baz explained that he'd need the main room—a large parlor complete with a bar—for the temporary lab he intended to set up. He didn't unpack right away, though; he was ready for that drink I'd promised him. So we left everything in the room and caught the elevator back downstairs.

The hotel bar is located in the casino, but I didn't want to drink in a place where the bartender is decked out like a Barsoomian warlord and the waitresses are dolled up as princesses of Helium. The John Carter is the only place on Mars where anyone looks like that; no one in their right mind would wear so few clothes outside, not even in the middle of summer. So we returned to the jeep and I got away from the strip, heading into the old part of town that the tourists seldom visit.

There's a good watering hole about three blocks from my apartment. It was still late afternoon, so the place wasn't crowded yet. The bar was quiet and dark, perfect for conversation. The owner knew me; he brought over a pitcher of ale as soon as the professor and I sat down at a table in the back.

"Take it easy with this," I told Dr. al-Baz as I poured beer into a tallneck and pushed it across the table to him. "Until you get acclimated, it might hit you pretty hard."

"I'll take your advice." The professor took a tentative sip and smiled. "Good. Better than I was expecting, in fact. Local?"

"Hellas City Amber. You think we'd have beer shipped all the way from Earth?" There were more important things we needed to discuss, so I changed the subject. "What's this about wanting blood? When you got in touch with me, all you said was that you wanted me to take you to an aboriginal settlement."

Dr. al-Baz didn't say anything for a moment or so. He toyed with the stem of his glass, rolling it back and forth between his fingers. "If I'd told you the entire truth," he finally admitted, "I was afraid you might not agree to take me. And you come very highly recommended. As I understand, you're not only native-born, but your parents were among the first settlers."

"I'm surprised you know that. You must have talked to a former client."

"Do you remember Ian Horner? Anthropologist from Cambridge University?" I did indeed, although not kindly; Dr. Horner had hired me to be his guide, but if you'd believed everything he said, he knew more about Mars than I did. I nodded, keeping my opinion to myself. "He's a friend of mine," Dr. al-Baz continued, "or at least someone with whom I've been in contact on a professional basis."

"So you're another anthropologist."

"No." He sipped his beer. "Research biologist . . . astrobiology, to be exact. The study of extraterrestrial forms of life. Until now, most of my work has involved studying Venus, so this is the first time I've been to Mars. Of course, Venus is different. Its global ocean is quite interesting, but . . . ."

"Professor, I don't want to be rude, but do you want to get down to it and tell me why you want the blood of a"—damn, he almost got me to say it!—"an aborigine?"

Sitting back in his chair, Dr. al-Baz folded his hands together on the tabletop. "Mr. Ramsey . . ."

"Jim."

"Jim, are you familiar with the panspermia hypothesis? The idea that life on Earth may have extraterrestrial origins, that it may have come from somewhere in outer space?"

"No, I've never heard that . . . but I guess that when you say 'somewhere,' you mean here."

"That is correct. I mean Mars." He tapped a finger firmly against the table. "Have you ever wondered why there's such a close resemblance between humans and Martian aborigines? Why the two races look so much alike even though they're from worlds over seventy million kilometers apart?"

"Parallel evolution."

"Yes, I expect that's what you've learned in school. The conventional explanation is that, because both planets have similar environments, evolution took approximately the same course on both worlds, the differences being that Martians . . . aborigines, sorry . . . are taller because of lower surface gravity, have higher metabolisms because of colder temperature, have significantly darker skin because of the thinner ozone layer, and so forth and so on. This has been the prevalent theory because it's the only one that seems to fit the facts."

"That's what I've heard, yeah."

"Well, my friend, everything you've known is wrong." He immediately shook his head, as if embarrassed by his momentary burst of arrogance. "I'm sorry. I don't mean to sound overbearing. However, several of my colleagues and I believe that the similarities between *Homo sapiens* and *Homo artesian* cannot be attributed to evolution alone. We think there may be a genetic link between the two races, that life on Earth . . . human life in particular . . . may have originated on Mars."

Dr. al-Baz paused, allowing a moment to let his words sink in. They did, all right; I was beginning to wonder if he was a kook. "Okay," I said, trying not to smile, "I'll bite. What leads you to think that?"

The professor raised a finger. "First, the geological composition of quite a few meteorites found on Earth is identical to those of rock samples brought from Mars. So there's a theory that, sometime in the distant past, there was a cataclysmic explosion on the Martian surface . . . possibly the eruption of Mt. Daedalia or one of the other volcanoes in the Albus range . . . which ejected debris into space. This debris traveled as meteors to Earth, which was also in its infancy. Those meteors may have contained organic molecules that seeded Earth with life where it hadn't previously existed."

He held up another finger. "Second . . . when the human genome was sequenced, one of the most surprising finds was the existence of DNA strands that have no apparent purpose. They're like parts of a machine that don't have any function. There's no reason for them to be there, yet nonetheless they are. Therefore, is it possible that these phantom strands may be genetic biomarkers left behind by organic material brought to Earth from Mars?"

"So that's why you want a blood sample? To see if there's a link?"

He nodded. "I have brought equipment that will enable me to sequence, at least partially, the genetic code of an aborigine blood sample and compare it to that of a human. If the native genome has nonfunctional archaic strands that match the ones found in the human genome, then we'll have evidence that the hypothesis is correct . . . life on Earth originated on Mars, and the two races are genetically linked."

I didn't say anything for a few seconds. Dr. al-Baz didn't sound quite as crazy as he had a couple of minutes earlier. As far-fetched as it might seem, what he said made sense. And if the hypothesis was true, then the implications were staggering: The *shatan* were close cousins to the inhabitants of Earth, not simply a primitive race that we'd happened to find when we came to Mars.

Not that I was ready to believe it. I'd met too many *shatan* to ever be willing to accept the idea that they had anything in common with my people. Or at least so I thought . . .

"Okay, I get what you're doing." I picked up my glass and took a long drink. "But let me tell you, getting that blood sample won't be easy."

"I know. I understand the aborigines are rather reclusive . . ."

"Now, *that's* an understatement." I put down my glass again. "They've never wanted much to do with us. The Ares 1 expedition had been here for almost three weeks before anyone caught sight of them, and another month before there was any significant contact. It took years for us to even learn their language, and things only got worse when we started establishing colonies. Wherever we've gone, the *shatan* have moved out, packing up everything they owned, even burning their villages so that we couldn't explore their dwellings. They've become nomads since then. No trade, and not much in the way of cultural exchange . . ."

"So no one has ever managed to get anything from them on which they may have left organic material? No hair samples, no saliva, no skin?"

"No. They've never allowed us to collect any artifacts from them, and they're reluctant to even let us touch them. That outfit you saw Tito Jones wearing? It's not the real thing . . . just a costume based on some pictures someone took of them."

"But we've learned their language."

"Just a little of one of their dialects . . . pidgin *shatan,* you might call it." I absently ran a finger around the rim of my glass. "If you're counting on me to be your native interpreter . . . well, don't expect much. I know enough to get by, and that's about it. I may be able to keep them from chucking a spear at us, but that's all."

He raised an eyebrow. "Are they dangerous?"

"Not so long as you mind your manners. They can be . . . well, kinda aggressive . . . if you cross the line with them." I didn't want to tell him some of the worst stories—I'd scared off other clients that way—so I tried to reassure him. "I've met some of the local tribesmen, so they know me well enough to let me visit their lands. But I'm not sure how much they trust me." I hesitated. "Dr. Horner didn't get very far with them. I'm sure he's told you that they wouldn't let him into their village."

"Yes, he has. To tell the truth, though, Ian has always been something of an ass"—I laughed out loud when he said this, and he gave me a quick smile in return—"so I imagine that, so long as I approach them with a measure of humility, I may have more success than he did."

"You might." Ian Horner had come to Mars with the attitude of a British army officer visiting colonial India, a condescending air of superiority that the *shatan* picked up on almost immediately. He learned little as a result and had come away referring to the "abos" as "cheeky bahstahds." No doubt the aborigines felt much the same way about him . . . but at least they'd let him live.

"So you'll take me out there? To one of their villages, I mean?"

"That's why you hired me, so . . . yeah, sure." I picked up my beer again. "The nearest village is about 150 kilometers southeast of here, in a desert oasis near the Laestrygon canal. It'll take a couple of days to get there. I hope you brought warm clothes and hiking boots."

"I brought a parka and boots, yes. But you have your jeep, don't you? Then why are we going to need to walk?"

"We'll drive only until we get near the village. Then we'll have to get out and walk the rest of the way. The *shatan* don't like motorized vehicles. The equatorial desert is pretty rough, so you better prepare for it."

He smiled. "I ask you . . . do I look like someone who's never been in a desert?"

"No . . . but Mars isn't Earth."

I spent the next day preparing for the trip: collecting camping equipment from my rented storage shed, buying food and filling water bottles, putting fresh fuel cells in the jeep and making sure the tires had enough pressure. I made sure that Dr. al-Baz had the right clothing for several days in the outback and gave him the address of a local outfitter if he didn't, but I need not have worried; he clearly wasn't one of those tourists foolish enough to go out into the desert wearing Bermuda shorts and sandals.

When I came to pick him up at the hotel, I was amazed to find that the professor had turned his suite into a laboratory. Two flat-screen computers were set up on the bar, a microscope and a test-tube rack stood on the coffee table, and the TV had been pushed aside to make room for a small centrifuge. More equipment rested on bureaus and side tables; I didn't know what any of it was, but I spotted a radiation symbol on one and a WARNING–LASER sticker on another. He'd covered the carpet with plastic sheets, and there was even a lab coat hanging in the closet. Dr. al-Baz made no mention of any of this; he simply picked up his backpack and camera, put on a slouch cap, and followed me out the door, pausing to slip the Do Not Disturb sign over the knob.

Tourists stared at us as he flung his pack into the back of my jeep; it always seemed to surprise some people that anyone would come to Mars to do something besides drink and lose money at the gaming tables. I started up the jeep, and we roared away from the John Carter, and in fifteen minutes we were on the outskirts of town, driving through the irrigated farmlands surrounding Rio Zephyria. The scarlet pines that line the shores of Mare Cimmerium gradually thinned out as we followed dirt roads usually traveled by farm vehicles and logging trucks, and even those disappeared as we left the colony behind and headed into the trackless desert.

I've been told that the Martian drylands look a lot like the American Southwest, except that everything is red. I've never been to Earth, so I wouldn't know, but if anyone in New Mexico happens to spot a six-legged creature that looks sort of like a shaggy cow or a raptor that resembles a pterodactyl and sounds like a hyena, please drop me a line. And stay away from those pits that look a little like golf-course sand traps; there's something lurking within them that would eat you alive, one limb at a time.

As the jeep wove its way through the desert, dodging boulders and bouncing over small rocks, Dr. al-Baz clung to the roll bars, fascinated by the wilderness opening before us. This was one of the things that made my job worthwhile, seeing familiar places through the eyes of someone who'd never been there before. I pointed out a Martian hare as it loped away from us, and stopped for a second to let him take pictures of a flock of *stakhas* as they wheeled high above us, shrieking their dismay at our intrusion.

About seventy kilometers southeast of Rio, we came upon the Laestrygon canal, running almost due south from the sea. When Percival Lowell first spotted the Martian canals through his observatory telescope, he thought they were excavated waterways. He was half-right; the *shatan* had rerouted existing rivers, diverting them so that they'd go where the aborigines wanted. The fact that they'd done this with the simple, muscle-driven machines never failed to amaze anyone who saw them, but Earth people tend to underestimate the *shatan*. They're primitive, but not stupid.

We followed the canal, keeping far away from it so that we couldn't be easily spotted from the decks of any *shatan* boats that might be this far north. I didn't want any aborigines to see us before we reached the village; they might pass the word that humans were coming and give their chieftain a chance to order his people to pack up and move out. We saw no one, though; the only sign of habitation was a skinny wooden suspension bridge that spanned the channel like an enormous bow, and even that didn't appear to be frequently used.

By late afternoon, we'd entered hill country. Flat-topped mesas rose around us, with massive stone pinnacles jutting upward between them; the jagged peaks of distant mountains lay just beyond the horizon. I drove until it was nearly dusk, then pulled up behind a hoodoo and stopped for the night.

Dr. al-Baz pitched a tent while I collected dead scrub brush. Once I had a fire going, I suspended a cookpot above the embers, then emptied a can of stew into it. The professor had thought to buy a couple of bottles of red wine before we left town; we opened one for dinner and worked our way through it after we ate.

"So tell me something," Dr. al-Baz said once we'd scrubbed down the pot, plates, and spoons. "Why did you become a guide?"

"You mean, rather than getting a job as a blackjack dealer?" I propped the cookware up against a boulder. A stiff breeze was coming out of the west; the sand it carried would scour away the remaining grub. "Never really thought about it, to be honest. My folks are first-generation settlers, so I was born and raised here. I started prowling the desert as soon as I was old enough to go out alone, so . . ."

"That's just it." The professor moved a little closer to the fire, holding out his hands to warm them. Now that the sun was down, a cold night was ahead; we could already see our breath by the firelight. "Most of the colonists I've met seem content to stay in the city. When I told them that I was planning a trip into the desert, they all looked at me like I was mad. Someone even suggested that I buy a gun and take out extra life insurance."

"Whoever told you to buy a gun doesn't know a thing about the *shatan.* They never attack unless provoked, and the surest way to upset them is to approach one of their villages with a gun." I patted the utility knife on my belt. "This is the closest I come to carrying a weapon when there's even a possibility that I might run into ab-origines. One reason why I'm on good terms with them . . . I mind my manners."

"Most people here haven't even seen an aborigine, I think."

"You're right, they haven't. Rio Zephyria is the biggest colony because of tourism, but most permanent residents prefer to live where there are flush toilets and cable TV." I sat down on the other side of the fire. "They can have it. The only reason I live there is be-cause that's where the tourists are. If it wasn't for that, I'd have a place out in the boonies and hit town only when I need to stock up on supplies."

"I see." Dr. al-Baz picked up his tin cup and mine and poured some wine into each. "Forgive me if I'm wrong," he said as he handed my cup to me, "but it doesn't sound as if you very much approve of your fellow colonists."

"I don't." I took a sip and put the cup down beside me; I didn't want to get a headful of wine the night before I was going to have to deal with *shatan* tribesmen. "My folks came out here to explore a new world, but everyone who's come *after* those original settlers . . . well, you saw Rio. You know what it's like. We're building hotels and casinos and shopping centers, and introducing invasive species into our farms and dumping our sewage into the channels, and every few weeks during conjunction another ship brings in more people who think Mars is like Las Vegas only without as many hookers . . . not that we don't have plenty of those, too."

As I spoke, I craned my neck to look up at the night sky. The major constellations gleamed brightly: Ursa Major, Draco, Cygnus, with Denes as the north star. You can't see the Milky Way very well in the city; you have to go out into the desert to get a decent view of the Martian night sky. "So who can blame the *shatan* for not wanting to have anything to do with us? They knew the score as soon as we showed up." Recalling a thought I'd had the day before, I chuckled to myself. "The old movies got it wrong. Mars didn't invade Earth . . . Earth invaded Mars."

"I didn't realize there was so much resentment on your part."

He sounded like his feelings were wounded. That was no way to treat a paying customer.

"No, no . . . it's not you," I quickly added. "I don't think you'd be caught dead at a poker table."

He laughed out loud. "No, I don't think the university would look very kindly upon me if my expense report included poker chips."

"Glad to hear it." I hesitated, then went on. "Just do me a favor, will you? If you find something here that might . . . I dunno . . . make things worse, would you consider keeping it to yourself? Humans have done enough stupid things here already. We don't need to do anything more."

"I'll try to remember that," Dr. al-Baz said.

The next day, we found the *shatan*. Or rather, they found us.

We broke camp and continued following the Laestrygon as it flowed south through the desert hills. I'd been watching the jeep's odometer the entire trip, and when we were about fifty kilometers from where I remembered the aborigine settlements being, I began driving along the canal banks. I told Dr. al-Baz to keep a sharp eye out for any signs of habitation—trails, or perhaps abandoned camps left behind by hunting parties—but what we found was a lot more obvious: another suspension bridge, and passing beneath it, a *shatan* boat.

The canal boat was a slender catamaran about ten meters long, with broad white sails catching the desert wind and a small cabin at its stern. The figures moving along its decks didn't notice us until one of them spotted the jeep. He let out a warbling cry— "*wallawallawalla!*"—and the others stopped what they were doing to gaze in the direction he was pointing. Then another *shatan* standing atop the cabin yelled something and everyone turned to dash into the cabin, with their captain disappearing through a hatch in its ceiling. Within seconds, the catamaran became a ghost ship.

"Wow." Dr. al-Baz was both astounded and disappointed. "They really don't want to see us, do they?"

"Actually, they don't want us to see *them*." He looked at me askance, not understanding the difference. "They believe that, if they can't be seen, then they've disappeared from the world. This way, they're hoping that, so far as we're concerned, they've ceased to exist." I shrugged. "Kind of logical, if you think about it."

There was no point in trying to persuade the crew to emerge from hiding, so we left the boat behind and continued our drive down the canal bank. But the catamaran had barely disappeared from sight when we heard a hollow roar from behind us, like a bullhorn being blown. The sound echoed off the nearby mesas; two more prolonged blasts, then the horn went silent.

"If there are any more *shatan* around, they'll hear that and know we're coming," I said. "They'll repeat the same signal with their own horns, and so on, until the signal reaches the village."

"So they know we're here," Dr. al-Baz said. "Will they hide like the others?"

"Maybe. Maybe not." I shrugged. "It's up to them."

For a long time, we didn't spot anyone or anything. We were about eight kilometers from the village when we came upon another bridge. This time, we saw two figures standing near the foot of the bridge. They appeared unusually tall even for aborigines, but it wasn't until we got closer that we saw why: each of them rode a *hattas*—an enormous buffalo-like creature with six legs and an elongated neck that the natives tamed as pack animals. It wasn't what they were riding that caught my attention, though, so much as the long spears they carried, or the heavy animal-hide outfits they wore.

"Uh-oh," I said quietly. "That's not good."

"What's not good?"

"I was hoping we'd run into hunters . . . but these guys are warriors. They can be a little . . . um, intense. Keep your hands in sight and never look away from them."

I halted the jeep about twenty feet from them. We climbed out and slowly walked toward them, hands at our sides. As we got closer, the warriors dismounted from their animals; they didn't approach us, though, but instead waited in silence.

When the owners of the John Carter hired a basketball star to masquerade as a *shatan,* they were trying to find someone who might pass as a Martian aborigine. Tito Jones was the best they could get, but he wasn't quite right. The *shatan* standing before us were taller; their skin was as dark as the sky at midnight, their long, silky hair the color of rust, yet their faces had fine-boned features reminiscent of someone of northern European descent. They were swathed in dusty, off-white robes that made them look vaguely Bedouin, and the hands that gripped their spears were larger than a human's, with long-nailed fingers and tendons that stood out from wrists.

Unblinking golden eyes studied us as we approached. When we'd come close enough, both warriors firmly planted their spears on the ground before us. I told Dr. al-Baz to stop, but I didn't have to remind him not to look away from them. He stared at the *shatan* with awestruck curiosity, a scientist observing his subject up close for the first time.

I raised both hands, palms out, and said, *"Issah tas sobbata shatan"* (Greetings, honored *shatan* warriors). *"Seyta nashatan habbalah sa shatan heysa"* (Please allow us human travelers to enter your land).

The warrior on the left replied, *"Katas nashatan Hamsey. Sakey shatan habbalah fah?"* (We know you, human Ramsey. Why have you returned to our land?)

I wasn't surprised to have been recognized. Only a handful of humans spoke their language—albeit not very well; I probably sounded like a child to them—or knew the way to their village. I may not have met these particular warriors before, but they'd doubt-less heard of me. And I tried not to smile at the mispronunciation of my name; the *shatan* have trouble rolling the "r" sound off their tongues.

"(I've brought a guest who wishes to learn more about your peo-ple)," I replied, still speaking the local dialect. I extended a hand to-ward the professor. "(Allow me to introduce you to Omar al-Baz. He is a wise man in search of knowledge.)" I avoided calling him "doc-tor"; that word has a specific meaning in their language, as someone who practices medicine.

"(Humans don't want to know anything about us. All they want to do is take what doesn't belong to them and ruin it.)"

I shook my head; oddly, that particular gesture means the same thing for both *shatan* and *nashatan*. "(This is not true. Many of my people do, yes, but not all. On his own world, al-Baz is a teacher. Whatever he learns from you, he will tell us students, and therefore increase their knowledge of your people.)"

"What are you saying?" Dr. al-Baz whispered. "I recognize my name, but . . ."

"Hush. Let me finish." I continued speaking the native tongue. "(Will you please escort us to your village? My companion wishes to beg a favor of your chieftain.)"

The other warrior stepped forward, walking toward the profes-sor until he stood directly before him. The *shatan* towered above Dr. al-Baz; everything about him was menacing, yet the professor held his ground, saying nothing but continuing to look the *shatan* straight in the eye. The warrior silently regarded him for several long mo-ments, then looked at me.

"(What does he want from our chieftain? Tell us, and we will decide whether we will allow you to enter our village.)"

I hesitated, then shook my head again. "(No. His question is for the chieftain alone.)"

I was taking a gamble. Refusing a demand from a *shatan* warrior guarding his homeland was not a great way to make friends. But it was entirely possible that the warriors would misunderstand me if I told them that Dr. al-Baz wanted to take some of their blood; they might think his intent was hostile. The best thing to do was have the professor ask the chieftain directly for permission to take a blood sample from one of his people.

The *shatan* stared at us for a moment without saying anything, then turned away and walked off a few feet to quietly confer with each other. "What's going on?" the professor asked, keeping his voice low. "What did you tell them?"

I gave him the gist of the conversation, including the risky thing I'd just said. "I figure it can go one of three ways. One, they kick the matter upstairs to the chieftain, which means that you get your wish if you play your cards right. Two, they tell us to get lost. If that happens, we turn around and go home, and that's that."

"Unacceptable. I've come too far to go away empty-handed. What's the third option?"

"They impale us with their spears, wait for us to die, then chop up our bodies and scatter our remains for the animals to find." I let that sink in. "Except our heads," I added. "Someone will carry those back to the city in the middle of the night, where they'll dump them on the doorstep of the nearest available house."

"Please tell me you're joking."

I didn't. The professor was scared enough already, and he didn't need any stories about what had happened to explorers who'd crossed the line with the *shatan*, or the occasional fool stupid enough to venture onto aboriginal territory without someone like me escorting them. I hadn't exaggerated anything, though, and he seemed to realize that, for he simply nodded and looked away.

The *shatan* finished their discussion. Not looking at us, they walked back to their *hattases* and climbed atop them again. For a moment, I thought that they were taking the second option, but then they guided their mounts toward Dr. al-Baz and me.

"*Hessah*," one of them said (Come with us).

I let out my breath. We were going to meet the village chieftain.

———

The village was different from the last time I'd seen it. Since the *shatan* became nomads, their settlements are usually tent cities, which can be taken down, packed up, and relocated when necessary. This one had been there for quite a while, though; apparently the inhabitants had decided that they'd stay at the oasis for some time to come. Low, flat-roofed adobe buildings had taken the place of many of the tents, and scaffolds surrounded a stone wall being built to enclose them. But if the place had a name, I wasn't aware of it.

Dr. al-Baz and I were footsore and tired by the time we reached the village. As expected, the warriors had insisted that we leave the jeep behind, although they allowed us to retrieve our packs. They'd slowly ridden abreast of us all the way, only reluctantly letting us stop now and then to rest. Neither of them had spoken a word since we'd left the bridge, but when we were within sight of the settlement, one of them raised a whorled shell that looked like a giant ammonite. A long, loud blast from his horn was answered a few seconds later by a similar call from the village. The professor and I exchanged a wary glance. Too late to turn around now; the inhabitants knew we were coming.

The village seemed empty as we entered through a half-built gate and walked down packed-dirt streets. No one to be seen, and the only things that moved were *hattases* tied up to hitching posts. The tent flaps were closed, though, and the narrow windows of the adobe houses were shuttered. No, the place wasn't deserted; it was just that the people who lived there had gone into hiding. The silence was eerie, and even more unsettling than the spears our escorts pointed at our backs.

The village center was a courtyard surrounding an artesian well, with a large adobe building dominating one side of the square. The only *shatan* we'd seen since our arrival peered down at us from a wooden tower atop the building. He waited until we'd reached the building, then raised an ammonite horn of his own and blew a short blast. The warriors halted their *hattases,* dismounted, and silently beckoned for us to follow them. One of them pushed aside the woven blanket that served as the building's only door, and the other warrior led us inside.

The room was dim, its sole illumination a shaft of sunlight slanting down through a hole in the ceiling. The air was thick with musky incense that drifted in hazy layers through the light and made my eyes water. Robed *shatan* stood around the room, their faces hidden by hoods they'd pulled up around their heads; I knew none of them were female because their women were always kept out of sight when visitors arrived. The only sound was the slow, constant drip of a water clock, with each drop announcing the passage of two more seconds.

The chieftain sat in the middle of the room. Long-fingered hands rested upon the armrests of his sandstone throne; golden eyes regarded us between strands of hair turned white with age. He wore nothing to indicate his position as the tribal leader save an implacable air of authority, and he let us know that he was the boss by silently raising both hands, then slowly lowering them once we'd halted and saying nothing for a full minute.

At last he spoke. *"Essha shakay Hamsey?"* (Why are you here, Ramsey?)

I didn't think I'd ever met him before, but obviously he recognized me. Good. That would make things a little easier. I responded in his own language. "(I bring someone who wants to learn more about your people. He is a wise man from Earth, a teacher of others who wish to become wise themselves. He desires to ask a favor from you.)"

The chieftain turned his gaze from me to Dr. al-Baz. "(What do you want?)"

I looked at the professor. "Okay, you're on. He wants to know what you want. I'll translate for you. Just be careful . . . they're easily offended."

"So it seems." Dr. al-Baz was nervous, but he was hiding it well.

He licked his lips and thought about it a moment, then went on. "Tell him . . . tell him that I would like to collect a small sample of blood from one of his people. A few drops will do. I wish to have this because I want to know . . . I mean, because I'd like to find out . . . whether his people and mine have common ancestors."

That seemed to be a respectful way of stating what he wanted, so I turned to the chief and reiterated what he'd said. The only problem was that I didn't know the aboriginal word for "blood." It had simply never come up in any previous conversations I'd had with the *shatan*. So I had to generalize a bit, calling it "the liquid that runs within our bodies" while pantomiming a vein running down the inside of my right arm, and hoped that he'd understand what I meant.

He did, all right. He regarded me with cold disbelief, golden eyes flashing, thin lips writhing upon an otherwise stoical face. Around us, I heard the other *shatan* murmuring to one another. I couldn't tell what they were saying, but it didn't sound like they were very happy either.

We were in trouble.

"(Who dares say that *shatan* and *nashatan* have the same ancestors?)," he snapped, hands curling into fists as he leaned forward from his throne. "(Who dares believe that your people and mine are alike in any way?)"

I repeated what he'd said to Dr. al-Baz. The professor hesitated, then looked straight at the chieftain. "Tell him that no one believes these things," he said, his tone calm and deliberate. "It is only an hypothesis . . . an educated guess . . . that I want to either prove or disprove. That's why I need a blood sample, to discover the truth."

I took a deep breath, hoped that I was going to get out of there alive, then translated the professor's explanation. The chieftain continued to glare at us as I spoke, but he seemed to calm down a little. For several long seconds, he said nothing. And then he reached a decision.

Reaching into his robes, he withdrew a bone dagger from a sheath on his belt. My heart skipped a beat as the light fell upon its sharp white blade, and when he stood up and walked toward us, I thought my life had come to an end. But then he stopped in front of Dr. al-Baz and, still staring straight at him, raised his left hand, placed the knife against his palm, and ran its blade down his skin.

"(Take my blood)," he said, holding out his hand.

I didn't need to translate what he'd said. Dr. al-Baz quickly dropped his backpack from his shoulders and opened it. He withdrew a syringe, thought better of it, and pulled out a plastic test tube instead. The chieftain clenched his fist and let the blood trickle between his fingers, and the professor caught it in his test tube. Once he'd collected the specimen, he pulled out a tiny vial and added a couple of drops of anticoagulant. Then he capped the tube and nodded to the chieftain.

"Tell him that I greatly appreciate his kindness," he said, "and that I will return to tell him what I have found."

"Like hell we will!"

"Tell him." His eyes never left the chieftain's. "One way or another, he deserves to know the truth."

Promising the chieftain that we intended to return was the last thing I wanted to do, but I did it anyway. He didn't respond for a moment, but simply dropped his hand, allowing his blood to trickle to the floor.

"(Yes)," he said at last. "(Come back and tell me what you've learned. I wish to know as well.)" And then he turned his back to us and walked back to his chair. "(Now leave.)"

"Okay," I whispered, feeling my heart hammering against my chest. "You got what you came for. Now let's get out of here while we still have our heads."

Two days later, I was sitting in the casino bar at the John Carter, putting away tequila sunrises and occasionally dropping a coin into the video poker machine in front of me. I'd discovered that I didn't mind the place so long as I kept my back turned to everything going on around me, and I could drink for free if I slipped a quarter into the slots every now and then. At least that's what I told myself. The fact of the matter was that there was a certain sense of security in the casino's tawdry surroundings. This Mars was a fantasy, to be sure, but just then it was preferable to the unsettling reality I'd visited a couple of days earlier.

Omar al-Baz was upstairs, using the equipment he'd brought with him to analyze the chieftain's blood. We'd gone straight to the hotel upon returning to the city, but when it became obvious that it would take a while for the professor to work his particular kind of magic, I decided to go downstairs and get a drink. Perhaps I should have gone home, but I was still keyed up from the long ride back, so I gave Dr. al-Baz my cell number and asked him to call me if and when he learned anything.

I was surprised that I stuck around. Usually, when I return from a trip into the outback, all I really want to do is get out of the clothes I'd been wearing for days on end, open a beer, and take a nice, long soak in the bathtub. Instead, there I was, putting away one cocktail after another while demonstrating that I knew absolutely nothing about poker. The bartender was studying me, and the waitresses were doing their best to stay upwind, but I couldn't have cared less about what they thought. They were make-believe Martians, utterly harmless. The ones I'd met a little while ago would have killed me just for looking at them cross-eyed.

In all the years that I'd been going out in the wilderness, this was the first time I'd ever been really and truly scared. Not by the desert, but by those who lived there. No *shatan* had ever threatened me, not even in an implicit way, until the moment the chieftain pulled out a knife and creased the palm of his hand with its blade. Sure, he'd done so to give Dr. al-Baz a little of his blood, but there was another meaning to his actions.

It was a warning . . . and the *shatan* don't give warnings lightly.

That was why I was doing my best to get drunk. The professor was too excited to think of anything except the specimen he'd just collected—all the way home, he'd babbled about nothing else—but I knew that we'd come within an inch of dying and that ours would have been a really nasty death.

Yet the chieftain had given his blood of his own free will, and even asked that we return once the professor learned the truth. That puzzled me. Why would he be interested in the results if the thought of being related to a human was so appalling?

I threw away another quarter, pushed the buttons, and watched the machine tell me that I'd lost again, then looked around to see if I could flag down a princess and get her to fetch another sunrise. Dejah or Thuvia or Xaxa or whoever she was had apparently gone on break, though, because she was nowhere to be seen; I was about to try my luck again when something caught my eye. The TV above the bar was showing the evening news, and the weatherman was standing in front of his map. I couldn't hear what he was saying, but he was pointing at an animated cloud system west of Rio Zephyria that was moving across the desert toward the Laestrygon canal.

It appeared that a sandstorm was brewing in Mesogaea, the drylands adjacent to the Zephyria region. This sort of weather isn't uncommon in the summer; we call them *haboobs*, the Arabic name for sandstorms on Earth that somehow found their way to Mars. From the looks of things, it would reach the Zephyria outback sometime tomorrow afternoon. Good thing I'd come home; the last thing anyone would want is to be caught out in the desert during a bad storm.

A waitress strolled by, adjusting a strap of her costume bikini top. I raised my glass and silently jiggled it back and forth, and she feigned a smile as she nodded and headed for the bar. I was searching my pockets for another quarter so that she'd see that I was still pretending to be a gambler, when my cell buzzed.

"Jim? Are you still here?"

"In the bar, professor. Come down and have a drink with me."

"No! No time for that! Come upstairs right away! I need to see you!"

"What's going on?"

"Just come up here! It's better if I show you!"

Dr. al-Baz opened the door at the first knock. Spotting the cocktail glass in my hand, he snatched it from me and drained it in one gulp. "Good heavens," he gasped, "I needed that!"

"Want me to get you another one?"

"No . . . but you can buy me a drink when I get to Stockholm." I didn't understand what he meant, but before I could ask he pulled me into the room. "Look!" he said, pointing to one of the computers set up on the bar. "This is incredible!"

I walked over to the bar, peered at the screen. Displayed upon it were rows of A's, C's, G's, and T's, arranged in a seemingly endless series of combinations, with smears that looked a little like dashes running in a vertical bar down the right side of the screen. A five-line cluster of combinations and smears was highlighted in yellow.

"Yeah, okay," I said. "Professor, I'm sorry, but you're going to have to . . ."

"You have no idea what you're looking at, do you?" he asked, and I shook my head. "This is the human genome . . . the genetic code present in every human being. And these"—his hand trembled as he pointed to the highlighted cluster—"are strands that are identical to the partially sequenced genome from the aborigine specimen."

"They're the same?"

"Exactly. There is no error . . . or at least none that the computers can detect." Dr. al-Baz took a deep breath. "Do you see what I'm getting at? The hypothesis is correct! Human life may have originated on Mars!"

I stared at the screen. Until then, I hadn't really believed anything that Dr. al-Baz had told me; it seemed too unlikely to be true. But now that the evidence was in front of me, I realized that I was looking at something that would shake the foundations of science. No, not just science . . . it would rattle history itself, forcing humankind to reconsider its origins.

"My god," I whispered. "Have you told anyone yet? On Earth, I mean."

"No. I'm tempted to send a message, but . . . no, I need to confirm this." The professor walked over to the window. "We have to go back," he said, his voice quiet but firm as he gazed out at the city lights and, beyond them, the dark expanse of the desert. "I need to get another blood sample, this time from a different *shatan*. If the same sequence appears in the second sample, then we'll know for sure."

Something cold slithered down my spine. "I'm not sure that's a good idea. The chieftain . . ."

"The chieftain told us that he wanted to know what we discovered. So we'll tell him, and explain that we need more blood . . . just a little . . . from one of his tribesmen to make sure that it's the truth." Dr. al-Baz glanced over his shoulder at me. "Not an unreasonable request, no?"

"I don't think he's going to be very happy about this, if that's what you're asking."

He was quiet for a few moments, contemplating what I'd just said. "Well . . . that's a risk we'll just have to take," he said at last. "I'll pay you again for another trip, if that's your concern . . . double your original fee, in fact. But I must go back as soon as possible." He continued to gaze out the window. "Tomorrow morning. I want to leave tomorrow morning."

My head was beginning to ache, dull blades pressing upon my temples. I shouldn't have had so much to drink. What I should have done was turn him down right then and there. But his offer to double my fee for a return trip was too good to pass up; I needed the money, and that would pay my rent for a couple of months. Besides, I was too drunk to argue.

"Okay," I said. "We'll head out first thing."

I went back to my place, took some aspirin, stripped off my filthy clothes, and took a shower, then flopped into bed. But I didn't fall asleep for quite a while. Instead, I stared at the ceiling as unwelcome thoughts ran an endless loop through my mind.

What would the chieftain do when Omar al-Baz informed him that *shatan* blood and *nashatan* blood were very much alike and that our two races might be related? He wouldn't be pleased, that much was certain. The aborigines never wanted to have anything to do with the invaders from Earth; as soon as our ships had arrived, they had retreated into the wilderness. This was the reason why they'd become nomads . . .

But they weren't anymore, were they? The significance of what I'd seen at the village suddenly became clear to me. Not only had this particular tribe built permanent houses, but they were also erecting a wall around them. That meant they were planning to remain where they were for some time to come and were taking measures to defend themselves. They were tiring of running from us; now they were digging in.

Until now, the human colonists had been content to ignore the *shatan,* thinking of them as reclusive savages best left alone. This would change, though, if humans came to believe that *Homo sapiens* and *Homo artesian* were cousins. Suddenly, we'd want to know all about them. First would come more biologists like Dr. al-Baz, more anthropologists like Dr. Horner. Maybe that wouldn't be so bad . . . but right behind them would be everyone *else.* Historians and journalists, tour buses and camera safaris, entrepreneurs looking to make a buck, missionaries determined to convert godless souls, real-estate tycoons seeking prime land on which to build condos with a nice view of those quaint aborigine villages . . .

The *shatan* wouldn't tolerate this. And the chieftain would know that it was inevitable the moment Dr. al-Baz told him what he'd learned. First, he'd order his warriors to kill both him and me. And then . . .

In my mind's eye, I saw the horrors to come. Wave upon wave of *shatan* warriors descending upon Rio Zephyria and the other colonies, hell-bent on driving the invaders from their world once and for all. Oh, we had superior weapons, this was true . . . but they had superior numbers, and it would only be a matter of time before they captured a few of our guns and learned how to use them. Ships from Earth would bring soldiers to defend the colonies, but history is unkind to would-be conquerors. Either we would be driven back, step by inexorable step, or we would commit genocide, exterminating entire tribes and driving the few survivors farther into the wilderness.

Either way, the outcome was inevitable. War would come to a world named for a god of war. Red blood would fall upon red sand, human and Martian alike.

A storm was coming. Then I thought of a different storm, and knew what I had to do.

Two days later, I was found staggering out of the desert, caked with red sand from my hair to my boots save for raccoonlike patches around my eyes where my goggles had protected them. I was dehydrated and exhausted to the point of delirium.

I was also alone.

Ironically, the people who rescued me were another guide and the family from Minneapolis whom he'd escorted into the desert just outside Rio Zephyria. I remember little of what happened after I collapsed at their feet and had to be carried to the guide's Land Rover. The only things I clearly recall were the sweet taste of water within my parched mouth, a teenage girl gazing down at me with angelic blue eyes as she cradled my head in her lap, and the long, bouncing ride back into the city.

I was still in my hospital bed when the police came to see me. By then, I'd recovered enough to give them a clear and reasonably plausible account of what had happened. Like any successful lie, this one was firmly grounded in truth. The violent haboob that suddenly came upon us in the desert hills. The crash that happened when, blinded by wind-driven sand, I'd collided with a boulder, causing my jeep to topple over. How Dr. al-Baz and I had escaped from the wreckage, only to lose track of each other. How only I had managed to find shelter in the leeside of a pinnacle. The professor's becoming lost in the storm, never to be seen again.

All true, every word of it. All I had to do was leave out a few facts, such as how I'd deliberately driven into the desert even though I knew that a haboob was on its way, or that even after we saw the scarlet haze rising above the western horizon, I'd insisted upon continuing to drive south, telling Dr. al-Baz that we'd be able to outrun the storm. The cops never learned that I'd been careful to carry with me a pair of sand goggles and a scarf, but refrained from making sure that the professor took the same precautions. Nor did they need to know that I'd deliberately aimed for that boulder even though I could have easily avoided it.

I broke down when I spoke about how I'd heard Omar al-Baz calling my name, desperately trying to find me even as the air was filled with stinging red sand and visibility was reduced to only arm's length. That much, too, was true. What I didn't say was that Dr. al-Baz had come within three meters of where I was huddled, my eyes covered by goggles and a scarf wrapped around the lower part of my face. And yet I remained silent as I watched his indistinct form lurch past me, arms blindly thrust out before him, slowly suffocating as sand filled his nose and throat.

My tears were honest. I liked the professor. But his knowledge made him too dangerous to live.

As an alibi, my story worked. When a search party went out into the desert, they located my overturned jeep. Omar al-Baz's body was found about fifteen meters away, facedown and covered by several centimeters of sand. Our footprints had been erased by the wind, of course, so there was no way of telling how close the professor had been to me.

That settled any doubts the cops might have had. Dr. al-Baz's death was an accident. I had no motive for killing him, nor was there any evidence of foul play. If I was guilty of anything, it was only reckless and foolish behavior. My professional reputation was tarnished, but that was about it. The investigation was officially concluded the day I was released from the hospital. By then, I'd realized two things. The first was that I would get away with murder. The second was that my crime was far from perfect.

Dr. al-Baz hadn't taken the chieftain's blood specimen with him when he'd left the hotel. It was still in his room, along with all his equipment. This included the computers he'd used to analyze the sample; the results were saved in their memories, along with any notes he might have written. In fact, the only thing the professor had brought with him was his room key . . . which I'd neglected to retrieve from his body.

I couldn't return to his hotel room; any effort to get in would have aroused suspicion. All I could do was watch from the hotel lobby as, a couple of days later, the bellhops wheeled out a cart carrying the repacked equipment cases, bound for the spaceport and the shuttle, which would ferry them to a marsliner docked at Deimos Station. In a few months, the professor's stuff would be back in the hands of his fellow faculty members. They would open the digital files and inspect what their late colleague had learned, and examine the blood specimen he'd collected. And then . . .

Well. We'll just have to see, won't we?

So now I sit alone in my neighborhood bar, where I drink and wait for the storm to come. And I never go into the desert anymore.

MATTHEW HUGHES

Matthew Hughes was born in Liverpool, England, but has spent most of his adult life in Canada. He worked as a journalist, as a staff speechwriter for the Canadian Ministers of Justice and Environment, and as a freelance corporate and political speechwriter in British Columbia before settling down to write fiction full-time. Clearly strongly influenced by Jack Vance, as an author Hughes has made his reputation detailing the adventures of rogues like Old Earth's master criminal Luff Imbry, who lives in the era just before that of *The Dying Earth*, in a series of novels and novellas that include *Fools Errant, Fool Me Twice, Black Brillion, Majestrum, Hespira, The Spiral Labyrinth, Template, Quartet and Triptych, The Yellow Cabochon, The Other*, and *The Commons*, and short-story collections *The Gist Hunter and Other Stories, 9 Tales of Henghis Hapthorn*, and *The Meaning of Luff and Other Stories*. His most recent books are the novels in his urban fantasy trilogy, To Hell and Back: *The Damned Busters, Costume Not Included*, and *Hell to Pay*. He also writes crime fiction as Matt Hughes and media tie-in novels as Hugh Matthews.

In the autumnal story that follows, he shows us that everyone sees the Mars that they want to see—and perhaps gets the Mars that they deserve.

The Ugly Duckling

MATTHEW HUGHES

IT TOOK FRED MATHER THE BETTER PART OF AN HOUR TO drive over the blue hills that stood between the base camp and the bone city. At the highest point of the switchbacking ancient road of crushed white stone, the thin Martian air grew even thinner. He had to take long, slow breaths to fill his lungs, while dark spots danced at the edges of his vision and he worried about steering the New Ares Mining Corporation's jeep over one of the precipices.

He could have gotten there more quickly—and more safely—by paralleling the dried-up canal down to the glass-floored sea. Then he could have plowed fifteen miles through its carpeting dust to the promontory girdled by a seawall that had not felt a wave's slap in ten thousand years. The towers of the dead Martian town stood like an abandoned, unsolved chess puzzle, white against the faded sky.

The road at the landward end of the town was lined on either side by low, squat structures, windowless but with arched doors of weathered bronze. He was just wondering if they might be tombs—nobody knew yet what the Martians had done with their dead—when the hand radio on the passenger seat squawked and Red Bowman's voice said, "Base to Mather, over."

He picked up the set, keyed the mike switch, and said, "Mather, over."

"How you coming?" said the crew chief. Mather thought he heard a note of suspicion in the man's voice.

"I'm just pulling into the town now."

There was a silence, then the radio said, "The hell you been playing at? You should've been there an hour already."

"I took the hill road."

"What the hell for?"

"I thought it might be quicker. It looked shorter on the map." Mather was lying. The reason he hadn't gone by the canal road was that he hadn't wanted to meet any other traffic. He had wanted, for a little while at least, to be able to pretend that he was the only Earthman on Mars instead of just the only archaeologist.

The radio crackled back at him. "We got a schedule to meet, egghead. Now you get those transponders planted, then you get your heinie back here mucho pronto."

Bowman hadn't said "Over," but Mather was about to confirm and sign off when the crew chief continued with, "And you come home by the seabed. You wreck that jeep, and you'll be going back Earthside on the next rocket, with a forfeiture of all pay and benefits!"

"Roger, over and out," Mather said. He put down the radio and steered the vehicle through a gateway of bone pillars carved in twin spirals that led to a small plaza surrounded by two-story white buildings, their walls pierced by narrow doors and slits for windows.

The Martians had been light-boned and graceful, brown-skinned and golden-eyed, though they had often worn masks when they went out—silver or blue for the men, crimson for the women, gold for the children. Back on Earth, he had seen the long-distance images recorded by the earliest expeditions—the ones that had failed, for reasons still unknown. There were no close-up, postcontact likenesses of Martians because between the third and fourth landings, Terran diseases to which they had no resistance had killed off almost all of them in a few weeks. Their flesh had dried to leaves and their bones had become sticks; the floors of their homes were littered with the stuff.

Mather would have loved to meet a Martian, though he knew they could be strange. Telepathic was the prevailing opinion among academics, though with brains that worked at a sideways tangent to what humans meant when they said, "Common sense."

You still heard tales of surviving Martians, spotted at a distance in remote places—such as the blue hills behind him. That had been another reason Mather had come that way, just in case.

He sat in the jeep and took a long, slow look at as much of the town as he could see from here. "Get a good overview," his graduate-thesis advisor used to say, "before you plunge into the detail. That way the details will form themselves into a pattern sooner and you may save yourself from running up a lot of blind alleys."

The plaza held only one object of note. At the center of the open space that surrounded him was a substantial circular structure, four ascending, concentric rings of white material that would probably turn out to be bone—there was a reason why the dead town was called "the bone city."

Mather could see a bronze pipe standing up from the smallest, highest circle. From it would have flowed water to fill the first round of the four, to trickle over the sides and fill the others in turn. Of course, not a drop of liquid had dampened the object in millennia: this part of Mars was believed to have been abandoned tens of centuries ago, after the seas had vanished and the soft rains that had gently sculpted the hills ceased to come over the green water.

Having finished his survey, Mather climbed out of the jeep, hooked the radio to his belt, and approached the nearest building. Its door was ajar, but he had to push it all the way open to squeeze through the narrow entry. He found himself in a circular foyer, its bone walls decorated with lines of copper—once gleaming, now a dull green—that had been inset into incisions in the white hardness.

Some of the lines were curved, some straight. They met at odd angles and somehow contrived to draw Mather's gaze into what seemed to be three-dimensional shapes. It seemed to him that the silence in the dead town had managed to deepen. Then, as he continued to stare, trying to make sense of the forms emerging from the matrix, the lines moved of their own accord. He experienced a growing vertigo. One moment, he was looking into an infinite distance; the next, he was about to fall into it.

He clapped his hands to his eyes and held them there while he slowly counted to ten. When he took them away, he was looking again at lines of verdigrised copper set into bone. But immediately they started their pull. He dropped his gaze to the floor, saw a spiral mosaic of gold and silver tiles, faded and half-obscured by dust that had drifted through the doorway. At least it did not move.

The radio hissed and squawked again. "Base to Mather," said Bowman's voice, "we're not seeing any transponder signals."

He went outside. "I'm in the town, just scoping for the best sites," he said.

The backseats of the jeep had been taken out to make room for a large wooden box with a hinged lid. Inside, nestled in packing straw, were dozens of small, black oblongs, each one a radio transponder with a telescoping steel antenna that could be pulled up from its top and a red on-off switch.

Mather's job was to place the devices in a rough grid. As he positioned each one, he was to throw its switch to *on*. The transponders would broadcast signals that would delineate the layout of the ancient town to the electronic brain of a huge tracked machine that was even now being slowly hauled from the base camp down to the dry seabed. Tonight, it would be eased down to the seabed, there to be loaded onto a multiwheeled transporter. Tomorrow, it would creep the rest of the way to the bone town, to be off-loaded at the base of a sloping ramp topped by a set of stairs from which, presumably, the ancient Martians had once launched their shining boats.

The leviathan would trundle up into the town, deploy its hydraulic grapples, and begin stuffing the bone city, piece by piece, into its mechanical maw. It would grind up the town, house by house, separating metal and stone from the ossiferous material that the Martians had built the place from. The valueless stone would be spat out, the metal compacted and excreted like cubic droppings.

The metal was valuable, but it was the bone that really mattered.

It would be pulverized, sacked, and stacked on a detachable trailer that rolled along behind the behemoth. As a trailer was filled, it would be detached and another put in its place. Then the loaded trailer would be hooked to a tractor, and the eight-wheeler would head off across the dry sea until it met the Martian road-and-canal network. Then it would go to one of the newly built Earthman towns that were surrounded by farms whose soil, even after lying fallow for thousands of years, was not all it might be.

The ground bones of Martian cities would fertilize the crops that would feed the tens of thousands of Earthmen arriving each month as the silver-rocket armada continued to cross the black gulf between the worlds.

Mather was one of the most recent arrivals. He had been unable to secure funding to come to Mars as an archaeologist. The new old world needed brawny pioneers, not pointy-headed academics, he was told. Archaeologists objected to the destruction of the ancient Martian cities, so the company was being careful not to let any of them anywhere near them.

So Mather had concocted a résumé that should not have withstood even the most cursory scrutiny, but New Ares Mining Corporation had lucrative contracts to fulfill and was desperate for men to mine the bone cities. Mather was on the next rocket out.

The trip was long and the quarters close. The men he would be working with soon deduced that Fred Mather had not come, as they had, from the coal mines of Kentucky or the oil leases of west Texas. His hands were too soft and his neck not rough enough. The crew chief, Red Bowman, a veteran of the Alaska gold fields, marked him down as a city-boy tenderfoot on a job that had no slack to cut for greenhorns.

Mather worked quickly, quartering the town on foot, placing the transponders according to a rough map made from an aerial photograph snapped by a New Ares rocket. Two hours after he began, he threw the switch on the last device, then walked back to where he had left the jeep.

He lifted the hood, removed the cover of the carburetor, and dropped a pinch of Martian grit into its barrel. Then he radioed base to say that the vehicle wasn't running right—he suspected dirt in the carburetor or fuel line—so he would stay the night in the town and repair the faulty part in the morning.

"I wouldn't want to risk overturning the jeep coming home in the dark," he said. "Those roads can ice up pretty bad, I hear."

Bowman was on his supper break. The radioman said, "Roger that. Talk to you tomorrow. Base out."

In the dwindling sunlight, Mather dug under the jeep's front seat for the scuffed satchel that contained his field notebook. He equipped himself with a heavy-duty flashlight.

"Okay," he said to himself, "let's see what we can accomplish."

It was no good saying to the directors and shareholders of New Ares Mining Corporation that the bone cities of Mars were a priceless asset. New Ares accountants and engineers had already worked out the figures: The cities were only priceless in that they were free for the taking; the profits from mining them, however, would start in the tens of millions and climb sharply into the hundreds. It was conceivable that, if Mars filled up and more of the bone-built dead towns were found, New Ares' earnings could eventually total a billion.

"Imagine," one of Mather's workmates had said on the trip out, as they swung side by side in their hammocks in the passenger hold. "A billion dollars. And we're gonna be part of that."

"Yeah," Mather had said. "Imagine."

The Martians had built their towns mostly out of stone and metal, crystal and glass. They had run water through channels in the floors—to cool the rooms and, Mather hypothesized, their slender feet—and grown fruit hydroponically from the walls.

But in some parts of the planet, there had once been a fashion—perhaps it was a ritual requirement—for building in bone. Martian architects had designed houses walled and floored in thin sheets of ossiferous material that must have been peeled like veneer from the huge bones of gigantic sea creatures. Sometimes, the great ribs and femurs were used whole as structural members, trimmed and squared or rounded to the needed dimensions, often ornately carved into pillars and lintels. Still more of the stuff had been crushed into powder, then bound together with burnt lime to make a durable concrete for roads and doorsteps.

Building in bone made for houses that were filled with a diffuse and airy light that threw no shadows. The material was also porous, so the rooms breathed even though the windows were narrow and sealed with bronze shutters. The walls also had the quality of absorbing rather than reflecting sound; Mather imagined that conversations in Martian rooms must have been muted, even the shouts and tumults of the aureus-eyed children softened and calmed.

He chose houses at random, traversing hallways and peering into chambers. The places were empty, the inhabitants having packed up in no apparent hurry. Occasionally, he found items of abandoned furniture—more bone, a couple of metal frames, the less durable wooden parts long since turned to dust.

In a corner of one upstairs room, he found a bone table on which rested a scatter of Martian books. He'd heard of these: sheets of thin silver inscribed in snakelike symbols of indelible blue ink. No one could read them, though it was said that someone had once done so and had become deranged. The subsequent murders had been hushed up.

Mather leafed through the books but could derive nothing from them other than that they had been beautifully made. He gazed at a page for almost a minute, waiting to see if he would be drawn into the twisting patterns as he had been with the wall design, ready to drop the book if anything untoward occurred. But nothing did. Finally, he placed the artifacts in his satchel—a willful violation of his terms of employment—and went outside.

The town sloped gradually from the landward end to the place where the sea had been, the finger of rock on which it was built also narrowing as it neared the vanished waves. At the very tip, the Martians had laid out a wide plaza, this one without a fountain. The pavement was fashioned from thousands of small tiles, their original bright colors now sun-faded to pale pastels, arranged in a border of stylized waves and sailing ships, blue against bronze, surrounding a great, sinuous sea creature with huge eyes and triangular flukes.

A broad flight of bone-concrete steps led down from the open space to the former harbor, where two curved moles enclosed a sheltered basin with a seaward opening only wide enough for two of the slim, burnished craft to pass at once.

The buildings that stood at the edge of the open space were grander than the houses he had entered so far. Their entrances were wide metal doors between carved pillars of bone. The surfaces of the doors were worked in raised snake-script in bas relief. Unlike the mouths of the houses, these were all closed.

It was natural for an archaeologist to wonder when presented with the unexplained behavior of vanished folk. Did the Martians, on the day they abandoned their homes, observe a ritual that decreed their doors must forever lie open? Was there a converse requirement to seal the entrances of public buildings, as Mather assumed the wide-doored edifices to be?

He did not know, would probably never know, but he would enjoy speculating in the professional journals when he returned at last to Earth, the only one of his kind to have done the fieldwork. And so it was with a frisson of anticipation that Fred Mather took hold of the handles of a pair of bronze doors and pulled.

The portals opened easily and he stepped into a wide, well-lit space. The building contained one high-ceilinged room, domed above in thinnest bone so that a translucent illumination fell upon the ringed tiers of seats that descended from the doorway to make a flat-bottomed bowl. In the middle of the amphitheater, rising from the floor, was a great cube of white stone, its top a little higher than the uppermost row of seats.

On the side facing Mather as he stepped down from tier to tier, the surface of the block was incised with a complex design, inlaid with greened-over copper, like the wall in the first house he had entered. It drew his eyes so that his steps began to falter. He lowered himself to a seat midway down the bowl. This time he would study the effect. He pulled his eyes away and fetched out his notebook, unclipped a pen from its wire-spiral spine, and took a deep breath.

Then he looked again at the cube. As before, he found that whichever part of the design he focused on, his gaze was pulled toward its center. Abruptly, the two-dimensional pattern took on depth, so that instead of staring *at* something, he was now peering *into* it.

Unable to look away, he flung a forearm across his eyes, then used the limb to restrict his vision as he made quick notes on the effect. At one point, he looked up to see if he could sketch the pattern of green on white, but immediately the pulling-in effect resumed— this time even stronger—and he had to use his arm to blind himself again while he noted this new observation.

From the satchel, the radio squawked. He paid it no heed, continued to write. Red Bowman's voice came, harsh and incongruous in this Martian space, "Base to Mather, over."

The archaeologist ignored the summons, continued to make notes. He had a sense that he was about to discover something new and remarkable, to acquire some transformative knowledge to which he would say, at first, "That's incredible!" followed almost immediately by, "But, of course!"

Bowman's voice intruded again on the moment. He reached inside the satchel to switch off the radio, but a momentary flash of cunning stayed his hand: If he didn't answer, they might think he was hurt; if they thought he was hurt, they might come to help him; if they came, they would take him away from . . . from whatever was about to fill him with—

"Base to Mather, are you all right?"

He keyed the mike switch. "Mather to base. What's up?"

"What took you so long?"

The lie came smoothly. "I was cleaning out the carburetor. Wanted to wipe my hands before I picked up the radio."

There was a silence. He could imagine the crew chief digesting the information, filtering it through his undisguised dislike of the greenhorn—an impersonal dislike that extended to all the Fred Mathers of the two worlds, with their soft palms, their long words and longer sentences. He probably suspected that people like him secretly hoarded books that should have been burned on the great bonfires Bowman would remember from his childhood, when the government had cleansed the people's minds.

At last, Bowman said, "We may have trouble getting the harvester down the ramp to the seabed tomorrow. It's steeper than it looked. So it might not arrive on schedule."

"Okay," said Mather. "Doesn't bother me."

"But we're all gonna be tied up with this. So if you can't get the jeep running, nobody's gonna come and get you."

"Okay."

"Or bring you any food or water."

Mather shrugged. "I've got sandwiches and a gallon or so. I'll get by."

"You say so," said Bowman. "I wouldn't want to spend too long in one of those places. People have seen ghosts."

"Ghosts don't bother me," said Mather. "Over and out."

He turned off the radio and put it back in the satchel. Then he methodically finished his note-taking. All this time, he had been shielding his gaze from the figured cube. Now he took a settling breath and said, "Okay, here we go."

He lowered his arm. The pattern seemed to reach out for him. A small, involuntary gasp escaped him, then he nodded and said, "Ah."

It was the evening of the Touching of the Sea. He had invited neighbors to dine before they went down to the gathering above the harbor. His wife cooked meats in the house, then brought them on golden plates out into the inner courtyard, where they sat on bone chairs and drank the fruited wine from his own trees.

The conversation was relaxed and mellow. The two couples were friends as well as each other's next-door neighbors. They talked of people they knew; the husbands compared their expectations for the coming season's hunt up in the hills; the wives discussed the plays they planned to see—mostly timeless revivals, though there was to be a new work by a playwright from across the sea who was developing a reputation for deliberately stimulating his audiences.

When the meal was done and the last, formal toast drunk, they went down to the festival, through darkening streets lit by crystal torches and aflow with golden-eyed folk in their holiday clothes. No one wore a mask this night; it was not a time for circumspection.

The plaza by the sea was thronged. All of the town was there, the oldest given places on the steps of the surrounding buildings, the youngest on the shoulders of their parents, so that all could witness the Touching. A coterie of musicians played the festival anthem and the crowd swayed, humming to the ancient song.

As the last notes died, all of them turned toward the harbor. The boats that usually filled most of the circular basin had been rowed to the sides, tethered to bronze rings set in the stones of the moles or to each other, so that a wide channel lay open from the foot of the steps to the gap where the enclosing barriers did not meet.

One musician struck a single, plangent tone from his harp. As one, the crowd craned forward. Now a sound somewhere between a sigh and a moan rose up from each throat. It mingled and became one common note, rising not in volume but in intensity. It filled the plaza like an invisible mist, then it flowed down the steps and across the harbor and out over the sea. And carried with it a single thought.

Minutes piled upon minutes, became almost an hour, the sound continuously pouring from the crowd, the thought uniting them. Then, out beyond the harbor mouth, the waveless summer sea rippled, once, twice. A triangular-fluked tail rose and slapped the surface gently. A dark, gleaming back showed, then disappeared, only to come up once more in the channel between the boats.

The monotonous song intensified. Golden eyes shone in the torchlight. A pressure wave rolled across the surface of the basin and wet the bottom steps. As the water ran back down, the sea parted. A broad-mouthed head broke the surface, its eyes as big as dinner plates, though these were not gold but resembled silver-rimmed onyx.

The sea beast's tail thrashed, driving its head and forefins clear of the water and up onto the harbor steps. The crowd's moaning song grew stronger still, the carried thought more imperative. The tail went deep, scraping the floor of the basin, the sinuous body hunched and straightened, and, as water ran from its dark, striated skin back into the sea, the summoned creature forced itself higher up the stairs, until its head touched the plaza's tiles.

Silence fell. The women took the children to join the old people, while the men descended the steps to stand on either side of the sea beast. The sky above the town was black, the stars like chips of bone. The harpist plucked another string. In one motion, the men drew their curved knives, then waited for the final note.

Fred Mather awoke to find himself in near-total darkness at the top of the steps above the dry harbor. The stars and the two small moons gave just enough light to show the bone town as a pale fog seen from the corners of his eyes, but when he looked straight ahead, he could see almost nothing. The sky was as black as it had been in the vision, but, near the horizon, he could see the small green orb that was

Earth. He did not know how long he had been standing at the top of the steps, but it had been long enough for the wind off the dead sea-bed to chill him. Shivering, he rubbed the pebbled skin of his bare forearms.

He had to make notes. He felt his way back to the amphitheater and to the seat where he had left the satchel. His notepad was not there, but the flashlight was. By its hard beam, he found the spiral-bound book outside. It lay on the tiled surface of the plaza, covering the eye of the sea-creature mosaic. He went and retrieved it, found the pen a few feet away.

But when he sat on a doorstep to write by the flashlight's glow, the making of ink marks on paper struck him as faintly ridiculous. The straight and curved blue lines would not always resolve themselves into words; they kept turning into mere chicken-scratchings, as if his ability to read was waxing and waning.

His mind kept going back to the vision of the festival: the death of the sea beast, the solemn taking of its flesh and the wrapping of the dripping pieces in squares of cloth the women had brought with them, the people walking home, leaving the creature's bones to be cared for by those who had earned that honor.

And something else. He did not know how he knew it, but he was aware that this Touching had been the last, that there were no more beasts left to call. He struggled to put that knowledge into words, then transpose the words into letters of blue ink scratched onto paper. But he kept losing the knack.

Finally, he abandoned the effort and lit his way back into the amphitheater. Some instinct told him to sit in another part of the great room, facing another side of the cube. He stared into its matrix of incised lines and instantly felt himself falling into . . .

They were four, all friends from boyhood, now grown to maturity. They had trained hard, challenging one another, encouraging one another, daring one another. And it had paid off: They had been victorious in the annual games and had thus won the honor of being the first hunting party into the blue hills above the bone town.

They ran now in single file along a trail they had known as children, when they had played at what they now did in earnest. They knew every curve and fold of the land, the ridges, shoulders, and valleys, and they knew as well that there was a certain place where the birds sheltered through the day, emerging at dusk to light up the night sky with their scintillating streaks and fire-trails, sparks falling like red snow.

It was a tall and narrow cave mouth, where the ground had parted a million years ago. But such was the lay of the land that the crevice was almost invisible unless viewed from a precise angle. The four men knew that angle, knew the chamber that widened behind the slit of the opening. In there, the birds would be sleeping, huddled together on the ground like a pool of banked embers, rustling and breathing together.

The four hunters crept to the mouth of the cleft, wire nets ready. Still in single file, they scraped backs and chests against the rough rock—it had been easier when they were boys—and eased into the cavern. Silently, breath abated, they ranged themselves around the sleeping quarry. Then, at a signal from the eldest, they cast their nets in a prearranged sequence.

The birds awoke as the first net fell, and rose up as one, swiftly bearing the wire mesh aloft. But the second net fell, its edges weighted, and the birds' upward motion slowed. Then came the third net, and the fourth. Weighed down, the overlapping meshes too dense to escape through, the creatures settled back to the floor with a mournful sound.

Elated, the hunters carefully brought the borders of the nets together, made a bundle whose gathered mouth they briskly tied with metal cords.

The birds, pressed into a sphere, flowed rustling over one another, like a boiling sun of gold and red. The men used their weapons to widen the crevice, then gently bore the captive birds out into the sunlight. The creatures voiced their displeasure, but the hunters struck up the traditional hymn of consolation with its promises of respect and good treatment.

The birds quieted, whether soothed by the blandishments or lulled by the sonorous rhythm of the song. Where the white road left the hills and ran down to the town, the men stopped to order their garments and brush off any dust or detritus. Then they hoisted the netted birds over their heads like a collective halo, and, at a measured pace, made their triumphant return.

Before they were halfway to the spiral-pillared gate, the people were coming out to sing them home.

The song was still echoing in Mather's mind when he came back to the here and now. He was not surprised to find himself outside the gate at the landward end of town. The shrunken sun was graying the Martian sky from somewhere behind the rumpled silhouette of the hills, making the road of crushed stone to shine ghostly at his feet.

This time, he did not even think to write any notes. He turned and walked slowly—he was unaccountably tired—through the dead town, back to the harbor plaza. Although he had not eaten or drunk in quite some time, he passed by the sandwiches and water can in the jeep without noticing them.

"He's mostly just dehydrated," said the roughneck who'd had first-aid training. "The air's so dry here, if you forget to keep drinking, you can start to get woozy pretty fast."

"Pour another cup into him," said Bowman, "then put him in the shade."

They'd found Mather facedown on the tiles of the harbor plaza when the truck carrying the mining machine arrived in the late afternoon of the second day. Now, as Bowman leafed through the notebook he'd found not far from the collapsed man, he knew why Mather hadn't been answering his radio calls since the day before.

Most of it was illegible scribbles, but a few words stood out—*communal, ritual, bonding*—enough to confirm the crew chief's long-held suspicion that Mather was another one of those long-haired intellectuals who got all Mars-struck and came out here thinking they'd find . . . What? Bowman had no idea what kind of foolishness filled a mind like Mather's. And he didn't want to.

He went to the top of the harbor steps and threw the notebook down toward where the mechanical behemoth's front tracks were already finding purchase on the bottom riser. Black smoke belched from the machine's exhaust as the operator goosed the throttle, and it began to climb, the bone steps cracking and powdering beneath grinding metal. The right-side track reached Mather's book and shredded it.

Bowman watched to make sure the miner was coming on in the way it was designed to. When it reached the top, and its front end crashed down onto the tiles, shattering them, he ordered the operator out and climbed into the control compartment. The machine's screen lit up, green on black, showing a gridwork based on bright points: the transponders Mather had placed, thankfully before he went outbacky-wacky, as Bowman had once heard an Australian desert prospector describe it.

The radio signals were all five-by-five. Bowman set the controls, stepped down from the cab, and watched as the great machine oriented itself and set to work. It labored over to the building nearest the harbor steps, deployed its heavy chain-link thrashers, and began to demolish the front wall in a spray of bone dust and chips.

"Looks good," the crew chief said, shouting to his men over the noise of the automated miner. "Let's get the jeep down here. I want to get back to base before it's too dark. First drink's on me."

When they were all loaded and ready to go, he sent a man to fetch Fred Mather. But Mather was gone.

The silvery-paged books were not really books, Mather now knew. The raised hieroglyphic squiggles weren't meant for the Martian eye but for Martian fingers. You ran the pads of the fingertips over the sinuous forms and out came, not text, but music. The songs formed in your head and played themselves out as you stroked the pages: all kinds of songs—from dancing tunes to soft ballads, from hymns to anthems, but each one tinged with a melancholic sweetness that he had come to associate with Martianness.

In his lucid moments, he contemplated the balance and the contrast that were inherent in the meeting of Martians and Earthmen: One race was fading into its purple twilight just as the other was setting out to see what the bright day would bring.

Over the music, he could hear Bowman and some other men calling his name. He was disappointed. He'd thought that when they set off back to camp, they'd report him as missing and forget about him. People did wander off on Mars, never to be seen again. And he had not made any friends among the miners. They'd all seen him for the ugly duckling he was.

But, as he sat in the birds' cave and thought about it, he recognized that they'd have had to come back to restart the machine. The morning after they'd left, he'd climbed aboard and thrown the big main switch that stopped it. The machine paused in its digestion of a house that stood halfway between the harbor and the gate. The land leviathan had been making substantial progress. Earthmen knew how to build reliable machinery.

But there were books to be gathered, and a few other objects that the Martians had left behind: masks, some children's toys, items of clothing, a cup that might have been carved from alabaster. He'd wanted to bring them to the cave. But when he'd gathered all that he could find and returned to restart the miner, he found that he did not know how to set its controls to follow the transponder grid. So he had left it with its engine idling in neutral, knowing that Red Bow-man would come out in the jeep to get it running again.

He had hoped that they'd think the miner had malfunctioned on its own, but the calling voices from outside the cave told him that the crew chief was not given to innocent explanations. Mather crept to the narrow mouth, which he'd made even harder to see by dragging prickle bushes into the cleft. Through the thin branches, he could see Bowman and the others. They were standing on a ridgeline, cup-ping their callused hands around their mouths to call his name. They had binoculars. They also had guns.

The men looked for him all day, but Mather remembered the Mar-tian hunting skills he'd acquired from the memory-visions—that's what he had taken to calling the phenomena—and he had no trouble avoiding capture. In the evening, the searchers climbed into the jeep and drove off across the empty sea. From the hills, he watched their dust plume hang in the air almost motionless, so slowly did the fine particles sift down in the lesser gravity and the windless Martian air.

When full darkness fell, he went down to the town. He had dis-covered that the lines incised into the walls of the houses performed a similar function to those graven into the sides of the cube. But, whereas the latter were memory-visions of public events, the ones in the houses were of private occasions. They were the Martians' family photo albums.

At first, he had thought he should disable the machine com-pletely, to save these intimate records. But after sampling several, he realized that they were all much the same: memories of births and deaths and unions, naming-day ceremonies, and other mundane rites of passage. But each was imbued with the same soft sadness that permeated the communal gatherings. These were not records taken from the middle of a community's life but from its end. They were memorials, left by the long-ago Martians when they packed up their possessions, and, leaving the doors of their houses open, went away forever.

Red Bowman was not happy. He had a production schedule to fulfill. Having the automated miner standing idle because crazy Mather had interfered with its controls threatened the crew chief's chances of winning the substantial bonus that would be due him if he delivered truckloads of bone fertilizer before the specified date. So when the jeep had gone far enough out across the seabed, he stopped it and got off, sending it on to base with the other men while he walked back along its vague track, trudging through the fine dust to the bone town.

Night fell before he got there, but he could see the white towers glimmering before him, occasionally lit by sparks and flashes as the tireless machine that was grinding its way through the walls encountered metal. But even if he'd been blind, Bowman could have found his way just by going toward the sound of the diesel engines. Or by the stench of its exhaust.

He came up the harbor steps and crossed the plaza. The sea beast's image was almost completely defaced by the miner's tracks. The behemoth's mechanical growls faded as it turned a far-off corner in its programmed course, putting walls between it and the Earthman. Bowman used the lull to listen for sounds of Mather's moving about the town. In a few moments, he heard something.

At first, he thought it was a wind wuthering beneath a building's eaves. But there was no wind, and the Martians' roofs were flat and no wider than the walls that supported them. He moved in the direction of the sound. It was coming from across the plaza, from one of the larger buildings that the behemoth would not reach for a couple of days.

The place had a bronze door, figured in the flowing script that Bowman did not like to look at; it reminded him of snakes, and snakes reminded him of the Devil. He sometimes wondered if there had been a deal between God and Lucifer: God would rule on Earth and the Devil would have Mars.

He eased through the door, a flashlight ready for use in his left hand, a pistol in his right. He didn't want to have to shoot Mather, but everybody knew the story of the man on the early expedition who'd gone mad and murdered his crewmates. He thought the fellow might have been an archaeologist—some kind of ologist, for sure—and he'd gone kill-crazy after rubbing up against too much Martian evil.

The sound came again, a keening, crooning note without words. It was like something a cat would sing, Bowman thought, maybe to a mouse it had caught. He didn't like cats either. Killing was all right when you had to, really had to, but you ought to do it clean.

He could dimly see the general layout inside the building: an open space, seats or steps in descending circles, a great white shape at the bottom. The sound came from the opposite side, louder now that Bowman was inside the place and the hoo-hooing was echoing so softly around the bone walls. The hairs on his neck and forearms rose of their own accord. He slid his thumb over his weapon's safety catch, making sure it was off.

He edged around the upper deck of the amphitheater. Against the white vagueness, he saw a dark shape, seated halfway down the tiers. He readied the pistol, then thumbed the flashlight's switch.

A Martian sat in the middle of the terraced seats, clad in a robe of metallic cloth that dully reflected the beam. His whole head was enclosed in a cloche-mask of silver, the facial features chased in gold, the thin eyebrows elevated, and the mouth pursed in an expression of permanent surprise. Bowman could not see the color of the eyes through the mask's slits, but the figure's gaze did not turn to him. Instead, it remained fixed on the side of the cube down in front.

The Earthman played the flashlight's beam over the man. He could see the hands, five-fingered instead of six. From beneath the robe came the cuffs of the blue jeans they all wore, and the scuffed boots were also New Ares company issue.

"Mather!" Bowman called. The man in Martian garb gave no sign of having heard. The crew chief moved in on the runaway, keeping the beam on him, with the pistol lined up just beside and behind the flashlight. "Mather!"

The masked head did not turn, the limbs did not move. Bowman stood beside him, poked his shoulder with the muzzle of the gun. "Snap out of it!"

Still no response. Bowman set the flashlight down on one of the tiered seats so that it illuminated the still figure. Then he hooked his fingers below the rim of the head-enclosing mask and yanked upward.

The Martian warriors marched to battle in gleaming companies of 144. Six companies made a battalion of 864. They carried shields of hammered bronze that matched their burnished armor and guns capable of spitting streams of metal insects that, finding flesh, would sting and burrow. On their flanks and scouting ahead raced knee-high electric spiders, their joints clicking with a rhythm that combined into a continuous whir.

Six battalions had gone out through the bone gate of Ipsli, almost the town's entire male complement. They took the coastal road toward Huq, and, by midday, they arrived at the chosen field, a place where the hills fell back to widen the coastal plain. They formed up, four battalions in front, two in reserve, and sat down to await the enemy.

The Huq army came late, earning themselves some justified mocking from Ipsli. Questions were shouted across the open ground as to whether they'd had something better to do today, whether their beds had been too comfortable to leave. Or their wives.

The Huq replied with taunts of their own, recalling past encounters when Ipsli's war aims had not been realized. Then the heralds went to meet in the space between the two hosts, to decide on the order of battle. As usual, it would be individual combats first, then small groups. Ipsli's first battalion was anxious for a rematch with their Huq counterparts; it was felt that last year's engagement was decided more by the state of the ground—it had rained the night before—than by the relative skills of the combatants.

Youths fought first, with minimized weapons. Then came the midranked warriors, in pairs and quatrains. Ipsli was doing well, only two deaths and one maiming, while several Huqs had had to be carried from the field. Sentiment within the ranks was leaning toward ending the day with a general melee.

There came a break for lunch while the spiders fought their bouts. Huqs and Ipslis wagered against each other on the outcomes, the heralds holding the takes and disbursing the winnings. Then it was time for individual champions to take the field.

Fred Mather was in the form of Ipsli's paramount, wearing his great-great-grandsire's armor of laminated strips of bronze overlaid with polished electrum. When, late in the afternoon, the trumpets called his sign, he took up the long spear, its black shaft bound with strengthening wire. He disdained to fight with a shield.

As he stepped out in front of Ipsli, the spear over his shoulder, a shout went up from the battalions behind him. He strode toward the center of the field, watching as the Huq champion came to meet him. Unlike last year, his opponent had chosen only the long, two-handed electric sword. It would be a memorable contest, Mather thought. Next year, they might well be singing songs about today.

He had gotten used to the strangeness of being two persons in one mind. The Martian memory-visions were like the documentary dramas he had seen on television at home, where actors took the parts of historical figures—except that here the spectator took the actor's place. He had wondered at first if the experience was similar to what fiction books had done to readers, before the cleansing of the world.

Now Mather-as-warrior strode calmly to where the heralds waited on the fighting ground. He grounded the butt of his spear, then tipped back his helmet to rest it on the crown of his long, narrow head. The man who had come out to face him set his sword's point against the turf and tilted back his own headgear. His golden eyes gazed at Mather with no sign of fear.

The first herald sang the traditional song. As he heard the last line begin, Mather gripped the shaft of the spear, took a slow and steady breath, and pulled his helmet down. He assumed the ready stance. The swordsman also covered his face and raised his blade.

Bowman yanked the cloche-mask clear of the lunatic's face, but it fit too tightly to come all the way off. Mather's eyes, in the flashlight beam, were wide and opaque. For a moment, they looked almost golden, but the crew chief put that down to a reflection of the pale bone walls in the man's grossly dilated pupils.

Mather blinked, once, then after a moment, twice more.

"Snap out of it!" Bowman said. He poked him again with the pistol's muzzle.

The archaeologist came up off the bench, turning toward the crew chief in one fluid motion. With the back of his left hand, he brushed the pistol away, while his right struck out at Bowman's belly. But the blow did not connect, and not just because the other man stumbled back.

Mather looked down at his right hand, as if puzzled. From the way he held it, Bowman first had the impression that there was something in the madman's grasp—did the Martians have invisible knives?—and that he had tried to stick him with it. But then, as he saw Mather blink, Bowman realized that the crackpot must be see-ing things.

Somehow, that made him more angry than anything yet. It wasn't right that this soft-handed college boy's insanity was threat-ening Red Bowman's bonus and the life it would buy for him here on Mars: a place of his own and a solid business to run. He was will-ing to work hard for what he wanted, and no dreamy-eyed book-fiend was going to rob him of his earned reward.

He stepped forward and smacked Mather across the side of the head with the pistol barrel. But the steel did not hit flesh. Instead, it struck the dull gleam of the Martian head covering. The sound of the impact was a musical note, but the helmet seemed to absorb the shock. Mather barely registered the blow.

Yet something had gotten through. The archaeologist blinked again, and now it seemed for the first time that he was actually focusing on the crew chief. He looked down again at his right hand, curled around empty air. Then he shook his head as if coming out of a daze.

"You're coming with me," Bowman said. He raised the gun, and so that the madman would have no doubt as to the consequences of disobedience, he thumbed back the hammer.

Mather's shoulders slumped. He reached up with both hands and wriggled the silver cloche-mask free of his head. He lowered it and gazed sadly at its polished, figured surface, the perpetual surprise that looked back at him. Then, when Bowman said, "Move it," he flung the metal object up and into the crew chief's face.

Bowman fell back, blood spurting from his nose. He lost his footing and toppled over the bench seat beside him, banging the elbow of his gun arm. The pistol fell, clattering on the bone floor right beside his foot, and he was glad it did not go off. But by the time he had recovered the weapon and swung the flashlight around, he had only enough time to catch Mather disappearing through the door to the plaza, the Martian robe flying like a flag from his shoulders.

He hunted for the madman all night, light and gun at the ready. He steeled himself to shoot on sight, but when the thin Martian dawn came he was still alone.

The mechanical behemoth ground on, house by house, street by street, filling its hoppers with the dust of millennia-dead sea beasts, excreting its cubes of gold and silver, copper and bronze, still warm from the atomic smelter. Bowman fretted that Mather would return from his hiding place in the blue hills and try to stop the work. He took men from other projects, gave them guns, and put them on guard.

The sentries reported seeing occasional flashes of sunlight on metal up in the blue hills, but the madman made no more attempts to interfere with the reduction of the bone city. Finally, the day came when they reloaded the automated miner onto its multiwheeled transporter and prepared to move it across the dusty, glass-bottomed sea to the next deposit. The operation proceeded without incident.

Red Bowman's bonus was safe again. He had been a man short for a while, but had managed to make up a full crew's complement by hiring an experienced hard-rock mining man who had come to Mars hoping to get rich prospecting in the barrens but had found nothing.

The crew chief watched the transporter slowly carry the leviathan away, followed by its floating contrail of pale dust. Then he started up his jeep and drove through the scar where the town had been. The houses were gone, as well as the pavement of the streets on which they had stood for thousands of years. The miner had scraped right down to the packed earth beneath, and in places to the rufous Martian bedrock. After it had uncovered the first urn buried beneath a courtyard, Bowman had called in the technician to reset the automatic controls. The machine had then proceeded to find scores of the gold, silver, and electrum containers, increasing the operation's precious-metals yield by a solid percentage. New Ares had awarded Bowman an "attaboy" bonus for showing initiative.

He came to where the gate had stood and put the jeep onto the ribbon of crushed white rock. He drove slowly toward the hills, then up into them as the road began to climb. He moved his gaze from side to side, watching for flashes of light.

The hills always gave him the creeps. They were as silent as the ancient towns, but somehow the silence was different here. The towns were not human-made, but they had been manufactured by beings who, for all their peculiarities, shared some commonalities with Earthmen. The land itself, though, that was pure Mars. It had never had any connection to humankind, not all the way back to the gelling of the planets. Men might come and build on it, but they would never be *of* it. And those who tried to be of it, like Mather, would always be driven mad.

That was Bowman's way of thinking, and before he moved off to the next demolition, he wanted to talk about it with the one man he knew who might understand. So he drove higher into the hills, stopping every now and then, his head turning from side to side, waiting for the bright wink.

Late in the afternoon, he saw it from the corner of an eye and turned toward the long, boulder-strewn slope from which it had come. There was a group of tall rocks halfway up the hill. They might have been a natural occurrence, or they might have been placed there for some obscure Martian purpose. But when he trained his binoculars on the formation, he saw motion through a gap between two of the stones.

He got out of the jeep and walked toward the place, his hands held out to show that they were empty. "Mather!" he called. "We're leaving! Nobody's going to come after you!"

A voice came from the rocks, thin on the less substantial Martian air. It had a flutey quality, as if a musical instrument were speaking. "What do you want?"

"I just wanted to say good-bye," Bowman said. He was closer now, close enough to see between the gaps in the rocks. He saw silver and touches of gold. "You know," he said, "that mask rightly belongs to New Ares Mining."

"No," said the thin voice, "I don't know that."

"Doesn't matter," Bowman said. "We'll get it later, I suppose. After you die."

There was no response to that.

"You are going to die, you know," said the Earthman, trudging up the slope. "Fact is, I don't know how you've managed to survive this long without water. Were you sneaking in at night to steal it?"

"No."

"Then how?"

Again there was no answer. Bowman had reached the rocks. He could see glimpses of Mather through the gaps. The man was wearing the Martian robe and another mask, this one with an expression of serene amusement. "Come out and we'll talk," he said.

"About what?"

The crew chief shrugged. "About what you're going to do, how you're going to live."

"Does that matter to you?" said the musical voice.

"A little. Listen, at first, I was angry at having you on my crew because I didn't think you'd pull your weight. Then I got scared that you'd screw up the operation and wreck everything."

Bowman waited a moment to see if the other man would respond, then said, "But once you left us alone to get on with it, you were not my problem anymore. And now that we're pulling out, I can afford to wonder about what you think you're achieving up here."

He waited again, this time letting the silence extend. It made him uncomfortable. He was thinking that it wasn't just a silence between him and Mather; it was a silence between him and the hills, between him and Mars.

Finally, the man behind the rocks spoke. "There's nothing to achieve."

"Then what are you doing?"

"There's nothing to do. Nothing to be done."

"I don't understand."

"It's all *been* done," said Mather. "That's the point. That's what Mars is."

"I still don't understand."

"I know." There was another silence, then, although Bowman

had heard no footsteps, Mather's musical voice came as if from far-ther away. "Good-bye."

The Earthman skirted the standing rocks and climbed above them. There was no sign of the other man. He called his name, twice, but heard only the eloquent silence of the Martian hills.

Bowman went back to the jeep, back to the base camp, then on to the next job. In later years, he would sometimes tell people, "Just because you can come up with a question, that doesn't mean there's an answer."

Some years later, a prospector came by, his picks and shovels and magnetometer clattering with each step of his walking machine. He spotted the cube of white stone that the automated miner had left as valueless and went to take a look. To one side, he found a mummi-fied corpse clothed in Martian cloth, seated on a chair carved from Martian ironwood. A silver mask rested on the desiccated lap.

At first, the prospector thought that he'd discovered a genuine Martian, though people said they were all gone now. It was the eyes that fooled him: wide and dried, and turned toward the cube, they had looked from a distance like golden coins.

But the mask was a good one. The prospector's day had not been wasted.

DAVID D. LEVINE

David D. Levine is a lifelong SF reader whose midlife crisis was to take a sabbatical from his high-tech job to attend Clarion West in 2000. It seems to have worked. He made his first professional sale in 2001, won the Writers of the Future Contest in 2002, was nominated for the John W. Campbell award in 2003, was nominated for the Hugo Award and the Campbell again in 2004, and won a Hugo in 2006 for his story "Tk'Tk'Tk." A collection of his stories, *Space Magic,* won the Endeavour Award in 2009. In January of 2010 he spent two weeks at a simulated Mars base in the Utah desert, which led to a highly regarded slide show and *The Mars Diaries,* a self-published hardcopy collection of his and his crewmates' blogs. His story "Citizen-Astronaut," a science-fiction novelette partially based on his "Mars" experience, won second prize in the Baen Memorial Contest, was published in *Analog,* and came in second in the 2011 AnLab Readers' Poll. David lives in Portland, Oregon, with his wife, Kate Yule, with whom he edits the fanzine *Bento.* His website is www.daviddlevine .com.

Here he takes us to Mars in a way that NASA probably never thought of . . .

The Wreck of the *Mars Adventure*

DAVID D. LEVINE

WILLIAM KIDD KNELT UPON THE COLD STONE FLOOR IN THE complete blackness of the Condemned Hold in Newgate Prison. Heavy iron shackles lay loose upon wrists and ankles grown far thinner than when they'd first been fitted, the skin torn and scabrous from too-long acquaintance with the cold, rough metal. Chains rattled as he shifted into a somewhat less uncomfortable position.

All of these were familiar, and could be ignored. But the commotion in the hall beyond his locked door was new, and a terrible distraction. No doubt some of the other prisoners were celebrating the imminent demise of their most famous neighbor.

"Keep quiet out there!" he cried, or tried to. "Leave a condemned man to make peace with his Lord!"

There was no possibility that the revelers could have heard Kidd. His Dundee brogue, once powerful enough to carry across a hundred yards of open ocean in the midst of a gale, was now reduced to little more than a whisper. Yet, almost at once, the babble of voices dropped away to nothing.

A moment later came the rattle of keys in the lock.

This too was unexpected. For anyone at all to enter Kidd's cell was a rarity, by order of the Admiralty Board and the House of Commons. A visit in the middle of the night was unprecedented. And on the very eve of his execution . . .

Kidd levered himself up into a sitting posture, chains clanking as he settled back on his haunches. Weary from months of imprisonment, despondent from years of rejection, disappointment, and defeat, he could think of no reason for such an untimely visit other than more bad news. Perhaps the House had decided to advance his execution to the small hours of the morning for some political reason. Or perhaps they intended to shave his head, or perform some other indignity, before marching him to the gibbet. He'd long given up any thought of comprehending the constant fickle changes of Parliamentary whim.

Whatever the news, Kidd meant to take it as a man should. Exerting himself to his utmost, he strained to rise to his feet. But he had barely struggled up to one knee when the door clashed open.

The dim, flickering light of torches blinded him. He tried and failed to raise an arm to shield his eyes. But before he could do so, two burly keepers entered and pinned his arms behind him. New irons clasped him at elbow and wrist, tight and hard and cold, and new chains ran clattering down to the ringbolts fixed in the stone floor. The guards forced Kidd to his knees, and in a moment he was trussed immovably in place. A hand gripped the back of his head, forcing his gaze to the floor. Was he to be beheaded here in his cell?

"P-prisoner secured, m'lord." The voice belonged to one of the prison's harshest and most brutal wardens. What could reduce this man to stammering servility?

"Leave us." A cold, brusque voice, one used to immediate compliance. It had an accent Kidd couldn't place. Dutch?

"M'lord?"

"Leave us. Alone."

The warden gulped audibly. "Yes, m'lord," he whispered.

The hand released Kidd's head and two sets of feet shuffled out of the cell. A moment later, the door creaked closed, shutting more quietly than Kidd would have thought possible.

A single torch remained, and the sound of one man breathing.

Kidd raised his head.

The stranger was tall, over six feet, and the dark cloak that covered him from head to toe could not disguise his imperious bearing. He held an embroidered handkerchief to his nose, no doubt soaked in vinegar to combat the prison's stench.

"To what do I owe the privilege, m'lord?" Kidd rasped, masking his terror with ironic courtesy.

The man pushed back his hood. "Surely an investor can pay a visit to his client?"

For a moment, Kidd failed to recognize the face, with its proud black eyes and its hard, humped beak of a nose. Then he gasped and ducked his head. Though they'd never before met in person, he'd seen that face in profile on a thousand coins. "Your Majesty," he whispered, though cold anger burned beneath his ribs.

William III, King of England and Ireland, also William II of Scotland, placed the vinegar-soaked cloth again beneath his nose. "My time here is short," he said, his voice muffled. "Even men as deeply stupid as my beloved advisers cannot be counted upon to miss my absence for long. So I must come directly to the point." He drew the cloth aside, his dark eyes fixing Kidd's. "I am here to offer you a pardon."

At first, Kidd could form no reply. Surely this was only a dream? Or a cruel jape, intended only to deepen his suffering? Hope warred with anger and disbelief in his breast. "Your Majesty?" he managed.

"You heard me," the king snapped. "I will spare your filthy, piratical neck from the noose my Parliament has woven for you from your own ill-considered words."

Kidd matched the king's level stare. "I but spoke the truth."

"The truth is nothing against politics! And were it not for politics, I'd never find myself here in this stinking rathole with you." The king sighed. "You are troublesome, Kidd. You and I both know you are no pirate, but my advisers would see you swing for the damage you've done your backers' reputation. And with your impetuous bravado and your damned honesty, you've made so many enemies I could never defend you in public without losing the whole Whig party. But for all your faults, and for all the stories your enemies have spread about you, you're too good a captain to waste on the gibbet. So, again, I have come to offer a pardon." A small strange smile played upon his lips. "But if you accept this pardon, you will be required to undertake a certain charge for me. When you hear the charge, and the conditions, you may wish to decline this offer of clemency."

"What charge and conditions," Kidd snarled through gritted teeth, "could make a man esteem the hangman's noose above a king's pardon?"

Infuriatingly, the smile broadened. "I desire that you plan, outfit, equip, crew, and carry out an expedition to the planet Mars."

Rage flared in Kidd at the king's callous jest, but he held his tongue; he did not even allow the contempt he felt to show on his face.

This prudence was a new thing for Kidd. Even one year ago, freshly detained on false and libelous charges, he would have railed and spat and fought at such a ridiculous slight. But capricious imprisonment had taught him caution.

He paused and gave due consideration to the words of a king—a king not known for levity or insanity. This was a new century, a time of exploration and discovery and wonders. With the New World now nearly as well mapped as the Old, men were setting out in search of even newer worlds. Balloons were rising from all the capitals of Europe, and after Dampier's successful circumnavigation of the Moon, a journey to Mars, though outlandish, was not entirely inconceivable.

"I've heard the charge," Kidd said, swallowing his anger. "And the conditions?"

"*Primus,*" the king said, holding up one finger, "you may not disclose the terms of the pardon to any man, upon penalty of death. *Secundus,* you will be placed under the command of the physiologer John Sexton. You will obey his orders, serve him faithfully, and remain within one hundred feet of him *at all times* until the successful completion of the expedition, under pain of death. *Tertius,* you will be held personally responsible for the safety of the said Sexton. Should any harm whatsoever befall him, you will suffer death." He put down the hand with its three extended fingers and crossed his arms on his chest. "On the other hand, if you should somehow manage to return to London with your own head and Sexton's intact, you'd have the gratitude of a king. Perhaps even a baronetcy."

Kidd considered the king's words, considered them most seriously. He knelt in chains, in the darkest cell of the worst prison in England, faced with a choice between an impossible task—an insane expedition, from the attempt of which neither he nor any man he might recruit would be likely to return—and certain death upon the morrow.

And he began to laugh.

Rough, hacking chuckles burst from a throat left parched and ruined by a year of prison food, prison water, prison air. The king took a step back, the white cloth held tight against his nose, as though he feared Kidd might somehow burst his manacles and attack the royal person.

"I accept your pardon, Your Majesty," Kidd gasped when the fit had passed. "I never could pass up a challenge."

Kidd strolled down Salisbury Court, heading for an appointment with Yale, the chandler whom he had engaged for water, cordage, and comestibles. Five weeks out of prison, it was still a wonder to walk unencumbered, to move for more than ten feet without encountering a wall, to breathe air untainted by the exudations of a thousand condemned prisoners.

Sexton, the physiologer, walked with him. A lean, pale-eyed man of twenty-eight—half Kidd's age—he was not only a member of the Royal Society and a lecturer at Gresham College, but had also invented a novel method for projecting the surface of the spherical Earth onto a flat paper map and discovered two new species of beetle. His theories on interplanetary shipcraft and navigation were, apparently, very highly regarded by his philosophic peers.

And, for all his brains, he had the common sense of a turtledove. Though Kidd's strength was improving, he still walked with a stick. But despite this handicap, he made better speed than Sexton, who paused periodically to converse with strangers, peer curiously at unusual bits of stonework, and scribble notes in a small notebook. The man was like a jackdaw—always darting hither and yon, his attention drawn to any shiny object, and easily startled into flight.

Kidd had originally thought that the secret terms of the king's pardon compelled him to remain close to Sexton to prevent him, Kidd, from escaping. He now believed that the real reason for this requirement was so that Kidd could protect Sexton from being run down by a coach, falling into a canal, or simply forgetting to breathe.

"Please, Dr. Sexton," Kidd called over his shoulder. "We are already late, and Mr. Yale is a busy man."

"Just a moment, Mr. Kidd," Sexton replied, stooping to inspect a weed that grew in the crack between two foundation stones of the building they were passing.

"*Captain* Kidd," Kidd muttered under his breath. He no longer bothered correcting Sexton, but the omission still rankled, especially given how insistent Sexton was upon his own title of Doctor.

"This is the ship?" said Edmonds, Kidd's old shipmate.

"Aye," Kidd replied.

The grizzled old sailor stood silent for a long time, casting a practiced eye on the little ship as she bobbed in the Thames. Edmonds had responded eagerly enough to Kidd's call for a quartermaster; they'd served together upon the *Sainte Rose,* and Kidd would trust him with his life.

"This'd be the strangest ship I've e'er served upon," Edmonds said at last.

To that assertion, Kidd merely nodded. "I'll not argue with that."

The ship was tiny, barely seventy feet from stem to stern, and would carry a crew of only sixty men. But not only was she small, she seemed . . . *spindly.* Everything possible had been done to lighten her weight—bulkheads were screens woven from rattan rather than solid wooden panels, carved rails had been replaced by simple ropes, and canvas sheeting took the place of hatch covers. And Kidd knew of many other changes invisible to the eye, such as the deck planks planed down to half their usual thickness.

"But *sweeps*?" Edmonds asked, incredulous, pointing to the row of oarlocks on either side. "In this day and age?"

Kidd set his chin. "I'd not sail without them. Wind and waves cannot be trusted, but a man at an oar can always be counted on to pull a ship out of trouble. Sweeps have saved my skin more than once."

He did not mention that the sweeps that would be fitted to those oarlocks were made to push air, not water. Sexton had designed them to Kidd's specifications, but Kidd could but hope they would work as well as Sexton promised—along with every other one of the thousand untried, theoretical pieces that made up the strange little ship.

Edmonds left off his critical inspection of the ship and turned to Kidd with a questioning eye. "D'ye think she'll really swim?"

Kidd nodded. "She's a strange one, all right, but there's a reason for it, and if you'll sign on with me, you'll learn what it is."

"Aye, but do ye *trust* her?"

There came a long, considering pause then.

It didn't really matter what Kidd thought. He was bound by the terms of his pardon to sail with Sexton, no matter the circumstances, and not to reveal the reason. But still, he felt he owed his old ship-mate an honest answer.

Though many of Sexton's designs seemed completely daft at first, the man had an enormous brain, and where Kidd could follow his logic, it seemed unassailable. And Kidd himself had supervised the ship's construction and provisioning, using the best men and materials the king's money could buy. If he could assemble a whole crew as good as Edmonds . . .

"I trust her well enough to sail in her myself," Kidd said. "And it'll be a long, long journey." *In miles, at least,* he added silently, though Sexton theorized it would take but two months all told. There were no plans to land upon Mars, merely to survey it for a later expedition.

Edmonds pursed his lips a long moment, then with a firm nod of his chin he stuck out his hand. "If she's good enough for Captain Kidd, she's good enough for me."

With genuine pleasure, Kidd took Edmonds's hand and shook it. "Welcome aboard, Mr. Edmonds. Welcome aboard the *Mars Adventure*."

Kidd shielded his eyes from the rising sun, trying to ignore the babble of the crowd on the wharf as he inspected the ship's bizarre rigging.

He had warned the king that rumors would begin to spread once the crew was hired, and, indeed, in the last few weeks the press of the public for more information on the strange ship, with her secret mission and her infamous captain, had become intense. But Kidd kept a tight rein on his men and kept Sexton busy with his drafts and charts, so that little real news had gotten out. But when they'd begun to inflate the balloons after sunset last night, word had traveled fast and the rabble had begun to gather almost immediately.

Soon everyone would know the secret of the *Mars Adventure*.

Nine balloons bobbed and swayed above the little ship, nine taut white globes of fine China silk filled with coal-warmed air, glowing like enormous pearls in the light of the rising sun. Already the ship rode impossibly high in the water, and the tug of the Thames on her keel combined with the action of the breeze on her balloons to give her a sick, disturbing motion unlike anything Kidd had ever experienced before. Sexton had assured Kidd that, once airborne, the ride would be smooth.

"Make fast that stay, there!" Kidd called, pointing. The bosun repeated his order, and two of the men scrambled up the great purse of netting that restrained the balloons to repair the flaw Kidd had spotted. *Stays* was what Kidd and the men called the great ropes that held the balloons to the ship, though they were no true stays at all; so much was new and unprecedented in this ship that they'd been forced to stretch existing sailing language to cover it all. It was better than the Latin that Sexton insisted on using.

Sexton appeared at Kidd's elbow. "Are we nearly ready to depart?" he said, his eyes darting about. "We must rise with the sun or the lift will be insufficient."

"Very nearly," Kidd replied, turning his attention to the wharf. "We only await . . . ah, there he is."

The crowd parted like the Red Sea before a surging retinue of colorful and bewigged gentlemen, in the midst of which the king strode like Moses. As word spread through the crowd, heads bowed in rings like ripples from a dropped stone.

"Good morrow to you, my subjects!" the king called once the clamor of his arrival had subsided. "I bring you good news! On this most momentous day, a new era of exploration and discovery dawns for England! Today my philosopher, John Sexton, together with a brave crew of handpicked men, sets sail on a most extraordinary voyage . . . an expedition to the planet Mars!"

Pandemonium. Cheers, gawps of astonishment, and hoots of derision greeted the king's announcement. Some of the most amazed reactions came from the crew, many of whom had greeted Kidd's revelation of the ship's destination with knowing winks and the assumption that the *real* purpose of the voyage would be disclosed later.

For his own part, Kidd, bristling at his own dismissal as merely part of "Sexton's crew," whispered a few commands to his bosun. "Aye, sir," the bosun replied, and scurried off to pass the word to the rest of the men.

Kidd understood that the king might wish to distance himself from a notorious, though pardoned, pirate. But he didn't have to like it, and he wasn't going to let the slight go unpunished.

If the king wanted a momentous day, he would have one.

On the wharf, the king blathered on and on, while Sexton peered through his fingers at the ever-rising sun. "We're losing too much time!" he whispered to Kidd.

"Patience," Kidd replied.

Just then, the bosun returned. "All's ready," he murmured in Kidd's ear.

Kidd grinned. "On my signal."

"This is a marvelous day for England," the king declaimed, "and for the glorious House of Orange-Nassau . . ."

That was more than enough royal self-aggrandizement for Kidd. He turned and bellowed, *"Cast off! Away ballast!"*

In one coordinated motion, sailors in the four corners of the ship slipped the mooring lines that held the ship down. A moment later came a rushing rumble from belowdecks, as other men opened the valves that let the ship's ballast—thousands of gallons of Thames water, rather than the usual stones—run out to rejoin the river.

With a great lunge that sent Kidd's stomach rushing toward his boots, *Mars Adventure* sprang into the sky.

The crowd's reaction made its previous outburst seem a paltry whisper. Great cries of astonishment and delight leapt from a thousand throats; a storm of hats soared into the air; coats and shirts waved like banners.

And in the midst of this uproar, the king's face glared up at Kidd with mingled fury and admiration.

Kidd raised his hat in salute. "See you in two months, Billy-Boy," he muttered under his breath, an enormous smile pasted on his face. "You conniving bastard."

Kidd stood at the rope, which on any ordinary ship would be the taffrail, his stomach troubled.

All of his seafaring instincts told him that his ship was completely becalmed. Floating beneath her balloons, she drifted along with the wind, so no breath of breeze freshened the deck. Sexton, with his instruments, assured Kidd that they were making good progress, but still he worried.

An unimaginable distance below, the whole great globe of the Earth lay spread out to his sight: a shiny ball of glass, swirled in blue and white, suspended in the blue of the sky. He could span the width of the world with two hands held out at arm's length, thumb to thumb and fingers spread.

The drop was now so great that the view had passed from terrifying to interesting.

Sexton stood nearby, peering upward through his telescope, and Kidd moved closer to him. "Dr. Sexton," he said, speaking low so that none of the other quarterdeck crew might hear, "I must confess myself uneasy. I've sailed through storms, battled pirates, and faced death by hanging, but this is the first time in my whole career I've felt such a tremulous sensation in my gut. My head is light as well, and my feet unsteady, and furthermore, the quartermaster has told me he feels the same. Could this be some disease of the upper atmosphere?"

Sexton snapped the telescope closed. "'Tis nothing more than the reduction of gravitational attraction."

With all his learning, Sexton sometimes lapsed into Latin without realizing he had done so. "What is the treatment?" Kidd asked. "Bleeding? An emetic?"

At that Sexton laughed. "Fear not. It is no disease, but a natural consequence of our distance from the Earth. This phenomenon was predicted by Newton and confirmed by Halley on his first attempt to reach the Moon. As we travel farther from the mother sphere, the attraction of her gravity—in layman's terms, our weight—will grow less and less. Already we weigh only three-quarters as much as we would at home." He bounced on his toes, and Kidd noticed the man's wig bounding gently atop his head.

Kidd too bounced on his toes, and was astonished to find the small effort propelled him several inches into the air.

"Before the day is out," Sexton continued, "we will pass out of the Earth's demesne and into the interplanetary atmosphere. There we will exist in a state of free descent, and will feel ourselves to have no weight at all. That is the point at which we will be able to retire the balloons and continue with sails alone."

No matter how many times Sexton had explained this phenomenon, Kidd had never quite been able to comprehend it. But now, with his thirteen stone pressing so lightly against his feet, he felt that he was beginning to understand. Again, he hopped lightly into the air, feeling himself float giddily for a moment before his boots struck the deck. "I see," he said.

While Kidd had been bouncing, Sexton had resumed his telescopic observations. "Of course," he said, peering upward through the instrument, "we must first traverse the boundary between the planetary atmosphere, which rotates along with the Earth, and the interplanetary atmosphere, which orbits the Sun." He collapsed the telescope. "There may be a bit of turbulence."

"You call this 'a bit of turbulence'?" Kidd shouted in Sexton's ear.

The two men clung for their lives to the whipstaff that controlled the ship's great sail-like rudder. Not only did it require the full extent of the two men's strength to keep the ship on course through the air, but only by clinging to the staff could they be certain they would not be blown overboard, to vanish immediately into the vastness of the air. Two of the crew had been lost before Kidd had ordered the men to tie themselves to the masts.

The ship tumbled dizzily through the air, lashed by torrential rains, tossed this way and that by capricious winds that blew with hurricane force not just from north, south, east, and west, but also above and below. Even Kidd, who'd survived a storm in the Strait of Bab-el-Mandeb without the least sickness, had sent his supper overboard.

"I had no idea!" Sexton yelled back. "Neither Halley nor Dampier ever encountered the like!"

"Sheet home the t'gallants, damn ye!" Kidd cried to his men. But all Kidd's seacraft was of no avail; no matter how he set the sails, the ship only reeled and veered like a drunken madman.

Kidd had never in his life felt so disoriented. Storm clouds roiled in every direction; the compass spun crazily in its binnacle. Even the basic, eternal verities of up and down had been left behind. "How do we escape this chaos?" he asked Sexton.

"Watch for a bit of blue sky and steer toward it!"

But steering the ship with Sexton's air-rudder was easier in Sexton's theories than it proved in practice, achieving little more than a dizzying spin. And shipping sweeps in this gale would most likely either snap the oar in two or fling the oarsman overboard.

An eternity passed, an eternity in a sailors' hell of unending, omnipresent wind and lightning, before a patch of blue appeared ahead on the starboard side. But though Kidd and Sexton jammed the rudder hard a-larboard and the men worked the sails with skill and alacrity, they achieved nothing but another wild tumble. "God *damn* this weather!" Kidd cried.

"Do not take the Lord's name in vain," Sexton responded. "But trust in Him, and He will provide." And then he pointed.

Another patch of clear blue air, no bigger than an outstretched hand, had opened off the starboard beam. And, just at that moment, the wind happened to be blowing from the larboard side, pressing the ship toward it.

An inspiration seized Kidd. "Set the mainsail!" he called. "Brace sharp up on a larboard tack!"

The bosun, who had lashed himself to the mizzenmast, stared at Kidd as though he doubted his captain's sanity. At the beginning of the storm, following long-standing naval custom, they'd struck all the sails and the balloons, facing the storm with bare masts rather than risking the sails being torn away; since then they'd set only the bare minimum of sail to control the ship. But now Kidd was telling him to raise the largest sail and turn it so that it would catch as much wind as possible.

"Smartly now!" Kidd cried, reinforcing his command with a demand for rapid action.

"Aye, sir!" the bosun replied. He and the maintop men unlashed themselves and crept cautiously, with at least one hand clutching the shrouds at all times, up the mainmast. Only the diligence, skill, and bravery of their decades of experience made it possible for them to unfurl the sail and sheet it home, the yard running fore and aft so that the wind from the larboard side caught the sail full-on.

No sooner was the sail set than it snapped open, filling with the rushing air. The frightening sound of tearing canvas could be heard even over the wind's roar, but the ship surged beneath Kidd's feet, lurching directly sideways toward the patch of blue. At sea, this sort of maneuver would be impossible, but with nothing but air beneath the keel, the game had entirely changed.

"Set all sails!" Kidd cried. "Brace all sharp on a larboard tack! Smartly now!" This stratagem could only succeed if they managed to press on all sail while the favorable wind continued.

The crew set to with a will, sheeting home one rain-lashed sail after another. With each new stretch of canvas, the ship rushed faster toward the open air.

The force of the gale on the crowd of sails also tumbled the ship to the side, heeling her so hard over to starboard that her keel pointed directly into the wind.

Kidd and Sexton clung hard to the whipstaff, but though the ship now lay entirely on her side, the Earth's pull had grown so weak that no man fell overboard.

The patch of blue, now above the mainmast, grew larger and larger.

And then the ship rushed through it, tumbling up into blue and clear air. The storm fell away behind, a horrific ball of lightning-whipped black cloud.

"Thank God," Kidd cried, "for able seamen!"

———

Kidd, Sexton, Edmonds, and the ship's carpenter floated in the air off the ship's starboard hull, each secured from drifting by a light line tied to an ankle. The storm lay three weeks behind them, but they'd passed within sight of many other such—great untidy knots of roiling cloud—and Kidd and Sexton had argued the whole time over how best to prepare for the next that could not be avoided.

The carpenter had chalked a large X on the hull, between the dried barnacles and shipworm holes. "This'd be the spot, Captain," he said. "If'n you're sure . . ."

Kidd wasn't sure, not at all. He cast a baleful eye at Sexton. "This is madness. To cut holes in our own hull?"

Sexton glared right back. "It is the only way."

For three weeks, the ship had been subject to the whims of the interplanetary atmosphere, tossed here and there by every changing breeze and tumbled every which way as it flew. Though they'd fastened down everything they could, the men still floated freely in the air, and the ship's unpredictable turns and tumbles had resulted in many injuries and several men nearly lost overboard. Kidd had learned much about how to sail in this new world, but still the ship seemed to fight him at every turn.

Sexton had proposed a new sail plan of radical novelty. The mainmast and mizzenmasts would be unshipped and remounted forward on the lower hull, sticking down and out to form a great equal-armed Y with the foremast. According to Sexton's theory, putting all sail forward in this way would cause the ship to present her stern to the prevailing wind rather than constantly heeling over; distributing the sails equally in the vertical plane would give them control over the ship's direction and her orientation in the air. But no ship in history had ever had masts below the waterline!

"We'll have to saw the masts from the keelson!" Kidd protested. "She'll never be whole again!"

Sexton patted the air placatingly. "I promise this new design will balance the ship out," he said. "If you can but make the masts secure in their new locations."

Kidd and his men would have to work out an entirely new system of rigging to support the masts. But their spare cordage was limited, and it would have to work perfectly the first time: If the rigging proved inadequate to hold the sails against the pressure of wind, the remounted masts would tear the hull apart. He shook his head. "I don't know if it can be done. Give me time, damn it! We can yet learn to sail her as she stands . . ."

"No. We've bickered enough." Sexton crossed his arms on his chest and glared down his nose to where Kidd floated some feet closer to the hull. "We must gain better control of the ship, and quickly, or come the next storm we'll wind up lost and tumbling, or broken to bits."

Kidd strove to relax his clenched jaw. "Is that an order?"

"If I must."

The two men held each other's gaze for a long, tense moment. Edmonds and the carpenter looked on, their eyes darting from the captain to the philosopher and back.

Once, Kidd had been captain of his own fate. Now he found himself subordinate to a scraggy, wispy-bearded schoolboy, and he rankled at the diminution.

But still . . . Sexton's ideas had gotten them this far. And if they could but complete their mission, the legend of Kidd-the-voyager-to-Mars might eclipse the slanderous lie of Kidd-the-pirate.

He bent down and looped the line from his ankle over his shoulders, cinching up the slack and leaning back to press his bare feet against the rough, barnacled hull. "Give me the axe," he said to the carpenter. Then he hauled off and began chopping through the X.

If anyone was going to murder Kidd's ship, it would be Kidd himself.

Mars shimmered in Kidd's telescope, a great, dull, copper-colored sphere. Where the Earth had gleamed like glass, the sun shining off her clouds and oceans and lakes, Mars seemed lusterless as dry, unpolished wood. A dead world.

Snapping the telescope shut, Kidd gazed at the approaching planet with his unaided eye. Mars's disc was already too big to cover with a thumb, and growing visibly day by day.

It should have been an exciting time.

The disaster had arrived imperceptibly, by stages. *Mars Adventure* had left London with food and water for three months, a month more than the longest possible round-trip voyage predicted by Sexton's theories. The outbound voyage had taken nearly eight weeks, longer than expected, but once they had refitted the masts and sorted out the working of the ship in air, Sexton's bizarre new sail plan worked beautifully. At the six-week mark, all hands had agreed to accept short rations and press on to Mars, expecting a quicker return trip.

When they'd broached the first empty water cask, they'd thought it just a fluke. But the second and the third dry cask began to raise alarms in Kidd's mind. He and the quartermaster had gone into the hold and thumped every remaining barrel.

Nearly one-third were dry. Even on half rations, they'd surely die of thirst long before they reached London.

"Damn that Yale!" Kidd muttered, clenching the telescope in his hands as though it were the accursed chandler's neck. But even more than Yale, Kidd cursed himself. Years hunting pirates, only to be betrayed and abandoned by his own backers, should have taught him better than to extend any trust beyond his own two hands.

Suddenly, Sexton's hand clapped down upon Kidd's shoulder, startling him out of his reverie. "Do not curse the chandler," he said, entirely too brightly. " 'Tis not his fault."

"How so?" Kidd replied, struggling to regain his composure. "Either he cheated me—that is, the king—or else he is incompetent."

Sexton shook his head. "I realized last night what the reason must be. Those casks were full when we loaded them, but they were built for Earthly climes. Have you not noticed how parched of moisture the atmosphere has become?"

"Aye . . ." Kidd licked chapped lips with a tongue dry as old leather. The air had been growing steadily colder and drier as Mars drew near.

"The air's thirst first dries out the casks' wood, then draws the water out through the seams between the staves. On our next voyage, we can line the casks with wax or lead to prevent this evaporation."

"Next voyage?" Kidd laughed without amusement. "There'll be no next voyage for us." He cast his eyes out over the empty, cloudless air and the dead, dry planet below. "The sea may be an inhospitable mistress, but at least she offers the occasional island, with a spring or pond of freshwater. There are no islands in the air."

"No islands, perhaps. But there are . . . canals."

Kidd blinked. "Canals?"

"Give me your glass." Sexton peered through Kidd's telescope at Mars, then handed it back, pointing. "There. Near the planet's limb."

For a long time, Kidd saw nothing. Then, wavery and blurry, a few thin straight silvery threads appeared, glinting in the reduced sunlight.

Kidd lowered the instrument from his eye. "Mere mirages."

"Canals," Sexton insisted. "And what could be in them but water? If the ship can but make landfall and rise from it, we might yet survive."

Again Kidd licked his dry lips, considering. Then he turned to the bosun. "Send word for the carpenter," he said. "The ship'll need some sort of legs if we're to land on sand."

Mars now loomed above the bow, glowing red and huge as the dome of St. Peter's at sunset. The great north polar cap gleamed white and pristine atop the ruddy globe, but Sexton had rejected Edmonds's idea of landing there to melt water from snow, fearing that the air of the polar regions might be so cold that their limited supply of coal could not heat it sufficiently to raise the ship again. Instead, they were aiming for an area at about forty degrees north longitude, where several great canals converged. Sexton swore he'd seen through his telescope evidence of a city at that nexus; Kidd's eyes, twice as old, could not confirm this. But, at least, the presence of multiple canals increased their chances of finding water.

Assuming, that is, that those silvery threads were indeed canals and did contain drinkable, liquid water and not some unknown Martian substance. And also assuming that they could land where they intended and survive the landing.

Even Sexton had no idea what conditions they might encounter on the fast-approaching Martian surface.

The winds were now shifting hard and fast as the ship entered the zone of turbulence where the interplanetary atmosphere met Mars's own rotating sphere of air. But Kidd's crew was now seasoned in aerial seamanship, the ship's rigging well proven, and unlike on Earth there seemed to be no storm clouds in the offing. "The air here's too dry for storms," Sexton opined through lips as cracked as every other man's. "Or even clouds, for that matter."

All they had to do now was to wait for a favorable wind, then raise sails to catch it. When that wind shifted or died, as they invariably did, they'd strike the sails and coast on in the same direction until encountering another favorable one. The work was exhausting for the men, but, using this technique, they were making excellent time. Sexton estimated they'd be close enough to Mars to deploy the balloons in just a few days.

Kidd peered through his telescope, seeking the tiny scudding bits of airborne flotsam whose motion he'd learned would predict a shift in the breeze. But suddenly a flock of silvery fluttering shapes burst across his view.

Sexton had given the creatures a Latin name that Kidd could never recall. The men called them flying fish, though they resembled fish only superficially in shape and not at all in taste, and they did not so much fly as row through the air. But over the past weeks Kidd had learned that such a flock often rode the leading edge of a hard-blowing wind . . . which was exactly what Kidd had been hoping for.

"Set royals and t'gallants!" he cried, and the crew leapt into action, many of them literally leaping twenty or thirty feet through the air to their stations. They'd become adept at maneuvering through the air, hands and feet propelling them swiftly from line to yard to sail in the absence of weight—Sexton insisted that the phenomenon should be called "free descent," though there was no descending at all. Kidd worried what would happen to the men when they returned to Earth, where a fall from a height could again kill them.

Kidd hauled himself hand over hand along the rope taffrail from one side of the quarterdeck to the other, peering over the sides at the mainmast and mizzenmasts. But the crews of all three masts knew their business now, and within minutes the sails were sheeted home.

A moment later, the hard gust hit them. The whole ship shuddered at the impact, yardarms rattling and masts groaning, and some of the men whooped as they bounced at the ends of their safety lines. Kidd and Edmonds leaned against the whipstaff, feet skidding on the deck as the air fought their attempts to turn the ship into the wind. But the rigging held, the oft-repaired sails stayed in one piece, and the ship shot forward, the planet growing with satisfying speed.

A few minutes later, Kidd was startled by the approach of Sexton, who scrambled down the length of a safety line with a panicked expression on his face. Somewhere the man had lost his wig.

"Stop! Stop!" Sexton called over the rush of air. "We're already well into the planetary atmosphere! I was a fool not to realize that Mars's gravity is less than Earth's. His atmosphere must be less dense, and thus deeper!"

"I've no time for natural philosophy, Doctor!" Kidd shouted back.

"You don't understand, Captain! We're beginning to fall!"

Sexton's announcement made Kidd realize consciously what his body had been trying to tell him for some time. The ship's rapid and increasing forward motion was, in fact, the formerly familiar sensation of falling. And not only was the ship speeding downward toward the planet, but Kidd's own weight was beginning to return, dragging him along the whipstaff and toward the ship's bow. "Inflate balloons!" he called. "Smartly now! And make yourselves fast to whatever you can!"

Immediately, the waisters scrambled to the great chests on deck where the balloons had been stowed weeks before. It had taken them a full day to inflate them back on Earth; now they would have to do it in far less time and in the midst of a gale.

Kidd returned his eyes to the sails, constantly adjusting their tack to keep the ever-shifting wind from tearing the ship apart. Should he strike them completely, losing all control, in order to reduce speed?

But before he could answer that question, his attention was drawn back to the ship's waist by a hideous screech of dismay. It was the captain of the waist. "Ruined!" he cried in anguish. "All ruined!"

In his hands he held a length of black and rotting silk.

Kidd dashed to the waist, rushing from chest to chest to assess the damage. Every balloon was more or less rotted where it had touched the wood of the chest. The parts in the middle of each bundle were still whole, but because of the way the balloons had been packed, every one was riddled with holes. There was no conceivable way that even one of them could be made to hold air in the limited time available.

Kidd looked down at the rotted cloth held taut between his fists.

It had been he, personally, who had packed the balloons away. He'd known how important they would be to their survival upon return to Earth, and he'd made sure they were properly folded and stowed.

What he had not considered at the time was that they had already been wetted by the first rains of the storm before being deflated and struck. The moist silk, no matter how carefully folded into the chest, was fated to mildew and decay.

Kidd, himself, had doomed *Mars Adventure*. He'd treated delicate silk like common sailcloth, and the sensitive stuff had wilted and died under his care.

Helplessly, he raised his eyes to Mars, the ruddy glowing ball rushing inexorably toward them, a great sphere of sand and rock against which the ship would now surely be dashed to flinders.

Sexton appeared by his side. Without a word, Kidd showed him the rotting silk. "Are they all like this?" the philosopher asked.

Kidd nodded, not trusting himself to speak. Had he not been nearly weightless, he might have collapsed in despair upon the deck.

Sexton immediately drew out his telescope, staring through it with such concentration it seemed that he intended to burn a hole through the storm with the intensity of his gaze alone. But at last he collapsed the instrument and turned to Kidd with slumped shoulders. "We cannot sail our way out of this," he admitted. "We are already too deep into Mars's planetary atmosphere; his gravitic attraction holds us fast." He sighed. "If only we could flap our fins and fly away, like the caelipiscines."

It took Kidd a moment to recognize the Latin as the name Sexton had given the flying fish. "Or row our way out of trouble." So many times in his career, Kidd had put out sweeps to shift the ship in a situation where wind and wave had failed him.

But though Kidd's heart lay heavy within his breast, Sexton's eyes showed the light of inspiration. "The oars," he said. "The oars! Perhaps they may be of use . . ."

"In this gale? They'd snap like twigs!"

Sexton shook his head. "Consider the fins of the caelipiscines."

Struggling to follow Sexton's reasoning, Kidd nevertheless tried to consider the fins. Great broad filmy things they were, stiffened with slim ribs of tough spiny tissue.

Each rib was no thicker than a pigeon's quill, but there were so many of them that each one bore only a small proportion of the strain as the fish flapped through the air.

No. They didn't exactly flap, not like birds. The action was more like rowing.

"Dear Lord," Kidd said, understanding.

"But we must reduce our speed at once," Sexton said, "or we'll have no chance."

"Strike all sails!" Kidd called. "And send word for the sailmaker, the rigger, and the carpenter!"

After the carpenter, the sailmaker, and the rigger had finished their work, there was barely room to move on the deck.

The least rotted parts of the balloon silk had been cut into strips, each strip then fastened between an oar and its neighbor; the whole assemblage was intended to form on each side a vast spreading wing like the sail of a Chinese junk. But at the moment, the ship's waist seemed no more than a vast fluttering mass of white fabric streaked with black. Loops and billows of loose, rotted silk luffed wildly in the wind of the ship's descending passage through the Martian air. Even two strong men could barely hold their oar steady against the pull of it.

The oarlocks had been reinforced with blocks, great knots of oak and cordage, and loops of the heaviest cable connected each block to its partner on the opposite gunwale. Running under the keel, the network of cables cradled the ship in a vast basket of rope.

"This will never work," Sexton muttered. "I was a fool even to suggest it."

It was unlike Sexton to lose faith in his own ideas. Usually, he would cling to a notion, no matter how impractical it seemed to Kidd, until indisputable success or failure settled the question definitively. But now, with the whole crew's lives riding on this one mad inspiration, the philosopher was shivering in near panic.

"It will work," Kidd said, clapping Sexton on the back—though he himself was far from certain of it. "It must."

Ahead and below, Mars now bulked so large that he could no longer be encompassed by the eye as a sphere. Instead he seemed a horizon, albeit a horizon unnaturally curved. Mars's proximity and the pressure of his atmosphere upon the ship's hull also gave Kidd a feeling of weight, a pressure of the deck against his boot soles he'd not felt in nearly two months. Sexton said that the pressure would never amount to more than a third what it did on Earth, which was good, because after so many weeks adrift, Kidd's knees felt as weak and wobbly as a newborn fawn's.

Or perhaps that was merely terror.

Kidd strode to the forward edge of the quarterdeck to address the crew, doing his best to put confident strength into his step. On an ordinary ship, he'd have climbed into the rigging of the mizzenmast, but *Mars Adventure*'s mizzenmast was now fastened to her starboard hull. "We'll not be rowing, lads!" he called above the rush of air. "Not in the ordinary way. You all know the command 'hold water,' d'ye not?"

A chorus of confused assent. "Hold water" was never used on a ship this large; it meant to brace the oar with one's body, to bring a small boat to a rapid halt.

"That's what we'll be doing. First, we'll point oars astern, then, at the command, we'll all bring 'em forward, smooth and handsome. Then *hold* those oars, hold 'em for dear life, for the whole ship'll be hanging from them!" He glanced at Sexton for confirmation and received a nervous nod. "Then listen for commands to raise or lower your oars. But only shift them a wee bit! Just like trimming sail."

He could only see a few of the men's faces, appearing and disappearing behind waves of flapping, rotted silk. They seemed nervous and unsure of themselves.

Yet those faces also showed hope, and trust . . . hope and trust in *him.*

Kidd set his jaw. He would prove himself worthy of that trust, or die in the attempt. "Point oars astern!" he cried, and "Fasten oars to oarlocks!"

With the best discipline they could muster, the men struggled to comply with a command that no captain had likely ever uttered before, using equipment no ship had ever seen before. The forest of oars fell astern, the patched and rotten silk strung between them flapping with a series of sharp reports like small-arms fire as the men worked to tie each oar firmly into its reinforced oarlock.

"Ready, Captain," the bosun reported after far too long a time.

Kidd took a breath. This was the moment that would prove Sexton's mad idea or else doom them all. "Hold water!" he cried in a bellow as firm as any he'd ever possessed. "Handsomely, now!"

The men put their backs into it, grunting with effort as they worked to lever the oars forward. Though they pressed against only air, not water, the force of the ship's great speed on the tattered silken membrane that stretched between each pair of oars was enormous.

They were good men, the best. They'd been fed well, on the finest rations the king's money could buy. But would even their able seamen's strength be enough?

The ship shuddered and yawed as the oars and their burden of fabric spread gradually wider, the rushing air snapping the silk taut. Men and timbers groaned under the strain, and Kidd felt himself pressed forward as the surge of air began to slow the hurtling ship. "Steady, lads!" he called, holding tight to his hat.

Juddering, trembling, fighting like a gaffed marlin, *Mars Adventure* began to transform herself from a ship of the air into something like a gigantic flying fish.

By now, the great ruddy curve of Mars's horizon had begun to straighten. A few thin wisps of cloud scudded by to either side, and even above. Sexton, bracing himself against the binnacle with his telescope, called out directions and made broad hand gestures, which Kidd fought to interpret into commands to his men. "Larboard sweeps up a point!" he called, and "Starboard, hold steady!" The roar of the wind in the rigging was deafening.

Kidd didn't always understand what Sexton was asking him to do. He suspected that Sexton himself didn't know either. Often the men overcorrected, or misinterpreted Kidd's commands— commands they'd never heard before. The ship rolled and pitched violently whenever a pair of men lost control of their oar for even a moment. Yet somehow no oar snapped and no man was lost overboard; nor did the ship tumble into an uncontrollable spin. And though the water-damaged silk continued to shred, it did not fall completely to bits . . . at least, not yet.

Closer and closer the ship drew to the land beneath, now whipping past in a red-and-ochre blur beneath the keel. Strange mineral formations sped by on either side, fantastical shapes of orange stone like nothing Kidd had ever seen in all his travels. A broad canal filled with shining water, straight as a spar and stretching from horizon to horizon, appeared, then fell behind in a flash. And then came an astounding city—towering spires, broad streets, and just a glimpse of what might be the scuttling inhabitants. Kidd gaped at the apparition as it receded astern.

"Captain!" cried Sexton.

Kidd turned about to find a tremendous dune of red sand looming ahead, Sexton gesturing madly with his arms.

"Starboard sweeps down five points!" Kidd cried. "Larboard up five!"

The men groaned with effort as they strained to comply. The whole ship creaked and shuddered as she leaned heavily to starboard. Kidd and Sexton put their whole weight into the whipstaff, providing what little help they could with the rudder.

Ponderously, grudgingly, the hurtling ship's course changed.

But not enough. They would not escape collision with the dune.

"All for'ard sweeps up! All aft sweeps down! Hold fast! And God save us all!"

With an enormous lurch, the prow rose up into the air, the horizon tilting madly as the ship reared back on her heel. Men cried out as the sudden change in bearing drove their sweeps hard against their bodies; one lost his grip and fell screaming down the length of the deck. Everywhere came the sound of ripping silk and the shuddering crack of tearing wood.

Kidd and Sexton scrabbled across the tilting deck to the binnacle and held on for dear life.

And then, with a horrific splintering crash, like God's own broadside, the ship ran hard aground.

Kidd knelt in the cold sand, head bowed in an attitude of prayer. But he was not praying; he was merely resting his weary bones. Idly, he wondered if God heard the prayers of men on Mars.

The ship lay largely intact on the breast of the great soft dune of sand upon which she'd run aground. But the two lower masts had been smashed to splinters, and the hull bore two great gashes where they'd been rooted. The landing legs the carpenter had rigged had also torn away, taking with them several hull planks each. Cargo and coal lay scattered across a mile of sand. Somewhere out there, too, lay the bodies of three men who'd been thrown from the ship in the crash. Two more had died of their injuries; most of the rest were expected to recover. Kidd himself carried his left arm in a sling, counting himself lucky to have endured no more than a wrenched shoulder.

By day, the climate of Mars's surface was not dissimilar from that of the air in the planet's vicinity: cold and dry, with a thin wind that whistled across the vastness and whipped up dancing whirls of dust. But when the sun had set an hour after the wreck—the first darkness they'd seen after two months of sailing the shadowless air between planets—the cold had grown far deeper, biting hard even through Kidd's heaviest coat. Most of the men had not even that much clothing to protect them. None of them had slept much, and the rising of the weak, wan sun had done little more than make the dismal situation more visible.

A chuffing sound of boots on sand made Kidd look up. It was Edmonds, the quartermaster, looking haggard and worn. "We've finished the inventory, sir."

Kidd merely waited.

"There's beef and pease for two months at half rations. But them water casks . . ." Edmonds shook his head. "Half of 'em sprung in the crash, sir. We've maybe two weeks."

Kidd took a breath, not knowing what to say. Before he could form a reply, there came a shout from above. One of the men stood atop the ship's prow, one foot braced on the fractured bowsprit, waving his arms and crying out words whose meaning was swept away by winds and lost in the vast thin desert air.

Awkwardly, Kidd levered himself to his feet and cupped his good hand behind his ear. "Say again?" he called.

The man made a speaking trumpet of his hands. *"Martians!"*

The natives somewhat resembled crabs—man-sized crabs with only four limbs, drawn out lengthwise and walking about on their hind legs. But though they had two arms and two legs, those limbs bent in all the wrong places, and both limbs and body were covered with a hard shell that shaded from white on the belly to the same red-ochre as the sand on the back. There was no distinct head, only a bulge at the top of the torso from which sprouted two black eyes on flexible stalks, like a lobster's, and a vertical mouth like the working end of a blacksmith's pincers. Each hand resembled a crab in itself, the fingers tipped with vicious-looking claws.

They waited in a group on the sand. There were over a hundred of them.

Kidd lowered his telescope and turned to Sexton. "D'ye suppose the savages speak English?"

Sexton looked terrible: his finery a shambles, wig long vanished, and cheeks gone black with stubble. "Unlikely. But they're no savages."

"How so?"

Sexton peered again through his telescope, and Kidd did the same. "Their clothing. Note the colors and patterns—very sophisticated. Somewhat reminiscent of Persian carpet. And especially that one in the center, the one with the hat. He appears to have jewelry at his shoulders and wrists."

Kidd squinted, but still could not make out as much detail as the younger Sexton. "All I see is the swords." Each native carried a long, thin sword, curved like a Persian shamshir, thrust scabbardless through his belt; smaller blades, likewise slim and curved, were also in evidence. They gleamed in the pale sunlight.

Sexton scoffed. "We are armed as well, are we not? And we are no savages."

To that, Kidd had no reply.

Kidd did his best to hold his head high as he slogged awkwardly down the slope of soft sand, but between his injured arm and the satchelful of materials for negotiation—gold coins, glass beads, dried beef, a flask of water, a Bible—he had a hard time keeping his balance. The Martians, he noticed, had wide flexible feet well suited for walking on sand; their lower garments were loose pantaloons like the Hindoos', cuffed at the knee, leaving the red-carapaced lower legs bare.

Focusing on these details helped keep Kidd from curling up on the sand in a terrified ball.

Sexton preceded him, holding out his open, empty hands. "We greet you in the name of King William III of England and Ireland, and II of Scotland."

The Martian with the hat stepped forward from the rest. He had a distinct but not unpleasant odor, something between horses and cinnamon, and the bright metal fixed to his carapace at several points had the appearance of real gold. Chittering and clattering in his own language, he pointed one chitinous hand up to the sky, then swept it downward in a gesture that encompassed the *Mars Adventure*, the Englishmen, and the Martians as well. Then he stood silent, with folded hands.

Sexton and Kidd exchanged a glance. Even the natural philosopher was plainly baffled by this display. "Perhaps we should show him the Bible?" Kidd suggested. "He waved up at Heaven . . ."

"I've no better notion," Sexton confessed. Kidd handed him the heavy book, and he opened it to Genesis. "This is our most sacred book," Sexton said to the native, presenting it reverently, "and this is the story of the creation of the universe."

The Martian took up the book, examining it on all sides with chittered commentary to his fellows. He ran crab-leg claws down the columns of text, as though reading, and tapped delicately at the leather cover and spine. He held the book close to his face, the eyes bending in together in a most disturbing manner.

Then, to Kidd's horror, he slowly and deliberately tore out a page, folded it, and crammed it between his hideous jaws.

Rigid with mortification, Kidd and Sexton could do nothing more than stand and stare round-eyed as the Martian chewed and swallowed the page with an apparent attitude of careful contemplation. No London gourmand in his favorite club had ever sampled a glass of wine with such keen attention. Even the black and lidless eyes appeared to lose focus, the native seemingly concentrating on the flavor of the vellum and ink.

Sexton was nearly vibrating with rage. "That is the word of the Lord!" he spat.

Kidd, too, was offended, but not so much as Sexton, and he was keenly aware of the dozens of armed Martians who had moved in to surround them on all sides. "Easy, Doctor," he muttered low, putting a hand on Sexton's shoulder.

With a visible effort, Sexton calmed himself. But Kidd had to physically restrain him when the Martian tore out a second and a third page, tearing each one into smaller bits and sharing them out among the other Martians nearby.

"It seems they find the word of our Lord quite . . . palatable," Kidd said as he held Sexton back with his one good arm across Sexton's narrow chest. He himself was so stunned by the Martians' blasphemous feast that he felt near to breaking out into a fit of hysterical giggles.

Sexton took a deep breath, then patted Kidd's hand. Kidd released him. "Forgive them, Lord," Sexton said, casting his eyes heavenward, "for they know not what they do."

While the two men had been talking, the lead Martian had handed the Bible to one of the others. A third native now came forward bearing a squat glass bottle, which the leader took and presented to Sexton. Spiraling marks, possibly writing, were etched into the bottle's surface; the contents were a deep amber in color.

Sexton and Kidd exchanged a quizzical look. It was Kidd who removed the stopper, which was made of some kind of flexible resin, and delicately sniffed the liquid within. He quirked an eyebrow, not trusting himself to speak, before tasting.

The flavor was unusual, with hints of ginger and pine, but the rich mellow burn as the liquid slid down Kidd's throat was so familiar that a tear stung his eye.

"It's not quite Ferintosh," he said to Sexton, "but *damn* me, that is fine whisky!"

Sexton blinked, then turned and bowed to the Martian. "It seems we have a basis for commerce," he said.

Kidd warmed his hands over a Martian prince's fire, marveling at how very far he'd come from Newgate Prison.

Despite the difficulties of communication, the Martians had been eager to trade their goods for books, belts, and anything else made of leather. The Martian meats were palatable, though spicy and a bit gamey in flavor, and Kidd and his men had been allowed the use of a small rounded building that appeared to have been carved seamlessly from a single piece of sandstone. Sexton theorized that the "stone" was in fact merely sand fused together with the Martians' own saliva, but Kidd tried not to think about that.

As for Sexton, he was as happy as a clam at high tide. He occupied himself studying the Martian flora and fauna, the language, and astronomy—he said he'd found that the planet had two tiny moons. He seemed perfectly content to remain here for the rest of his life.

But the ship's stores of acceptable trade items were limited. Some of the men had had success exchanging their labor and entertainments, such as playing on the pennywhistle, for the Martian liquor and other sundries, but they couldn't go on like this forever. Already, Kidd thought, the Martian with the hat was beginning to cast inhospitable looks upon them with his protuberant black eyes.

Kidd stood up from the fire pit and made his way across the crowded common room to where Sexton sat studying one of the Martian "books"—a long spool of thin steel etched with spindly writing. Martian steel was plentiful and much better than English steel, easily the equal of the best Spanish steel.

Sexton sat engrossed for some time before noticing Kidd's presence. "I think this may be a verb," he said, holding up an inscribed strip of metal.

"I have a question for you," Kidd said. "Of natural philosophy."

"Oh?"

"Come outside with me."

The two of them drew cloaks about themselves—rich, soft cloaks of the brightly colored Martian fabrics—for the tiny weak sun was long vanished from the sky. The street outside was quiet and very dark, the Martians being generally stay-at-homes at night, and a million stars stared down unwinking.

"Which of them is the Earth?" Kidd asked, clouds of breath puffing from his mouth.

Sexton looked upward for a moment, then pointed. "Just beyond the eastern horizon, I believe. She should rise within the hour."

"I see." Kidd gazed in the indicated direction. "What would it take to get there?"

"New balloons, of course," Sexton replied without hesitation. He'd plainly considered the question in detail already, if only as an intellectual exercise. "But there's plenty of this fine fabric available." He rubbed his cloak between two fingers. "Food and water can be obtained from the natives, likewise coal to heat air for the ascent. The biggest problem is replacing the masts."

"Aye, the masts." The Martians did not seem to use wood for construction at all. In this city of stone and steel, they'd seen no wood bigger than kindling.

"And repairing all the other damage from the crash. But the masts are the sticking point." Sexton clapped Kidd on the shoulder. "Still, it's not so bad here, eh? Now come inside. 'Tis cold."

"In a moment," Kidd replied.

While Sexton returned to his books, Kidd stared off to the east, as though he could will the bright blue star of Earth to rise more quickly.

Kidd grubbed through the box of knuckle-roots near the fire pit, looking for the ones that were the least scrawny and fibrous. The white, knobby roots were tough and flavorless, but the Martians too cared little for them; a hundredweight could be obtained for just a few hours' labor. Kidd suspected the roots of being animal fodder but preferred not to inquire too deeply into the question. They were keeping him and his men alive.

The ship's books and leather had all been eaten weeks ago, putting an end to trade for luxuries such as meat and rum and sweets. But water and wood had to be hauled on Mars as well as anywhere else, and the men, with the Earthborn muscles of able seamen, could lift and haul far more than any Martian. There were things to herd, which were nothing like sheep and yet acted very much like sheep, and the canals required constant maintenance. All this work kept them supplied with food, of a sort, and water and coal. But it was no life for a sailor.

Selecting several roots from the pile, Kidd prepared to roast them, but when he went to stoke the fire, he found the cloth basket that served as a coal scuttle empty. Kidd cursed; bad as they were when roasted, raw knuckle-roots were completely inedible. "Sexton," he called, tossing the basket his way. "Bring us some coal from the pile, would you?"

While he waited for the coal, Kidd arranged the roots in the fire pit, bemoaning his fate. But by the time he'd placed the last root, Sexton and the coal had still not appeared. "Damn you, man," he called over his shoulder, "what's the delay?"

But Sexton did not reply, and was nowhere to be seen.

Sighing with exasperation at the easily distracted philosopher, Kidd rose and stalked into the next room, where he found Sexton standing by the coal pile with the half-filled basket at his feet, staring with great intensity at a lump of coal. "Surely," Kidd snapped, "you can leave off your studies for five minutes for the sake of our supper?"

In reply, Sexton thrust the filthy thing into Kidd's hands. "What think you of this?"

The black lump was not coal at all but wood covered in coal dust. The Martians used small fragments of wood as kindling; this lump was much bigger than those, nearly as large as a fist, but apart from that it was not unusual. "It's wood," Kidd said with a shrug. "What of it?"

"The rings, man! Look at the *rings*!"

Kidd rolled his eyes, then peered closer . . . and his heart began to race. "From the curvature . . . this must have come from a tree at least three feet in diameter."

"Exactly!" Sexton pointed to several similar lumps in the cloth basket. "And these are the same. Yet there's not a tree to be seen anywhere near here." He picked up a chunk of wood and held it up between them. "We must discover their source!"

———

Kidd slogged to the top of a dune, surveying the horizon ahead through his telescope. "Nothing!" he called to Sexton. "Not a damned thing."

Not awaiting a response, he headed back down the dune, his feet sending cascades of the fine, cold sand sliding toward where Sexton sat rubbing his feet.

The natural philosopher's face showed vexation and exhaustion both. "I would have *sworn* that adjective he used indicated a distance of between two and ten miles." He took a drink from his waterskin. "My water's over half-gone. Perhaps we should turn back."

Kidd looked back along the well-trodden track they'd followed for the past four hours, then forward to where it vanished around a curve. "You're certain he indicated this path? And that he understood what you were looking for?"

Sexton shrugged. "It's a pox'd difficult language."

Kidd took a sip of water, shielding his eyes against the sun, and considered their situation. It was nearly noon, and all they'd seen in four hours of walking was endless sand and mineral formations that had once seemed exotic. Though his own waterskin was not as depleted as Sexton's, he too was tempted to abandon this snipe hunt. Yet it was the only hope they had.

He stared out across the desert. So much like an ocean, yet red and dry and motionless. And, unlike the sea, with its constant rush of wind and wave, oppressively silent.

No . . . not quite silent. Could that be . . . ?

"My feet are—" Sexton began.

"Hush!" Kidd snapped, and cut him off with a gesture.

Kidd listened hard. And heard a sound he'd not heard in many months.

Axes. Axes chopping wood. The sound had been hidden from them before by the noise of their own feet on the sand.

They hurried forward, around the curve, and soon found themselves on the edge of a canyon perhaps two hundred feet deep. They'd been only a few hundred yards from it and had not even suspected its existence. A sandy track, apparently carved from the canyon wall by Martians, switchbacked down from the desert's surface. And at the bottom . . .

"My God," Kidd said.

The bottom of the canyon was thick with trees. Enormous trees, a hundred or even a hundred and fifty feet tall, each honey-blonde trunk rose straight and smooth from the dark loamy floor to a single great tuft of foliage just below the canyon's lip. Groups of Martians moved among them, tiny at the feet of these towering giants.

As they watched, one of the trees fell gently, slowly, to the canyon floor. The Martians leapt upon the fallen giant and began hacking it into tiny pieces with their axes.

"What in God's name are they doing?" Kidd cried.

"The growing conditions at the bottom of this canyon must be nearly unique," Sexton mused. "But, as we've seen, coal is plentiful here. Perhaps they are so accustomed to burning coal that they must cut their wood into coal-sized chunks."

Kidd shook his head. "Prisoners of habit."

While Kidd stared down into the canyon, Sexton paced excitedly. "I must determine how these trees survive in the midst of a desert!" he muttered. "This could be my life's work!"

At that statement, Kidd's eyes went wide, and his already-dry mouth grew drier still. These trees were the final piece in the puzzle of how to return to Earth, but if he returned without Sexton, he'd face the noose anew.

Furthermore, he realized, he'd grown rather fond of the silly goose.

"But Sexton," Kidd said, placing an arm around the philosopher's shoulders, "if you make of these trees your life's work, who will help us to rebuild the ship? Surely there are improvements to be made in the design."

"Surely . . ." Sexton said, his eyes unfocusing as he considered the question.

"And once we are airborne, we must find a new prevailing wind to bear us homeward. For this, we may require new theories of the motions of air."

"A difficult problem indeed." Sexton patted his pockets for his notebook.

"Consider, too, the problem of bringing the trees, whole, out from this canyon, transporting them to the ship, and raising them up as masts."

Sexton's head came up suddenly. "Masts?"

"Masts," Kidd acknowledged.

"But that's exactly what we need!" said Sexton, and laughed. "Masts!"

"Masts!" Kidd cried, and he too burst out laughing.

The two men held hands and danced around and around, bouncing with glee high into the thin Martian air.

Mars Adventure floated fifty feet above the sand, straining against her mooring cables. Above her loomed eight vast balloons, each slightly larger than before—an enormous crazy patchwork of bright Martian colors. They had taken up nearly every yard of fabric in the city, purchased with many weeks of backbreaking labor, but both Martians and Englishmen seemed pleased with the exchange.

The new masts were astounding—straight and smooth and so very light that they'd taken only half the crew to hoist out of the canyon and fit into place. And this was not merely the lighter weight of everything on Mars . . . these trees, products of a tiny, dry, and alien planet, bore a wood lighter and stronger than any on Earth. They'd packed the hold with as many logs as they could cram in. "We'll build a whole fleet of airships!" Sexton swore, "and come back for more! We'll make our fortune with these logs!"

"Not I," Kidd told him.

Sexton blinked in astonishment, then grinned. "Surely the famous Captain Kidd does not lack in avarice?"

Kidd returned Sexton's grin. "Have no fears on that score. Upon my return, I expect the gratitude of a king! And with those proceeds, I intend to settle down in Scotland, my ancestral home, with all the Ferintosh I can drink." He leaned over the taffrail, looking down upon a city full of Martians, all a-chitter with excitement to see the great ship fly. "Fare thee well, ye great crabs!" he cried, then turned to the bosun. "Cast off!"

The men leapt into action, and, a moment later, with a great soaring bound, *Mars Adventure* sprang away into the blue Martian sky.

S. M. STIRLING

Considered by many to be the natural heir to Harry Turtledove's title of King of the Alternate History novel, fast-rising science fiction star S. M. Stirling is author of the Island in the Sea of Time series (*Island in the Sea of Time, Against the Tide of Years, On the Ocean of Eternity*), in which Nantucket is cast back to the year 1250. He's also produced the *New York Times* bestselling Change series: a first trilogy (*Dies the Fire, The Protector's War, A Meeting at Corvallis*), followed by *The Sunrise Lands, The Scourge of God, The Sword of the Lady, The High King of Montival, The Tears of the Sun,* and *Lord of Mountains,* and his most recent book, *The Given Sacrifice.* Another alternate history series, The Lords of Creation, has two volumes: *The Sky People* and *In the Courts of the Crimson Kings,* set in a universe in which Mars and Venus were terraformed by mysterious aliens in the remote past. Most recently, he started a new series, Shadowspawn, which consists of *A Taint in the Blood, The Council of Shadows,* and *Shadows of Falling Night.* He has also written stand-alone novels such as *Conquistador* and *The Peshawar Lancers,* and collaborated with Raymond F. Feist, Jerry Pournelle, Holly Lisle, and *Star Trek* actor James Doohan, as well as contributing to the *Babylon 5, T2, Brainship, War World,* and *Man-Kzin War* series. His short fiction has been collected in *Ice, Iron and Gold.* Born in France and raised in Europe, Africa, and Canada, he now lives with his family in Santa Fe, New Mexico.

If something important is stolen from you, sometimes you have to go to extreme lengths to get it *back,* no matter how dangerous the quest—or how many corpses you have to pile up along the way . . .

Swords of Zar-tu-Kan

BY S. M. STIRLING

Encyclopaedia Britannica, 20th edition
University of Chicago Press, 1998

Mars—Parameters:

Orbit:	1.5237 AU
Orbital period:	668.6 Martian solar days
Rotation:	24 hrs. 34 min.
Mass:	0.1075 x Earth
Average density:	3.93 g/cc
Surface gravity:	0.377 x Earth
Diameter:	4,217 miles (equatorial; 53.3% x Earth)
Surface:	75% land, 25% water (incl. pack ice)

Atmospheric composition:

Nitrogen	76.51%
Oxygen	20.23%
Carbon dioxide	0.11%
Trace elements:	Argon, Neon, Krypton.
Atmospheric pressure:	10.7 psi average at northern sea level

The third life-bearing world of the solar system, Mars is less Earth-like than Venus . . .

Zar-tu-Kan: Avenue of Deceptive Formalities

"WELCOME TO *ZHO'DA*," SALLY YAMASHITA SAID.

"I've been on Mars over a month now!"

"Kennedy Base is on Mars, but it isn't really on *Zho'da*," she said. The Demotic word meant something like *The Real World.*

She swept her mask over her face with a practiced gesture as she walked out of the street-level stage of the airship landing tower, against air as dry and acrid as the Taklamakan Desert and nearly as thin as Tibet's.

A second later, Tom Beckworth followed suit. The living, quasi fabric writhed, then settled down, turning her face into a smooth black oval below the tilted brown eyes. You didn't absolutely have to think about the fact that you were plastering a synthetic amoeboid parasite over your mouth and nose. His matched his medium ebony skin much more closely.

Sally always enjoyed getting back to Zar-tu-Kan, the main contact-city for the US-Commonwealth Alliance of explorers and scientists on Mars. It was honestly *alien*. While Kennedy Base was . . . sort of like a major airport that had somehow landed in Antarctica with everyone stuck in a second-rate hotel by bad weather. She was probably going to live out the rest of her life on Mars, and with antiagathics cheap at the source, that could be a long time.

Beckworth was gawking, though with restraint; this was the real thing, not training. Slim tulip-shaped spires reared hundreds of feet into the air between warrens of lower-slung, thick-walled compounds, their time-faded colors still blazing against a sky of faded blue tinged pink with the dust of the Deep Beyond. The towers varied in pointillist shadings like the memory of rainbows seen in dreams. Lacy crystalline bridges joined them, and transparent domes glittered below over lineage apartment houses or the homes of the rich and powerful, full of an astonishing flowering lushness. The narrow serpentine streets below wound among blank-faced buildings of hard, glossy, rose-red stone whose ornamental carvings were often worn to faintest tracery . . .

Zar-tu-Kan had been an independent city-state and ancient when the Tollamune emperors of Dvor-il-Adazar united Mars. It had outlived the Eternal Peace of a planetary empire that lasted thirty thousand years, and was a city-state again. The elongated forms of its native citizens moved past one another and the draught-beasts and riding-birds in an intricate, nearly silent dance, with the loudest sound the scuff of leather and pads on stone. Occasionally a voice; now and then a tinkle of music, like bells having a mathematical argument.

"Mars isn't older than Earth. It just *feels* older," Tom Beckworth said, as they walked, renewing a discussion they'd been having off and on all the way from Kennedy Base on the icebound shores of the Arctic sea.

Shipping people between planets was *expensive,* even in this year of grace 1998, and only the very best got to make the trip. Unfortunately, sometimes smart, highly educated people invested a lot of their mental capital in defending preconceptions rather than challenging them.

"Martian *civilization* is a lot older than ours," Beckworth went on. "But there have to be commonalities. And frankly, they've done less with their time than we have with ours."

She smiled to herself. This wasn't Venus and you couldn't play Mighty Whitey Sahib in a pith helmet here. He would learn. Or not.

She stopped and made a sweeping gesture with her arm. "This is it," Sally said. "Home sweet residence."

The building was a smooth three-story octagon, featureless on the outside save for low-relief patterns like feathery reeds, with a glassine dome showing above its central portion, typical of the Orchid Consort style in the Late Imperial period. Maintainer bugs the size of cats and shaped like flattened beetles crawled slowly over the crystal in an eternal circuit.

"Helloooobosssss," a thin, rasping, hissing voice said, in thickly accented English.

The man started violently as a skeletal shape uncoiled itself from beside the doors. In outline it was more or less like a dog covered in dusty russet fur—a fuzzy greyhound on the verge of starvation, with a long whip tail, teeth like a shark, and lambent green eyes under a disturbingly high forehead and long, prehensile toes.

"Hi, Satemcan," Sally said. "Anything to report?"

"Quietttt," the animal said, dropping back into Demotic; the greeting had exhausted its English. "Possibblytoooquiettt."

It bent forward and sniffed at Beckworth's feet. "Smelllsss unusual. Like you, but . . . more."

She reached into one of the loose sleeves of her robe and tossed a package of *rooz* meat. The not-quite-animal snapped it out of the air and swallowed flesh and edible preservative packaging and all, licking his chops with satisfaction. Then she stripped the glove from her right hand and slipped it into a groove beside the door. A faint touch, dry and rough, and the portal of time-dulled tkem wood slid aside.

"You'll need to give the house system a taste," she said, as they passed into the vestibule and tucked their masks back into pockets in their robes. "There."

Beckworth put his hand in the slot in a gingerly fashion.

"It *bit* me!" he exclaimed.

"Needs the DNA sample," she said.

The inner door with its glossy surface slid aside to reveal an arched passageway in the foamed stone. That gave onto an inner courtyard about a hundred yards across. The air was blissfully damp—about like Palm Springs or Bakersfield—and smelled faintly of rock, growth, and things like marjoram and heather and others that had no names on Earth. The pavement was ornamental, a hard, fossil-rich, pale limestone that was replaced every few centuries. Little of it could be seen beneath the vegetation that covered the planters, rose up the slender fretwork pillars that supported the arcaded balconies that overlooked the court, and hung in colored sheets from the carved-stone screens. It wasn't quite a closed system like a spaceship, but fairly close.

"I extend formal and impersonally polite greetings to the lineage and residents," she said quietly in fluent Demotic. "This is my professional associate, denominated Thomas, casual/intimate form Tom, lineage designation Beckworth. He will be residing with me for some time as is contractually permitted by my lease."

That took all of ten words and a couple of modifiers, in Martian. Half a dozen people looked up from chores or narrow books that hinged at the top or games of *atanj*, gave a brief inclination of the head, then ignored her, which was reasonably courteous; none of them were wearing their robes, or much of anything else.

"We're on the second floor," she said, leading the way.

"Nobody seems particularly interested in us," Beckworth said.

"They've seen Terrans before," Sally said, with a shrug.

"There are only a couple of hundred of us on Mars. I'd have thought we'd attract more attention. A Martian sure as shit would in Oakland!"

"They're not like us, Tom. That's the point."

The door to her suite opened its eye and looked at her, the S-shaped pupil swelling. She met the gaze, letting it scan her and her companion. It blinked acknowledgment and there was a dull *click* as the muscle retracted the ceramic dead bolt.

They racked their sword belts and he looked at her pictures with interest. There was one of her parents, one of the winery they ran in Napa, and a couple of her siblings and nieces and nephews and one of a cat she'd owned, or vice versa, in university.

The apartment was large, several thousand square feet, paradisical after you got used to spaceships or space habitats or that habitat-on-Mars called Kennedy Base. The furniture was mostly built into the substance of the walls and floor, with silky or furry native blankets and rugs folded on top, some stirring a little as they sensed the Terrans' body warmth. The extra two degrees tended to confuse them.

Homelike, in a sort of chilly detached alien way, she thought, and went on aloud:

"There's a bed niche over there, let's sling your duffle."

"Where's the bathroom?"

"That way. Wait until you make the acquaintance of the Zar-tu-Kan style of bidet," she added, and grinned at his wince.

"When do we eat?"

"I'll whip us up a stir-fry," she said.

"Martians make stir-fries?" Beckworth said, surprised.

"No, *I* just like stir-fries."

"Want me to lend a hand?"

"You're not going anywhere near my cooking gear," she said. "It took *years* to get everything just right."

As they stowed his modest baggage, Beckworth said quietly: "What's with the canid?"

"Satemcan? He's . . . ah, he's a very helpful gofer. Especially out in the field. His food doesn't cost much."

He raised an ironic eyebrow, and she went on reluctantly, in a lower tone: "And yeah, a bit of a rescue thing. He's got . . . problems. He was lucky not to get needled and stuffed in the digester long ago."

"So much for the cold-blooded, ruthless *puppy-rescuing* Old Mars Hand," he said, grinning wide and white.

Sally raised one arm, made a fist, and elevated her middle finger as she went back to the kitchen nook.

"*Rooz*, the meat vegans can eat," she called as she sliced and stirred, and Beckworth joined in the laugh as he set out two flat-bottomed globes of essence on the table and pushed in the straws.

Martians regarded the idea of *killing* a domestic animal to get meat from it as hopelessly inefficient. The *tembst*-modified bird-dinosaur-whatevers the rooz came from grew flaps of boneless meat where their remote ancestors' wings or forelimbs had been, and they regrew when sliced off.

"And it does taste like chicken," Beckworth said.

She put the fry-up aside for a moment in an insulated bowl and poured batter into the wok, swirling it and then peeling out a half dozen tough but fluffy pancakelike rounds of vaguely breadlike stuff in succession.

"More like veal, this variety, and there's this spice that tastes a bit like lemon and chilies—" she began.

Satemcan whined, his ears coming up and nose pointing toward the door.

It opened without the chime. A green paralysis grenade came rolling through, but Satemcan was already getting to his feet; he made a desperate scrambling leap and struck, batting the barrel-shaped handful of ceramic back out through the open portal.

It sailed out on an arc that would—unfortunately—take it right over the balustrade and into the courtyard. There were shouts of *Fright! Alarm!* from below, abruptly cut off as it shattered on the stone and everything nearby with a spinal cord went unconscious the instant one of the nanoparticles touched skin.

Three masked figures in robes with the hoods up came through her door on the heels of the projectile, swords and bulbous, thin-barreled dart pistols in their hands. They checked very slightly; she realized it was surprise at finding the Terrans still in their robes in-doors, and the fabric was good armor against the light needles.

Sally pivoted on one heel and threw the bowl of sizzling-hot oiled meat and vegetables into the face of the first Martian through the door. He toppled backward, tangling his companions for an instant as she dove forward in a ten-foot leap from a standing start, one arm up in front of her face. A dart gun hissed in a stink of burnt methane tinged with sulfur, and something struck her elbow painfully through the fabric.

That was one pistol out of commission for twenty seconds while it recharged. She hit the ground rolling, stripping her sword out of the belt hanging beside the door; no time for the Colt .45.

Everything felt dreamlike, swift but smooth and *stretched* somehow; partly the adrenaline buzzing in her blood, partly the gravity. Jumping around on Mars *was* dreamlike, and so was the softer way you hit the ground.

Satemcan leapt out the door; there was a round of scuffling and thudding and savage growling and a Martian voice screaming:

"Pain!Suddenextreme*pain!*" in a tone that told of sincerity. *"Emphatic mode!"*

And Tom Beckworth fell to the ground with a limp boneless *thump,* a red spot on his throat showing where a soluble crystal dart had hit as he charged forward like an enraged bull. The third Martian came in at her with a running flèche and all thought vanished as pointed steel lunged for her left eye, blurring-fast and driven by a longer arm than hers.

Parry in tierce, a desperation move, her blade whipping up and to the side and wrist pronated, jarring impact through her fingers. Smooth *ting-shring* of steel on steel, and she stepped in with a quick shuffling advance and punched with the guard as the elongated figure began an agile backing recovery. That was a bully-swordsman's trick that would get you disqualified in any salon on Earth, but she wasn't on Earth and there weren't any second prizes here.

The Martian made a hissing sound as the Terran's heavier bone and muscle ripped the hilt of his or her gloved fingers, probably breaking something in the process. Sally Yamashita had just enough time to begin a savage cut from the wrist toward the other's neck before she felt the slight sting on the back of hers. There had been three Martians to start with.

Oh sh—

Blackness.

The unconsciousness didn't last long, and the anesthetic dart didn't leave a hangover. Something rough and wet was touching her cheek. She blinked her eyes open and saw Satemcan's bloodied muzzle.

"Bossss . . ."

The canid's paw-hand dropped the applicator from her belt pouch that had administered the antidote. Blood leaked away from the dagger wounds in his throat and torso, slowing as she watched. Volition returned and she rolled upright, trying to staunch the wounds with her hands.

"Good dog," she said. *"Optimal canid."*

Satemcan whined. A face looked around the doorjamb, one of the lineage.

"Medical care, imperative tense!" Sally barked.

That brought someone in with a clamshell-shaped platform running at their heels on many small, unpleasantly human feet. It opened to display a bed of writhing wormlike appendages that divided and subdivided until pink filaments too fine to actually see glittered and weaved. Sally grunted as she levered Satemcan inside and the chitin top closed with a clumping sticky sound like two raw steaks being slapped together. A few moments later a voice came from behind a pierced grille in the shell, unstrained through consciousness as the organic machine spoke:

"Hybrid canid, standard format. Extensive exsanguination, moderate tissue trauma, minor damage to motor nerves. Stabilizing . . . prognosis excellent but requiring additional proteins and feedstocks."

"I authorize the expenditure," she snapped, holding herself from slumping with relief; Mars didn't run to national health plans. "Maximum accelerated healing."

For a moment she touched the shell of the trauma unit.

Come on, boy, you can make it!

She came to her feet; the robe had shed the blood, and scuttling things were coming out of tiny holes in the walls to clean up the rest before they returned to feed it and the spilled food to the house digesters. The platform trotted off *pad-pad-pad-pad* to plug itself into the . . . more or less . . . veins of the building.

"How much were you paid to let them in?" she asked.

The lineage head—his name was Zhay—was gray-haired and wrinkled, which meant he'd probably been born when Andrew Jackson was president of the United States and Japan was a hermit kingdom run by knife-fanciers with weird haircuts who spent all their spare time oppressing her peasant ancestors.

"One thousand monetary units, and in addition a conditional threat to kill or excruciate several of us if we declined," he said. "The perpetrators were independently contracting Coercives, persons self-evidently given to short-term perspectives."

Which is a devastating insult, locally.

He went on: "I would estimate that they were highly paid, however."

Sally made herself count to five before replying in an even tone: By local standards she simply didn't have any grounds for being angry, and she had to conform if she wanted to be taken seriously. Nobody here would *expect* the residents to risk their relatives or their own lives to protect someone like her. And if they were going to rat her out, why shouldn't they make a profit on it? A thousand monetary units was a lot of money.

Somebody was willing to pay high for a Terran, or for Tom specifically. Or maybe they wanted both of us, but they were too banged-up to take us both.

The apartment's lineage had had the medical platform standing by, which actually showed goodwill. She *really* couldn't afford to unload on them.

"But it would feel so *good* to go completely ripshit," she said to herself through gritted teeth, in English.

"Take this to my consulate and you will receive reasonable recompense," she went on, when the throbbing in her temples had subsided, typing quickly on her personal computer and loading it onto the data stick.

She hadn't known Tom Beckworth long enough to care about him really deeply.

Not as much as I do about Satemcan, if we're being completely honest, she thought.

But he was a Terran where those were damned few, and a fellow American where they were even thinner on the ground, and more important, looking after him while he was still green here was her *job.*

"Please note that if there is any repetition, my associates at the consulate will invoke an arbitration council and propose a heavy fine for implicit violation of the mutual-protection provisions of my lease."

Zhay looked as if he were going to protest—it was an arguable point, since that clause really only applied to random street crime and burglary. Instead he simply gestured acknowledgment again and accepted the little plastic rectangle.

She didn't bother to threaten him with the consulate's influence with the local government. Robert Holmegard was a good man, but she'd learned right down in her gut what the Alliance consul still had trouble accepting over there in the palace district: government just didn't *matter* nearly as much here as it did back on Earth, where variations on social democracy were pretty well universal outside the EastBloc.

And I am better informed about this *side of Martian life than a diplomat. Much, much better.*

"I will be out for a considerable period," Sally concluded. "I need to find a Coercive of my own. Please leave on the porch light; I'll be back after midnight."

It didn't rhyme in the monosyllabic tonalities of Demotic, but the puzzled frown was worth it. They *really* didn't get folk rock here.

A Martian staggered out of the *Blue-Tinted Time Considered as a Regressing Series,* cheap inert fabric mask dangling and a smile—a slack grin, by local standards—on his face. He hummed a tune, then called out:

"Eu . . . Eu . . . *euphoriaaa!* Is there anyone within heeeearringggg intent on parareproductive coitus?"

Sally stiff-armed him as he stumbled toward her. The lightly built Martian gave an *ooof* and bounced back into the wall, still giggling.

"Three inhabited planets in this fucked-up zoo of a solar system, and you can't get away from irritating drunks on any of them."

He sank against the wall and slid down it, tittering, then started to hum the same tune as he sat splay-legged. Several adolescents eyed him, waiting to see if it was safe to lift his possessions, but blinking and backing a little when she glared at them.

It was that sort of neighborhood. She pushed through the doors. Teyudza-Zhalt was usually to be found here when she wasn't working a contract. It was a canal-side dive where the crews of the long-distance canal boats and the landships that sailed the desert plains and caravan traders down from the highlands hung out . . . and where the little sign with the glyphs reading *Professional Practitioner of Coercive Violence* on her table wasn't at all out of place.

Silence fell as Sally entered the inner door, and heads moved to consider her.

"Vas-Terranan," someone murmured—which was insulting, but at least subtly so.

There was a slight clatter as weapons were laid back on tables or holstered. The light had an unpleasant greenish cast; someone was underfeeding the glow-globes. The murals on the walls looked dusty and faded, outlining a big circular room on the ground floor of a tower more than half-abandoned. The adamantine stone of the floor was worn deep enough to show ruts in places, and it was set with circular tables cut in slabs from the perfectly circular trunks of tkem timber. They were nicked and battered, which took some doing with a wood that contained natural silica monofilaments.

The air was dry and cool, of course, but it somehow smelled of ancient ghosts and lost hopes and all the labyrinthine history of *Zho'da,* the Real World.

Teyud sat with a tiny incense-burning brazier empty and swept clean beside her, but leaving a faint musky fragrance in the air when you got close. She was playing *atanj,* left hand against right, and occasionally taking a sip from a globe of essence as she considered the moves of her pieces or threw the dice.

Beside the folding game-set her table held a bowl of sweet dipping sauce and a platter of black-streaked crimson flowers. She crunched one, swallowed, sipped, and inclined her head in Sally's direction.

"I express amiable greetings, Sally Yamashita," she said, in a voice that had an undertone like soft trumpets. "This match will be completed shortly."

The Coercive was on the tallish side of average height, around seven feet, but the color of her huge eyes was distinctly odd, a lambent amber-gold. Her robe was of a reddish khaki, excellent blending colors nearly anywhere on the planet, but the hood was thrown back to show hair caught back in a fine metallic net. Hair and metal both had a sheen like polished bronze. She was slender, but not with the impression of birdlike frailty common among Martians. Unless the bird was a golden eagle, the type Mongols had used to hunt wolves with back in the old days.

Thoughtful Grace, the emperors of the Crimson Dynasty had called the *tembst-*modified warrior caste that had enforced their will and kept their peace. They were rare now that the Tollamunes controlled nothing except the old capital of Dvor-il-Adazar and its environs, but it wasn't only Martian manners that ensured a ring of empty tables around Teyud.

Sally didn't intrude on the game; they took their *atanj seriously* here. The Coercive threw the dice one more time, moved a Transport piece to the square of the left-side Despot, nodded very slightly, and began to pack the set away. When the pieces were in their holders she folded it shut and tucked it into a pocket in the sleeve of her robe.

"I profess amiable greetings in return, Teyudza-Zhalt," Sally said.

She took one of the flowers and dipped it in the sauce. *Amiable greetings* included an invitation to share. The texture was slightly chewy and the flavor sort of like frangipani-scented sweet-and-sour pork; her stomach growled.

Murder and sudden death, but you still get hungry if you don't eat . . . and I literally threw away dinner.

"Contractual discussion?" she went on to the Martian.

"You have recently been engaged in lethal or near-lethal conflict," Teyud said thoughtfully. "You were struck by an anesthetic dart there—" She tapped the back of her neck. "You are not accompanied by the . . . unconventional canid. I request details; then we may discuss contract terms in accordance with degrees of uncertainty, calculable risk, and difficulty."

They did, and in a marked concession to Terran custom, the mercenary shook hands to seal the deal; hers was firm and dry and extremely strong. It wasn't the first time she'd worked for Sally or other members of the Alliance mission here.

"This will be an interesting task," she said.

"I need to get my colleague back," Sally said grimly.

"That is the point of interest," Teyud said, finishing her globe of essence. "That he was removed indicates that immediate lethality was not the object of the attackers. They were—metaphorical mode—operating as if intent on armed robbery, even though they stole nothing else. They wished to steal a vas-Terranan. Surely even the most eccentric of collectors would not do that simply to have one on hand? I am pleasantly at a loss for an explanation."

The clock on the wall began to sing in the poetic-aesthetic mode, with a tone like the grief of diamonds:

Hours like sand
On the shores of a bitter sea
Flow on waves of time;

Twelve hours have passed
Since last the Sun
Rose in blind majesty;
It shall yield heedless to night
In one more—

"Bit him, emphatic mode! Bit, bit, *bit* him!" Satemcan said viciously, snarling . . . literally. "I bit the intruder on the territory of my social reference group!"

"Yes, you did," Sally said patiently, patting the canid on the head.

"I will—future-conditional intentional case—bite him again, emphatic mode!"

You *couldn't* just say you absolutely would do something in the future in Demotic; the assumptions built into the structure of its grammar forbade certainty about uncontrollable events. Satemcan was coming as close to that as possible.

The canid wasn't looking at his slightly scruffy best; the areas over his wounds were naked and glistening with the pseudoskin that covered them. He was moving well enough, though, and the medical *tembst* used organic glues to hold things together internally. They'd be absorbed as the accelerated natural healing took place.

And there was a crazed look in his reddish eyes. *Not a happy camper,* Sally thought. *Well, neither am I.*

"Canid," Teyud said. "Can you track these individuals?"

"Yessss," Satemcan said, all business for a moment.

He began to walk away from the apartment building, nose working as his deep red tongue came out to lap over it. After a moment he sniggered, which was something to see:

"He-he-he-he! Here they triggered an antiscent aerosol. I express derision! Utter futility! My exceptional sensitivity and practiced skill easily uncover the scents of blood and fear pheromones."

He trotted on. Teyud was keeping her eyes up, watching for movement on the low rooftops without seeming to strain.

"Intriguing," she said softly. "This resembles minor-unit confrontation tactics more than most private commissions."

Martians weren't any braver than Terrans, on average; they were just more straightforward. Teyud was, though. They'd worked together before, and it could get stressful. But right now, Sally didn't give a damn.

"I express regret at the risk you must undergo," Sally said.

The Coercive didn't look around, but there was slight surprise in her voice:

"I chose to be involved." Thoughtfully: "You vas-Terranan are the first new thing to come into the Real World in a very long time. Working with you is less demoralizing than sitting and contemplating the time when the Deep Beyond spreads over the final cities and the last atmosphere plants wither."

"It will be a long time before that happens, too," Sally said; it didn't bother most Martians much.

She was checking their six; it would be difficult to detect a tail, but not impossible.

"Not so long as the time that has passed since the date when the First Emperor reigned," Teyud said. "Ah, your canid halts."

"Here," Satemcan said, casting around under the feet of irritated pedestrians. "Multiple trails, but the freshest leads into this structure."

"Oh, *shit*," Sally added, as the canid looked up with tail waving, expecting praise. "Ah . . . good job, Satemcan."

The glyphs on the building read:

Cooperative Agency for Aggrandizement, Zar-tu-Kan Franchise.

"What are we going to do?" she said. In English: "Here at Yakuza Central?"

"I recommend following the exhortation on the wall: *Enquire Within*," Teyud said.

The waiting room was a large arched space; it had a rack for scrolls, which was the equivalent of a stack of magazines, and a vending device for essences. And there were advertising posters on the walls:

Have you lost the desire for self-preservation but lack the fortitude for conventional suicide? Then consider tokmar *addiction, the most subjectively pleasant form of slow dissolution for individuals with your psychological malfunction! Initial samples available gratis!*

Or:

Few satisfactions equal the excruciation of those who have antagonized or superseded you. Indulge spite and envy! Our specialists . . .

"It's not the differences that are really disturbing, it's the goddamned similarities," she muttered, avoiding the helpful illustrations. "Or maybe it's both. We do the same stuff, but they're so fucking up front about it."

Satemcan had his ears laid back as they entered; he must be getting a snoutful of unpleasant scents far too faint for human or Martian nostrils.

"Apprehension," he whined. *"Fear."*

"Did they come through here?"

"That way," he said, pointing with his nose.

That way was effectively the receptionist's desk, the one with a helpful sign:

Past This Point Those without Authorization Will Be Killed without Warning.

"You wish?" the receptionist said.

Then he took in Teyud, and Sally could see his pupils expand. He brought his hands out of his sleeves and laid them carefully flat on the table.

"You wish, most refined of genome?" he repeated—this time using the honorific mode.

Three Coercives in black robes stood behind the slab of gray smooth stone, and she thought there were probably more in the offing. This *was* thug central. It was some consolation that their eyes were traveling between her and Teyud with a certain nervousness; she'd been here long enough to read Martian body language well. It gave her an advantage, since the locals she dealt with didn't have nearly as much experience with Terrans.

It's bullshit that they don't have emotions, whatever those Far Frontiers *episodes say. They're just less self-reflective about them.*

Sally took a deep breath; she wasn't entirely confident of getting out of here alive, but the odds would be much worse without Teyud.

"My residence was attacked . . ." she began.

When she had finished, the receptionist blinked at her and bent to whisper into a grille. Teyud's ears pricked forward; so did Satemcan's. A tendril extended and the receptionist plugged it into *his* ear. The conversation that followed went entirely silent; he nodded several times, then extracted the intercom thing (or possibly data-retrieval thing) with a *plop* and spoke:

"Three independent Coercives contracted with a third party for the operation you mention four days ago, through our employment placement service, with the usual finder's fee. They also purchased tactical information on your habitual schedule. Early this morning they returned here with a vas-Terranan prisoner, whom they turned over to the third party. They then purchased fairly extensive medical care for bone fractures, burns, and canid bites and departed Zar-tu-Kan bound for Dvor-il-Adazar. We will not sell you their identities because their affiliation contracts contain a nondisclosure clause."

International Union of Thugs, Local 141, she thought bitterly. *They've had a long time to come up with rules to cover every contingency.*

The receptionist blinked; evidently Sally's expression was showing more than she wanted. Earth-human body language wasn't exactly the same as Martian, but it wasn't impossibly different either for basics like humor or anger. The problem was that each species found the *reasons* for the other's emotions weirdly opaque. Add in that Martians had only one language and one set of social rules and hence were unaccustomed to dealing with different reactions, and crossed wires were more common than not.

There was more cultural variation in San Francisco than on this entire planet. She made the muscles of her face relax one by one.

"The nondisclosure policy is not negotiable, by permanent directive," the receptionist said cautiously. "Killing or excruciating myself or any of our other associates here will not alter this; the policy is set at higher levels, to whom we are of little consequence."

Sally schooled her face and glanced aside at Teyud. The Thoughtful Grace made a very small gesture with two fingers of the hand resting on her sword hilt: *Don't push it.*

"I'm more interested in the person who employed the three . . . associates of your cooperative," Sally said grimly.

"We will inform you of the identity of the third party for a fee of 2,750 monetary units, with financing available on the following terms at an interest rate of . . ."

"No nondisclosure clause?"

"No, none was purchased. This was an imprudent excess of thrift that increases the probability of suboptimal results from the client's perspective! Note that we will include a nondisclosure agreement with *you* for a modest additional fee of—"

Ten minutes later they were back on the street, and Sally was looking at the name and address written on a scrap of paper-equivalent.

"What do we do now?" she said.

Teyud smiled. "As to our course of action, we engage in reconnaissance, then attack."

Here I am, invading Harvard with fell intent. Or maybe Oxford.

Even by the standards of Zar-tu-Kan, the Scholarium was *old*. Old enough that it hadn't originally been under a dome, or laid out whole in one of the fractal-pattern mazes Martians had gone in for under the Crimson Dynasty. They'd improvised during the Imperial era as it grew; now the reduced students and staff rattled around in buildings that ranged from the size of her apartment block to things bigger than the Solar Dome in Houston or the Great House of People's Culture in Beijing; the bigger ones were mostly garden now, and they were all linked together by tunnels below and translucent walkways etched in patterns like magnified snowflakes above.

Sally suppressed a start as she saw herself in a reflective patch of one of them. She and Teyud wore student robes—slightly threadbare and gaudy—and Scholarium-style masks. Hers was a Spinner-Grub, modeled on the pupal stage of an insect used for textile production—a freshman style, and something of a dry joke in local terms. Teyud's was a jest of her own, a delicate golden mask representing the face of a Thoughtful Grace sword-adept . . . which she actually was. Here it could mark someone studying the martial arts, or military history. The fact that most people wore masks and clothing that covered everything to the fingertips made sneaking around in disguise *much* easier.

And Teyud had a rather ironic sense of humor. When Sally mentioned the fact, she nodded slightly.

"More. In their origins, the Thoughtful Grace were Coercives concerned with maintenance of rule and regulation deference . . . what is that Terran word . . ."

"Police," Sally said quietly.

"Yes. And now I am pursuing a similar function, particularly for you."

She chuckled slightly. Sally didn't feel like laughing; it was a bit too personal.

"And so I still serve *Sh'uMaz*, in—metaphorical mode—a way," Teyud said, and touched the Imperial glyph in the forehead of her mask that represented that concept. "Even though I am not in the service of the Kings Beneath the Mountain."

Sh'uMaz meant *Sustained Harmony*, the program and motto of the Tollamune emperors. The Eternal Peace of the Crimson Dynasty was a nostalgic memory on Mars now, but there was some undertone in Teyud's voice stronger than that.

A section of the walkway curled downward in a spiral like a corkscrew. They slid down it in a way practicable only because the gravity was a third of Earth's, then walked out into the space under a dome. The buildings around the edge were wildly varied, but most of the identifying glyphs bore variations on the beaded spiral that signified *tembst*. This was the science faculty, more or less.

Pathways of textured, colored rock wound through the open space, interspersed with low shrubs and banks of flowers. Colorful avians flew or scurried about. One of the birds stopped and hovered before her face.

"Food?" it said hopefully.

"Buzz off," she replied, and it did.

Students sat or sprawled along the pathways and planters and benches, arguing or reading or occasionally singing. Apart from the eternal *atanj* a few played games that involved throwing small things with bundles of tentacles that tried to snag your hand. You won by catching the tip of a tentacle and whirling the . . . thing . . . at the next player. If it missed, it scuttled back to the one who had the next turn.

She couldn't understand why anyone here would abduct a Terran biologist for his knowledge; Martians were simply better at it, and Tom had come to this planet to learn himself. That left something on the order of *I need a lab rat with a particular genetic pattern* as motivation. Which meant that anything could be happening to him.

Anything at all.

"Information," Teyud said smoothly to a passerby. "Knowledgeable Instructor Meltamsa-Forin?"

The student had a mask whose surface mimicked something that had a swelling boss of bone on its forehead.

"Ah, Meltam the Neurologically Malfunctioning," he said.

Or Meltam the Eccentric or Meltam the Mad, she translated mentally.

"Identity, function?"

The student pointed to one of the buildings. "Be prepared to listen to exquisitely reasoned arguments from faulty premises."

"Specialty?"

"Agri-*tembst,* with a more recent subsidiary field in Wet World biotics," the student said. Grudgingly: "In the latter, he has considerable data. Though the subject is arcane and of little immediate utility, it has some interest."

He tilted his head and left, having comprehensively dissed a professor. Under other circumstances, Sally would have found it humiliating: the glyph on the building he'd pointed out was roughly translatable as *Veterinary Science.* Of course, it also meant *Engineering Malfunctions and Their Remedies.*

"Tom was kidnapped by *veterinarians?*"

The building itself was old enough that it had high, arched windows, filled with foam-rock aeons ago. Most of it was included in the later dome, but a tower reared high above, a smooth stone cylinder that flared outward at the top like a gigantic tulip.

"Ah," Teyud said. "Yes. A straightforward entry has limited possibilities. But there are alternatives available."

"What alternatives?"

"There are advantages to being of the Thoughtful Grace genome, which compensate for the increased caloric intake necessary." She frowned in thought and ate another flower. "In your terms . . . I am *owed favors* and have *serious mojo* with the local Coercives in the service of the Despot."

"They'll intervene?" Sally said, surprised and pleased.

"Not directly. But . . . *off the books.*"

"I would have preferred a high-altitude insertion with directional parachutes," Teyud said a few hours later. "There is a small but calculable risk of the airship's being spotted."

"No," Sally said; that was less impolite in Demotic.

The blimp was very nearly silent; the engines were panting—literally—because they'd pulled it into a position upwind and were now drifting with the breeze quietly and slowly toward the Scholarium. Zar-tu-Kan passed below the transparent compartment in the belly of the dirigible, less stridently bright than a Terran city from the air, a mystery of soft glow and points of light. It was cold, well below zero, but the robes and undersuit were near-perfect insulation. Only the skin across her eyes was exposed, and that only until . . .

Teyud extended a case unclipped from her belt. Sally winced slightly but bent forward. The lid snapped open, and tentacles swarmed out and webbed around her face. The optical-beast pulled itself out of the case with a sticky *plop* and settled firmly; it only weighed a couple of pounds, and it felt like the slightly tacky play-goo kids used. Everything went blank, and there was a slight sting at her temples as the fine tendrils plugged into her veins. Another sting at the corners of her eyes, and a sensation like blurs of static and a very brief headache as even finer filaments integrated into her optic nerves.

Then everything went brighter, like an overcast day. Teyud glowed very slightly; the animal sensed ambient heat as well as magnifying light.

"Functioning," she said.

If she looked anything like Teyud, she was now giving a fair imitation of a Bug-Eyed Monster from an ancient magazine cover; the optic the Thoughtful Grace wore turned the upper part of her face into a smooth bulging surface like the eyes of an insect . . . which was more or less what it was. This was Imperial-era military *tembst*, and Teyud had said there was a very slight possibility it would kill Sally when she tried to use it, despite her providing a blood sample for prior authorization.

Too small a probability for serious consideration, was the way she'd put it.

The intercom whistled, then said: "Coming up on target. Prepare to deploy. I express a desire that random factors eventuate in a favorable pattern."

Satemcan whimpered slightly as Teyud picked him up, and he clamped on to her harness with both paw-hands. Sally checked her equipment; her sword was across her back, in that cool-looking position that meant you had to be careful to *not* slice off your ear when you drew. She wore a native dart pistol, after a bit of an argument from Teyud. Her own Colt had a much higher rate of fire—it didn't depend on a chamber generating methane. On the other hand, shooting someone with a bullet didn't drop them instantly, and it was much louder.

Cables uncoiled from the roof of the assault transport's ceiling. Sally clipped one to her harness and gripped it in her gloved hands.

Down below, the dome of the Science Faculty glowed like an opal beneath the moon—Phobos was up here, a third the size of Luna from Earth, and Deimos crawled past it. The airship's props whirred briefly as it corrected course.

"Deploying . . . *now!*"

The transparent doors beneath them opened, and her weight came onto the harness. The cable dropped away, coiling into space, and dangled as they approached the swelling top of the tower. Teyud's head moved, calculating.

"*Now*," she said, and squeezed the release.

Sally followed suit, and they swooped down into the not-darkness. She *hoped* the falling-elevator sensation in her stomach was all physical. The tower's roof was flat or nearly—shedding rain wasn't much of a problem here, and from the markings there had been Paiteng perches there once. She didn't try to gauge her own speed; Teyud was the specialist, and she just followed as closely as possible. There was a sudden flexing in the cable; the bundle of sucker-equipped boneless limbs at its end had clamped down on the target. She clamped her legs together and extended them as the roof rushed up at her, then hit the release and tucked and rolled the way she would have from a parachute drop; she'd done that on Earth, of course, but never here.

Whump.

"Oooof!" and a muffled yelp from the canid.

Things thumped and gouged at her and the wind jolted out of her lungs. The boots and padding protected her, a bit. She thought the impact would have broken bones on Earth; it would have broken bones here, for most standard-issue Martians. Teyud was up on one knee, the edges of her blackened sword blade glimmering and the dart pistol in the other.

Sally drew likewise, the steel a comforting weight. The pistol was in her left and much lighter, but she didn't have the Thoughtful Grace's advantage of being ambidextrous. Satemcan staggered for a moment, shook his head, and slunk over to her heel.

There were a couple of packages of Semtex in her belt, part of her *other-job* kit as she thought of it. Hopefully . . .

They came erect and padded over to the door. It opened its eye— slowly, which was the sign of a system reaching the end of its life span. Teyud leaned forward swiftly and pressed her optic mask to the opening. Things made rather ghastly wet, sticky sounds as the commando optic used one of its functions to take over the other biomachine, and the door swung open.

"Poor security maintenance," Teyud said very softly.

A spiral staircase led down from the landing stage, curling around a shaft that held—or had held, once—a freight lift. Teyud went down with a rapid scuff-scuff-scuff leaning run not quite like the way a Terran moved and only slightly more like the way a standard Martian did. Sally simply hopped down three or four steps each time, quiet enough in padded-sole boots if you were careful. There were occasional glow-globes, but they were nearly dormant; the optics gave them a sort of twilight view, in which footprints glowed slightly from remnant heat.

Every once in a while, they'd pass a door, one that led to rooms in the thickness of the tower wall. Most were unoccupied. Some—

Phufft.

Teyud fired before the door was fully open. The student toppled backward, a surprised look on his face. One hand held a pancake-tortilla thing wrapped around some filling, the other a top-hinged book. Teyud moved in a blur, getting her pistol arm underneath him before he struck the ground, lowering him gently and leaving the book and the more-or-less burrito on his chest.

Sally covered the stairwell while she worked. Shooting someone here wasn't really like doing it at home, not if you used anesthetic darts; it was more like paintball, in a way, with the only real risk that of bonking your head when you collapsed. She *had* played a fair amount of what amounted to paintball with Teyud and her friends now and then. It was fun and excellent training, though she never beat the Coercive. Other Martians yes, but not the Thoughtful Grace, though she came close occasionally.

Of course, out on planet Reality and away from the padded obstacle course you couldn't *tell* if someone was using lethals until it was too late. The instant unconsciousness was the same, but with the real thing you had instant brain-death too.

"Here," Teyud whispered, in a flat, noncarrying tone.

Here was a door with more than its share of faintly glowing footprints. Sally tapped Satemcan on his head, and he sniffed long and carefully, then nodded.

"Sssssamesssstrangesssssssmelll," he whispered.

Teyud went through the eye-capture routine again. Then she looked up and nodded to Sally before she pushed gently on the door.

It swung open, and her optic mask stepped down the brighter light. A voice came through:

". . . many years of declining fees and contributions by organizations and the Despot. This is suboptimal in the medium to long term! Contact with the Wet World—"

Which was colloquial Demotic for Earth.

"—presents both unprecedented risks and opportunities for maximizing the utility of the faculty of—"

Under the tiger alertness, some distant part of Sally Yamashita's mind quietly boggled.

Am I really listening to an evil-mastermind academic veterinarian monologing about cutbacks in his fucking budget? that part of her asked.

The chamber was large and had scattered consoles and lab benches, and what Sally recognized as an isolation tank, a glassine cylinder. Tom Beckworth was in it, naked and glaze-eyed and fastened to a frame with living wormlike bonds. An elderly white-haired Martian was striding up and down in lecture mode, dressed in a dark coverall fitted with dozens of loops to hold instruments, most of them alive.

There were a half dozen younger Martians, probably the equivalent of grad students. She checked a half step at the seventh, a tall, hard-faced man in a gray uniform. He had blond hair cropped to a bristle cut, but his cheekbones were nearly as high as hers and his eyes slanted. One of the grad students was fitting a glassine tube to the side of the isolation chamber and preparing to press a plunger.

Teyud simply walked toward the group. Sally followed, taking deep, slow breaths. Then—

The EastBlocker turned, and his eyes went wide. A hand sped toward the Tokarev at his waist, very fast. Sally leapt—

Pfutt!

The student slumped to the floor before he could press the plunger, and Teyud's dart pistol was out of action for twenty seconds as the methane chamber recharged.

—and the blond man leapt back, but the tip of her sword scored across his hand and the automatic pistol went flying—

Crack and Teyud's sword punched through another student's eye socket and into her brain and out again, as the rest scrambled for their sword belts if they weren't wearing them. The professor stood glaring with indignation.

Ting, and the EastBlocker had his own blade out, settling into a classic European academic épée stance and beating aside her flèche and riposting with a stop-thrust.

Cling-ting-crash and Teyud was moving through the press of grad students in a whirling blur, with blood misting into the air in arcs as she did. *Pfutt,* and another dropped bonelessly to the floor. A scream and growl as Satemcan leapt onto the back of one angling to get behind Sally's back.

Ting-crash-ting, and the point of Sally's blade slid into the man's throat, with an ugly sensation of things crunching and popping and yielding.

She froze for a moment, watching him fall slowly to the floor and lie kicking as the astonishing amount of blood a human being contained flowed out.

"Mat' . . ." he gasped once: *Mother.*

"You came a very long way to die," she murmured, suddenly conscious of a wound along her ribs that she hadn't even noticed. She swallowed as she felt it; just an inch or two farther in . . .

The last of the grad students broke and fled for the door. Teyud's dart pistol came up: *Pfutt.*

Something crunched as he fell face-first.

Sally wiped her sword on the arm of her robe and sheathed it, throwing back the hood of her robe and keeping her pistol trained on the white-haired professor. She removed her mask and the optic, regretting it as the thing scuttled across the floor and flowed up Teyud's robe, opening a container and stuffing itself inside. It wasn't the light, which was adequate; it was the smell. Martians and humans both tended to be very messy when they died.

The robe she was wearing would take care of her wound until she had time to do something more formal. She reached for the ampoule plugged into the side of the isolation chamber.

"Careful!" Tom said.

She looked up; he was gray with either pain or shock or both, but alert.

"Dr. Cagliostro there was about to test that on me, he liked explaining every step. It's a virus that makes you suggestible. The East-Blockers . . . or maybe that guy on his own . . . were paying him to develop it. Then they were going to tell me to forget about it and let you rescue me . . . so I could spread it."

"Sounds like them," Sally said grimly. "There's a protection?"

"Vaccine," Beckworth said.

Teyud came back from the door, considering the veterinarian with her head to one side.

"You are elderly and frail," she said. "Attempting to resist excruciation would be pointless."

Sally smiled thinly as she worked the controls of the isolation chamber. There were times when she *did* like the way Martians thought.

Sally Yamashita yawned as she finished her essence, a taste like raspberries and mango with an alcoholic subtang. The glow-globes of her apartment were turned down low; Tom needed all the sleep he could get.

"I am an *optimal* canid," Satemcan said sleepily, curling up on his rug.

She yawned again. "Damned straight," she said. "Best damned dog on Mars."

MARY ROSENBLUM

One of the most popular and prolific of the new writers of the nineties, Mary Rosenblum made her first sale, to *Asimov's Science Fiction,* in 1990, and has since become a mainstay of that magazine and one of its most frequent contributors, with more than thirty sales there to her credit. She has also sold to *The Magazine of Fantasy & Science Fiction, The New Space Opera, The Dragon Book,* and to many other magazines and anthologies. Her linked series of "Drylands" stories, about an American Southwest rendered uninhabitable by prolonged droughts, proved to be one of *Asimov's* most popular series, and now, alas, seems more germane than ever. Her novella "Gas Fish" won the Asimov's Readers' Award Poll in 1996, and was a finalist for that year's Nebula Award. Her first novel, *The Drylands,* appeared in 1993, winning the prestigious Compton Crook Award for Best First Novel of the year; it was followed in short order by her second novel, *Chimera,* and her third, *The Stone Garden.* Her first short story collection, *Synthesis & Other Virtual Realities,* was widely hailed by critics as one of the best collections of 1996. She has also written four mystery novels under the name Mary Freeman. Her most recent books include a major new science-fiction novel, *Horizons,* and a reissued and expanded version of the Drylands novel and novelettes entitled *Water Rites.* A graduate of Clarion West, Mary Rosenblum lives in Portland, Oregon.

In the poignant story that follows, we learn that living caught between two worlds can be difficult and painful—especially when you're the only one who can see one of them.

Shoals

MARY ROSENBLUM

MAARTIN XAI GRABBED HIS COVERALLS FROM THE HOOK BY the door, checked the charge on his breather, and headed down the street to the public lock, the one closest to the garden domes. Outside, the usual afternoon winds swirled, twisting dust devils across the red-and-ochre plain that stretched beyond the dome, bounded by the spires that edged the canal. A half dozen dust devils skittered across the dull green-brown of the cyan fields, raising thin trails of red dust.

That's where Dad was, off with the other grown-ups, planting more cyan fields where they found enough water, down deep. Making oxygen.

Dad couldn't see it the way it really was. None of them could. He strolled toward the garden dome until he was out of range of the lock cams, tasting Mars on his tongue, even as breather air filled his lungs. The dust devils changed course and zigzagged toward him and he smiled. Soreh, who ran the weigh room, had been complaining last night as she drank beer with Dad that the dust devils hung around the settlement, that they followed her. Dad had laughed at her.

She was right, but he didn't tell her. She'd told Dad that he must have gotten brain damage in the blast.

Out of cam range, he hiked away from the low garden domes. Have to stop and check the lines on the way back. Not now. The leading pair of dust devils converged as he reached the edge of the cyan field, their passage a dry scuff in the thin atmosphere. He stopped, braced himself as they twirled around him. Let his eyes go blurry.

He stood on a mosaic plaza, the tiles of shimmering green,

ruby, and deep azure laid out in swirling arcs radiating from a cluster of crystal basins. Water leaped in the center of each basin, giving
off the tinkle of glass chimes as it splashed back down, overflowing
the rim and trickling across the plaza in snaking streams. The two
Martians stood in front of him. He smiled at them, recognizing
them. He'd named them Rose and Shane because he liked the
names. He wasn't sure that "name" was something that they understood. It wasn't like they talked in words.

Tall and skinny as the winter trees he'd seen vids of from Earth,
they pirouetted, bathing him in their smiles. Well, it felt like a smile.
He pirouetted with them, laughing without his mouth because they
heard that. Their faces had looked weird at first, with a ridge pushing out down the middle from forehead to chin, so that their elongated, cloudy eyes were set back on either side of the ridge. Their
mouths were perfectly round, mostly closed with pale lips, although
now and again they opened wide to show darkness and nothing like
teeth that he could see. He had no idea what they ate, had never seen
a Martian eating.

They fluttered their long, six-fingered hands, and he followed
them toward the canal along a long, curving street paved with azure
tiles edged with silver so that it flashed in the sunshine, a ghostly
image overlaid on red dust and rock. Tall, twisted spires of buildings
rose on either side and the tall, slender Martians strolled in and out,
crossing the spaces between the buildings on narrow, arching rib-
bons of crystal, like graceful tightrope walkers he'd seen in vids of
old-days circuses. Only, you could see in the circus videos that the
tightrope walkers were afraid of falling.

Nobody here was afraid.

Five more Martians had joined them, fluttering their hands as
they strolled along the azure path in a ghostly shimmer, their half-
length robes fluttering in the breeze, a shifting rainbow of color, like
an oil slick on the air. Small thorny plants covered with pink blossoms lined the path here, barely visible in the noonday sun, and the
spires were less crowded. Maartin stopped, fascinated, as one of the

plants began to rock back and forth. It slowly worked thick rootlets free of the soil. The rootlets, pink and fleshy, flexed like fingers, stretching and elongating, reaching away from the path to bury themselves in the reddish soil. Slowly, the rootlets contracted, pulling the plant away from the neat row along the path.

A Martian hurried up, long fingers of one hand fluttering furiously. The other hand held a slender black wand. The Martian poked the tip of the wand into the soil where the plant had anchored its rootlets. The rootlets whipped out of the soil, coiling tightly under the plant's thorny branches. It shook its dull green leaves with a threatening rustle and all its thorns slowly aligned to point at the Martian with the wand. The Martian shook its fingers at the plant and poked the wand tip into the soil again. Slowly, the rootlets extended on the far side, and the plant began to drag itself back to the path and the space it had left between its neighbors. Just like the school av'. Maartin covered a smile because moving his mouth made his Martian friends finger-laugh at him. The plant looked defeated, its leaves drooping slightly, its thorns no longer erect.

A finger of urgency prodded him and he looked up. The group of Martians had stopped and were looking back at him. Rose stepped forward. It was her urgency he'd felt. Her. He shrugged as he hurried to catch up. She *felt* like a her, and he wasn't sure why, but she did. She looked the same as Shane and *he* felt like a he.

The canal lay ahead. Towers soared gracefully along its rippling expanse. Barges floated on the water, moving slowly along. When he sneaked out at dusk, the water looked almost solid, but in the sunshine, you could see the empty bed through the barges and the water. Colorful awnings flapped in the breeze, and, in their shade, Martians reclined on footed cushions, their fingers flickering in conversation. A trio stood at the bow of one barge, blowing into polished and twisted horns that branched into multiple mouths. He couldn't hear anything, but they gave out a soft blue smoke and suddenly he was filled with gentle feelings, sort of like the way he felt at night, when Mom used to tuck in the covers and say good night. He swallowed, and Rose drifted back to walk close to him, floating along on her long toes, as if she was nearly weightless. She waved her fingers in front of him and her head dipped, mouth opening briefly.

Sharing his sorrow. He blinked. They had never paid this much attention to him before. Sometimes they walked with him, but there was no . . . communication. He felt them some, but they usually didn't really feel *him*.

Maybe that was changing.

He closed his eyes, remembering. Mom and her gentle hands, her touch on his face, the way she laughed when Dad looked at her. A tear slid down his face and he wiped it away, Mars dust gritty on his skin, his eyes on the crystal spires, the sparkling water of the canal. *Mom* would believe him. That he saw . . . *this*. The way it really was.

If she was here.

An explosion shattered the quiet, and Maartin flinched as an invisible hand shoved him. The canal, the barges, vanished. On the far side of the canal, where the Rim rose against the pale greenish sky, a burst of red dust fountained upward and a narrow and elegant tower of rock dissolved into a waterfall of pulverized fragments. More clouds of dust billowed outward, and a faint thump followed. Dust devils skittered around him, zigzagging angry patterns across the ground, and he blinked, his eyes tearing as they filled with dust.

Miners. He swallowed. Hard. Felt the swallow turn to stone as it sank into his belly. He blurred his eyes, tried to see the spires again, the barges, through the drifting curtains of dust. He could see them to the left, to the right, way down the canal. Martians stood on the barges, fingers flickering and pointing.

In front of him, only dust, the canal bed empty and dry.

The pile of rubble that had been the rock tower seemed to smoke as dust seeped from it. Machines crawled around the edges, swallowing broken red stone, spewing tails of red dust and rock now. On either side, more columns of rock twined skyward, forming the rim, twisted like the horns of the unicorns he'd seen in the kiddie videos he used to watch. Carved by the wind, Dad said, they all said. The dust devils drifted across the plain toward the dust cloud, zigzagging around the machines. One of the figures grabbed at his full-face breather as a dust devil snatched at it, and one of the machines bogged down and stopped. More figures hurried to it.

He veered left, to the crumbled edge of the canal, where you could scramble down to the bottom. The sides were mostly still clean and vertical. Only here and there had they crumbled so that it wasn't a sheer drop to the floor. He slid down, dust a red flag trailing away in the always-wind, stretched his eyes, trying to see water, barges.

"Hey."

He froze. Looked over his shoulder.

"What the hell are you doing down here?" A short, squat figure, bulky in dull, metallic-colored coveralls, stepped forward to block his path. Maartin had missed him in the morning shadow.

A miner.

He stared into hard gray eyes behind safety goggles, a weathered face with a scraggle of beard sweating beneath a full-mouth breather mask.

"I asked you a question, kid." A gloved hand clamped down on Maartin's arm. "You coulda been under that rock when it came down. You wanta die?"

He shook his head, his stomach twisted up in his throat.

"Hey, we warned you folk at the settlement to stay away, didn't you hear?" The gray eyes softened a bit. "We're gonna be blowing another outcrop. You're underneath, you could get dead."

Dad hadn't said the miners were coming. He wouldn't. He struggled to find words.

"Hey, I got a kid brother about your age." The miner let go of his arm. "I wouldn't want to see him get hurt, neither."

"You . . . killed . . . Mother." That burst out, as clear and edged as broken glass. He swung at the man's face, wanting to hurt him, wanting to . . .

"Hey, hey, whoa!" The man put his hands up, held him off, ducking the swings. "Cool yer jets, kid. We don't kill anybody."

Maartin grabbed at his breather hose, struggled as the man gripped his arms. The words were gone as abruptly as they had come and his tongue knotted, threatening to choke him.

Another figure came around the bend in the canal. "Hey, Jorge . . ." The man stopped, fists planting on narrow hips, his lean face sharp-edged as a Rim rock in the morning light. "Jeez, these hogs don't have the sense God gave rocks, do they? Don't they get it that they gotta stay clear? Bring 'im in." He started to turn back. "We'll ship 'im back, prosecute for trespass. Maybe that'll keep 'em away."

"Ah, it's a kid, Ter."

"Can it, Jorge, you're a damn softie." The skinny man stepped forward, pulling plastic cuffs from his belt. "C'mere, kid. You're in trouble now."

Suddenly, the air was full of hissing as dust devils circled, zigzagged. The skinny man yelled as a rock bounced off his forehead and Maartin caught a glimpse of bright blood. The other man, Jorge, ducked as a rock screamed past his head. Maartin tore free and ran, pushing off the smooth floor of the canal, stretching out and really traveling now, the walls flashing past, the man, Ter's, shout torn away by distance. The dust devils danced around him, to the side, behind, so that he ran curtained by red dust, the canal an open path ahead. He didn't slow to climb out where he'd come down, just kept running, settling into a rhythm so that his breather could keep up.

Anger filled him, deep and dark, heavy as stone, an anger as big as the planet.

He looked back, and the dust devils veered, so that he could see through the thinning dust. They weren't chasing him—but they couldn't catch him if they did. He could outrun any of the grown-ups in the settlement. Adaptation, Dad had called it when Maartin started winning their races, back when he was ten. "The planet is shaping you."

They weren't going to catch him. His breather was working hard and he slowed, kind of pushing himself off with his toes, letting his body do the work, like the Martians moved, like their bodies could sort of float. He could see them again now—they weren't dust devils anymore—pushing along beside him with the same floating gait, but lighter than he could do it. Rose drifted beside him and anger hummed in the air, making his back teeth ache.

It would never be there again. The canal. The barges and the towers. He'd only see red rock if he came this way again. His stomach cramped up and he skidded to a stop. There was another collapse a klick farther on. He walked now, trudging along the smooth floor of the canal. The vague shapes of barges drifted above him on the surface of the water that used to be. The floor was like glass but not as slick. Dad said he'd looked at it . . . or one just like it . . . from Earth, when he was a boy and wanted to come here.

Long time ago.

Maartin stopped. The Rim came right down to the canal, as if the rock spires were ready to step into the water that used to flow here. He found the small fall of rock that let him climb the smooth face of stone to the foot of the Rim. Above him, two spires twisted skyward like dancers, upraised hands joined. A soft whisper tickled his mind.

Grief. Anger. Maartin leaned back against the stone. Maybe it was dead for them, too, the canal, the water, the barges and players? A slow, depthless sadness filled him, *their* sadness. He blurred his eyes and looked out at the canal. Here, water still sparkled in it and on the far side, glittering crystal spiderways arched and twisted, crisscrossed and vanished into the distance. The people floated along the strands, long fingers waving at each other. Vines twined around the base of the spiderways here, thick with red, purple, and orange leaves. Their leaves were shaped a little like the tomato plants in Kurt Vishnu's plot, even if the leaves weren't green. Other plants that looked like spiny melons dotted the ground. That kind moved, too.

He watched as one tall one stretched its branches, bruise-purple leaves quivering.

A Martian drifted up and over the canal on one of the tall, looping arches that crossed it, coming quite close to where Maartin was standing. *He,* Maartin thought. The Martian stepped off the web strand where it ran past the Rim and looked at him. Really *looked.*

Only Rose and sometimes Shane had looked at him, up until now. He shivered, couldn't look away, and that dark sadness filled him, streaked with fiery veins of anger. He couldn't look away. It was as if he were diving into red dust, dry, suffocating. He gasped. Jerked back. The long fingers curled, just so.

A smile?

He curled his fingers, felt . . . amusement. Approval.

Another blast rocked the ground.

The web and the water and the Martian all shimmered and . . .

. . . were gone.

Maartin slumped back against the rock tower, his gut hollow.

He could see the towering plume of dust, couldn't see which spire they had blown apart this time. How much more had died? He pushed himself to his feet, broke into a trot, measuring his breathing. Time to get home before Dad got back with the cyan crew and found him gone.

To his left, all he saw was the empty red dust and scattered rocks on the canal floor. He slowed to a walk as the rows of low, inflated greenhouses came into view. Bad to show up panting. No reason to hurry. Their plot was at the far end, closest to the vestibule. He entered, sealed the door, and opened the inner door. The rush of warm, humid air soothed his dry lips, and he pulled off his breather for a moment, so that he could smell the rich green-and-dirt-scented air. Too bad you had to use a breather in here, but the air from the settlement filters was heavy in carbon dioxide, very low in oxygen. He'd passed out once, and Dad had had a fit. He pulled the door closed behind him. Seaul Ku was working in her plot, just across from theirs. "Were you lost?" Her narrow dark eyes, nested in smile-wrinkles, fixed on his face. "I saw you out there, following the dust devils. You looked lost." She shook a blue-gloved finger at him. "You should not follow the dust devils. They can knock you down. Break your breather. Then what would you do?"

"They . . . wouldn't." His tongue struggled, let the words out. Mistake. Too late to call the words back now. "I . . . I'm care . . ." He gave up, pulled his pad out, tapped it. *I watch how the wind is blowing them along and stay clear.* He smiled, but her eyes had narrowed with *that* look. Oh well. *Your beets are bigger than ours.* He gave her a big smile. *Howcum?*

"Ah, it's that greenish rock you find sometimes." She wagged her finger at him again, her back not quite straight, even when she stood upright, so that she had to tilt her head up to look at him. "It's got a lot of phosphorus in it, I guess. And the beets love it. Only because you help me when my back hurts." She gave him a conspiratorial wink. "Try it, but don't tell anybody else, especially not Sascha. He thinks he's such a hot gardener." She cackled. "You're always wandering off, keep an eye out for it, bring some back. Bring some back for me, too, since I told you." She gave him a sly look. "And I won't tell your dad that you were out there. Your legs are younger than mine. Soreh told me that Rav, the market guy from town, asks specifically for *my* beets. And pays extra for them, too. Now, he'll pay extra for yours, too."

Soreh said a lot of things. *Won't tell anybody. U want help?* He didn't need her headshake to know she didn't, he could always see it when she was in pain, sort of like a heat shimmer in the air. Wasn't there today. He nodded, waved, and stepped over the plastic tape that marked the boundary of each plot. "Dad . . . back . . . ?"

"Ah, they're already in." She squatted amidst the beet rows, gently loosening the reddish soil around each crown of dark green leaves. "I guess the patch wasn't as big as Gus said it was and they got the seeding done early. He came by to see if you were here." She kept her eyes fixed on her cultivator as she worked the moist soil.

"I . . . said I didn't know where you were. But you shouldn't go wandering off like that." She shot him a quick sideways glance. "You could get lost. Those dust devils could knock you down."

He shook his head, knelt, and started checking the drip lines, looking for any telltale dry or soggy patches that might mean a leak of too much precious water or a plugged line. He hurried. The longer Dad wondered where he was, the more likely he was to check back on the house database. Sure enough, he managed to find a couple of drippers that were partially plugged. Dad would probably go over to Canny's place. She brewed beer out of all kinds of stuff, and he'd heard Dan Zheng say that this batch was really good. Dad was pretty easygoing about his skimping on lesson time after a couple of beers.

The sun was pretty low by the time he headed in, and he didn't have to blur his eyes very hard to see the plaza and the fountains. Four or five musicians were piping pink and green mist from the twisted horns, over near the fountain. Some of their spinach was ready for market, and he detoured to the settlement-warehouse entrance. The weigh room was cold, right down near freezing. He set the unit basket on the scale, entered his dad's code and contents. The scale beeped, uploading the weight of spinach contributed to their ag total for the month. Rubbing his stinging hands together, he headed for the door.

Just as it scraped open.

"Darn dust gets into everything. You gotta replace bearings here all the time." The mayor, Al Siggrand, shoved the door all the way open. "Hey, your dad's lookin' for you!" He gave Maartin a fake scowl. "You weren't wandering out there by yourself again, were you?" He talked a little loud, as if Maartin couldn't hear right. "You know your dad told you not to do that. Do you remember?"

Maartin nodded, but his eyes went to the man standing behind the short, squat mayor, dressed in a full miner's suit. The miner he'd talked to.

"Maartin, meet Jorge." The mayor jerked his chin at the miner. "I guess these guys are tired of freeze-dried. They're willing to pay good market price for some fresh stuff for a change."

Oh great, and now he'd tell the mayor that Maartin had been in the canal. Maartin swallowed.

"Hey, Maartin." The miner was smiling at him. He had a long, freckled face and hair that wasn't quite the color of the Martian dust that coated the spots where the breather mask didn't cover. "Nice to meet you. Want to sell us some of your produce? What do you and your dad grow?"

Maartin pushed past them, out into the settlement alley.

"Don't mind him." The closing door couldn't quite block out the mayor's words. "He's not quite all there, got a head injury in a rock-fall accident a couple years back. Can't talk anymore. He gets lost, wanders off. We all kind of look out for him."

Fists jammed into his pockets, Maartin headed left, toward their rooms. He could feel the old city around them. Through the transparent skin of the settlement dome, dust devils danced in the fading light, weaving complex and angry patterns across the barren ground beyond the garden domes. The spires and spiderways shimmered in the bloody light of the setting sun.

Angry?

He stopped at the intersection to their alley. Blinked.

Yes. *Angry.*

Their door slid open to dark rooms. Dad would be at Canny's. He headed there, feet scuffing up a thin haze of dust that seeped in no matter what you did. Canny's big two-room place was just around the corner on the street and the door was open, which made the mayor mad because the rooms were all a higher O_2 concentration than the dome itself, but with the jam of bodies crowding the space, you could see why. A half dozen people stood around the doorway, mugs in hand.

"Hey, Maartin." Celie, who made the mugs and some pretty cool dishes from the red Martian dust and sold 'em to the produce buyer from City, waved hers at him. "Give your dad time to finish his pint, eh?" She winked at him, her round face framed by gray curls.

"Th . . . mayor . . . selling . . ." His tongue struggled with the words. *To the miners,* he tapped out. He faced her, horrified to feel a hot sting behind his eyelids.

"Honey, it's okay. Really." She put her arm around him. "It's a good thing they're buying from us. They're not the bad people who were responsible for the accident. They like our veggies. And they're going to pay us a lot of money."

It wasn't an accident and everybody knew it. And now they were killing the city. He blinked, struggling to hold in the tears.

"Hey, Maart, where were you?"

Dad saved him, face flushed, pushing through the crowd. "Darn, kid, I was worried. And then Seaul texted me and said you were cleaning drippers after all, that she figured you were working on someone else's plot out there and that's why she hadn't seen you. Was that where you were?" His face relaxed some as Maartin nodded. He had the tears buried deep now.

". . . helping," Maartin stuttered. He nodded some more.

"Okay, then, you text me next time, let me know where you are." Dad put an arm around his shoulders. "I don't want to be organizing any search parties for no reason, hear?"

He nodded, got a head tousle from Dad. He smelled faintly of cyans and a little bit like drying-out water. Maartin had helped them seed a few times, mixing in the cyanobacteria spores, setting up the pumps and microdrip system that brought the deep-drilled moisture up and wicked it into the soil. They didn't need a lot of water, the cyans. They were engineered, just went into biosuspension when it got too dry, came back to life with more water. Sometimes Dad would squat over an established patch and take off his breather. He said you could smell the oxygen, that before Maartin died, he'd be able to walk around without a breather. Maartin couldn't smell anything but cyans. He walked around without oxygen all the time in the dome.

Dad got him a mug of juice and Maartin retreated to his usual perch on a plastic bin that stored bar towels and stuff, over in the corner. Nobody much noticed him, it was kind of dark there and, sitting, he was down low. People didn't much look down when they were drinking Canny's beer; they looked at each other or around the room at other faces. Four or five kids were playing some kind of chase game, running in and out. Celie yelled at them for it. He knew them. The girls were okay, he pretty much steered clear of the boys. Especially Ronan. He was the smallest, but he made up for it in meanness. Whenever the adults weren't around, they did a great job of illustrating the pack behavior he'd read about in his school programs. He wondered if the Martians behaved like humans. He'd never seen any sign of conflict on the streets or the spiderways. No yelling. No pushing. Or maybe they weren't all that different, just used *another* way to push one another around and call one another names.

Rising voices snapped him out of it. The kid pack was back, hanging around the door. Hanging around five miners. Maartin stiffened, pulling back into the shadow beneath the makeshift bar.

"Hey, folks, nice to meet you, just wanted to stop in, sample the local brew." Jorge was in front, smiling and easy.

"You guys aren't finding any veins of your druggie-ore running our way, are you?" Celie spoke up and it went quiet, *right now*. Maartin watched as people moved or didn't move. A small space opened up around the miners, and the hellos were halfhearted from the ones that didn't move.

The mayor bustled through the door, slapped one of the men on the shoulder. "This round's on me!" He beamed, but he was looking to see who moved and who didn't, too. "Let's show these hardworking boys our hospitality. Fill 'em up, Celie!"

The moment broke. Celie opened her mouth, but already people were crowding to the counter, their mugs in hand. And Dad? Maartin didn't wait to see. He slipped to the wall, away from the rush to the bar, slipped along the wall to the door and out.

"Hey, it's the retard!"

Maartin flinched as a hand closed on the back of his shirt and yanked him backward, around the corner and out of sight of Canny's doorway.

"They texted an alert, retard, and we had to go lookin' for you." Ronan's breath was hot in his ear, stinking of garlic. "That was my time on the game-net and I had like five minutes left by the time they said we could quit lookin'." He twisted his fist, and Maartin choked. "Retard, somebody's gotta pay for my game time!"

It was going to hurt. Maartin closed his eyes, but he could feel the other two boys, hanging just back from Ronan. Hunger. It felt like hunger. He shivered.

"So." Ronan's voice was buttery and he twisted the shirt harder. "How do you think you oughta pay, retard?"

He couldn't breathe and in a minute he was going to start to struggle, his body wouldn't obey him anymore. Red and green spots flashed against the blackness of his closed eyes and his chest was going to explode.

Ronan yelped and let go. Maartin stumbled on his knees, barely feeling the impact, sucking in painful shuddering breaths that made him dizzy.

"You got a thing about picking on people?" a slow, familiar voice drawled.

Maartin scrambled on his knees. Jorge had Ronan by the back of the neck, was holding the boy about a foot off the ground, the way you'd hold a bag of fertilizer. Ronan's eyes were wide and his skin had gone about three shades paler.

"I'm talkin' to *you*, kid." Jorge shook him very very gently, and Ronan squeaked as Jorge let go suddenly and dropped him to his feet.

He bolted to the corner. "I'm gonna tell the mayor," he yelled back. "You can't do that!"

"Go tell him." Jorge smiled. "And I just did it." He looked down at Maartin for a long moment. "You need to learn how to do something to people like that, kid." He held out his hand. "C'mon. Get up."

Maartin sucked in a breath. "Hit . . . ?" The words came this time.

"Yep." His eyebrows rose and he tilted his head, frowning. "You're not retarded. So how come people say that about you?"

Maartin shrugged, looked away.

"I mean, you act like an idiot, sure. Nobody oughta be runnin' around out on a strange planet on their own. You get hurt, could be a while before your people get to you. I've seen miners die a couple miles from a dig just because they wandered off and didn't tell anybody. This planet's got more bad luck than a picnic's got ants."

Maartin frowned. Shook his head. "Not . . . luck. Not . . . *alone.*" And he clamped his lips together. Those words had come out on their own, he didn't mean to let them.

"Yeah, I heard you got invisible buddies out there. I hope they can carry you home when you bust a leg." But his eyes had gone very narrow, and Maartin had to look away again. "What do you see out there?"

He sounded funny . . . as if he maybe didn't think it was just imagination. Or the head injury, like Dad did. He shrugged, stared down at the patterns the dust made on the street.

"I know why you hate us now. Celie in there, she made sure I knew. She's got a tongue on her, that gal. I'm sorry, Maartin. I'm sorry that you got hurt, that your mom got killed. Yeah, you got some rogue companies, and man, you just don't know what it does to guys, thinkin' they got their hands on enough money to go back home, live like a prince. Most of us . . . we're never gonna get home." Shadows moved in his dark eyes. "Costs a fortune to pay transport and you never really get your ticket out here paid off, it's too easy to spend what you get on beer, or booze, or chemicals so you can go home the easy way." He laughed harshly. "Only way you're gonna make more than your ticket back is to find a shoal. That . . . I guess that was what made those guys crazy. You hear about 'em. Pearls all over the place, the whole crew can go home in style, awake, no danger of cryodamage from steerage. Buy that palace when they get there. Take care of their families."

Maartin looked up. He sounded so . . . sad. "Why . . . people want . . . pearls?" The words were coming easier now, easier than with Dad even. "Why . . . so much?"

"You never held one?" Jorge chuckled and reached into his pocket. "I guess they do different stuff to different people. Mostly, they make sex feel really really great." He winked. "Kind of like you're givin' and takin' at the same time. That sells really well back home, you better believe it. Up here, sometimes you can see weird stuff." He held out his hand. "Pick it up."

Maartin looked at the small ovoid on Jorge's palm. It was the color of dust, but veins of silver and gold swirled through it, and, as he stared at it, tiny starbursts of light seemed to flicker off and on, deep in its depths.

"I should turn it in, I guess, but I . . . I see stuff. Pretty stuff. Cheaper than the drugs." He laughed that harsh laugh again. "Kind of holds your eye, doesn't it?" He pushed his hand closer. "Pick it up. See what it does for you."

Maartin reached for it and just before he touched it, the hum of the city around him intensified, rising instantly to a howl as his fingers brushed the smooth . . .

He let the flow of the crowd carry him along the wide boulevard, where conversation flowed like the sparkling waters of the canal in the distance. Happy, comfortable, belonging. All around him, slender residents of the city floated along the twisting spiderway . . . the name for it flashed in his mind. They were all heading toward the canal, and suddenly, the happy/comfortable feeling cracked, streaked through with ugly red anger. *Anger.* He looked ahead, where the spires twisted into the sky and the fragile bridges crossed the canal in soaring arches. And winced as he spied the empty, dry, ugly space where the miners were working. The anger was building, building, building . . . washing back across the plain, choking him, turning the sky and air the color of dead dust, blurring the lovely spires, blurring . . . All around him people stretched out long-fingered hands, reached death from the air, held death like silvery spears that shimmered and twisted, humming, humming, humming, death . . . He gasped for air, choking on anger-dust, struggling . . .

"Maartin? He's waking up."

Dad's voice.

Arms were holding him. Dad? He blinked, his eyelids gummy, sticky, forced them open.

He was in the infirmary. Everything was white, and a screen winked numbers and flickering graphs beside the bed. Dad leaned over him, his face blocking out the screen and the people strolling through and around his bed, fingers flickering in conversation. "You had some kind of seizure, son. Jorge here brought you in. He said it happened when he touched a Martian pearl."

It wasn't a pearl, what a silly name. A pearl was from the shell of a mollusk, a creature from Earth's oceans, how dumb to think that this was from some kind of sea creature. The people standing around his bed waved their fingers in agreement, flicking laughter at him. Silly comparison, not-too-smart, not-worth-our-attention. *They just don't know.* His fingers twitched on the white sheet covering him and he absently noticed the garbled sounds coming from his . . . from his mouth. It took him a moment to remember the right word.

"Maartin? What are you trying to say? Stay with us, son."

He blinked, and the strolling people faded a little. He could see through them now, see Dad's face again, more worried now, see Jorge standing at the foot of the bed.

"Maartin?"

"I . . . oh . . . kay. Dad." He shaped the words carefully, closed his hands into fists as his fingers tried to move. Mouth. Focus. "Fain. Ted?"

"Hello, Maartin, how are you feeling?" Another face swam into focus, pushing Dad aside. Dr. Abram, the settlement's health-tech person. Dr. Abram was smiling one of those too-wide smiles that meant stuff was wrong. "So what happened? Mr. Moreno here says that some of the boys were getting a little rough. Did you hit your head on something?"

He could feel the pressure of their attention, Dad and Jorge. His fingers twitched again, trying to explain. He clenched his fists more tightly, made his head rock forward and back. A nod. The word for the gesture came back to him. He nodded again. "On. Wall." It was getting easier to find the words for the lie in the tumbled chaos inside his head.

"I told Al that the boys were bullying Maartin." Dad's voice rose as he faced Abram. "But no, he's not gonna do anything but shake his finger at those punks. When did that ever do any good? And now this . . ."

"Easy, Paul." Abram put his arm on Dad's shoulder. "There's no hemorrhaging, no pressure on the brain or areas of injury, according to the scans. Apparently the bump caused something like a short and sparked a lot of unusual brain activity, that's all. The root cause is probably the earlier accident, the original brain trauma." He was speaking very soothingly, and Dad looked away. He was trying not to cry.

Maartin looked at Jorge. He was frowning. Yeah. He knew that the doctor was wrong. Maartin waited for him to say so, but he didn't say anything. Instead, he gave Maartin a crooked smile. "Glad you're feeling better, Maartin. Hey, you get better, okay?" He lifted a finger to his forehead in a kind of salute and left the room.

"I'm . . . I'm glad he came along." Dad looked after him, his face tight. Nodded grudgingly. "Good to know a few of 'em are okay." He turned back to Abram, anger in his eyes once more. "I'm going to go talk to Al. Right now. This is a matter for community intervention."

"You heard what the boys had to say." Abram shook his head.

"They're lying."

"He's going to be fine, Paul. Kids are rough. They act like bullies once in a while. This scared 'em. They learned from it."

"Maartin, I'll be back in a little while." Dad was talking to him like the mayor talked to him. Too loud and too slow. Maartin swallowed sadness. Nodded.

"You're going to be fine, Maartin." Abram wasn't looking at him, was looking at the screen with all the numbers and graphs. "But we're going to keep you here a little while longer." He gave that too-wide smile again, but he still wasn't looking at Maartin. "You were unconscious for over three days."

Three days? Maartin nodded, but the doctor wasn't looking at him and didn't notice. He lay back on the pillow and let the crowd in the plaza come back into focus. It had thinned now. People walked away, through the walls as if they weren't there at all, and he could see the buildings, the road, the spiderways arching overhead. The curved wall of a building crossed through the room, right through the end of the bed. He watched Abram walk through it and right through a trio of people fluttering an intense conversation as they strolled into its wide, arched doorway. He shoved a foot out, tried to feel something as his foot pushed into the building's wall. Nothing. One of the people rippled her fingers in a smile and said something that didn't quite make sense, but almost. About his foot. And the building.

"What are you seeing?"

He startled and red flashed on the screen. Jorge stepped forward quickly and touched it. The red went away and he glanced furtively at the door. "Man, they've got the alarms set way high. I guess the doc is afraid you're gonna seize again." He perched awkwardly on the foot of the bed, oblivious to the two people who hurried through him. "So what do you see?" His dark eyes were intent on Maartin's face.

"I . . . the city. Spiderways. People." He let his fingers talk, too. It helped the words come. Jorge stared at them.

"With long fingers and they wave 'em all the time, right? Silvery hair? Skinny? Kind of weird."

". . . Beautiful. Like . . . spires."

"Yeah." Jorge sighed. The sound was tired. Old.

Maartin squinted at his face, at the shadows in his eyes.

"So it's not just me." He rubbed his face with both hands. "I couldn't figure out how I came up with this stuff. What are they, Maartin? Do you know?"

". . . people."

"Martians?"

Maartin shrugged. Silly question.

"Ghosts?"

Maartin frowned. Shook his head slowly. "Ghosts . . . dead people."

Jorge groaned and buried his face in his hands. "I've been asking around. For a long time. Yeah, the guys who handle pearls see stuff, but nobody keeps a pearl very long. Well, me. But I wanted to figure out what I was seeing. I figured they were ghosts." He raised his head and fixed his eyes on Maartin. "I did some checking. Found the old news post about your . . . about the accident. You and your mom got caught in a debris slide from a blast. It took out a small dome."

They'd been visiting Teresa, Mom's friend. She'd laughed a lot and taught him to play poker. Maartin closed his eyes as once again, the dome above them buckled, split, and red dust and rock flowed in like water. Screaming split his ears, then silence, darkness, and . . .

. . . people.

"I'm so sorry."

Maartin opened his eyes as something brushed his face. Jorge was wiping tears from his cheeks.

"That was the richest shoal of pearls ever found. People . . . people went crazy. So, what are they?" Jorge was whispering now. "The pearls. Do you know?"

Maartin thought about it. He did know. He wasn't sure he had the words, wove a faltering explanation in the air with his fingers, biting his lip, waiting for the breath-words to come. They didn't.

"What does that mean? What you're doing with your fingers?"

Maartin shook his head. "I . . . I think they . . . like . . ." He drew a deep breath. ". . . a soul. No." He shook his head. ". . . projector? From long ago?"

"So they are ghosts."

He sounded so relieved. Maartin shook his head. ". . . not dead. Alive." He struggled to find words that would explain, as his fingers quivered. "Dif . . . different way . . . of being." He raised his head, stared into Jorge's dark eyes. "They live forever. But . . . when . . . when you take . . . pearls away . . . they . . . die. Everything. City. Spires. Spiderways."

"No." Jorge spun to his feet, heading for the door. "Kid, you're dreaming. They're not alive, they're just visions. Yeah, they seem real, but that's all they are. Ghosts. *Visions.*"

"No." Maartin clenched his fingers into fists. ". . . alive. You kill them."

Jorge left.

Maartin listened to his footsteps fade. Around him, the city hummed with life. People slid across the spiderways and a trio of musicians shook bouquets of delicate silver wands that gave off a shimmering, crystal music that rose and fell, filling the air with curtains of rose and golden light. A city. He strained his eyes so that the dome faded away and all he saw were the streets, the free-form plazas paved here with opalescent tiles, the silvery arches of the spiderways overhead, the delicate walkways that connected the tall buildings' soaring spires.

Full of people.

Full of life.

A shoal.

Dad took him home the next day, treating him as if he were made of delicate glass and might break. He had rented a mover, as if Maartin had a broken leg. Maartin felt silly, perched in the seat next to Dad as they hummed past people walking to their gardens or shopping or doing whatever. They all looked at him as soon as they could. He didn't have to turn around, he felt the stares like prodding fingers on his back. But he found he could let the Martian city come into focus and didn't have to feel them. But even that wasn't comfortable. The feel of the city was changing and that anger-hum threaded through everything. Everything. South, toward the canal, the empty red space where the spiderways ended and the canal gaped barren and dry nagged like a missing tooth. When they got back to their rooms, Maartin told Dad that he didn't feel good and Dad gave him one of the pills Dr. Abram had given him. The pills made him sleep and he didn't even dream about the city. Dad was relieved when he took the pill. Now he could go return the mover and didn't have to worry.

The city got in his way. He had to concentrate in order to keep the dome in focus. If he forgot, if he lost focus, the city buildings and the people and the spiderways tangled up with the corridor walls and the dome and he stopped when he didn't need to or ran into people. Or walls. Everybody was really nice about that, they'd all heard about the "seizure." They just walked him back home, even if that wasn't where he wanted to go, saying soothing things in too-loud, too-simple voices. Their kids slunk away whenever they saw him.

But the anger-hum was fading. Dad took him to Canny's one night and he heard people talking about how the miners had quit blasting, that they weren't finding any pearls, that they were doing some test digs, but if nothing turned up, they'd move on.

He hadn't seen Jorge since he'd walked out of the infirmary.

Dad took him back to Dr. Abram again and asked the doctor to do another brain scan.

"Yes, there has been an increase in random activity in the temporal lobes." Abram didn't bother to lower his voice even though the door was open between his office and the exam room where Maartin was sitting. "It's a significant increase since the scan I ran after the initial accident." The doctor reached across his keyboard to put a hand on Dad's arm. "Speech, hearing, visual processing . . . it all comes from that area. Think of an old-fashioned Earthly thunderstorm. The lightning made the lights flicker, caused static on the radio, interfered with old-fashioned cable TV. That's what's going on in Maartin's brain." He sounded almost cheerful now. He loved lecturing, Maartin thought. He'd logged in to some of Dr. Abram's video lectures on health issues and they were pretty good.

Not this one.

Dad's sadness dimmed the city plaza that overlay the office. One of the people strolling by flickered sympathy to him and he rippled a weak appreciation. "Is there any way to fix the problem?"

Abram shook his head. Such a crude gesture when the slightest curve of his third finger could have conveyed so much more. Maartin watched Dad's shoulders slump. "The drugs quiet the activity, but since they sedate him . . ." Abram shrugged. "And a lower dose doesn't seem to do any good."

Well, it dimmed the city some, but that was all.

"What about his hands . . . they twitch and spasm all the time."

"I don't know what's causing that." Abram frowned.

Thunderstorms. Maartin frowned. Dad was feeling pretty bleak and Dr. Abram was patting him again. A shoal, Jorge had said. Lots of pearls in that avalanche of dust and rock when the miners blasted the escarpment above Teresa's settlement? And he'd been buried in them for a whole day. That's what Dad told him after, anyway. It had taken that long for someone to dig him out. Sleeping in the pearls, touching them? Thunderstorm?

Two people carrying purple flowers paused as they crossed the plaza and flickered a negative at him. Not quite right. The taller one fluttered rapid fingers, waved emphatically. Rippled a smile.

We fixed you.

You are whole now. You were broken. Imperfect unit. They rippled smiles, comfort, and approval and strolled on their way, their arched feet barely brushing the polished tiles.

Wait! He waved both hands. They paused, looked back. *Fix the miners! Fix them!* His fingers snapped together with urgency and both of them curled disapproval at his tone, but softened their fingers into a long arc of understanding. Imperfect unit, still. They rippled a shrug and went on. Maartin flinched as his father's hands closed over his.

"Easy, son." His eyes were full of pain. "Try clasping them together when they want to do that."

You don't understand. His fingers writhed in his father's grasp.

"They . . ." He forced out the crude huff of air. "Don't." His fingers twitched, stifled in his father's grip. "Care."

"Who doesn't care?" The smile looked artificial. "The miners, Maartin? These aren't the bad men who . . . who hurt you."

I want them to make you whole, too. His fingers struggled. *I want you to see. We're not alone here. She share. We just don't see.*

He started going to the garden domes every day, weeding all the beds. They'd built the beds on a pretty plaza, a graceful, free-form space tiled with pale blue and soft green octagons that sparkled with crystal dust. Two fountains played watery music and soft blue and pink mists spread from the slender black tubes that rose from the tumbling water. Sometimes one of the people stopped to speak to him. He recognized them by feel; Soft-sweet-happy, or Firm-thoughtful—he had had word names for them once, but he couldn't remember those. Then there was Sharp-edge-alert. Sharp-edge-alert didn't speak often. He thought about the miners a lot, Maartin could tell. He sometimes *felt* Maartin. Well, *felt* wasn't quite the right word, 'cause they couldn't really touch each other, like you'd touch a plant or dirt or a stone. But he would sometimes put a hand on Maartin and it would . . . sink into him.

Maartin didn't like the feeling much. It didn't hurt, but it felt . . . wrong. Like something was stuck in his flesh and shouldn't be there. When the others "touched" him, their hands brushed his skin the way any human hand would do, but he didn't feel anything. If he tried to touch them, he found, they shied away if he let his hand slide into them. So he didn't.

Only Sharp-edge-alert pushed his hands into Maartin, and Maartin never saw him do that to any of the people.

The human residents mostly left him alone, although Seaul Ku, who weeded there a lot, too, sometimes talked to him. But even she did the slow-talk thing and used baby words. So he didn't try too hard to talk back, kept his fingers working in the soil. She wasn't there the afternoon that Jorge came to the gardens.

He looked *old*. Maartin straightened to his knees, his fingers asking what was wrong, scattering soil crumbs across his thighs.

"What are they?" Jorge squatted to face him. "What are the people you see if they're not ghosts?"

His fingers danced, explaining. He shook his head. Groping for words. They were getting harder to find. "They . . . *are* . . . the pearls." Inadequate. "Like . . . like . . ." He thought hard, running through all the earth-things he'd learned. "Projector? Storage? They . . . live . . . forever. Until the sun . . . eats the planet." Gave up, slumping, his fingers snapping and weaving his frustration in the air between them.

Jorge was staring at them. "Live forever?" He shook his head. "They can't be alive. Like you said, they're images. Ghosts. Not real. The pearls are *rocks*." He lifted his head to meet Maartin's eyes.

He wanted Maartin to say yes. Wanted it a lot. Maartin shook his head. He studied the explanation as his fingers rippled and twined it in the air. "Spectrum." That was close. "Energy?" Not quite. "Different spectrum. They live."

Jorge closed his eyes, and when he opened them, the hope was gone. "Cory and Bantu have been scratching around here when nobody was watching." His voice was hoarse. "Your settlement is sitting on a shoal."

Maartin didn't bother to nod. Sharp-edge-alert had drifted up behind him. It occurred to Maartin that Sharp-edge-alert always seemed to be close by.

"I'm . . ." Jorge sucked in a ragged breath. "I'm going to warn your mayor. To leave. Just clear out of here. The settlement. I've . . . you can't talk to them. It's all about . . . going home. Like I told you."

They would destroy the settlement, the way they'd destroyed the other one. Worse, because the shoal was beneath them, not up in the rocks above. He closed his eyes, imagining the mayor, his father, when the big earth-chewers rolled up to the gardens. "The mayor . . . will call the Planetary Council." Maartin groped for the words, forced them out. "They'll help."

"No, they won't." Jorge shook his head, looked away. "We got better weapons and they know it. We'll pay off the people who need paying off—you can do that when you've got a shoal's worth of pearls. Everybody wants them, Maartin." His voice was harsh. "Everybody. You better ask your Martian buddies to defend you if you want to stay here." His laugh came out as bitter as the bleakness in his eyes. "Nobody else is gonna do it. Come on." He grabbed Maartin's arm. "I gotta get back before they suspect I came over here to warn you, or I'm dead meat."

"You'll kill . . ." His fingers writhed outrage. "You'll kill . . . the city."

"The settlement, you mean? Not if you guys don't fight back." Jorge was dragging him along the path now, toward the exit lock.

He didn't mean the settlement. Sharp-edge-alert drifted along behind.

Anger.

And then he left, loping across the pastel tiles. Everybody in the plaza stopped and turned toward him. The water in the fountains subsided into low, burbling mounds and the mists drifting from the pipes turned an ugly shade of brownish green. Cold sweat broke out on Maartin's skin, and he thought he was going to faint as Jorge yanked him into the lock and closed the inner door.

They found the mayor at Canny's. Maartin hadn't realized how late it was; the sun was sinking into the red crags beyond the city and the canal. Most people were there. Dad was leaning on the bar-plank, and he looked about as old as Jorge. Maartin hadn't noticed it before. There was a lot of gray in his hair now. A crowd of people streamed through the room, heading toward the canal, slipping through the settlers, through the walls, hurrying. He'd never seen one of the people hurry. Maartin peered after them, the anger-hum intensifying steadily, making his bones ache.

"What the hell are you saying?"

The mayor's angry bellow yanked Maartin's attention back to the room. Jorge stepped away from him as the settlers gathered to face him, eyes hard, mouths grim. The people streamed through them, more of them now. Maartin doubled over with the pain of the anger-howl. Jorge retreated a step. "There's nothing you can do." He spread his hands. "You fire a shot at them, they'll raze this settlement. Get your stuff and get out now and we'll try not to damage too much."

"You do that and the Planetary Council will issue death warrants in a heartbeat." The mayor stepped forward, chin out. "You'll all die."

"You think so?" Jorge stopped retreating, his eyes as bleak as they had been in the garden dome. "I lied to you." He was speaking to Maartin now, only to Maartin. "I was there, I was part of the crew that brought the rock down on the settlement over near First Down. I . . . knew what they were gonna do. I just quit, walked away. But I didn't warn the settlers. I . . . I'm sorry." His eyes were dark as night. "I'm sorry, Maartin." He faced the mayor again. "Every one of those men got a death warrant. Every one went home. *Rich.*" His voice grated, harsh and loud, in the sudden silence. "You got real pearl-money, the death warrant gets kind of delayed. Until the next ship leaves. Got it?"

"Paul, get the rifles. We've got twelve in the vault in my office." The mayor blocked Jorge as he edged toward the door. "Grab him."

Jorge lunged, went down with a half dozen settlers on his back. Somebody shoved through the crowd with restraints from the little jail room behind the mayor's office and they strapped his hands behind him, feet together.

"You're not going to stop 'em." Jorge shouted the words, his mouth bloody. "You don't have to die! Just get out! They'll pay damages after, if you don't scream to the Council."

"Fifteen years." The mayor stood over him, fists at his side. "We've been culturing those cyan beds for fifteen years! And you're just gonna plow 'em all up? And then go home? We *can't* go home, and we want to breathe." He kicked Jorge in the side. "Let's go!" He turned, grabbed a projectile rifle from someone behind him. "They're gonna pay for this! We'll spread out, take cover, and drop a hell of a lot of 'em, soon as they come in range."

"You do that, and they'll kill every last one of you!" Jorge yelled from the floor. "There won't be anything left here!"

Nobody listened.

"Come on, Maartin." Dad grabbed his arm. "I can't leave you here. God knows what they'll do when we start shooting. Stay close!" He dragged Maartin along with the settlers pressing through the door, grabbing breathers.

Dad was scared. His whole body shivered with it.

Wait, wait, wait, don't go, don't go that way! His fingers snapped with urgency, but Dad didn't look, didn't notice. "No!" He finally forced the word out. "Wait!"

"We can't wait, son. It'll be too late." Dad wasn't speaking slow, wasn't really paying attention as he dragged Maartin along.

No one would pay attention. The anger-hum was squeezing his brain, his organs. The plaza was undulating under his feet so that he stumbled, and Dad lost his grip on his arm. He yelled, trying to turn back, but the press of settlers swept him on. The others pounded past him, ignoring him. The spires swayed with the anger and the spiderways shivered; clouds of silvery sparks spouted from the columns in the now-dry fountain, hissing and crackling with an ugly sound.

Dad and the mayor and Celie and all the others were way ahead of him now. He cut right, following his shortcut to the canal. That was the way they'd come. He could get there first. His teeth felt as if they were loosening in their sockets and he clenched them, leaning against the anger-hum, homing in on it.

The people stood in a graceful, curving line, hes and shes, facing the oncoming rumble of the earth-eaters. The machines wallowed along on their heavy treads, churning up clouds of red dust, open maws like fanged mouths ready to suck in red dirt and rock, sieve out the pearls, the city. They rumbled through spires and a land-scaped garden of paths and sculpted shrubs surrounded by flocks of creeping plants with purple and silvery blossoms.

The tread didn't harm the plants or the paths. Not yet.

Not until they started digging up the pearls.

They couldn't see the people. Neither could Dad. Or the mayor.

The anger formed like milky clouds over the heads of the people, thickening as he watched, a pale fabric that floated above them, a sickly color. They raised their hands, all together, fingers weaving, shaping, twining the scalding energy of the anger into that thickening fabric. Some were turning to face Dad and the mayor. Celie was marching along beside Dad, and, behind her, Seaul Ku panted to keep up. She carried one of the projectile rifles. A small part of Maartin's brain noticed it and was surprised.

He leaped in front of the people, hands in the air, shrieking to them, fingers wide, hands waving. *Not them. They are not bad. You do not understand. We are not the same.*

At first, he thought that none of them would look, but they did. The weaving and spinning slowed and the fingers flickered sharply.

Defective. Defective units.

Not bad, no harm, we live here, too. They do not. And Maartin flung his fingers out to point at the miners, saw a faint ripple of shock at his terrible rudeness. But most of the fingers snapped and flickered discussion, too fast for him to follow, flashing and twisting.

Sharp-edge-alert brought his hands down in a slashing gesture, faced the miners. Maartin spun to face the settlers. "Stand back!" The air words came to him, his fingers spread stiff and still, silent, in front of him. "Stand back, the people are going to destroy the miners."

At first, he thought they'd ignore him, although he saw Dad's eyes go wide. Then they halted, murmuring, and fear shrilled the murmur, brought their hands up, pointing crudely.

He turned.

As one, the people pulled the woven fabric of the anger-hum from the air and . . .

. . . tossed it.

Lightly.

It drifted over the oncoming machines, over the miners trudging purposefully along on either side with energy weapons in their hands. Settled lightly, gently, over them.

They began to scream, backs arching, breathers ripped from their faces as they convulsed, limbs spasming, flopping like the pictures of fish that Maartin had seen on vids, pulled out onto a riverbank to die. The sickly veil dissipated, leaving twitching bodies and machines that lumbered slowly forward. One of the big earth-chewers ran over a body, grinding the man's torso into the dust.

"Holy crap!" The mayor's harsh voice rose above the machine rumble. "What the hell happened?"

"Get the machines stopped." Dad ran forward, grabbed a handhold, and swung into the seat of the lead earth-chewer. He fumbled for a moment or two and it stopped, tracks grinding to a halt. Dad leaped clear as the machine behind it ground into it, slewing it sideways.

The mayor leaped onto that one, and now everybody was running—toward the machines or to the fallen miners or back to the settlement. In a few moments, all the machines had been stopped. None of the miners were moving. Settlers were standing up, shaking their heads, their eyes scared, faces pale.

"My God, storm . . ." "Dust devils . . ." "Nasty little twisters . . ." "Like little tornadoes, like they were . . . attacking . . ."

The settlers were all looking at Maartin.

The people were drifting away, heading back to the plaza or stepping up onto the spiderways. A few strolled in the garden and one man played a trio of twisted purple tubes that drifted lavender mist streaked with silver into the air.

"What did you do, son?" Dad's voice was hushed.

They had gathered in a semicircle between him and the settlement. Scared of him. Looking around. For more dust devils? Maartin faced them, the air words playing hide-and-seek, his fingers weaving an explanation, flickering and twining.

"He sees the Martians. They *live* here. Right where your settlement is." Jorge panted up, his wrists welted angry red from the too-tight restraints. "I can see 'em just a little when I hold a pearl. I guess they . . . they killed the crew." He swallowed. "I . . . did you tell them not to kill us, too, Maartin?"

He flickered affirmative. Gave up on the air words.

"I think he means 'yes.'" Jorge stayed back with the crowd, didn't get too close to him. "I . . . I caught a few glimpses."

Everybody wanted to know about the Martians. They asked him questions for a while but gave up when only his fingers explained, talked to Jorge instead. Jorge got things wrong, but Maartin didn't bother to try to correct him. Dad put an arm around his shoulders and led him away, back to their rooms. Dad asked questions too, but Maartin kept his hands clasped, and, after a while, Dad stopped asking.

They reported the incident to the Planetary Council, and a few people came out. They listened, shook their heads at the evolving interpretation of hidden Martians and long-range energy weapons, and, for a while, everybody was afraid, looking out at the hills as they walked through the strolling musicians on the plaza or through the lower curves of the spiderways.

They were afraid of *him*, too, but that was actually better than before, since they no longer led him home when the plaza and the walls got tangled up and he walked into something.

And, after a while, they stopped looking for Martians they couldn't see, and they stopped being afraid of him. The abandoned machines got hauled away and settlers grumbled in Canny's that the settlement should have been able to claim salvage rights, not the Council. And they went back to planting new cyan beds, and Dad started talking about smelling the oxygen again.

Mostly, Maartin weeded the garden because he liked the smell and feel of the soil, and Seaul Ku had decided he was still the same old Maartin, and he liked that, too. And when he got tired, he strolled in the plaza with Soft-sweet-happy or Firm-thoughtful. Sharp-edge-alert didn't follow him anymore; he hadn't seen him since the attack on the miners.

One day, Jorge came into the garden. He'd been working with Dad planting the new bed and had rented a room a few doors down from Canny's. He squatted down in front of Maartin. "I'm leaving. Gotta stakeholder grant in a new one just going in, over a day's ride south of City." His dark eyes held Maartin's. "I can't mine anymore." He fumbled in his pocket, drew out his pearl. "I need to put this back. Where does it go?"

He reached for it and lifted it from Jorge's palm before he could pull it away. Soft-sweet-happy was crossing the plaza and he called her over with a flick of his fingers, offered it to her. She touched it, vanished it back to its place, and smiled as they both felt the tiny ripple of its return.

"What did you just do?" Jorge was staring at his empty palm. He raised his head. "I hope you're happy." He said it softly. "I hope they're friends with you."

Pity, Maartin thought. Did he need pity? He thought about it. What needed pity was gone, he decided. His fingers flashed and flickered as he told Jorge about how, even now, his every action, every vibration of every molecule in his flesh was feeding into . . . a pearl.

He would stroll this plaza, share the mist-music, wander the cities and spiderways forever, once it was done.

No. No pity.

"We. Will. Protect." He managed to find those three words.

Watched the fear creep back into Jorge's eyes. "The story's got around among the miners." He expelled the breath-words on harsh puffs of air. "But stories get ignored. When there's money."

Maartin shrugged. Sharp-edge-alert had learned what he needed to know. About imperfect units.

Jorge headed for the lock, taking his fear with him.

It did not matter. The transfer completed.

He stood, stretched, and strolled through the dome and across the plaza, savoring the drift of mist from the fountain, heading for the spiderway where Soft-sweet-happy flickered him a greeting.

No longer imperfect.

Behind him, very faintly, he heard the harsh sound of breath-words.

MIKE RESNICK

Mike Resnick is one of the best-selling authors in science fiction, and one of the most prolific. His many novels include *Kirinyaga, Santiago, The Dark Lady, Stalking the Unicorn, Birthright: The Book of Man, Paradise, Ivory, Soothsayer, Oracle, Lucifer Jones, Purgatory, Inferno, A Miracle of Rare Design, The Widowmaker, The Soul Eater, A Hunger in the Soul, The Return of Santiago, Starship: Mercenary, Starship: Rebel,* and *Stalking the Vampire.* His collections include *Will the Last Person to Leave the Planet Please Shut Off the Sun?, An Alien Land, A Safari of the Mind, Hunting the Snark and Other Stories,* and *The Other Teddy Roosevelts.* As editor, he's produced *Inside the Funhouse: 17 SF stories about SF, Whatdunnits, More Whatdunnits, Shaggy B.E.M. Stories, New Voices in Science Fiction, This Is My Funniest,* a long string of anthologies coedited with Martin H. Greenberg—*Alternate Presidents, Alternate Kennedys, Alternate Warriors, Aladdin: Master of the Lamp, Dinosaur Fantastic, By Any Other Fame, Alternate Outlaws,* and *Sherlock Holmes in Orbit,* among others—as well as two anthologies coedited with Gardner Dozois, and *Stars: Stories Based on the Songs of Janis Ian,* edited with Janis Ian. He won the Hugo Award in 1989 for *Kirinyaga.* He won another Hugo Award in 1991 for another story in the Kirinyaga series, "The Manamouki," and another Hugo and Nebula in 1995 for his novella "Seven Views of Olduvai Gorge." His most recent books are a number of new collections, *The Incarceration of Captain Nebula and Other Lost Futures, Win Some, Lose Some: The Complete Hugo-Nominated Short Fiction of Mike Resnick,* and *Masters of the Galaxy,* and a new novel, *The Doctor and the Rough Rider.* He lives with his wife, Carol, in Cincinnati, Ohio.

In the fast-paced adventure that follows, he takes us to the remotest wilds of Mars, on a search for the Tomb of the Martian Kings, lost for eons, and spins a story of greed and betrayal and the lust for riches—and how sometimes it might be better *not* to find what you're looking for.

In the Tombs of the Martian Kings

MIKE RESNICK

IT WAS CROWDED IN RAZZO THE SLUG'S.

There was no reason why it should be. There were twenty-three ramshackle bars surrounding Marsport, each with a don't-hear-don't-tell policy, but for some reason Razzo's was the one that was always crowded.

Razzo himself wasn't much to look at. It was Cemetery Smith who'd first remarked that he looked like a slug, and it stuck. No one knew where he came from, though it was clear from his accent and some of his mannerisms that it wasn't from any of the inner planets. Not that anyone cared as long as he didn't water his whiskey too much, provided an endless array of dancing girls from half a dozen worlds and moons, and made sure that nothing he heard was ever repeated.

The bar was long, made of some gleaming alien metal, and different sections raised or lowered as it sensed the size of the various races sidling up to it. On the wall behind the bar was a large holographic representation of whatever world Razzo had come from, and it usually made the assembled drinkers glad that they'd never set foot on it. There were two robotic bartenders, but Razzo spent most of his time behind the bar as well. The common assumption was that he stayed there to make sure the robots didn't fill the glasses too high.

Right at the moment, Razzo's was playing host to fifteen Martians, a dozen Venusians, a pair of miners from Titan, two more from Ganymede, and a scattering of Earthmen. The only one who drew any notice was the Scorpion, and that was mostly because of his companion.

The Scorpion's real name, which hardly anyone ever knew or used, was Marcus Aurelius Scorpio. He was tall, a good six or seven inches over six feet, and lean, and hard. He had a thick shock of brown hair that was just starting to show specks of gray, a week's worth of stubble on his cheeks and chin, and pale blue eyes, so pale they seemed colorless from certain angles.

He was dressed in nondescript browns and tans, and he made no attempt to hide the burner he carried in a small holster on his hip. Most observers couldn't tell that he had a smaller one tucked in the back of his belt and a wicked-looking knife in one boot.

There was really nothing about him to attract any attention— except for the creature lying on the floor at his feet. At first, it seemed like a dog, but there weren't any dogs on Mars, and certainly not any that approached the size of a lion. It had four nostrils—two in front, one on each cheek—eyes that seemed to glow even though they were totally shielded from the dim lights, and a tail that ended in such a sharp point that it could very well be used as a weapon. The animal was covered by a dull blue curly down, and when it yawned, it displayed a double row of coal-black fangs.

All the patrons gave the table—and the creature—a wide berth. The diminutive Mercurian waiter, who was used to him, paid him no attention as he brought Scorpio a drink and continued making his round of the tables.

Scorpio lit one of the local cigars, took a puff, and settled back to watch a Martian woman gyrate in a slow dance that looked awkward to him but was clearly driving the Martian customers wild. The music wasn't quite atonal but was so alien that he was sure he couldn't hum it if he heard it around the clock for a week.

Scorpio sipped his drink, trying not to make a face as it burned his throat on the way down, and puffed away on his cigar. After a minute, he pulled something out of his pocket and tossed it to the blue creature, which caught it, chewed it as it made loud, cracking sounds, and finally swallowed it.

The Martian girl's dance ended, the Martians in the audience cheered and uttered those strange hoots that were unique to their species, and then a girl from Io climbed onto the stage to complete indifference.

The Martian girl was walking to a dressing room behind the bar, but she stopped at Scorpio's table.

"You are here again, Scorpion," she said.

"I like to visit my money," he replied.

"Did you like my dance?"

"It was unique."

"Perhaps I should perform another, just for you."

"I'm always open to new experiences," said Scorpio.

This is silly, said a voice inside Scorpio's head. *Tell her to go away.*

Scorpio looked down at the blue creature. *Do I interfere in your sex life?* he thought.

Damn it, Scorpio! Why are you wasting time? She's a Martian, for Podak's sake. She couldn't accommodate you even if she tried.

Scorpio smiled a very cynical smile. *Love will find a way.*

"You're talking to your dog again," said the girl.

"He's not a dog, and you haven't heard me say a word."

"You lie to me," she said. "All the time you lie to me."

"Of course I do," answered Scorpio. "We're in Razzo the Slug's. It might even be against the law to tell the truth here."

She uttered a Martian obscenity. "Earthman!" she added contemptuously, stalking off.

Happy? asked Scorpio.

Thrilled, came the answer. *By the way, someone's looking for you.*

The girl went and got a weapon?

The creature snorted. *By the door. The Martian with the bag.*

Scorpio looked across the bar at a Martian who had just entered. He was small, stooped over (which was rare in the lighter gravity), showing signs of age, and carrying a cloth bag over what passed for his shoulder.

You're sure he's for me? thought Scorpio.

Of course I'm sure, came the reply. *Not everyone requires speech to communicate, you know. Some of us evolved beyond that eons ago.*

Then why were you living in a swamp when we met? asked Scorpio with that unique, not quite humorless, smile of his.

Why are you in a bar with criminals and reprobates from all over the solar system? I went to the swamp where the food was, and you go where the money is so you can buy the food, an extra step my race has no use for.

Scorpio stared down at the creature. *So why do you hang around with such a primitive being as me?*

You're the deadliest being I have ever encountered, came the answer. *There's always the chance of fresh food when I'm with you.*

Scorpio watched the Martian approach. *Okay, you're the telepath. What does he want?*

He's come a long way. I'll let him tell you.

Why bother? I'm just going to send him packing.

I don't think so, replied the creature.

Then the Martian reached the table and stood there, staring uneasily at Scorpio.

"You are the Scorpion?" he asked hesitantly.

Scorpio nodded. Then he remembered that most Martians didn't know that nodding was an affirmative. "Some people call me that, yes."

"May I . . . May I sit down?" asked the Martian, indicating an empty chair opposite Scorpio.

"Go ahead."

The Martian took a step toward the chair, then realized that he would have to pass very close to the blue creature. He froze and just stared at it, afraid to move.

"It's all right," said Scorpio when he realized that the Martian might well stand there motionless all night. "His name's Merlin. He's my pet."

Your pet?

Why tell anyone what you really are? It works to our advantage to have them think you're a dumb animal.

I may just bite your leg off.

"I have never seen anything like him," said the Martian timidly.

"Not many people have," replied Scorpio, as the Martian carefully walked around Merlin and seated himself. "What can I do for you?"

"I have been told that you are the one being best suited for the work I am preparing to do," said the Martian.

Who does he want killed, I wonder? said Merlin wordlessly.

You could tell me right now.

Me? I'm just a dumb animal.

"Just what kind of work do you have in mind?" asked Scorpio.

"Perhaps I should properly introduce myself first."

Scorpio shrugged. "Whatever makes you happy."

"My name is Quedipai, and I spent more than a century as a professor of ancient history at the university in Baratora, which you know as New Brussels."

"Okay, so you taught history and you're not a kid anymore," said Scorpio. "What has this got to do with me?"

Quedipai leaned forward and lowered his voice. "I believe that I have discovered the location of the lost Tomb of the Martian Kings."

Scorpio snorted contemptuously. "Sure you have."

"But I *have!*"

"On my world, it's King Solomon's Mines. On Venus, it's the Temple of the Forgotten Angel. On Mercury, it's the Darkside Palace. And on Mars, it's the Tomb of the Martian Kings."

"There have been two attempts on my life already," said Quedipai. "I need protection. More than that. I am an academic. I need someone who is aware of all the hazards I will encounter in the wildest section of the western dead sea bottom, and who can avoid or neutralize the worst of it."

"I wish you luck," said Scorpio.

"You will not accompany me?"

"Not interested."

"You have not heard my offer yet."

"I've been to the western sea bottom. It's called Balthial, and whoever told you it was dangerous understated the case," said Scorpio. "I'm happy right here."

"Will you at least let me name a price?" said Quedipai.

"Buy me another whiskey and you can talk your head off."

"What kind?" asked the Martian, getting to his feet.

Scorpio held his empty glass up and studied it. "I'm tired of this stuff. I'll have a glass of that bluish joyjoice they brew in Luna City."

The Martian went to the bar and returned with a glass, which he set down carefully on the table in front of Scorpio, then took his seat.

"It's smoking," he noted.

"It's old enough," replied Scorpio, lifting the glass and taking a swallow.

"You are not my last chance, Scorpion," said the Martian. "But from everything I've been able to find out, and I am a *very* thorough researcher, you are my *best* chance." Scorpio stared at him patiently and with very little interest. Finally, he took a deep breath, leaned forward, and said so softly that no one else could hear: "Four hundred thousand *tjoubi*, the hunt not to exceed fifty days."

Quick, thought Scorpio. *What's that in real money?*

A quarter of a million credits, answered Merlin.

You can read his mind. Is he telling the truth, and has he actually got the money?

Yes, and yes.

Scorpio stared at the Martian. "What was your name again?"

"Quedipai," was the answer.

"Cutie Pie," said Scorpio.

"*Quedipai*," repeated the Martian.

"Right," said Scorpio, nodding. "Cutie Pie, you've got yourself a deal. Half down, half on completion, and we're yours for the next fifty days."

Quedipai pulled out a sheaf of large-denomination bills. Scorpio took it and stuffed it in a pocket.

Don't you want to count it?

Flash that much in Razzo's? Don't be silly. We'll count it later. If he's short, we're not going anywhere till he makes it up.

"You mentioned 'we'?" asked the Martian curiously.

"Merlin and me. Like I told you, he's my pet."

Quedipai stared at the creature.

You wouldn't believe what he's thinking right now.

"Trust me," said Scorpio, "if we run into any trouble, you'll be glad he came along."

"I will take your word for it," said the Martian. He took the bag from his shoulder and placed it on the table. "Is it safe to show this to you now?"

"If I can't protect you in a bar, I sure as hell can't protect you once we leave what passes for civilization around here," answered Scorpio.

Quedipai reached into the bag and pulled out a very old map. He opened it and spread it on the table.

"Okay," said Scorpio, "it's Balthial."

"Do you see this small mark here?" asked the Martian, pointing a triply jointed finger toward it.

"Looks like a speck of dust."

"It is three miles across."

"Okay," said Scorpio, unimpressed. "There's a three-mile speck of dust on the sea bottom."

"I cannot give you an accurate translation," said Quedipai. "The closest I can come is the Crater of Dreams."

Scorpio frowned. "I've heard of that, a long time ago."

"Some say that it was caused by an asteroid," said Quedipai. "Others say it is the result of an ancient war when we had horrific weapons that are completely forgotten today. Still others say it occurred when an underground city collapsed beneath it."

"And what do you say?" asked Scorpio, staring not at the map but the Martian.

"I say it was caused by the fist of God."

"Why should you think so?"

"My race is not the first to inhabit this world," answered Que-dipai. "Before us, there was a race that strode across Mars like the giants they were. A tall man like you would not come up to the waist of even the smallest of them. Nothing could stand in their way, but soon their triumphs made them arrogant. It was when they decided that they themselves must be gods that the true God brought His fist down and flattened their kingdom with a single blow."

"Did you learn this in history class or in church?" asked Scorpio sardonically.

"You do not believe me, of course," said the Martian.

"For four hundred thousand *tjoubi*, I'll believe you for fifty days and nights, starting"—he checked his timepiece—"four minutes ago."

"I do not blame you for your doubts," said Quedipai. "Until last week, I shared them."

If he tells me he had a vision, I'm quitting, money or no money.

Just listen to him, responded Merlin.

"We have many religions on Mars," began Quedipai. "Most of them stem from historical incidents, or occasionally the origins of these beliefs can be found in the works of the great philosophers. But there is one religion—it is pronounced *Blaxorak;* there is no translation or approximation for it in Terran—that has survived lon-ger than any other. Its temples have all been demolished, its monu-ments torn down and broken into rubble, only the sacred Book of Blaxorak still exists. And in the rarest and most obscure of our an-cient writings, I have found enough clues to convince me that an-swers can be found in the Crater of Dreams."

Scorpio frowned. "*What* answers?"

"The clues I have put together lead me to believe that the Tomb of the Martian Kings actually exists in or beneath the Crater, and within the golden tombs, I will find the one remaining copy of the sacred Book of Blaxorak, interred with the greatest of the kings. Even if the existence of the book is a myth, even if there is no truth to it whatsoever and there is nothing but a series of empty tombs, it will still be the most important historical find of the millennium."

"*Golden* tombs, did you say?" said Scorpio.

"Jewel-encrusted," replied Quedipai.

Is he telling the truth?

He believes that he is, answered Merlin.

And he's really a scholar who specializes in this stuff?

Yes.

"Where are you staying?" asked Scorpio out loud.

"At the hotel across the street."

"The Fallen Torch?" said Scorpio.

"Yes."

"I suggest you go there right now and get some sleep. I plan to start this expedition at daybreak tomorrow."

"But I have more to show and tell you," protested the Martian.

"You'll show and tell me along the way," replied Scorpio. "Suddenly I'm anxious to get this show on the road."

"But I've barely mentioned—"

"Your wildly evocative descriptions bring the past back to life and make me want to see it for myself," said Scorpio, getting to his feet. "Come on, Merlin."

"Where shall we meet?" asked the Martian.

"I'll pick you up in your lobby at sunrise," said Scorpio. He took a few steps toward the door, then turned back. "Pay my bar bill before you leave, Cutie Pie."

Scorpio had counted out the money, the total was correct, and he drove Quedipai to the airfield in the morning.

"I have the coordinates right here," announced the Martian, indicating his shoulder bag.

"Keep them where they are," replied Scorpio, climbing out of the three-wheeled iron-plated vehicle, a leftover from a recent war.

"But surely you didn't study the map long enough to pinpoint the location!" protested Quedipai.

"That's right."

"Then—?"

"You told me there have already been two attempts on your life," said Scorpio, lighting a cigar. "Were you just trying to impress me, or were you telling the truth?"

"I do not lie," said the Martian with all the dignity he could muster.

"Then that means that someone besides you thinks you know where the Tomb of the Martian Kings is," continued Scorpio, "and you don't have to be a master scientist to be able to track a planet-bound flyer once it's aloft. We'll land a couple of hundred miles from the edge of the Crater and waste a day there before we head toward it, just to put anyone who's watching us off the scent. I'll have plenty of time to study the map."

Quedipai's dark eyes opened wide. "I never considered that."

"You don't have to," answered Scorpio. "That's what you're paying me for."

"I chose the right person for the job."

"Let's hope so," said Scorpio. "We'll leave as soon as Merlin arrives."

"He is missing?"

"He hates driving in these landcars. He'll be here in another minute or two."

"Which flyer is ours?" asked Quedipai.

"That one," answered Scorpio, pointing to the oldest, most beat-up flyer in the area.

The Martian gave his race's equivalent of a frown. "It looks like only the dirt and the rust are holding it together."

"If you want to treat us to a new one, be my guest."

Suddenly Merlin trotted up. *You'll be pleased to know that the Martian dancer didn't cry herself to sleep.*

Go ahead, break my heart, responded Scorpio wordlessly. *Climb into the flyer and remember you're a pet. Don't mess around with the controls.*

"How did he know you were driving to this location?" asked Quedipai.

"This is the only place in Marsport that I ever drive to," answered Scorpio.

Hah!

He'll buy it, thought Scorpio confidently. *Why would I lie to him?*

Wait until he knows you better.

I don't lie to anyone who's paying me a quarter million credits to stand guard while he wastes a couple of months looking for something that never existed. Well, not unless I have to, anyway. This should be a piece of cake.

I don't eat cake.

"Shall we climb aboard?" said Scorpio to Quedipai.

The Martian ascended the stairs to the hatch, and was soon strapping himself into the cocoonlike chair. Scorpio followed suit, didn't bother checking Merlin, who entered last and refused, as always, to be strapped or secured to anything, and soon they were aloft and heading toward the Crater, which was some seven hundred miles distant.

"Shouldn't we head west, then circle around, in case we're being watched?" asked the Martian.

Scorpio shook his head. "You've come three hundred miles east from New Brussels. Why would you go right back to it? I hope the opposition's that stupid, but let's assume they're not."

"I defer to your experience."

"Okay," said Scorpio. "Let me put this thing on autopilot and cruise at nine thousand feet while you show me the map again."

Quedipai pulled the map out of his shoulder bag and opened it. "Here is the Crater of Dreams," he said, pointing to the area. "There are no cities in it, no outposts, nothing."

"It looks like there's a city not five miles to the north of it," noted Scorpio.

"A deserted ruin," answered the Martian.

"Let's hope so. Are there any water sources below the ground?"

"In the Crater?"

"The Crater, the city, anywhere in the area."

"I don't believe so."

"So if someone *is* waiting in the city, they probably figured out that you were coming to the Crater of Dreams," said Scorpio. "As opposed to waiting indefinitely for *someone* to come."

"It is deserted," said Quedipai with conviction.

"If it isn't, we'll find out soon enough," said Scorpio grimly. "Okay, the Crater's, what, three miles in diameter?"

"It is thirteen *borstas*," replied the Martian.

Merlin?

It comes to about two and three-quarters of a mile.

"It looks flat as a board. Surely if this tomb exists, it's not thirteen *borstas* across, so where would you start digging?"

"I cannot tell you yet."

"If you don't trust me, we might as well call this whole thing off," said Scorpio.

The Martian shook his head. "You misunderstand. I cannot tell you because I do not yet know."

"When *will* you know?"

"Some of the ancient writings that I have uncovered describe certain landmarks."

"Cutie Pie, this is going to come as a shock to you, but landmarks change over twenty or thirty millennia," said Scorpio.

"Not these," said Quedipai confidently.

Does he know what he's talking about? Scorpio asked Merlin.

Probably.

What do you mean, probably? He does or he doesn't.

Probably these landmarks still exist.

You'd better be right. I don't relish spending the next seven weeks digging holes in the damned Crater.

"Tell me more about this deserted city," said Scorpio.

"Its ancient name was Melafona, but it has had five other names since then. It played host to every Martian civilization except the current one."

"Good."

"Good?" repeated Quedipai.

Scorpio nodded. "That means there should be water there, unless that's why no one lives there anymore. And if there's water, and it's deserted, we'll make it our headquarters."

"But it's more than twenty *borstas* from where I believe the tomb to be!"

Scorpio looked at the Martian and sighed. "There have been two attempts on your life. Unless you were dallying with the wrong Martian ladies, we can assume those attacks were either to prevent you or anyone else from finding the tomb, or because the attackers know what you know and want to get there first. Either way, do you think it's a good idea to camp out, unprotected, on the featureless floor of the Crater of Dreams?"

"I see," said Quedipai. "Of course, we shall do what you suggest."

"We probably won't have to walk to the site every day," said Scorpion. "The flyer's too small to carry any ground transportation in the cargo hold, but since the city's been used in the past, we should be able to find or rig some kind of wagon and harness. Merlin likes to feel useful; I'm sure he'll enjoy pulling us."

I think I've put off killing and eating you long enough.

Fine. You and Cutie Pie can sleep out in the middle of the Crater. I'll walk out from the city every morning and visit your remains.

"Whatever you say," agreed Quedipai.

When they hit the outskirts of the Balthial sea bottom, which marked the halfway point, Scorpio decided to set the flyer down next to the ruins of a deserted village.

"Why have we landed?" asked the Martian. "We're still hundreds of miles away."

"Remember, I told you we'd waste a day out here in case anyone's tracking us," said Scorpio. "We'll stretch our legs, relax, and grab some lunch."

It may not be that easy, warned Merlin.

Why not?

There's a family of carnivores living in the village.

Big ones?

I can't tell. But they're hungry ones.

Scorpio climbed down from the flyer, then helped Quedipai out. Merlin leaped lightly to the ground on his own.

Are they smart enough for you to read their thoughts?

They're not sentient, Scorpio. The only thing I read is hunger. It's been a few days since they made their last kill.

How many are there?

Five. Maybe six.

You can't tell?

There may be one who's too weak from hunger to be transmitting.

Scorpio walked around to the cargo hold, opened it, and pulled out a sonic blaster. He checked it to make sure it was fully charged, then carried it over to the Martian.

"You know how to use one of these?" he asked.

"No," said Quedipai.

"Ever seen anyone use it in an entertainment video?"

"Yes."

"Same thing. This is the firing mechanism. Just aim and push this button."

"Who are you expecting?"

"It's more a bunch of *whats* than a *who*," answered Scorpio. "And make sure you don't hit Merlin."

"Why would I fire at Merlin?" asked Quedipai.

"He'll be our first line of defense. If we're attacked, he'll be fighting whatever's attacking us before you even raise the blaster to take aim."

Soon. They know we're here.

"I'm going to get another weapon out of the cargo hold," said Scorpio. "Keep on your toes."

Quedipai looked puzzled. "I don't *have* any toes," he said.

Damn! They're big!

Before he could even open the hold the Earthman turned to see five shaggy, bearlike six-legged creatures, each a dull gray, armed with vicious canines and long, curved claws on each foot, slinking out of the city and spreading out, as if to cut off all escape routes.

Quedipai was shaking like a leaf, so Scorpio walked over to him and took the sonic blaster, which the Martian relinquished gratefully.

Who's the leader? he asked Merlin.

Second from the left.

He's the smallest of the lot.

He's a she, and the Martian duxbollahs *live in matriarchies.*

Scorpio aimed the blaster at the female and pressed the firing mechanism. She screamed in pain and surprise as she was hurled ten feet through the thin Martian air by an almost solid wall of sound. The other *duxbollahs* looked around nervously, trying to pinpoint the enemy that had sent their leader flying, never associating it with Scorpio and his weapon.

No sense letting them get organized. Wish me luck.

No sooner had Merlin sent the thought than he launched himself at the still-groggy female, ripping into her with claws and fangs. She tried to fight back, but it was clear that the Venusian was slowly tearing her to pieces. Finally, uttering a shrill scream, she turned tail and raced back to the ruins. The four males hesitated for a moment. Then Merlin charged the largest of them. He immediately followed the female, and the other three also raced back to the ruins in a wide semicircle that took them as far from Merlin as possible while still heading for safety. The Venusian loped after them in a leisurely manner to make sure they didn't change their minds, then turned around and returned to the ship.

"Still wonder why he came along?" asked Scorpio with a smile.

"He's quite awesome," said Quedipai. "I didn't think there was any animal around that could scare off five *duxbollahs* at once."

Did I hear right? Did he just call me an animal?

For what he's paying, he can call you a lot worse than that. Just keep an eye out in case those things return. They're not going to get any less hungry in the next couple of hours.

"Let's keep alert for hungry visitors," said Scorpio to Quedipai. "And in the meantime, tell me a little more about what you think you're going to find."

"As I told you: the Tomb of the Martian Kings—and hopefully, inside the tomb, the Book of Blaxorak."

"There have been a lot of Martian kings over the eons," said Scorpio. "Why are these so much more difficult to find? This isn't a very big planet, and it hasn't got all that many weird places where you could successfully hide a tomb for thirty or forty thousand years."

"They are more than well hidden," answered Quedipai. "If my research and our legends are correct, they are *protected*."

"Protected?" repeated Scorpio. "By who or by what?"

"They are the tombs of the Krang Dynasty," said the Martian. "The Krang were a special race. Some say they were not even native to the planet but that a small handful came here and conquered the entire world in something less than a year. They built no cities and left no edifices, which suggests that they were . . . *visitors*."

"As far as I can tell, you were always a warrior culture until your wars finally almost destroyed the whole damned planet. What kind of special race could conquer you in under a year?"

"I don't know," admitted Quedipai. "They were said to be huge, but that could be relative. Huge compared to what? I assume if they had the technology to come here from another world, they doubtless possessed weaponry in advance of ours, and there are hints, rumors, legends, that the Book of Blaxorak gave them powers that were so close to being supernatural as to make no difference."

"But you don't know for sure that they *did* come from another world," Scorpio continued.

"True. Nor do I know why they all died or vanished—or left in a short period of time. Those are some of the answers I hope to discover when we find the tomb."

"*If* we find the tomb."

"If we find the tomb," amended Quedipai. "But I truly think we will. I have been studying the Krang for most of my adult life."

"Can I ask a question?" said Scorpio.

"Certainly."

"Why?" he said. "If they existed at all, they lived tens of thousands of years ago. They were here just long enough to conquer the planet, after which they left or went extinct. As far as I can tell, they left nothing behind—no artifacts, no monuments, nothing but a few myths and legends. Why spend your whole life trying to learn about them?"

"We are not all creatures of action like you and your friend."

"My friend?" repeated Scorpio.

"Merlin. It is now obvious that you are in psychic or telepathic rapport with him."

Well, good for you, Quedipai! thought the Venusian.

"Anyway, I learned what I could about you before I approached you, Scorpion," continued Quedipai. "You have been to all of the inner planets, as well as Triton, Titan, Ganymede, Io, and Europa. You clearly have a desire to see what lies beyond the next planet. I, too, am interested in the next world. My worlds are just defined differently than yours."

"Makes sense when you put it that way," said Scorpio.

Quedipai turned to Merlin. "And I apologize for thinking you were merely an animal."

Merlin stared at him and remained motionless.

Come on, thought Scorpio. *He's apologizing. Lick his hand or something.*

That's disgusting. Maybe I'll just bite off six or seven of his fingers. Martians have too many fingers anyway.

"He appreciates your apology and accepts it," said Scorpio aloud.

"Good, I would hate for him to be annoyed with me."

What has annoyed got to do with it? I'll face five duxbollahs a day for my half of what he's paying us.

I had no idea you valued money was Scorpio's sardonic thought. *I thought you were a superior species.*

We are. But we need money when dealing with inferior species, like Earthmen.

"Did the Krang leave any written records?" asked Scorpio.

"They themselves? No. But some of the races they conquered did. The question remains: How much of those records can we believe?"

"Why not all of them if they were written by the Krang's contemporaries?"

Quedipai allowed himself the luxury of a very toothy smile, one of the few Martian smiles Scorpio had ever seen. "Tell me, Scorpion, are you a Christian?"

"Not much of one," answered Scorpio with a shrug.

"*Did* Jesus say the things that are credited to him? After all, they were reported by his disciples—but were they reported accurately?"

Another shrug. "Who the hell knows?"

And another smile from Quedipai. "Now you know the problem we have with the Krang. Are the writings factual, or myths, first-hand or hearsay?"

"Okay, I see," replied Scorpio. "The subject is closed."

"Until we enter the tomb."

"Let's not worry about entering it until after we find it."

They waited by the flyer until twilight, not wanting to wander too far from it while the *duxbollahs* were still nearby. Then Scorpio announced that they were ready to leave, and soon the flyer was heading toward the Crater again.

"You are a very thorough man," said Quedipai, as Scorpio kept checking to make sure there were no other planes aloft anywhere near them.

"The graveyards are filled with men who weren't thorough," replied the Earthman.

Merlin, check a map back there and see if this city we're heading to has got a landing field.

This is a sophisticated flyer, answered Merlin. *You don't need one.*

I know. But if there's a landing field, it stands to reason that there's a hangar. Why leave the flyer out where anyone can see it?

I'll look. I wonder if they even had flyers back then.

And a moment later came the answer.

No luck.

All right. It was worth a try.

"Has this city we're heading to got a name?" Scorpio asked the Martian.

"It has had several," said Quedipai. "In the days of the Krang rulers, it was Melafona. Later, during the Sixth Pleistar Dynasty, it became Bechitil. And its last name, before it was sacked a little over five centuries ago, was Rastipotal." He sighed. "And today it has no name at all. Even when it appears on maps, it is designated only as the abandoned ruin of a deserted city."

"Given the area it covers, it looks like it might have held half a million people, maybe more," said Scorpio.

"It did once," confirmed the Martian.

"Why has it been standing empty for the last few centuries? Did the populace get tired of being sacked?"

"You know very little of Martian history, Scorpion," said Quedipai.

"I skipped that course of studies," said Scorpio.

You skipped school entirely.

"The war of five centuries ago is known informally as the Germ War," said Quedipai. "It was fought not with guns and explosives, not with heat rays and sonic weapons, but with living viruses that wiped out entire populations. And those that didn't die were geneti- cally mutated. They produced a generation of malformed monsters, and there was a planetary purge of them." His face tensed. "It is the era of which almost every Martian is least proud."

"I can see why," said Scorpio. "Well, that explains why the city is empty . . . *if* it is."

"There is no way to find out, short of landing and exploring it," said the Martian.

"Merlin will tell us," said Scorpio. "It would be nice if something was living there—a Martian, a *duxbollah, something.*"

Quedipai frowned in puzzlement. "Why?"

"I'd like some physical proof that the virus that wiped out the city is gone, or dead, or so weak it can't harm whatever's living here."

"It is safe," said the Martian. "Its art treasures reside in the mu- seum that is associated with my university. Somebody was able to procure them and bring them back unharmed."

"For all you know, they were removed *before* the virus was un- leashed, or possibly they were collected by men . . . well, Martians . . . in protective suits."

"Then perhaps we should stay in the Crater, as I originally wanted."

"We'll decide when the time comes," answered Scorpio.

They soon were cruising low over the city, looking for a likely landing spot, and Scorpio found one right in the city center. He set the flyer down gently, killed the lights and motor, sat still for a few moments, and finally turned to Merlin.

Well?

I don't think—began the Venusian. Then he suddenly tensed. *Wait! We're in luck!*

What is it?

Merlin frowned as he concentrated. *Three thieves, on the run from the law.*

Martians?

Two from Titan, and an Earthman.

How long have they been hiding here?

Six days.

And they're still healthy? Okay, we can leave the flyer.

"Looks a little like Pompeii, or maybe that deserted city on Mercury's dark side," commented Scorpio, staring at their surroundings.

"If you say so," replied Quedipai. "I have never been off the planet."

"It's an interesting solar system," said Scorpio. "You should try to see some of it."

"We each have our passions. Mine is—"

"I know," Scorpio interrupted. "Merlin, how close are they?"

"They?" repeated the Martian uneasily.

"Three outlaws, hiding from the authorities," answered Scorpio. "Is it safe?"

"They've been here long enough to prove that the city's probably safe from any virus. Whether we're safe from *them* is another matter."

"Perhaps we should stay in the ship," suggested Quedipai uneasily.

"They know where *we* are. I'd like to know where *they* are too." He turned to the Venusian. "How about it, Merlin?"

I'm trying to pinpoint them. It's more difficult with Titanians than with most races.

"I've been sitting here long enough," said Scorpio, opening the hatch and jumping down to the ground. He helped Quedipai down, then stood aside as Merlin leaped out and landed lightly.

I love this gravity, thought the Venusian.

"Avast there!" cried a human voice.

"Avast?" repeated Scorpio, half-smiling. "Do people still say 'Avast'?"

"Who are you and what's your business here?" continued the voice.

"Just some travelers looking for a place to rest," answered Scorpio, still unable to see the man who was speaking.

"You're welcome to stay here as long as you want," said the voice.

"Thanks."

"For ten thousand credits a night," added the voice.

"Does that include running water and kitchen privileges?" asked Scorpio, withdrawing his burner.

The voice laughed. "I like you, fellow Earthman!" it said. "It would be a shame to kill you over something as trivial as a few thousand credits. Put the burner away, pull out your money, and we can all be friends."

"All?" said Scorpio.

"Did I neglect to mention that you're surrounded?"

"By two naked monkeys from Titan and an Earthman who hasn't got the courage to show himself?" replied Scorpio. "I may just faint dead away from fear."

Where are the other two?

One's twenty degrees to the left of where you're facing, the other is thirty degrees to the right.

I don't know from degrees. Give me a reference point.

One's in front of the doorway to the crystal building on the left, and if you follow the right wing of the flyer straight out seventy meters you'll find the other one.

You'd better be right, thought Scorpio, pointing his burner at the crystal building, pressing the firing mechanism, and moving the barrel so that it covered the entire front of the building.

There was an inhuman scream. Scorpio dropped to one knee, fired where the right wing of the flyer was pointing, and was rewarded with a wail of agony an instant later.

"I'll kill you for that!" cried the human voice.

Stand next to me—quick!

Scorpio grabbed Quedipai and pulled him over to where Merlin was crouching. The ground where they had been standing exploded a second later.

"Nice try," yelled Scorpio. "But now you're outnumbered three to one. Maybe you'd like to call it quits. Just put ten thousand credits on the ground and walk away safe and sound."

He was answered by a curse and another explosion, this one blowing the landing gear off the flyer.

"We'd better do something soon," said Scorpio softly. "If he hits the ship broadside, we're hundreds of miles from any transportation."

"*He* must have transport," offered Quedipai. "He couldn't have walked here if he's trying to elude the law. And the natives of Titan are bigger than Earthmen, so clearly his transport can accommodate all three of us."

"Cutie Pie, you're getting better at this all the time," said Scorpio. "Okay, Merlin, we won't worry about the ship. Let's just concentrate on taking him out."

But the Venusian was no longer there.

"Here!" said Scorpio urgently, handing his burner to Quedipai. "Start firing it nonstop, and aim about ten or fifteen feet above the ground." The Earthman got the sonic blaster and began doing the same.

"I assume there's a reason for this," said Quedipai.

"Merlin's gone," said Scorpio. "That means he's after the man, and we don't want to hit him by accident. We just want the man to be concentrating on us."

"Will Merlin be able to find him?"

Scorpio nodded as he continued firing. "His eyesight's none too good, and his sense of smell is no better than mine, but somehow he can home in on thoughts. Any politician would want to shoot him on sight."

The far side of the flyer took a direct hit and caved in.

"Damn!" muttered Scorpio. "He's getting close."

Distract him.

He'd damned well better have come in a flyer, thought Scorpio. Aloud he said: "Cutie Pie, turn the burner on the flyer!"

"What?" said the Martian, confused.

"Just do it!" snapped Scorpio as he aimed the sonic blaster at it and blew out all the windows.

Quedipai followed suit, and a second later the interior to the flyer was ablaze.

And almost instantaneously, they heard a single hideous scream from about ninety yards away in the darkness.

"Okay, you can stop now," said Scorpio.

"We were creating a distraction, were we not?" asked Quedipai.

"Well, a confusion, anyway," replied Scorpio.

A moment later, Merlin trotted back to the ship.

"You okay?"

A little bruised, but that will just make dinner taste all the better.

Dinner?

Don't ask.

What about their weapons?

Old and not very efficient. Ours are better.

I trust you destroyed them?

Of course.

"Well," announced Scorpio, "there's no sense staying in or near what's left of the ship. Let's see what the city has to offer in the way of lodging."

The three of them set off to explore the ruins. The first order of business was to find the outlaws' flyer, and they accomplished that in ten minutes. The outlaws' hideout was just some fifty yards away. They had raced out the second they realized Scorpio was preparing to land, and they'd left their quarters—the ground floor of an ancient building—illuminated, which made it stand out in the dark. There was a beat-up landcar parked nearby, and Scorpio checked it to make sure it was working, then led his companions into the building. There were bedrolls on the floor, the Earthman had brought along several days of condensed rations, and Quedipai assured his companions that he and Merlin could both eat some of the Titanians' food with no ill effects.

"We might as well set up housekeeping here," announced Scorpio. He examined the walks and floor, found a loose floorboard, and stared down beneath it. "I assume no one else is likely to show up, but just the same I'd advise you to leave anything you don't want to carry and don't want stolen in this storage area below the floorboard."

Quedipai walked over to a bedroll, adjusted it so that he could sit and lean against it as it covered the lower section of a wall, and gingerly lowered himself to the floor. Scorpio lay down on a similar bedroll at the far end of the room.

Merlin walked to the doorway. *I'll be back later.*

You're really going to eat an Earthman?

The Venusian wrinkled his nose. *Have you ever tried to clean one of those things? I'm off to dine on uncooked Titanian.*

And then Merlin was gone, the other two fell asleep, and when they awoke, it was morning and Merlin was sleeping by the doorway.

"Shall we have some breakfast before we begin?" suggested Scorpio.

"I'm too excited to eat!" responded Quedipai. "I'm finally here!"

"You're going to be a little less excited and a little hungrier after we traipse across the floor of the Crater," said Scorpio.

"I'll bring food with me."

How about you?

I'm dying. My eyes were bigger than my stomach.

Given the size of that bloated section of your body, your eyes must be larger than basketballs.

Whatever they are.

Merlin got painfully to his feet. Scorpio stared at him and smiled.

You ate both of them? Didn't your parents ever teach you moderation?

Go ahead, make fun of me. I'll remember this the next time someone's trying to kill you.

"Shall we begin?" asked Quedipai, walking to the door.

"If we can," agreed Scorpio, still grinning at his partner.

The three of them walked outside to the landcar and climbed in. They followed the street, which curved back into itself, took another route that soon ended at a building with no discernible entrance, and after two more false starts, finally found a route to the edge of the city. Scorpio kept melting edges of buildings with his burner so that they could find their way back at the end of the day, and made a mental note to be sure to return before it was totally dark and he couldn't see the marks he was making.

In another fifteen minutes, they had left the ancient city of Melafona—it had many names, but Scorpio liked the oldest of them—and had taken their first steps on the flat, reddish sand that covered the floor of the Crater.

A comet, do you think? suggested Merlin.

Too big and too fast; not enough damage here. Probably an asteroid, or more likely just part of one. Back then Mars had a little more atmosphere; it would have burned up a good part of it before it hit.

"So," said Scorpio aloud, "where are these landmarks?"

"You are looking at one of them," replied Quedipai, indicating a jagged red peak at the far side of the Crater.

"That thing was here eons before your Krang," remarked Scorpio.

"Of course," answered the Martian. "It couldn't have been in the ancient writings if it was not itself ancient."

"Point taken." Scorpio looked around. "What else?"

"I beg your pardon?"

"What other landmarks are we looking for?"

"We shall find one of them at the north end of the Crater."

Scorpio pulled out his positioning device. "Okay, we're about three-quarters of a mile away from it," he said, angling off to his left.

They stopped after ten minutes, and Quedipai began walking around the area, examining the ground ahead of them. Finally his entire body tensed.

"I think . . ." he began. "Yes! Yes, it is!"

"What do you see?" asked Scorpio.

"My second landmark," said Quedipai, pointing just ahead of them. "Study it and you will see it too!"

"Son of a bitch!" said Scorpio. "I *do* see it."

They approached a totally flat, perfectly circular rock some eight feet in diameter. It was mostly covered by the shifting Martian sand, but once Scorpio realized what it was, it seemed to jump out at him.

"I was right!" said Quedipai with obvious satisfaction. "I was right."

"Okay, what next?" asked Scorpio.

"We proceed eighty-three paces due west from the westernmost part of the circumference."

Scorpio began measuring off the steps.

"No," said Quedipai.

"What's the matter?"

"It was measured by a Martian. My steps are shorter than yours."

"All right," said Scorpio, moving aside while Quedipai walked the eighty-three paces.

Scorpio and Merlin joined him and looked around.

"I don't see any tombs," said the Earthman.

"You won't," answered Quedipai. "They are buried beneath the surface of the Crater."

Scorpio stared at him. "Do you see an entrance?"

"Not yet."

"Not yet?" repeated Scorpio, frowning.

"That is correct," said Quedipai. He pulled some foodstuffs out of his shoulder bag. "I might as well have some nourishment, since we cannot leave this spot."

"Before you eat anything, I think an explanation is in order."

"When the sun is ten degrees past its peak, all will be revealed," said the Martian, then added softly, "I hope."

"And that's all you plan to tell us?" said Scorpio.

"I could be wrong."

"We're being paid whether you're right or wrong, so it makes very little difference to us."

"It means everything to me," responded Quedipai.

Scorpio decided that further questioning would be fruitless and sat down cross-legged on the Crater floor.

Do I have to watch him eat? complained Merlin.

No, you can crawl off and die in splendid isolation if you prefer.

I hate you.

I *didn't eat two entire citizens of Titan.*

If I'm still alive, wake me at noon. Merlin closed his eyes.

Scorpio wished he'd brought a book along, though he didn't know why since he hadn't read one in years. Finally, he settled for just staring at the peak and fondly remembering a seemingly endless series of women, some human, some not, all of whom he was sure at one time or another that he loved, none of whom he loved enough to settle down and remain in one place.

He checked the sky now and then, and when the sun was directly overhead he got to his feet.

"Can you confide in me yet?" he said.

"Soon," whispered the Martian.

Merlin was on his feet too, and his bloated belly was back to its normal size. Scorpio marveled once again at how much the Venusian could eat, and how quickly he could digest it.

The three of them stood, waiting, for twenty, thirty, forty minutes, then—

"Now!" cried Quedipai, pointing—and suddenly a shadow appeared, stretching from his feet to a previously unseen crevice in the wall of the Crater. *"There* is where the entrance will be!"

He actually knew, thought Merlin. *Who'd have guessed it?*

They approached the crevice, and, as they did so, the sun glinted off something that clearly wasn't part of the Crater wall.

"Looks like metal," said Scorpio.

"The top of a railing," confirmed the Martian.

Scorpio approached it and found himself looking down a long, spiral staircase, the bottom of which was lost in shadows.

"I have found it!" said Quedipai, more to himself than his companions. "They scoffed, and they laughed, and they disbelieved, but I have found it!"

"What you've found in the entrance to *something*," said Scorpio, shining a light down the stairs. "Let's go find out what it is."

"I will lead," announced the Martian, beginning to descend the stairs.

Anything alive down there?

Nothing sentient. I think I sense some animals, but I can't tell what kind.

Given the bad light, they'd better be cuddly.

Scorpio fell into step behind Quedipai. They descended some sixty feet, but to their surprise, they were not immersed in total darkness. The walls seemed to glow with some luminescent property. The light wasn't bright, but at least they could see their way around, and Scorpio turned off his own light.

Suddenly, Scorpio reached forward and grabbed Quedipai by the shoulders, pulling him backward until the Martian was sitting awkwardly on the stairs.

"Why did you do that?" he demanded angrily. "I told you I would lead."

"Yeah," said Scorpio, "but I thought you'd like your head and your body to lead in concert."

"What are you talking about?"

Scorpio pointed to a thin, knife-sharp, almost invisible metal fiber stretched across the stairway. "You walk into that at normal speed, moving down the stairs, you'll be decapitated."

"I apologize for my outburst of temper," said Quedipai. He stared at the fiber. "How did you know to look for it?"

Scorpio pointed to a headless Martian body at the base of the stairway, which was finally visible. "You aren't the first one to enter this place."

Merlin edged past them, descended the stairs, and examined the body.

It's mummified. It's been here at least for centuries, possibly for millennia.

When they had reached the bottom of the stairs and walked around the body, Scorpio turned to Quedipai. "That's probably not the only booby trap down here. You'd better let me go first. Merlin will guard the rear."

"I consent," replied the Martian.

Scorpio withdrew his burner and began walking along the corridor that led from the stairwell. The corridor twisted and turned but never branched off, so he had no trouble following it. He was just starting to relax, thinking that the metal fiber might have been the only hazard, when he received a sharp mental warning.

Stop!

He froze, and Quedipai bumped into him, but despite the collision, he stood his ground.

"What is it?" Scorpio said aloud.

Something I've never encountered. But it's approaching.

From in front?

Kind of.

What the hell does that mean?

Above! It's right over your head!

Scorpio looked up. There was nothing but the top of the corridor, composed of the same faintly glowing stone as the walls.

You're wrong. There's nothing there.

Here it comes!

And suddenly, an ugly head with huge, razor-sharp fangs and glowing red eyes burst through the ceiling exactly above Scorpio. He pushed Quedipai back, hurled himself against a wall, and fired at the head. It didn't quite roar and didn't quite hiss, but made a sound that was halfway between the two. The burner had blown one of its eyes out and melted a fang, but still it came at him, and as he backed away, firing his weapon, it stretched out to four, five, six, seven feet in length.

Finally, Scorpio extended his weapon and arm in the thing's direction. It opened its mouth to bite or perhaps swallow both, and he pressed the firing mechanism one last time, burning the beast's brain to a crisp and blowing a hole in the back of its head.

It hung, motionless, from the ceiling, almost touching the floor, while the trio stared at it.

"What the hell *is* it?" asked Scorpio.

"Even I cannot pronounce the ancients' name for it," answered Quedipai. "It is not quite a snake, because it has very small limbs and claws that are still above the ceiling, but I suppose the closest definition is a cave snake, a snakelike *thing* that lives within the walls of caves."

This isn't a cave, noted Merlin.

Same thing, responded Scorpio. *Besides, what difference does it make? You want to call it a tomb snake, be my guest.*

Do you get the feeling that these kings don't want to be disturbed?

Scorpio began walking again, and after another hundred yards the corridor broadened out and the walls actually glowed a little brighter. They finally came to a fork in the corridor, and Scorpio paused, wondering which direction to go.

"This is too easy," he said at last.

"Easy?" repeated Quedipai, surprised.

Scorpio nodded. "Keep alert and you don't have a problem on the staircase. And I didn't have to shoot the snake thing; I could have just run ahead. He can't go through stone as fast as I can run. Whoever designed this had to know that most intruders would get this far."

He stared at both corridors again and couldn't make up his mind. Finally, he retraced his steps to where the dead creature still hung down from the ceiling. Reaching into his boot, he withdrew a wicked-looking knife and soon cut the thing's head off.

"What are you going to do with that?" asked Quedipai, staring at the severed, mutilated head with horrified fascination.

"You'll see," said Scorpio.

He carried the head back to the fork, took a couple of steps into the left-hand corridor, then rolled the head down it like some nightmare bowling ball.

When it had rolled about forty feet there was an audible *click!* and the floor opened up. The head plunged down into a deep, seemingly bottomless pit.

Did you see where it stopped and started?

Yes. Let me go first, while I've still got it pinpointed.

Be my guest.

Merlin began trotting down the corridor. When he had gone just short of forty feet he reached a forepaw out and gently touched the floor.

Nothing happened.

He moved forward another foot and repeated the procedure, and this time the floor opened just as it had for the snake's head.

Merlin leaped across the pit with ease.

It's no more than four feet wide, he signaled back. *Deep as hell, and the walls are absolutely smooth, so don't trip.*

Scorpio turned to Quedipai. "Can you jump?" he asked.

"I don't know," answered the Martian uneasily.

"How can you not know?" demanded Scorpio. "Either you can jump or you can't."

"I can jump. But I am very old. I don't know if I can jump that far."

"All right," said Scorpio. "We'll do it the hard way."

"The hard way?" repeated Quedipai.

Scorpio scooped the Martian up in his arms, ran down the corridor, and measured his leap to begin a few inches before the pit began. It didn't sense him and remained shut until he landed on the far edge. The floor dropped away from him, but his momentum carried him forward. As he released his grip on Quedipai, both of them rolled down the corridor behind the pit.

"That was terrifying!" moaned the Martian.

"These guys knew their stuff," commented Scorpio. "It's amazing that it still works after all these thousands of years."

They walked cautiously, looking for more traps, for another hundred yards. Then the corridor curved to the left and terminated at a massive golden door that had a series of hieroglyphs carved into it.

Quedipai walked up to the first set of hieroglyphs and studied them intently. Finally, he stood back.

"Well?" asked Scorpio.

"This is the Tomb of the Lesser Kings," he said.

"*Lesser* Kings?" repeated Scorpio.

"The Krang had seven kings. Six of them are interred in this vault."

"I assume the important one—the seventh king—is down the other corridor?"

"That seems likely."

"But it doesn't expressly say so on the door?"

"No."

"Well, we'll worry about it after we examine this tomb," said Scorpio.

Quedipai was about to push the door open when Scorpio grabbed his hand.

"*Don't!*" said the Earthman.

"What's the matter?" asked Quedipai.

"Let's assume the guys who designed this place meant business," replied Scorpio. He pulled his knife out of his boot and tossed it against the door, which immediately began sparking and crackling.

"Electrified?" asked the Martian.

Scorpio nodded. "Yeah. I'm surprised it still has power after all this time."

"What shall we do?"

"It's deadly," replied Scorpio, "but it's not unique. Merlin and I run into this kind of thing a lot." He pulled a small, complex device out of one of his many pockets and held it up. "A Nullifier. This little gizmo can negate any charge that's not strong enough to melt the door."

He pressed a switch, the device began humming, and he pressed it against the door. There was no repetition of the sound or sparks.

"Okay, let's see what's inside," he said, pushing at the portal, which slowly swung inward, creaking under its own weight.

The chamber was spacious. More, it was luxurious. The walls were gold, and reached some twenty feet high to an arched ceiling. There were a number of ornate cabinets, and spread evenly about the chamber were six exquisitely carved and freestanding mausoleums, each looking like a miniature temple.

Scorpio entered the first mausoleum and saw nothing but a pile of ashes.

All I'm finding are ashes, signaled Merlin.

Me, too, replied Scorpio.

He walked back out and saw Quedipai emerging from another mausoleum.

"What the hell happened here, I wonder?" said the Earthman.

Merlin opened a cabinet with his pointed tail. *Empty,* he observed.

Quedipai walked to a series of hieroglyphs that had been carved into the wall. "Do you see this?" he said, pointing to an inscription at the very bottom of the hieroglyphs.

"Yes?"

"It was added to the original approximately five thousand years ago, if I have identified my dynasties correctly. It was written by a grave robber who actually reached the tomb, only to find that it had been robbed millennia earlier. He stole what few artifacts remained and left this message for any who followed him."

"What does the message say?"

"That he looked for the Book of Blaxorak but couldn't find it. Either it is in the other tomb, or it never existed."

"As long as he got this far, why didn't he just go to the other tomb and see for himself?" asked Scorpio.

"He had three companions. Cohorts, I think one could call them. They all died trying to enter the Tomb of Xabo, and he decided to leave while he still lived."

"Xabo?" repeated Scorpio.

"He was the greatest of the Krang kings," answered the Martian. "It was said that he was capable of feats that seemed very little removed from magic." He looked around the tomb. "I am almost glad the thief's associates were killed. I hope Xabo's tomb is intact."

"Let's find out," said Scorpio.

They retraced their steps, the Earthman once again jumped across the pit while carrying Quedipai, and finally they came to the fork. This time they set off to the right, down another glowing corridor.

Anything alive up ahead?

Not so far.

The corridor twisted and turned, and suddenly they saw two ancient bodies sprawled on the corridor's floor about ten yards ahead. They stopped and stared at the scene.

"Do you see anything that looks wrong?" asked Scorpio.

He got negative replies from his two companions.

"Any marks on the bodies?"

No, but they're both facedown.

Scorpio studied the scene with a practiced eye. "No bloodstains on the floor or walls, so whatever killed them, it didn't break the skin." He paused, frowning. "Cutie Pie, didn't that hieroglyph say that the author lost *three* cohorts?"

"Yes," replied the Martian.

"So one of them got through." He paused as he considered the bodies. "We'll never know how he made it until we know what killed these two." He peered more intently at the farther body. "He's got a weapon in his hand, so I think whatever killed them, it wasn't something of flesh and blood that he could blow away."

He scratched his head, frowning. "Nothing living. And it couldn't be something that electrified the corridor. There are no burn marks, and one of them survived in each direction."

"*Each* direction?" repeated Quedipai. "I don't understand."

"We haven't come to a third body yet, so he obviously got through . . . and the one who wrote the message either stayed on this side of the carnage or found a way to get back through it unharmed."

Still nothing alive in the area, Merlin informed him.

"Well, once we've eliminated all the things that didn't kill them, we're left with just two possibilities: sound or gas. And I don't believe it was sound. These walls would turn the corridor into an echo chamber. Any noise that was strong enough to kill these two would have killed the others. It had to be gas."

"Why only two, then?" asked Quedipai.

"Air currents," suggested Scorpio. "Or, more likely, a lack of air currents. If you weren't standing directly where the gas was released, it didn't reach you."

"I don't see any vents in the walls or ceiling," said the Martian.

"It didn't have to happen right there," replied Scorpio.

"But you just said they had to be standing exactly where it was released," protested Quedipai.

"They did," confirmed Scorpio. "But they didn't have to die instantly. They take a whiff, they scream 'Run!' to their partners, and they go two or three or ten steps before they collapse and die."

"Then how can we tell where it was released?"

"We'll check for hidden vents between here and the bodies," answered Scorpio.

After ten minutes, they had to admit that there were no vents.

"You must have been wrong," said Quedipai at last.

"It happens," admitted Scorpio with a defeated shrug. "Let's proceed."

They had gotten to within five feet of the bodies when Scorpio yelled "Stop!" and both his companions froze.

"What is it?" asked the Martian.

"I'm an idiot," said Scorpio.

I already knew that.

"Put yourself in their place," he continued. "You know you've been attacked, been poisoned. You don't know what lies ahead, between here and the tomb, but you know it was safe up until you were gassed." He smiled triumphantly. "They weren't running *toward* Xabo's tomb. They were running back the way they came." He took a step past the bodies, studying the ceiling, took another five steps, then he froze, staring at the ceiling.

"Stand back," he said, pulling out his burner and aiming it at a tiny, almost invisible vent.

It melted and sealed the opening instantly, before any remaining gas could be released. They waited a few minutes, just to make sure no poison had escaped, and began walking toward the tomb again.

Finally, they came to a massive door, the sister of the one leading to the Tomb of the Lesser Kings.

"So where's the third body?" asked Scorpio, looking around.

"I see nothing," agreed Quedipai.

"Either the writer can't count, or his friend made it into Xabo's tomb."

"If that is true," said the Martian, "then they both made it, or the writer would not know that his cohort had died."

Still no sign of life?

None.

Scorpio pulled out his Nullifier again. "I assume this door's rigged the same way as the other," he said. "After all, if you touch one of them, you're not going to be around to touch the other."

He activated it, placed it on the door, then pushed it open.

"What the hell?" he muttered, as he found himself facing six mummified warriors standing guard around a mausoleum. It was larger and more impressive than those in the other tomb, made of pure gold, forty feet on a side. A throne, also gold, stood just in front of it.

Scorpio stepped forward and studied the warriors. Each was nine or ten feet high, and their facial features differed markedly from Quedipai's or any other Martian he had ever seen. Each stood—or had been positioned—at attention, and each held a wicked-looking spear in one hand.

"How many Xabos were there?" asked Scorpio, frowning.

"None of these is Xabo," answered Quedipai. "They *guard* Xabo."

"These guys look like they're in the prime of life," observed Scorpio. "Are you saying that they killed and preserved six warriors just to stand them down here and frighten off any superstitious grave robbers?"

"He deserved more," said the Martian, "but the Krang were not a numerous race. As I told you, they may not even have originated on this world."

There were four small anterooms attached to the main chamber, each filled with exquisitely carved cabinets. Scorpio walked over to an ornate cabinet and opened it. It was empty.

"Maybe they should have stuffed and mounted twelve warriors," he said, as Merlin pushed open the door of the mausoleum.

Scorpio—trouble!

What's the problem?

Come see for yourself.

Scorpio did so, and was soon staring at two bodies that were sprawled on the floor of the mausoleum.

Take a look. He's a member of Quedipai's race. He's been stabbed maybe fifteen times by spears. And the other is dressed from a different era, but he was speared to death too.

Scorpio stood, hands on hips, surveying the carnage with a puzzled frown on his face. Each clutched a sack or bag, and when Scorpio examined them he found them filled with what he assumed were the missing art objects.

I assume one of them is the third member of the gang?

Almost certainly.

"What the hell do you think happened?" he asked aloud.

You don't want to know my answer, thought Merlin nervously. *But I think we should leave, and the sooner the better.*

"It was Xabo's personal guard," announced Quedipai with certainty. "The guard is here for only two reasons: to safeguard the sacred book and to protect Xabo. Not his possessions, not his funeral gifts, nothing but the book and Xabo himself."

"I want a closer look at this," said Scorpio, stepping into the mausoleum.

"It is *here!*" cried Quedipai excitedly. "It is actually here!"

He raced up to a jewel-encrusted platform that held an ancient scroll.

"That's what you came to find?" asked Scorpio.

The Martian gently lifted the scroll. "It is the sacred Book of Blaxorak!"

Suddenly, they heard a heavy footstep behind them. Scorpio walked to the door of the mausoleum and looked out—and saw the six warriors slowly coming to life.

Merlin, get over here quick!

Scorpio pulled his burner and fired it in a single motion. A black, smoldering hole appeared in the chest of the closest warrior, but it had no other effect.

We can't kill them, Scorpio—they're already dead!

We can't kill them, but we can sure as hell turn them to ashes!

Scorpio stepped out into the chamber, pulled his smaller burner from where he kept it tucked at the back of his belt, and began firing both weapons, keeping his fingers pressed on the triggers.

The warriors were moving slowly, as if they were using muscles that had not been used in millennia, which was indeed the case. Scorpio kept ducking and dodging their awkward attempts to impale him, keeping the burners trained on the two nearest until they finally burst into flame, then aimed at the next two.

One of the two fallen warriors rolled across the floor and managed to kill the flames. The second he did so, Merlin leaped upon him and literally began tearing him limb from limb. Quedipai clutched the manuscript to his chest and stood motionless just inside the entrance to the mausoleum.

Scorpio saw one of the last two warriors approaching Merlin, who was still battling a fallen warrior. The Earthman quickly trained one of his burners on the warrior's spearhead, melting it before he could reach the Venusian. As he did so, a flaming warrior staggered against him, sending him rolling across the floor. As it came after him, he fired at its feet, burning them into a misshapen, useless pair of molten blobs.

It was over in less than three minutes. The remains of the six warriors were scattered across the chamber, still smoldering.

Well, now we know why there aren't more grave robbers in the Crater, thought Merlin.

We were damned lucky. I only had about twenty seconds of power left in my burner. Scorpio got to his feet and put new power packs into his burners. *Where's Cutie Pie?*

Believe it or not, he's just standing there, reading.

"Hey, Cutie Pie," said Scorpio, getting to his feet. "Let's get ready to go."

"No," said the Martian.

"Why not? You've got the book, we've killed the bad guys—if they *were* bad guys—and the rest of the place has been looted. It's time to head home."

"This is more important," insisted Quedipai, staring intently at the manuscript.

"Read it when we get back to the city," said Scorpio. "I'm sore and I'm tired and I want to lie down."

"No!" yelled the Martian. "I have found it!"

"I know you found it. Now let's take it with us."

"You don't understand!" said Quedipai excitedly. "I have found the prayer for resurrecting the king!"

"We just met his friends and relations," said Scorpio. "Let's let it go at that."

But Quedipai never looked up from the prayer, and finally he began reading it aloud.

On your toes, came Merlin's thought. *We're not alone anymore.*

And as Scorpion drew his burner and turned to see what the Venusian was referring to, a huge being, some twelve feet in height, resembling Quedipai but clearly not of the same race, clad in a jeweled military outfit, arose from where he had been lying.

Quedipai took one look at him and dropped to his knees. Scorpio and Merlin stood side by side in the mausoleum's entrance, the Earthman's burner aimed directly at the newcomer.

"I live again!" announced Xabo in a rich, deep voice, and although it was in a language neither Scorpio nor Merlin had ever heard before, they both understood it. Xabo's gaze fell on the burner in Scorpio's hand. "Put that away," he said. "I will forgive you your transgression this one time only."

Scorpio stared at the huge king for another few seconds, then holstered his burner.

"Who is *this*?" asked Xabo, indicating Quedipai, who had fainted dead away and lay sprawled on the floor, still clutching the manuscript.

"The one who brought you back to life," answered Scorpio.

"There will be a place for him in my kingdom," announced Xabo. He stretched his massive arms. "It is good to be alive again!" He turned back to Scorpio and Merlin. "And who are you, and this creature?"

"We're his protectors."

"Now *I* am his protector."

Scorpio shrugged. "He's all yours—once he pays us what he owes us." He paused for a moment, studying the massive king. "What are your plans, now that you live again?"

"What they always were," replied Xabo. "I will reestablish my kingdom and bring back the old ways and the old religion."

You know what I'm thinking. Are you game?

Go ahead, replied Merlin. *I'm with you.*

"You've been away a long time, Xabo," began Scorpio. "You may not know it, but no other member of your race has survived, and there's every likelihood that the current inhabitants of the planet may resent your giving them orders, resurrected king or not."

"What they want makes no difference," replied Xabo. "It is my destiny to rule, and I will do so with more justice and wisdom than any king has displayed since I was sealed in this tomb." Suddenly, he glared at the Earthman and the Venusian. "Or do you propose to stop me?"

"Not at all," replied Scorpio. "This isn't *our* world. We don't have a problem with you . . . but a lot of people will. People who know their way around today's Mars and especially today's weapons." He paused again to give that time to register. "Like it or not, you're going to need some help."

"Are you offering it?" asked Xabo.

"That's our business," replied Scorpio. He stepped aside so that Xabo could see the bodies of his warriors strewn across the floor. "And those are our bona fides." He pointed to Xabo's neck. "That's a very pretty gold necklace you've got there."

Xabo strode out of the mausoleum, stared at the bodies, and seated himself on his golden throne. "Let us talk," he said.

And while Mars slept, the ancient king, the Earthman, and the Venusian settled down for a long night of hard negotiations.

LIZ WILLIAMS

British writer Liz Williams has had work appear in *Interzone, Asimov's, Visionary Tongue, Subterranean, Terra Incognita, The New Jules Verne Adventures, Strange Horizons, Realms of Fantasy,* and elsewhere, and her stories have been collected in *The Banquet of the Lords of Night and Other Stories,* and, most recently, *A Glass of Shadow.* She's probably best-known for her Detective Inspector Chen series, detailing the exploits of a policeman in a demon-haunted world who literally has to go to Hell to solve some of his cases, which includes *Snake Agent, The Demon and the City, Precious Dragon, The Shadow Pavilion,* and *The Iron Khan.* Her other books include the novels *The Ghost Sister, Empire of Bones, The Poison Master, Nine Layers of Sky, Darkland, Bloodmind, Banner of Souls,* and *Winterstrike.* Her most recent book is the start of the Worldsoul trilogy, *Worldsoul.* She lives in Brighton, England.

Here she sweeps us along on a perilous hunt across the remotest and most dangerous parts of Mars, in a story where nothing and nobody are quite what they seem to be, and nobody's motives are to be trusted, even for a minute.

Out of Scarlight

LIZ WILLIAMS

THE TRIBES OF THE COLD DESERTS DON'T LIKE ANYONE WHO doesn't come from their blood. So I knew that they would not care for me, and that was quite apart from who I really was, or what. I rode up out of Scarlight, taking the road that led to the Cold Deserts, on a frost-rimed morning in early winter with the wind they call the Jharain kicking up the dust. I'd kept myself to myself in Scarlight, where the long trail had led me: It's that kind of a town. I'd taken care to stable my own tope, who didn't like other people, or even me, much, and he seemed glad to be out of the place as well. I'd spent the previous night awaking intermittently, as an occasional great thump from the stable below alerted me to the fact that the tope was trying to break down the door. So our progress up the mountain trail was brisk until we reached the summit of a ridge and I turned to look back.

Scarlight sits in a narrow valley, at a point where the Yss river is channeled between steps of stone, and cascades down to the canals of the plains in a series of dramatic chasms. At the top of Scarlight itself, an ancient arched bridge sits over one of these waterfalls, which then plummets several hundred feet to a dark pool, and on down through the town. Scarlight is one of those nexus places, where many roads meet, and they say that the pool is filled with the bones of those who have upset the lords of Scarlight.

They're probably right.

We, however, were following the Yss, and as the tope paused to drink noisily from the tumbling white water, I dismounted via the saddle steps and stood for a moment on dry, golden grass, burned into straw over the summer. Red earth showed parched and cracked:

the winter rains had not come into their own, and yet the river was full enough. I looked for tracks, but not much was visible: a mark that might have been half a footprint, some droppings that were clearly from the little verminous ulsas. There was a rank smell in the air, too, which I could not place, and it disturbed me. If I had not made a brief search of the area, I might have missed the tracks altogether, but they lay farther up over a patch of soil—a mount of some kind, traveling fast, and probably carrying more than one person. The footprints were reptilian, however, unlike the splayed feet of a tope. It had followed the river for a few paces, then bounded up over the rocks, and here the trail ended.

Thoughtfully, I rounded up my own mount, climbed back into the saddle, and jogged on. It might complicate matters if anyone else was up here—and by anyone else, I meant Nightwall Dair. Whether he realized it or not, we'd crossed paths all that year, first over the face of the plains, then most recently in Cadrada, and I was getting sick of it. If he knew me at all, it was as a man called Thane, and that cover had seemed to hold. If he found out who I *really* was, and what—a woman named Zuneida Peace—I was in deep trouble, and I didn't want that. Zuneida was a former temple dancer, a seductress of princes (and princesses), a poet—a very different person to my taciturn alias Thane, who hid black hair beneath a hat, and drops of juice in his eyes to conceal the blue, who wore a half mask allegedly to hide the damage done by a scar, who spoke as little as possible, and in an accent that betrayed the north.

Half a day later, and we were high up into the slopes of the Khor; another full day, and I estimated that we would reach the edge of the Cold Deserts themselves. I camped that night in the shelter of a high tor of rock, one of the inexplicable piles of stones left by a people long gone, and decorated with the stylized wings of birds. A ban-lion called once, a throaty gasp against the silence of the mountain wall, then the night birds sang. I lay in a fleece wrap and watched the stars wheel over me until I slept and dreamed of warm Cadrada and a night filled with jasmine and golden wine, and of someone, now gone, beside me in the dark.

Next morning, the temperature had dropped another couple of degrees. I washed as best I could in the icy waters of the Yss and brewed tea on a makeshift fire. The tope yawned and snorted in the morning air. Later, high on the slope, I looked down across the plateau that was opening up ahead of me and saw the tiny figure of a rider on a black-furred mount, speeding over the tundra toward a stand of trees. There was something oddly familiar about the mount, and I wondered if I had seen it down in Scarlight. Then it disappeared into shadow and was gone. I skirted the cliff, keeping close to the anonymity of the rock wall, just in case. I knew that the Tribes did not come down this far, preferring the higher plateau of the Cold Deserts.

At midday, I saw the first outpost of the Tribes: a squat tower made of blackened stone. This was not something that they had originally built but a remnant of some long-gone people that they had taken over, perhaps once a military fortification, perhaps a temple of some kind. It could have been either, and it was impossible to tell—whatever sense of the practical or the numinous that it had once possessed was also long gone, leaving it a gloomy shell. But there were signs of a recent fire scorching the stone of its floor and witch-marks daubed in soot around the walls. I smiled when I saw them, because I was one of the ones whom the marks were intended to deter, but they held no trace of power, not this far west. It was only when you reached the inner desert that the sand-singers knew what they were doing; these marks would have been made by a warrior, superstitious, and thus afraid. Something clattered high in the roof, and, outside, the mount gave a rumbling bellow. A bird, nothing more, one of the leather-winged shrikes that haunted the mountains. I went outside again and looked down the valley. There was the bird, a low shadow shooting over the grass.

It was too early to camp in the tower, so I set off once more, heading through a stand of desert birch whose bare trunks arched out of the soil like golden bones. It was as the mount was traversing its thickest point that I heard a distant cry, borne on the wind. I steered the tope to the edge of the little wood and looked down. The wood stood high on a ridge of rock, looking out onto the plain, and, against the pale grass, I saw again the man on the black tope, but this time I could see that he wore the emblem of a tribe upon his hat and that he had a pursuer.

The pursuer rode a green beast, one of the burrow-dwelling things that live in the hills of Ithness, and it was therefore a long way from home. Part reptile, part cat, it leaped along sinuously, and I could see its rider casting the malefic incantations that the sorcerers of Ithness are wont to employ, hurling poisons like bolts. I grinned. I should not get involved, and yet—well, I knew Ithness all too well, had danced for a time in their slave palaces, and for Cadrada itself I had a score to settle. Besides, bestowing an unlikely favor is never a bad thing. I kicked the mount forward and rode down onto the plain.

As I neared the two figures, I could taste the incantations on the air. It is said that in Ithness, sorcerers imbibe magic with their poisons, so that they emit wrongness whenever they utter words, and the air was bitter in his wake. I recognized those incantations, and the man behind them. I notched a barb into the nozzle of the gun and took aim, firing through a lace of salt-alder on the banks of a brackish rivulet. I watched with satisfaction as the sorcerer threw up his arms and toppled sideways from his mount. The green beast shrieked and ran. The man on the black-furred tope reined it in and hailed me, but I was already turning my mount, fleeing back up the slope, and was gone.

Cadrada, sometime before, and a girl was dancing. There was a blue-green fire in the center of the hall, and far below the city, the plains jackals were barking out their territorial boundaries. The girl danced to the beat of their song and her eyes caught the light like a forest fire. I watched her from the back of the hall and thought of the night before, when she had danced for me alone. Her name was Hafyre, and I was not the only one watching.

The sorcerer sat on a dais, cross-legged beside our host, one of the lords of Cadrada, a man named Halse, who had a jackal as his totem. Appropriately. Occasionally, I saw the sorcerer lean over to whisper to him, and the lord's cold, jaded face betrayed a flicker of interest. I noted that the sorcerer was typical of his kind: parchment skin and a yellowing rattail of hair, bound with a spiral of bone. The people of Ithness are always too pale, like mushrooms. His sleeves jingled with warding charms, and when he reached out a hand for his wineglass, I saw that it was tattooed with the sigil of his personal demon.

Later, looking for Hafyre, I saw the sorcerer again in the maze of corridors that led from the hall. He snapped his fingers and a spark of a spell arced through the air. Hafyre came meekly out of the shadows, took his sigil-decked hand, and followed him into the night. I did not think that the spell had much to do with it, however I might have liked to believe otherwise. That was Hafyre: She liked to circle herself with power and was not choosy about how she achieved it.

Then she had gone missing. No one knew where. Halse was predictably angry and had the slavemaster thrown off the battlements. He was not, it seemed, so jaded after all. He hired me to find her and bring her back. I did not know if he knew about Hafyre and myself, or if he would have cared. He knew me beneath the mask as Zuneida Peace, and men do not take women's affairs seriously, or, if they do, are intrigued rather than angered. And I was little more than just another servant for hire, after all.

Hafyre's trail, such as it was, led to Scarlight, and thus had brought me north. Now the pallid sorcerer was here, as well. And so, it seemed, was Nightwall Dair.

I left the plain far behind, and by dusk was deep into the mountains. The walls rose ahead of me, tower upon tower of shadow. When it grew too dark to see, I dismounted, lit a fire, and camped for the night. I slept, but with the strange dreams that I remembered from earlier times here, tormenting images of leatherblack wings and a girl's face, seen through fire.

When I woke, I lay blinking at the stars. I knew who that girl in the dream was, of course: Hafyre, my quarry. Her eyes glowed forest-green, her skin was golden, and her hair a brown-red, like soil. She smiled, turned her head, and beckoned, and, in imagination, I saw her move sinuously in the firelight. She wore the costume of a slave-girl, her bare torso striped with a hundred shifting bands of emeralds and her tunic trousers the color of leaves in spring. Desire flickered deep within me. She was all the shades of the world, but she was gone, fleeing with the morning, and soon I rode on.

By now, I had expected to see signs of the Tribes, and that I had not done so concerned me. It was cold, but I would not yet have expected them to retreat into their mountain fastnesses, the secret places that made the more credulous folk claim that they were nothing more than ghosts. Toward the middle of the afternoon, however, I came across more tracks, then, in the distance, a cluster of the round grey tents that the Tribes use in summer, sprouting like toadstools on a plateau of dead grass. Their mounts grazed nearby, and I saw the red-and-azure banner of the Ynar flying on a pole. I released a breath of relief: These were the most civilized, if you like, of the Tribes—they do not, at least, shoot on first sight. And they were also the ones I was looking for. I approached warily all the same.

When I was a short distance away, the priestess came out of a tent with a flail in her hand. She was not young, her skin scarred and splattered with indigo patterning. I saw the spike through her lower lip that told me she was a deathspeaker, and her headdress jingled with the beads of her wealth. She did not look pleased to see me.

"Shan-hai," I greeted her with her title, "I come with a message. From Cadrada."

"I know no one and nothing in the cities," the priestess snapped. "Do not lie."

"I'm telling you the truth." I dismounted and threw the scrap of fabric with the emblem of the Ynar upon it, above the personal totem. Her breath hissed in her throat as she saw it, and she snatched it from the ground as though I were going to steal it back.

"Where did you get this?"

"Give me water and I'll tell you. I cut it from no corpse, if that is what you're asking."

She stared at me for a long moment, then shook the flail and spoke a word of Protection from the carrion gods of the Ynar . . . "You won't need that for me," I said. Her eyes widened: the dark green of winter forests. I remembered Hafyre and held my breath. The priestess was not as old as I'd first assumed. She did better than water, making me tea from the bittersweet verthane of the high slopes and keeping a polite silence until I'd drunk the first three mouthfuls. Then she said, "I ask you again. Where did you get this?"

"From a slave palace." She had not yet realized that I was not a man. If I had my way, she never would. "What I was doing there—that's my business. But I met a girl, who told me that she was a princess of the Ynar. Her name was Hafyre. She gave me this." I pointed to the emblem.

"And you brought it back to us. Why?"

"I'm traveling across the Cold Deserts to Coyine. I want safe passage."

"And so you buy it with an emblem of the lost," she said, but consideringly, without condemnation. I could see that she was thinking fast.

"If you like."

She gave a swift gesture of assent. "Very well. What else did you understand of the girl? 'Princess' is not a term we know."

I affected disinterest. "I'm not familiar with your hierarchies."

"Very well, I shall explain them to you, though no man can apprehend how the Tribes are governed." She turned her head and spat. "You with your male-ruled cities—you cannot understand our matriarchies. Hafyre is ghost-touched, grass-haunted. There was a comet at her birth, and we believe that is a herald from the carrion lords who live between the winds, the land where death is. She is an oracle, a harbinger, and she is marked for power."

"Then you'll be wanting her back."

"As you say. She went missing a year and a half ago; we had thought her dead, but the wind brought no messages from her, and I confess that I did not understand why."

I looked away. "How do you plan to retrieve her?"

"Ah," the Shan-hai said, "I don't think it wise to tell you that."

"It's none of my concern, really. But you'll guarantee safe passage?"

"Yes. You have done me a service. Even though you are a man, I won't forget it. There'll be a ceremony tonight because of this—you will stay. I say this not because I wish to honor you: It is the best way to inform as many people as possible of your presence, at once."

"What does this ceremony involve?"

"A call to the winds and the gods who ride them. No more than that. You won't be expected to do more than watch. The priestesses run things here."

"Then it will be an honor indeed," I said, and saw her cold, forest-eyed smile.

To the citizens of Cadrada, these people are barbarians. Remembering Halse's palace, and the things that happened there, I rather think it is more even-handed than that. The ceremony to which I had been invited was held up in the rocks, on a low plateau looking out across the darkening plain and the red sun falling. The air grew colder swiftly and smelled of snow. Huge harps of sinew were threaded between tall poles, and, as the dusk breeze grew, they began to whine and sing. The priestess moved among them, whispering, in a dance that grew steadily wilder as the evening wore on. By the time the actual ceremony was due to begin, some three hundred people had gathered. I saw the banner of the Ynar again, but others, too. The women gathered about the fires; the men stood sullenly on the fringes, standing guard.

The Shan-hai called on the carrion spirits of the wind. They use an older tongue for these ceremonies, a language that has been dead for thousands of years and has nothing to do with the builders of the canals or the cities of the plain. It is wilder, stranger, not at all human. It made my skin crawl to hear it, and yet it filled me with a strange ascetic sense of longing: the reverse of the sex-songs that they sing in the palaces to inflame all those who hear them. This spoke of purity and deliberate isolation. Perhaps it was what I needed. I became lost in the thin harmonies, as the priestess berated or cajoled or implored the carrion gods; I did not know which. But then I became aware that someone was close to my shoulder. Casually, I turned.

His tea-colored eyes caught the firelight. His coat was frayed, but originally of good quality, and he wore a hat with an emblem upon it—the same form of emblem that I had brought to the priestess. Close to, his face was sallow and long, like a chiseled candle, under a fall of fawn-brown hair. I had last seen him on a black-furred mount, pursued by the sorcerer from Ithness.

"You rescued me," he said. He sounded amused. His voice was low, like silk and razors, with the sibilants of the plains. "Why?"

"I don't like Ithness."

"The hotels? The shopping?"

I inclined my head, though my smile was hidden by the mask. "Neither are good. The hotels are verminous and the shops overpriced. Their sorcerers are worse."

"This one isn't dead, by the way. Regrettably. You'd need a bolt or poison for that, or one of their own spells, not a barb gun. But it was a kind thing to do. And altruism always worries me."

"It worries me, too. That's why I never practice it. What did you do, to be pursued so far and so hard? Are you a traveler? You're no tribesman, yet you wear their sign."

"Well," he said, "I am indeed a traveler, and as for why I am permitted to wear the sign of the Ynar, that's a longer story. If this was Scarlight, I'd offer to discuss it over a drink. But here—"

"The tribes don't indulge in wine or spirits. Unless you like fermented tope milk."

"That's why I brought a hipflask."

We both deemed it prudent to wait until the ceremony was over before returning to a tent and pouring out measures. I was feeling insecure. He was flirting, I could have sworn it, and that was a problem. Either he knew me for a woman, or he thought I was a man. Neither possibility was reassuring. I kept to the shadows and made sure that the mask was securely tied, nor did I drink much, although the man I had rescued watched me all the while.

He had not told me his name, but he did not need to. He was called Nightwall Dair. He was the only man who had ever gone beyond the Nightwall of the far north, the great glacier that separates Heth from the plains, or at least the only man who had done so and lived. He had brought back a captive, a strange black thing with golden eyes, who had lived for a time before spilling its secrets to the sorcerers of Cadrada. I'd seen it, and him, at Lord Halse's palace, and, as I've said, we'd crossed paths on several occasions before that. Dair was a manhunter, just as I was, and a hunter of other things, too. Not an easy man to trick, and I did not know if I had succeeded.

We spoke of Scarlight, and Cadrada itself, lightly enough, as men do when they meet in a strange place. At length, he said, "I know you, I am sure of it."

I shrugged. "Perhaps we have met on our travels. There is something a little familiar about you."

"Many people know me," he said. He spoke as if it did not matter.

"Perhaps, then, we have met. But I have still not heard your name."

He gave a grin filled with teeth. "Just as well. If you had, you would have reason to be afraid."

"Many say the same of me." I rose to my feet. "It's getting late, and I have a long way to go."

There was a faint curiosity in his face. "Where are you headed?"

"Coyine."

"The Tribes don't like travelers."

"That's why I've paid for safe passage."

"They don't use money."

"I wasn't talking about money."

He laughed. "I think you've been here before."

"And you? But of course you have, with that emblem."

"Me? I've been everywhere." He put his head on one side, looking up at me from beneath the lock of hair that fell across his face. His long countenance was wry, amused, like one who anticipates a negative reply. "Do you want a companion for the night?"

"Not fussy, are you? You haven't even seen my face."

"As you say, I'm not fussy."

"Unfortunately, I've recently taken a vow of celibacy," I said.

He laughed again. "And you *have* seen my countenance. Well, I shall choose to believe you—it's more flattering than the alternatives."

I bowed, then headed to the tent that the priestess had told me I could use. I don't like tents. They're hard to secure, and I spent most of the night in a light doze with my blade over my knees, just in case. But Dair had obviously taken my refusal in good spirits: I knew that he would not have found entertainment among the tribes, who are prudish in the extreme, but he did not bother me.

In the morning, I woke to find the priestess sitting outside the tent.

"The woman you saw," she began, without preamble. "I want to use you for a divination."

"Very well," I said. The sun was only just coming up. "What did you have in mind?"

"I need to take you to the scrying pool."

"And if I prefer not to?"

"You still want safe passage to Coyine, I believe?" She glowered. "And my magic can fry any man at seven paces."

"Good point. I'd like some tea first, though." I wasn't at my best first thing.

"It's better on an empty stomach," she said, unsmiling.

The scrying pool lay up in the woods. A narrow track that looked as though it had been made by an animal led up to it, and when we sat down by its glassy black depths, the air rose cool and dank through the ferns. Red earth, green leaves . . . they reminded me of Hafyre.

"What do you want me to do?"

She was lighting something in a tiny censer, held by a dangling bronze chain. A pungent smell twined out in its smoke, making me cough. It reminded me of something: one of the strong perfumes of the south that are brought forth by heat.

"Close your eyes," she instructed. I did so, though not too trustingly. I felt a warm breath on the skin around my eyes, the only part of my face that was visible. The smoke penetrated the mask, seeping into my throat, and, against my better judgment, I felt myself grow slack and relaxed. I had a sudden vision of the long pale face of Nightwall Dair.

"No," I heard the priestess hiss. Another image floated before me: the girl with green eyes and hair the shade of earth. The priestess gave a breath of satisfaction. "There she is. Hafyre."

The girl's face was downcast. She stared down at something she was holding in her lap, a crystal globe with a spark at the heart of it, like a little flame. A shaft of lamplight came over her shoulder; she wore a filmy ochre shift. Her face was as beautiful as I remembered it, all ovals and symmetry and that sudden, flaming smile. The slave brand was stamped white on her shoulder and the priestess cursed when she saw it.

"Defiled!"

I'd met her in a slave palace, after all. They're not convents.

"This is the past," the priestess said, with authority. "She is not there now."

This was dangerous ground. I didn't want the woman looking into my head and discovering that the girl was the reason I was here, that I'd been sent to bring her back. That—well, I did not want to let her in and that was an end of it.

"Is it so?" I said, deceptively dulcet.

"Try to see where she is now." The smoke grew stronger. Against my will, I looked into the black and saw the girl. This time, she wore black leather riding gear and she was sitting beside a hearth of ashes. But she was still the same person I had known back in Cadrada, the girl who could, in an instant, throw another person into desire like the flick of a whip.

"Ahhhh," the priestess said. "I know where she is."

"Where?"

"Enough." The smoke abruptly ceased and my eyes fluttered open.

"Why did you choose me for this?" I asked. I didn't know whether she'd seen that I was a woman.

"An outsider is better, even a man." That answered that question. "Those of the Tribes—they bring too many assumptions to it." She stood and nodded thanks. "You can go now. You'll have safe passage to Coyine. When you reach the next ridge, you will find a settlement on the far side. Give them this." She handed me a token: a brass coin bearing a sigil. "They will exchange it for another. Thus, with luck, and if you do not meet too many wild beasts, you will reach Coyine alive." There was a flicker of contempt beneath her words.

And so I mounted up and rode swiftly into the morning light. I did not see Nightwall Dair again, but before I reached the ridge, I turned the mount and headed up into the woods. I doubled back until I could see the tents. The priestess was speaking to two warriors: They saddled up topes and she swung up behind the leader. Then they were riding northwest, fast. I followed.

By the middle of the afternoon, we were high into the mountains and the air had grown an icy bite. I was quite a long way behind, but when I came up over a ridge, they had halted and were standing below. The ruin was so decrepit that at first I failed to realize what it was: another stump of a tower. I reined in my mount and watched the little pantomime enacted below. The priestess came out of the tower and waved her arms. I got the impression that she was blaming the warriors for something. There was an argument, then they all mounted up again and rode off. Greatly entertained, I waited until they had disappeared from sight and rode down to the ruin.

Inside it was as I had seen it in the vision. There was no sign of Hafyre. The ashy hearth lay undisturbed, or so I thought at first. Then I looked closer. In the ash, someone had inscribed a few symbols. To anyone unfamiliar with the secret slave signs of Cadrada, which was most people, it would have looked like the footprints of a bird, or the scratchings of vermin. To me, it was a message.

Northwest, then west again. A rock below a star.

I digested this for a moment, then made a thorough examination of the ruin. She had not been the only person here. There had been someone with her, a man, I thought from the footprints. Someone had pissed up against the wall; it was still faintly damp. I knelt and sniffed. Not a native of the south, but someone else . . . It wasn't wet enough to have been one of the priestesses' warriors—not as recent—and it was too high on the wall to have been a woman. So someone else had been here with Hafyre, someone who did not know the slave-signs.

Someone from Ithness? Or had Dair beaten me to it?

Well, that was what I intended to find out. I went back out, cautiously, climbed back on the tope, and kicked it into a gallop in a westerly direction.

For some time, I'd been getting the impression that I might be being followed. A fleeting scent on the wind, a prickle at the back of the neck, nothing more. If so, there were two obvious likely candidates: the sorcerer and Nightwall Dair. But there wasn't a lot I could do about it. If I doubled back, my pursuer would know, and I stood little chance of losing him in this terrain; on the pale tope, I stood out like a moon in a clear sky. And the message hadn't exactly been clear, although once I'd been riding for a bit, I saw what she'd meant. The only possible westerly passage was a funnel of rock as the mountain wall closed in, channeling me in the direction of the setting sun. And at the end of it, as we rode into dusk, a pinnacle of stone reared up over the narrow valley, wearing the Lovestar like a hat. When I saw that, I smiled under the mask and spurred the mount on and under a lip of rock. Then I dove off it, falling the ten feet from its high humped back and sprawling with a gasp in the dust. The tope, astonished, bounded away. I knew it wouldn't go very far: it would come back eventually if it thought there was a chance of food. I lay in a twist of limbs.

I knew when he was close. I could smell the tope, and a shadow fell across my face. There was a light step, then a foot in my ribs. He reached down and snatched off the mask. I felt my hair spill down into the dirt. I didn't stir but lay still with my eyes shut. He didn't say anything, but I heard him laugh with surprise. He shoved me again with his boot. Then, when he still got no reaction, he picked me up and hoisted me up over the back of his tope. And that was when I kicked him in the head.

That's one of the good things about being a professional dancer. I felt his jaw snap back, then he was down in the dirt. I dropped onto him from the back of the tope and flattened him for good measure. Then I took a good look at him: at the long face and the fawn hair sprawling in the dust.

"Nightwall Dair. My apologies." I almost felt sincere.

I tied his arms behind him: I thought he was out cold, but I didn't want to take the chance that he'd try the same trick with me that I had with him, and I wanted his wrists secured, at least. He was too heavy to lift onto the puzzled tope, so I left him lying there and ducked back under the lip of rock, making my way down the canyon. I dusted off the mask as I went and replaced it. On the way down, I met my mount wandering back up. It was now almost dark.

"You stay there," I told it, and tied its harness to an outcrop. Then I looked for what I'd been expecting to find, and found it.

The ancestors of the Tribes, or those who came before them, had done something stupid once. I don't know what. Some kind of poisoning of the atmosphere, a souring of the soil, thousands of years ago. It had made them take to the mountains for a time, burrowing into the rocks against the killing cold. Their tunnels could still be found, used now as winterings, and a round stone door showed where the closest one lay. It stood half-concealed behind a boulder. I gave it a push, judging the pivot point, and when it opened, I climbed through. It led into a passage, traveling downward. I could smell a perfume that I knew well, plus sweat and smoke. I followed.

Hafyre was huddled in a makeshift bed of furs, still in her riding leathers. She gasped when she saw me, and I saw her become more sinuous, sliding into the furs as she assessed this new threat.

Slowly, I took off the mask and watched her face change.

"Zuneida Peace," she breathed. "All the way from Cadrada. I didn't think you cared." Her forest eyes were wide with surprise. "Of all the people I thought might come after me . . ."

"Your lord paid well."

"Good enough," she said, briskly. She got to her feet.

"Where is he? The sorcerer?" I demanded.

"He's gone to find my aunt," she said. "I don't know when he'll be back. I tried to get out, but I couldn't move the door from the inside."

"We need to go."

On the way back up the passage, I said, "Did he rape you? The sorcerer?"

"No." Our eyes met.

"What were you doing with him?"

"He took me from the palace. We'd been sleeping together." She told me this without a hint of shame, as though what she and I had experienced did not matter, and perhaps, I thought with bitterness, she was right.

"He bound me with a spell and took me out of Halse's palace through the cellars. I thought at first that he was taking me to Ithness, to the markets there. But he brought me here, instead. He wants leverage over the Tribes. He planned to use me as a bargaining chip with my aunt." She paused. Her face grew downcast and demure, a little sly. She ran a hand over my arm and murmured, "What are *you* planning to do?"

"Take you back to Cadrada."

I braced myself for resistance and fingered the little phial of amorphite in my pocket. It would knock her out immediately and keep her out for a while. But she perked up.

"Good! We both gain, then. You'll get your fee and I'll get a traveling companion back to the palace." She laughed at the expression on my face. "You don't think I want to *stay* here, do you? Shut up in a stuffy tent until it's time for me to be a broodmare, manipulated by my priestess aunt because of some moldy old prophecy? Or shut down in a wintering like this, not able to go out for a piss for six months because the cold freezes the snot in your nose, and living off dried ulsa meat? No thanks." She paused. "I suppose this has occurred to you already, but the roles of women in this society really aren't worth much, are they? When I was snatched from the Cold Deserts in the first place, it was the best thing that ever happened to me. I've got *opportunities* in the palace. Clearly, Lord Halse wants me back, but in three or four years, I'll be over the hill and too old for him. They'll give me a pension—it's happened to other women. Then I'll set up my own place. I know several girls who'd be happy to work for me, and I'd have my own regular clients." A meditative look entered her green eyes. "I fancy a place overlooking the Grand Canal—all those lovely gardens and a restaurant on every corner. I've got it all worked out."

"I see," I said, faintly.

"So." Hafyre bounced up. "Shall we get going?"

"We might as well," I replied.

I hoped Dair hadn't come round by the time we left; it would save embarrassment, but the body sprawled in the dust had gone. That made me doubly eager to get going. He'd freed my tope, but the mount hadn't gone far; after a moment of panic, I saw it trot nimbly down through the rocks with an air of affront. Hafyre had walked, apparently, since the edge of the mountains, and was more than happy to ride. All we had to do now was get out of the lands of the Tribes and head south.

But, however conscious I was of the missing Dair, I still wasn't paying quite enough attention.

Once we'd come through the canyon, the stars were fully out, spreading a pallid light over the rocks. I saw the sorcerer from Ithness out of the corner of my eye, suddenly rearing up on the edge of a ledge, and Hafyre cried out as I toppled, paralyzed, from the tope and hit the ground for the second time that day. There I lay, while the sorcerer leaped from the rock as lightly as a bird and onto the back of my mount. Hafyre shrieked curses and went abruptly silent. They disappeared down the slope at a run.

Some considerable time later, I became aware that a pair of boots had appeared in front of me.

"Tut, tut," said the voice of Nightwall Dair. "I see that the hand of immediate karma appears to have touched you. How ironic." He bent down and touched something cold and damp to the side of my neck, and suddenly I could move again. "I really should try to get over these disastrous impulses toward compassion. Never does me any good . . . Especially after what happened earlier." He helped me to my feet. His wrists were raw.

"Thanks," I mumbled. I wouldn't say that I felt abashed, precisely, but there was a slight element of the embarrassment I'd hoped to avoid earlier. Why I should have felt this way, I don't know: It must have been a professional thing.

"So, where is she? The girl?"

"The sorcerer from Ithness took her."

Dair swore. "I thought so. Bastard. Are you on a finders' fee?"

"Yes. You?"

"Yes, from a lord in Cadrada who took a fancy to her. One of Halse's rivals. I know who you are now, by the way. A man named Thane. Or a woman named Peace. I recognize you from Halse's palace. You were a dancer. Among, it seems, other things."

"I'm not sure it matters."

"We stand more chance of tracking her down together. I don't need the hassle of your interference, and I know this sorcerer; we've got a history."

"Very generous of you. I know him, too. *We* have a history. You could, of course, just kill me."

Dair looked pained. "I don't work that way. We can sort out the money later."

I knew that he had no intention of splitting it: He just wanted to keep an eye on me and perhaps get my help. But that was fine for the moment.

With me up behind Dair on his black tope, we tracked them as far as the edge of the plain, then lost the trail. The tope stood, swinging its head in indecision. Since the sorcerer had stolen my mount, I wondered what he'd done with his own. Maybe the lizard-thing was still roaming around the place.

"Might as well camp up for the night," Dair said, philosophically.

"I'm still not up for 'companionship.'"

"Now that I've found out you're a woman, actually, neither am I."

We took turns keeping watch. It was a quiet enough night, although for a time I heard sounds out on the plain suggesting the Tribes were having another jamboree. Dair woke me at dawn, handed me a leather cup of tea, and told me that we were getting going. I was quick enough to agree. I wanted to get out of tribal lands, before the priestess—Hafyre's aunt—discovered that we were still on her patch and sent her warriors out against us.

We'd gone far enough west already that by the time evening fell, we were back in Scarlight, and I was surprised to find how much I'd missed the place. At least, compared to the Cold Deserts.

We found a bar to sit out the early evening in a corner booth. I thought that the sorcerer, having presumably dealt with Hafyre's aunt, might come back through Scarlight. If he still lived. Whatever the case, I was resigned to Hafyre's loss. But by that time, I was also looking forward to a sweat lodge, and wine.

"You're quite attractive now you're not covered in filth," Dair said when I reappeared. I gritted my teeth. I was likely to get more attention as Zuneida than I had as the anonymous Thane, so I'd kept the mask on, rendering his remark even more irritating.

"I thought you didn't like women."

"I like some women. Just not for sex." He glanced around at the men in the bar.

"Trust me, that's refreshing."

"So," Dair said, primly. He poured me a glass of Ylltian white and watched as I took a sip. If he'd been going to poison me, I thought, he'd have done so earlier. "You've had a varied career."

"You noticed."

"Whereas I'm more single-track. I've always been a bounty hunter, ever since I was a young man. Followed in my uncle's footsteps."

"You're from Cadrada?"

"I'm from a lot of places. I was born in a desert village. Didn't have a name, it was too little. I got out on a barge down the Grand Canal and never went back. You?"

"Cadrada, but I don't know who my parents were. Brought up on the edge of the court, by a variety of people, then into the temple as a dancer. They used me to seduce visiting aristocracy. Reliable enough work." And it paid for my poetry, but I didn't really want to tell Dair that; I thought it might make me seem less threatening.

"Easier than bounty hunting."

"Only sometimes. Anyway, I wanted to travel." I was trying to be philosophical about Hafyre's loss, and failing. This is why one should never mix business and personal matters.

Dair was scanning the room behind me; he'd seen something, but I didn't want to draw attention by looking round. "I can understand that."

"This is decent wine," I said, loudly. "Want some more?"

His eyes remained on the back of the room. "Whatever you say, my friend." His free hand traced a couple of sigils on the tabletop: *northwest, leaving*. Then he stood. "There's a back way out behind the kitchen."

So that was the way I took, while Dair went out the front. I passed a greasy scullery and someone washing pans; she did not look up. The staff were probably used to it. I sped through an alley, seeing no one, and met Dair again outside the bar, standing in the shadows.

"They're here. The sorcerer is, anyway."

"Did you see her? Why would he have brought her back here and not to the Tribes?"

"I don't know. Negotiating on neutral ground? Or maybe he thinks it's safer now that he's found out we're on the scene. I only saw him. I don't think he saw us, though. But I can't be sure."

"Did you see where he went?"

"No."

"I want my tope back," I told him. A quick trip round the town's stables seemed in order, and, in the second, belonging to one of the cheaper guesthouses, we found my mount. He bellowed a welcome when he saw me, looking up from his steaming bucket of entrails and enveloping me in a blast of fetid breath. Dair said that he thought it was sweet. I did not bother to reply. We took the back stairs, weapons at the ready. Dair took a phial from his pocket, broke off the top, and threw it into the corner; after a moment, smoke billowed out, seeping under the doors.

"Fire!" Dair shouted, with a convincing note of panic.

We waited until there were a series of gratifying cries and people in various stages of undress bolted forth. At the far end of the hall, however, a door remained firmly closed. I ran through the clouds of smoke and kicked it in.

The sorcerer was standing by the window, in the act of throwing open the shutters.

Hafyre cried out, muffled by a gag. Her hands were tied behind her back. I sliced through the bonds while Dair fired a bolt at the sorcerer, who flung himself to one side. I stood up to get a clear shot with the barb gun, aiming at the sorcerer's face, but at that moment the room crackled with the cast of a spell.

I felt it hit me, and it felt as though it should have brought me down, but it broke over me like a fiery wave and was gone. There was a cry of fury and I turned to see the priestess, Hafyre's aunt, standing in the doorway. Her hand was outstretched; her face, bewildered. The sorcerer gave a sudden caw of laughter.

"That's the trouble with women's spells!"

My magic can fry any man at seven paces. Being a poet, I really should pay more attention to figures of speech, especially in other people's languages.

The sorcerer flung out a hand of his own. Dair tackled me low, clutching me around the waist and bringing me to the floor.

The bolts shot over my head like twin comets: one green and one blue. There was a sharp cry, a curse from Hafyre, then the ringing silence that follows concussive-weapons fire. The pressure of Dair's body on mine was abruptly released. He pulled me to my feet. A scorched outline against the opposite wall was all that remained of the sorcerer: Evidently rage had lent force to *that* particular spell. In the doorway, the body of the Ynar priestess, Hafyre's aunt, had slumped lifelessly to the floor. And a window banging against its own shutters was the only trace of Hafyre herself.

She'd stolen my tope, we discovered shortly. But there were no prizes for guessing where she was headed: Cadrada, decent restaurants, and a lifetime of business opportunities. We could have gone after her, but I couldn't help feeling that she deserved to have a free run.

Later, though—later I would return to Cadrada. Maybe with money in my pocket. The hope in my heart was already there, however misplaced.

Aloud, I said I thought that she was more trouble than she was worth. So Dair and I split the proceeds along gender lines: He took the sorcerer's cash bag and poison store, while I stripped the priestess's body of her coin belt and the wealth-beads in her hair. Then we dumped her body in the Yss and gave the guesthouse proprietor a bit over the cost of the room to keep her quiet. Even with this unexpected expense, over another bottle of Ylltian white, we calculated that we'd made slightly more than the finders' fees.

"Of course," Dair said sourly, a couple of hours later, "failure's not good for the reputation."

"True. But at least we don't have to go all the way back to Cadrada empty-handed. Although I don't think that the north is a very healthy place to be anymore." I was remembering the priestess's warriors. Dair turned the glass in his fingers.

"I was thinking of Yllt. Lovely at this time of year. And they do make a nice wine."

I smiled.

"Do you want a companion for the ride?"

"Not fussy, are you? Although I'm reminded that you no longer have a mount."

And so the next morning I once more rode out of Scarlight, on Dair's black tope, with the Jharain wind at my back, money in my pocket, and the vision of a girl's face before me, her eyes the color of forests.

HOWARD WALDROP

Howard Waldrop is widely considered to be one of the best short-story writers in the business, having been called "the resident Weird Mind of our generation" and an author "who writes like [a] honkytonk angel." His famous story "The Ugly Chickens" won both the Nebula and the World Fantasy Awards in 1981. His work has been gathered in the collections: *Howard Who?, All About Strange Monsters of the Recent Past: Neat Stories by Howard Waldrop, Night of the Cooters: More Neat Stories by Howard Waldrop, Going Home Again,* the print version of his collection *Dream Factories and Radio Pictures* (formerly available only in downloadable form online), and a collection of his stories written in collaboration with various other authors, *Custer's Last Jump and Other Collaborations.* Waldrop is also the author of the novel *The Texas-Israeli War: 1999,* in collaboration with Jake Saunders, and of two solo novels, *Them Bones* and *A Dozen Tough Jobs,* as well as the chapbook *A Better World's in Birth!* He is at work on a new novel, tentatively titled *The Moone World.* His most recent book is a big retrospective collection, *Things Will Never Be the Same: Selected Short Fiction 1980–2005.* Having lived in Washington State for a number of years, Waldrop recently moved back to his former hometown of Austin, Texas, something that caused celebrations and loud hurrahs to rise up from the population.

Historical re-creations are popular on Earth, with thousands reenacting Civil War battles and scenes from other conflicts, but here Waldrop shows us a historical re-creation taking place on Mars, one that takes us on a voyage on a historically accurate reconstruction of a *slimshang* out across the Martian deserts to the source of all life itself.

The Dead Sea-Bottom Scrolls

(A Re-creation of Oud's Journey by Slimshang from Tharsis to Solis Lacus, by George Weeton, Fourth Mars Settlement Wave, 1981)

HOWARD WALDROP

SO I AM STANDING HERE ON A COLD MORNING, BESIDE THE best approximation of a *slimshang* of which Terran science is capable—polycarbonates and (Earth) man-made fabrics instead of the original hardened plant fibers and outer coverings of animals long extinct. It looks fast, probably faster than any native-made *slimshang*, but it will have to do.

One thing it's missing is the series of gears, cogs, plates, and knobs with which a sort of music was made as it rolled. Martians spoke of "coming at full melody"—since the reproduction was mechanical, like a music box, the faster the *slimshang* went, the louder and more rackety the tune.

Instead, I have a tape deck with me, on which I have chosen to put an endless loop of the early-1960s tune "The Martian Hop."

It's appropriate and fitting.

What I am doing is to set out in the re-created *slimshang* to follow the route (if not the incidents and feelings) of Oud's famous journey from Tharsis to Solis Lacus.

It's the most famous Martian travelogue we have (for many and varying reasons).

Oud was the first thinking commentator on the changes Mars was undergoing in his (long) lifetime. Others had noted the transformation, but not the underlying processes. And Oud's personal experiences added much to the classic stature of his tale.

So on this cold morning at Settlement #6 (vying, like many, for the AAS to officially rechristen it Lowell City), I shook hands with the three people who had come outside the temporary bubble dome to see me off.

We stood exchanging small talk for a few minutes, then Oud's words came to me: "A Being has to do what a Being has to do."

So I climbed into my high-tech *slimshang*, up-sailed, waved to the others (who were already heading back for the haven of air they could breathe), and set my course west, playing "The Martian Hop" as I jumped some scattered pinkish dunes.

Think of Oud as a Martian Windwagon Smith.

He set out from Tharsis (on the old volcanic shield) toward Solis Lacus (the site of some till-then-inexact place of cultural revelation), and recorded what would have been to other Martians a pleasant (as we understand it) few-days jaunt in the equivalent of a hot-rod windwagon (which most *slimshangs* were, and Oud's definitely was; I'm assuming that his approached mine in elegance, if not materials).

That Oud started in winter was unusual. The weather was colder and the winds less predictable then, given to frequent planet-girdling dust storms. Winter and spring trips were not unknown, but most were taken in mid–Martian summer, when temperatures sometimes rose to the low forties Fahrenheit.

This tradition was left over from an earlier Mars (along with cultural patterns and the development of the *slimshang*). No one thought to do it any other way.

The Martians were nothing if not a tradition-bound species. But there's a lot to be said for customs that get you through 10 or 15 million years (the jury is still out).

I'm sure, in the future, someone will read my retracing of Oud's journey and point out the know-it-allness of earlier humans jumping in with inexact knowledge and pronouncements of age off by factors of three or four, and will comment on them in footnotes.[1]

From Oud: "Weather fine (for the time of year). Not much debris, sands fairly smooth and sessile. Skirted two or three eroded gullies. Smooth running till dark. Saw one other being all day, walking, near an aboveground single habitation. Pulled *slimshang* over at dark and buttoned up for the night. Very comfortable."[2]

He should have seen the place today. I had to dodge erratic rocks the size of railroad freight cars, and the two or three eroded gulleys now look like the Channeled Scablands of the northwest United States.

Oud lived, we think, at the start of the Great Bombardment (see later), before the largest of the geologic upheavals, the rise of the shield volcanoes and the great asteroid impacts that released untold amounts of suddenly boiling permafrost and loosed water vapor and pyroclastic flows that changed the even-then-ever-changing face of Mars.

After the now-eroded features of my first day's route, I was slowing myself where necessary to cover exactly the same distances as Oud: Only once in the whole trip had Oud's *slimshang*, which must really have been something, made better time than mine through (in his day) worse terrain. Give or take a boulder the size of an Airstream trailer, the ground was a gradual slope off the Tharsis plateau.

I settled in for the night, calling in my position to Mars Central, watched the sunset (which comes fast in these parts), and saw one of the hurtling moons of Mars hurtle by. Then, like Oud, millennia before, I went to sleep.

Day 2:

OUD, ON HIS ORIGINAL ROUTE, COMMENTED THAT, IN FORMER days, *slimshangs* had made part of this day's journey by "otherwise"—

---

[1] Well put. Weeton's guess was fairly accurate, one of the few times early colonists and philologists were. Other places, he's less reliable.

[2] Elenkua N'Kuba, ed. *Weeton's Oud Narrative:* A facsimile reproduction. Elsevier, the Hague: 2231.

i.e., water. He dismissed how easy such an old journey must have been—on land, water for most of the day, then back to land.

Oud (and I) had to make our way around more dried channels. In Oud's time, some still contained surface ice, as opposed to the open-water lakes they must have been in Oud's ancestors' times. Now not even ice remains, sublimated into the air. Just old worn watercourses, which made today's trip a tough mother. I thought once I might have damaged a wheel (I have spares, but changing one out is not easy), but had only picked up a small, persistent rock.

Oud was one of the first to notice that the air was getting thinner. Others had seen the effects but had attributed it to other causes. The loss of water was one. *Slimshang* sails had once been small affairs: By Oud's time, they were twice as large—my reproduction is 7/10 sail and sometimes that's not enough.

It was also on this second day that Oud saw an asteroid hit in the distance.

From Oud: "A sudden plume of dust and steam on the horizon that rose a *cretop* (five miles) high. Much scattering of debris. Had to trim the *slimshang* close-to to avoid falling boulders and navigate carefully around many more. The cloud hung in the air till sundown, and probably after."

My present course shows some remnants of Oud's event and later ones, including a string of frosted craters off to my right. There are also a couple of shield craters or later volcanic (still active) cones that followed on that cataclysm.

The navigating was even dicier than Oud's had been.

Some idea of the upheavals of Oud's time may be gained by his referral (in an earlier narrative) to what is now Olympia Mons as "the new hill."

So on went Oud on his winter journey, unconcerned by small things like the sky falling and mountains building on the horizon line.

It's only an accident of sound that Oud's name is the same as the English one for a Turkish mandolin. (I believe there is an album called *The Kings of the Oud on Oud,* put out by Picwick Records, supposedly music inspired by Oud's journey, done by a bunch of studio musicians, rumored to have included Lou Reed and Glen Campbell, among others. I have never heard it: People who have said that it was "pretty uninspired by anything.")

The third day of both our journeys was fairly downhill, uneventful, and of no great consequence. Night was the same. Oud did not even mention it.

The fourth day, I had some trouble with the rigging of the *slimshang.* Oud had troubles of a differing kind.

His narrative is deceptive. After complaining about the low quality of the foodstuffs he could find for his breakfast (he had noticed the decline in traditional plant life from his ancestors' time earlier in the narrative), and speculating about his probably paltry lunch ("slim mossings" is the phrase he used), a few hours into the day comes the line, "If I didn't know better, and this wasn't winter season, I would think I was undergoing *grexagging.*"

Well. I wasn't undergoing *grexagging* (no human ever had), but I was having the devil's own time getting over a series of long gullies without my sail luffing. I resorted to the last ignominy of *slimshanging*: I got out and pushed.

Eventually, I gained height and wind simultaneously and made off at a fast clip, Solis Lacusward.

I had left Oud in his travels sure that he was not undergoing *grexagging.* After some more navigational and observational entries, his next sentence may take the reader by surprise.

"Bud has the tiller now. Since he knows almost everything I know, but is only just learning to use his pseudopodia, I let him learn by experience what a glorious thing a *slimshang* is, but also how ungainly it can become in seconds."

Bud? asks the reader. Bud? Who is this? Where did he come from?

Oud cannot resist his little joke:

"I watch him clumsily take us around boulders and over dunes. I see how his movements and coordination become smoother and more assured as time—and miles—pass. He reminds me of myself when younger."

Of course he did. Oud had undergone *grexagging* (meiosis). Bud was a younger Oud.

This is the only time in Martian literature that a narrator has *grexagged* in the course of an ongoing narrative. *Grexagging* usually took place in one's domicile, attended by nest-brothers, and was celebrated with ritual exchanges of foodstuffs, chattel, and good wishes. *Grexagging* usually occurred in the spring or summer season, foretold by mood swings, dietary changes, and agrophobia.

It had happened to Oud in the winter, with no presaging except the *slimshang* wanderlust. He must have attributed his body's stirrings to that, sublimating the others.

Scientist to the end, he described his changes: "I have less weight than in 393rd year. To think I *grexagged* at such an advanced age, with no forewarnings, and in the winter season, is as surprising to me as anyone.

"It is said that Flimo of the (Syrtis Major) nest had an off-bud at 419 years, but that it was unviable and was ritually eaten at the Festival of Foregiving, and the nest stayed away for the customary year before being allowed to attend the next All-Nest Convention.

"Bud looks viable to me—in the last few hours, his handling of the *slimshang* has grown as assured as that of someone who'd been doing it for a century or so.

"We run now at full jangle across the flat of the former sea-bottom that stretches toward (Solis Lacus). It does a Being good to watch his bud-descendant proud and confident at the tiller of his *slimshang*."

It's still debated (especially by us first wave of humans on Mars) what event it was that took place at the cultural shrine toward which Oud and Bud made their way.

Before Oud, the literature was conflicting and rather noninformative. (On Earth, when anthropologists can't find instant meaning in any cultural artifact, they say, "This obviously had deep religious significance.")

What had happened in the dim Martian past? we asked, before Oud's manuscript was unearthed. Was there some Fatima- or Lourdes-type event? Was it a recurring event and ritual, a Martian Eleusinian Mystery? Rather than either, it appeared to have been a singular event, so important that its effects lasted for several million years. Whatever it was, it must have been a doozy. No Being ever really talked about it before Oud. It seemed to be part of them, a piece of general knowledge, perhaps as known to Bud a few hours after his off-budding as to Oud after his 394 years.

So onward they went toward Solis Lacus; so onward I followed them (some three hundred thousand to four hundred thousand years later), me happy in the long-gone companions of the journey; Oud proud of his new offspring; Bud probably hooting from the sheer joy of being alive and at the tiller of a fine *slimshang,* on a dying planet that was losing its oxygen, its water, and its heat.

"As with all nest-fathers," says Oud, "I instructed Bud on how to more efficiently rid himself of his waste products on waking in the morning and how to use his haze-eyes to better see distant objects. He only took a few minutes to learn those skills that would last him a lifetime."

Now Oud the scientist takes over the narrative:

"I notice that for the past two days we have had only dry snow (carbon dioxide frost), with only a few patches of real snow here and there. Not like in our ancestors' time, when dry snow was the rarity."

———

His (and their, and my) next day of the trip would bring us to our goal—changed though it was since their time.

On old maps of Mars, Solis Lacus (The Lake of the Sun) was a bright circular feature in the midst of a darker area, thought at the time to be an irrigated, heavily vegetated patch, with the stark circularity of Solis Lacus in its midst.

We now know that the dark part was heavy volcanic dust and ash and the bright roundness a raised area swept by winds and kept clear.

In Oud's time, it was a long fold of the edge of the old bottom of a remnant sea, like prehistoric Lake Bonneville on Earth. As they rolled toward it, Oud said, "Ancestors described the wonder and majesty of (Old Bitter Sea) with its rolled margin of amaranth and turquoise gleaming in the sunset after a long day's *slimshanging*. Now it's an almost featureless rise of the landscape, hardly worth a second two-looks."

Oud reefed his sail as they slid out onto the brightness of the middle of Solis Lacus.

Bud said, "It is quiet here, Father."

"Indeed," said Oud, "for here is where it started."

"Were you born here, Father?"

Oud looked around.

"We were all born here," said Oud. He pointed to the raised lump in the cold distance. "That is where the Life-Rock fell from the sky. From where we, and all living things, come. In the ancestors' days, we returned each year for the Festival of Wow, to appreciate that, and to think and wonder on its happening. It must have been something, then, all the nests gathered, all hooting and racket, such music as they had."

"Are you sad, Father?" asked Bud.

"Sadness is for those who have personally lost something," said Oud. "How can I be sad? I have made a fine journey in a good *slimshang*, in the low season. I have arrived at the place of our First-Birth.

And I have a new bud-son who will live to see other wonders on this elder twilight world. How could I be sad?"

"Thank you for bringing me here," said Bud.

"No," said Oud, "thank you."

Weeton here again. We leave Bud and Oud in a sort of valetudinarian idyll (I like to think), staring into the setting sun with Solis Lacus around them, and Thyle I and II far away.

Meanwhile, I'm out here on this empty rise where the edge of a sea once rolled, trying to find what is dragging on my retro-*slimshang*. The sun is setting here, probably adding to my anthropomorphization of those two Martians now dead four hundred thousand years.

After exploring the Life-Rock for a day ("If you've seen one rock, you've seen them all"—Oud), his narrative ends two days into the return journey back to Tharsis.

Oud, as far as we can find so far, never wrote another word.

Bud, except for his appearance in Oud's narrative, is unknown to history or Martian literature.

I hope, so far as I'm able, that they lived satisfying, productive Martian lives.

We'll never know. While Mars and the Martians were dying, we were still looking up, grunting, out of the caves, at the pretty red dot in the sky.

JAMES S. A. COREY

James S. A. Corey is the pseudonym of two young writers working together, Daniel Abraham and Ty Franck. Their first novel as Corey, the wide-screen space opera *Leviathan Wakes*, the first in the Expanse series, was released in 2010 to wide acclaim, and was followed in 2012 with a new Expanse novel, *Caliban's War*. Coming up is another Expanse novel, *Abaddon's Gate*.

Daniel Abraham lives with his wife in Albuquerque, New Mexico, where he is director of technical support at a local Internet service provider. Starting off his career in short fiction, he made sales to *Asimov's Science Fiction*, *SCI FICTION*, *The Magazine of Fantasy & Science Fiction*, *Realms of Fantasy*, *The Infinite Matrix*, *Vanishing Acts*, *The Silver Web*, *Bones of the World*, *The Dark*, *Wild Cards*, and elsewhere, some of which appeared in his first collection, *Leviathan Wept and Other Stories*. Turning to novels, he made several sales in rapid succession, including the books of The Long Price Quartet, which consist of *A Shadow in Summer*, *A Betrayal in Winter*, *An Autumn War*, and *The Price of Spring*. At the moment, he's published the first two volumes in his new series, The Dagger and the Coin, which consists of *The Dragon's Path* and *The King's Blood*. He also wrote *Hunter's Run*, a collaborative novel with George R. R. Martin and Gardner Dozois, and, as M. L. N. Hanover, the four-volume paranormal romance series Black Sun's Daughter.

Ty Franck was born in Portland, Oregon, and has had nearly every job known to man, including a variety of fast-food jobs, rock-quarry grunt, newspaper reporter, radio advertising salesman, composite-materials fabricator, director of operations for a computer manufacturing firm, and part owner of an accounting-software consulting firm. He is currently the personal assistant to fellow writer George R. R. Martin, where he makes coffee, runs to the post office, and argues about what constitutes good writing. He mostly loses.

In the tense story that follows, they show us that "honor" can mean many different things to many different people—and to nonpeople too.

A Man Without Honor

BY JAMES S. A. COREY

For the exclusive eyes of George Louis, by the Grace of God
King of Great Britain, France, and Ireland

30 September 172–

Your Majesty, I was once an honorable man.

I do not wish at this late date to recount the circumstances
under which Governor Smith revoked my Letter of Marque, nor the
deceptions by which I was then forced to choose between my
loyalty to the crown or my honor as a gentleman. I made my
choices then, and I have accepted the consequences of them. For
the greater part of a decade, I have led my crew through Caribbean
waters, the forces of personal loyalty, despair, and rude vengeance
changing me as a caterpillar in its chrysalis into the debased, cruel,
and black-hearted man that I was accused of being long before it
was true. I have sunk a dozen ships. I have ransomed members of
your own family. I have taken what was not mine by right but by
necessity. I have no doubt that you have heard my name spoken in
tones of condemnation, and rightly so, for I have made that original
calumny true a hundred times over. Nor shall I pretend any deep
regret for this. My loyalty and care were rewarded with betrayal,
and though it be a defect of my soul, such a trust once broken with
me can never be mended.

I have likewise no doubt that on this, the occasion of Governor
Smith's death, some part of the credit or blame for his demise
might be attributed to me. I write to you now not to ask pardon for
that which I have done or defend myself against accusations of

which I am innocent. It is my sole hope that you shall read my
words and through them understand better the circumstances of
the governor's death and my own role in it. I only ask that as you
read this you bear in mind these two things: I swear before God
that, though he had earned my vengeance a thousand times over, it
was not my hand that slew the governor, and that I was once an
honorable man.

Picture, then, my ship, the *Dominic of Osma*, as she rode upon
the August waves. A hurricane had assaulted the coast three days
earlier, and water and air held the serenity that only comes after
such a storm or before it. The sun shone with a debilitating heat,
looking down upon our poor sinners' heads like the eye of an
unforgiving God or else His counterpart, and we rode upon a sea
whose blue echoed the sky. I recall feeling a profound peace as we
moved between these two matchless vastnesses. I had a hold
stocked with salt pork, freshwater, limes, and rum. I had a crew of
men whose loyalty and ability I had reason to trust. We might have
spent weeks upon the sea without sighting land or fellow vessel
before I felt the first pang of anxiety.

But that was not to be.

Quohog was the first man to sight the doomed ship, and his
barbaric yawp sounded down from the crow's nest. In his accent,
one of the oddest I have heard in the widely traveled Carib, the call
of *Ship ahoy!* sounded more *Zeeah loy* and his further report of
smoke as *Awch*. For those of us who had shipped with him, there
could be no doubt as to the meaning of his garble, but as to the
intent of it, I believe we all hesitated. Quohog had a well-earned
reputation as a man who enjoyed a good joke, and none of us,
myself included, would have been surprised if he had invented the
sighting for the sheer joy of looking down at the deck and watching
us scatter. So it was that I made no order to change our sail until I
could, with spyglass in hand, climb aloft and confirm the existence
of this improbable ship.

She was a merchant fluyt, that was clear, and she rode low in the water. Sails once proud hung ragged from her arms, and smoke rose from her. The gunports were open, and her half dozen cannon stood openmouthed and unmanned. She flew the tattered flag of Denmark, and her rail and sides were splintered and burned. In retrospect, I believe it was the burning that led me astray, for I had seen the leavings of many battles at sea, and I had never seen scorching of that kind from a weapon of man. I assumed instead that I was looking upon a lightning-struck ship that had through ill chance or malice been caught in the open sea during the tempest just passed. Such easy prizes were rare but not unheard of, and with pleasure at our good fortune, I called the man at the wheel to turn us in pursuit.

I can recall still the slow movement of the derelict from a pinpoint on the horizon to a mass of black no larger than a coin held at arm's length. Her masts took shape even without the aid of a glass, and then as if between one breath and the next we were upon her. Close, the extent of the damage she had suffered became clear. The black char along her sides had reduced her higher planks to coal, and rough holes punctured her flesh. I had no doubt that she rode low not from the weight of her cargo but because she was taking on water. The smoke that rose from her was the pale white of great heat, and as we came alongside, my only fear was that the fire might reach whatever magazine the merchant possessed and detonate her powder while we were near enough to be harmed. The name on her counter was *Vargud van Haarlem*. I prided myself on knowing the waters where I plied my trade, and I had never heard of her. That alone should have been warning, but I was rash and, worse, curious. I ordered her boarded, gave command to my first mate Mister Kopler, and crossed to her ruined deck myself.

Upon my arrival, the first thing to command my attention were the bodies of the dead. Many were sailors in the rough canvas as common to ships of the line as to merchants or pirates, but several wore the uniforms of soldiers of the colonial guard. And among them were strange, jointed objects like nothing so much as the legs of massive crabs as thick as a strong man's thigh and as long as my own body. I instructed my men to step lightly and be ready to flee back to the *Dominic,* but I hardly needed to bother. I say without shame that there was something eerie about the *Vargud,* and I walked her decks mindful of tales of the Flying Dutchman and of plague ships that ride the ocean currents long after the crews have died. Her quarterdeck burned with a forgelike heat, but the pale flames remained oddly fixed. The sails were not of canvas, but an odd mineral weave that the heat would not consume. At the helm, the burned remains of a man stood, hands fused to the wheel. As I paused there trying to imagine what unholy conflagration could leave such damage behind it, the voice of my third mate, Mister Darrow, called out to me.

Mister Darrow was a New Englander, and though some may be his equal in seamanship, there has never been born into this world a man more laconic. To hear the alarm in his voice chilled me to the bone. I recall his precise words. *Captain Lawton, you're needed in the hold.* Seeing them written here, they seem prosaic, but I assure Your Majesty that at the time they seemed a cry from Hell. I drew my pistols and ducked belowdecks, prepared, so I believed, to find anything.

I was mistaken.

To those accustomed to the hold of a ship of the line, the belly of a fluyt is an improbable thing. They are large and robust, fit to fill with crates enough to make the journey between old world and new yield a profit. In the vast interior darkness of this ship, I found only a half dozen of my own men and two things more: a pallet stacked as high as my waist with gold in the shapes and designs I had come to know as Incan, and a woman standing before it, sword in one hand, pistol in the other, and soaked by her own blood.

Looking back upon the moment, there cannot have been so much light as I remember, but I swear to you I saw her in that dimness as clear as in full day. She stood half a head taller even than myself, and I am not a small man. Her skin was the color and smoothness of chocolate and milk, her hair only half a shade darker. She wore a man's trousers and a brocade jacket any gentleman of court would have been proud of, though it was cut to her figure. Her eyes were the gold of a lion's pelt, and the lion's fierceness also set the angle of her jaw.

I saw at once that she was grievously injured, but she blocked the path to the treasure with her body and would let no man pass. Indeed, as I stepped in, she shifted the barrel of her pistol neatly to my forehead, and I had no doubt that the slightest movement of her finger would end my life. Mister Darrow knelt on the deck, a junior crewman called Carter lying at his feet, hand to his shoulder.

"What's this, then?" I asked.

"Mine," the woman said. "What you see here is mine, and you will not have it without slaughtering me as you have my people."

"I've slaughtered no one, miss," I said, amending myself with, "or at least no one here. I am Captain Alexander Lawton."

"Lawton?" she said, and I thought a flicker of recognition touched her expression. "The same who stood against Governor Smith?"

"And lost," I said, making a joke of it. "I am the same."

"Then you are the answer to my prayer," she said. "You must return me to my ship."

Darrow cast a glance toward me, and I shared his thought. Her wounds had no doubt rendered her subject to delusion, for we stood within her ship even as she asked to be returned to it.

"Put down your weapons, and I will do what I can," I said. Her pistol did not waver.

"Give me your word of honor."

Your Majesty, I find myself hard-pressed to describe the emotions that arose in me with those words. She stood outnumbered and outgunned, and she did not beg. Her words were not a request, but a demand. For years, my word of honor had been hardly worth the breath it took to speak it, and yet she insisted upon it as if it were a thing of value.

"I cannot offer what I do not have," I said. "But I promise you will come to no harm."

Her expression grew serious. She lowered her pistol, and as if continuing the same motion, crumpled to the deck. It was all that I could do to kneel in time to break her fall.

"Carter's hurt," Mister Darrow said. "Tried to part the miss there from her gold."

"Seemed the right thing," young Carter said.

"Will you live?" I asked, lifting the unconscious woman up.

"Will or won't, sir," Carter said. "Either way, crossing her's a mistake I'll not make twice."

I left Mister Darrow in possession of the burning ship and transported the woman of whose name I was still ignorant to the *Dominic* and Doctor Koch. Your Majesty is perhaps aware of Doctor Koch's somewhat unsavory reputation, and I cannot claim that it is undeserved, for we were unsavory men, but when I appeared at his cabin with an unfamiliar and unconscious woman in my arms, I can truthfully report that his oath as a man of healing lent him an expression of concern better fitted to a mother dog nuzzling her injured pup. He bade me leave her with him to have her hurts attended, and swore that he would call for me as soon as she came to herself. It was not a promise that he kept, but given the circumstances, I cannot hold the fault against him.

I returned to the deck in time to hear Darrow's dry voice agreeing that the gold the *Vargud* had carried was a fair load. In the sunlight, the gold shone with a richness and beauty that I had never seen before, as if the metal were alive and aware. I have seen my share of treasures, but I sensed in that moment that the riches before me were of a different order than any I had known.

I gathered my breath to order it all taken below, when the cry *Zeeah loy* again interrupted the proceedings. I took the speaking trumpet and called up to Quohog. The first part of his reply—*Zeeah een, Catin. Ghana.*—was perfectly comprehensible to one who had shipped with him. A ship of the line, and worse, one that bore the personal flag that my old nemesis Governor Smith affected. The second part, however—*Eeah mantu!*—escaped me at the time. I was later to understand that my brave lookout had meant *He has monsters*. At once, my crew and I leapt to action. The planks laid between the *Dominic* and the *Vargud* were pulled back, the lines between us cut, and we hoisted sail.

I must presume that Your Majesty has not had occasion to spend some years aboard ship with the same crew. Allow me, then, to report that there is a rapport that grows between men in long association at sea, an unspoken comprehension that outstrips the mere anticipation of orders to a point where they become almost unnecessary. Please do not think I am boasting when I say that my crew worked as a single creature with a hundred hands and a single mind between us, for in this particular, as in everything I set down here, my sole ambition is to apprise you of the facts. When I say then that it was not five minutes of the clock before we were set free of the *Vargud* and under way, I am being generous. The *Dominic* claimed a shallow draft, a proud mast, and Mister Kopler's expert hand at the wheel. It was a combination that had seen us safely through a dozen pursuits. And yet, when I looked back across that wide sea, the governor's ship was closing fast. The wind was not high, and I had great faith that whatever fortunate current the governor had happened upon would soon fail him, and we would make good our escape.

I was mistaken.

Over the following hour, it became clear that the governor's ship was not only keeping pace with us, but gaining. Through my spyglass, I saw her prow cutting through the water as though driven by some invisible force. I also saw the unmistakable uniforms of the colonial guard upon her deck. There was something else, though, which I thought at first I only imagined. Upon the deck, towering over the soldiers, a massive statue stood reminiscent of nothing so much as a grotesque spider, and yet it was no spider. When I spied another such in the rigging, this one moving with the swift and sure motions of a thing alive, I recalled the objects on the *Vargud* that I had taken for crab's legs. Improbable as it seemed, this was no statue, but a living thing, a beast as terrible as if ripped from the pages of Revelation. And further, one of these beasts had met its end there before the doomed ship had managed to escape its pursuers, and now two more, the colonial guard, and Governor Smith himself were racing toward me to finish the job. They carried more cannon than we did. They had many soldiers with muskets. Governor Smith had, it appeared, allied himself with the forces of Hell. There was aboard the *Dominic* not a word of panic, no weeping or prayer, but only the concentration that fear can bring, for we had no doubt that if we were caught, we would perish.

So much did the governor's ship command my attention that I did not see or hear it when our guest regained the deck. I only caught a scent of blood and magnolia, took my spyglass from my eye, and she was beside me. Doctor Koch had bound her wounds in rag and gauze and strapped her left arm against her ribs, but she stood as sure as a woman uninjured. When she spoke, her voice was crisp.

"Where are we?"

I gave her our location in rough terms, and she insisted on seeing the charts. I watched her golden gaze flicker over my maps of the Carib Sea. She placed a single dusky finger on a place not far from our position.

"Here," she said. "Take us here."

"If we turn, they will intercept us."

"If we continue without turning, they will overtake us. One will not be better than the other."

"Is that where you were fleeing to the first time you were caught?" I asked.

"It is," she said. "And it is our only hope now."

I hesitated, I admit. Only a few hours earlier, I had seen this same woman ask to be returned to the ship on which she stood. I had carried her exhausted form in my arms. I had no cause to believe her in her right mind or to trust her judgment if she was. She sensed my reluctance and turned her eyes to me. In the dimness of the hold, when she had been half-mad with pain and fear, she had been a handsome woman. In the light of the Caribbean sun, she was unmatched. A joyful recklessness took me, and I smiled as fully and honestly as I had in years.

"Mister Kopler," I called. "Hard to starboard!"

The *Dominic* groaned under the sudden change, her flanks and spars bent by the weight of the sea and the power of the air. The governor's ship changed course as well, bringing her closer and closer to us. I could read the name on her side now. The *Aphrodite* bore down upon us so near I saw the puffs of smoke and heard the reports of rifles as the soldiers on her deck took aim on us, hoping for a lucky shot. The great spiderlike beasts were chittering and crawling along her yardarms and masts. Though she was not yet at broadsides to us, I saw her gunports beginning to open. The moment was very nearly upon us when flight would no longer be an option, and the battle would be joined.

Beside me, the woman's attention was fixed not upon the doom bearing down upon us but at the clear waters on which we rode. Your Majesty will not, I think, have made the journey to the Caribbean. But as a man who has known many seas, let me assure you that no European sea, not even that nursery of civilization, the Mediterranean, can compare with the glasslike clarity the Caribbean can on occasion achieve. If one can train one's eyes to see past the reflected sky, it is as though we rode upon empty air. I looked down with her at the mottled green of the ocean floor, nearer here than I had expected it to be, when, without warning, she let out a whoop of the purest joy. Far below us, that which I had taken for the ocean's bottom moved, turning slowly up toward us. The sea boiled, and the dismayed cries of the *Aphrodite* carried across the waves. Four great, arching walls rose up from the water, reaching, it seemed nearly to the sky. Then, like Poseidon closing his fist around us, the arching walls met and blotted out the sun.

A roaring sound filled the world louder than anything I had ever heard, and I felt a sensation of terrible weight, as though divine hands were pressing down upon every atom of my being. Around me in the sudden gloom, I saw my men pressed slowly to the deck, and heard the protests of the *Dominic* as the wood all around groaned. I feared to see the ocean lapping at the rail, but the weight, whatever it was, appeared not to affect our buoyancy.

The woman slipped to the deck as well, borne down by the same terrible heaviness. Her face was an image of triumph, and it was the last thing I saw before darkness took me.

There is a gulf between worlds, Majesty, greater than any ocean. Its emptiness is only relieved by an unsetting sun that burns in the blackness and an unimaginable profusion of stars. Those ships that sail that upper abyss are greater than any leviathan of the lower waters that I once knew. How can I adequately describe the glory of the vessel into which I woke? How can I tell you of the grace of her lines, the power that permeated her? Imagine stepping into the vast nave of St. Paul's Cathedral, where instead of stone, every arch is fashioned of living crystal that glows with light and power the improbable blue of a butterfly's wing. Imagine the poor *Dominic of Osma,* which had housed myself and my men these many years, lying on her side like a child's toy abandoned beside a stream while outside the vast window, the stars shine steady and unblinking as you have never seen through Earth's fickle air.

And the enemy. As beautiful as the doomed *Serkeriah* was, her pursuers were her echo in grotesquerie. Inhuman and insectlike, they swarmed through the void, the thousand filthy talons of a single demonic hand. Their carapaces were lit from within by a baleful light that spoke of brimstone and sulfur. Serrated claws reached out from each of these unclean bodies in a design that promised that to be touched by one was to be not merely cut, but infected. And it was on one of these, Your Majesty, that the Right Honorable Governor Smith rode with his diabolical masters.

But I precede myself, for I knew none of this in my uncanny sleep. Indeed, I knew nothing until an unfamiliar voice reached me and called me to myself.

"Captain," the strange voice said. "Please, Captain. Wake up!"

There is, as I am sure Your Majesty knows, no greater impetus that could call a man back from his own unconscious depths than the fear that those entrusted to his care and command might be in need. I roused myself only with a great effort of will, for my awareness had entirely left me until then. But when I managed to pry open my resisting eyelids, two surprises waited. The first was the man who spoke the words. Kneeling, he was still as tall as I might have stood. His hunched body was covered in a soft, tawny pelt, and his countenance, while expressive of distress and an almost unimaginable kindness, nevertheless seemed most like that of some serene, gentle, and unaccountably furry toad.

The second surprise was that his words were not directed to me.

"What is our situation, La'an?" the woman asked. It would be a mistake to call her voice weak. Rather, it was the voice of a strong person compromised by sleep or illness.

"The alloy you brought us has been recovered, Captain," the toad-man said, "but the Ikkean fleet is in pursuit. And the crew . . . ?"

"The crew is gone," the woman said, regaining her feet. "We were attacked on the sea, and I alone survived. Only blind chance and these men preserved me."

The toad-man made a distressed chirping deep in his throat, looking around at the motley lot of us. And ragged we were, Majesty, even for such a normally tattered bunch. Young Carter lay splayed out upon the crystalline deck, and Quohog beside him, like two men asleep. Mister Kopler had risen to his knees, his eyes wide as saucers as he took in the great structure that surrounded us. Doctor Koch, his head down, scuttled among the fallen men, his eyes blind to all wonders in his haste to care for the men. And I, I confess, sat in awe, struck dumb by the marvelous and terrible fate that had befallen us. When the woman rose to her feet, I found my own, more from a vestigial sense of propriety than from the conscious exercise of will. Only Mister Darrow seemed unaffected by our otherworldly surroundings. He, with the calmness of an attorney before the judge, tugged his forelock to the woman.

"My pardons," he said. "This alloy you were speaking of. That wouldn't be the Incan gold, would it?"

The woman and toad-man both turned, he startled and she amused.

"You are correct," she said. "It is not true gold, but the rare alloy formed in the volcanic crust of some worlds."

"See now," Mister Darrow said, turning to young Carter, who had only just regained consciousness. "I told you how it was too light. Real gold's got heft to it."

"You're very clever, sir," Carter said. "So. Are we dead, do you think?"

"Not yet," the woman who captained that strange vessel said. "But we shall be soon. Uncrewed, the *Serkeriah* cannot outrun my enemy."

"Madam," I said, "I fear I have underestimated both you and the severity of your plight. My men and I know nothing of how to man a vessel such as yours, but we have many years at sea together, and that unity of purpose is a power not to be discounted."

Her eyes met mine, and I felt her uncertainty of me almost as a physical sensation.

"You would have me give the operation of my ship to you?"

"Captain," the toad-man said, "what alternative is there?"

Imagine, Majesty, that our places had been reversed. That I had been aboard the *Dominic of Osma* but deprived of my most valued crewmen. Can I say I would not have balked at the prospect of giving gentle La'an the helm, even though we were trapped between reef waters and enemy cannon? I cannot. Control of a ship is a thing of terrible intimacy, and to deliver it into an unknown hand is a leap of faith among the faithless. Even as we both knew, she and I, that this marriage must be made, I saw the hesitance in her eyes.

"La'an," she said. "See these men to their stations and give them what assistance and guidance we can. Captain Lawton. If you will accompany me to the command node."

"A hostage to my men's good conduct?"

"If you choose to see it that way," she said. And, Your Majesty, I went.

As we passed through the vast interior of the *Serkeriah,* Carina Meer—for this proved to be the captain's name—did her best to apprise me of our situation, and I will do my best to summarize here what she said to me. That body that we call Mars was once home to a vast and flourishing civilization. Great cities of living crystal filled the mountains and planes, connected by a network of canals filled with sweet water. The seven races lived together there in harmony and conflict, peace and war, much in the fashion of the nations of our own world. She told me of being a child and looking up at the vast night sky to see the brightness that, to her, was our own world, and I found myself powerfully moved by the image. Those cities now lie in shards, the canals empty and dry. The Ikkean race, for reasons known only in their own insectile councils, turned en masse upon the other six races. The soft-shelled Manae, wise and gentle Sorid (of whom La'an was the first of my acquaintance), radiant Imesqu, vast and slow Norian, mechanical Achreon, and our own cousin Humanity were driven under the surface of the planet, to live in the great caverns where the Ikkeans feared to follow. The six conquered races lived in darkness and despair until Carina's brother, Hermeton, happened in his alchemical investigations upon a rare alloy capable of bring-ing enormous power. His new solar engines, it was hoped, might tame the Ikkean threat, should the alloy be found in sufficient quantity.

To this end, the conquered races had sent their agent to the rich profundity that is Earth, to gather from the violence of our planet's core the means of their liberty. Great was their fear of discovery, for while their power is vast, their position with the Ikkean threat is tenuous. An alliance between the Ikkean race and the humans of Earth would certainly have spelled doom to the six races. And their fears, as you will see, were not unjustified.

But let me also say this: As I walked the iridescent halls of the *Serkeriah*, I felt the power of the great ship. With one such as her— only one, Majesty—I should have made myself the Emperor of all Europe. No navy could have stood against me. No army could bring me to earth. No city, however mighty, would not quail in my shadow. Imagine then the power of the enemy that had brought her makers low, and thank merciful God that Ikkean ambition has not yet extended to England. But again, I run ahead of myself.

My crew worked manfully at their new posts. The experience of the high seas had given every man an instinctive understanding of motion and mechanics that no scholarship can best, and La'an and the few remaining of Carina Meer's crew did their all to train my men even as we fled through the void, our very lives at issue. I will not recount in detail the discomfort we all suffered as hours passed to days and days to weeks. The Ikkean ships did all that they could to outmaneuver us, to outrace us, to trick us into turning from our path. We slept when we could, worked as we had to, and suffered exhaustion and fear with the good humor and camaraderie I had known. As the red planet grew nearer, our pursuers became more desperate. For a time, I believed we might even achieve our goal. But our enemy had numbers and experience. They wore us down as a man might grind the proudest stone to dust.

And even at the end, surrounded as we were by the diabolical ships of the enemy, they knew to fear us. An animal cornered is at its most dangerous. So it was that I saw again Governor Smith.

Picture me if you will, Majesty, standing the wide bridge of the *Serkeriah*. Captain Carina Meer stood frowning down at the wide pool in which our vessel and our enemy's were charted in light as if by angelic hands. The smell of burning flesh still hung in the air, mute witness to our previous engagements. Gentle La'an and Mister Kopler stood their stations beside me, each coordinating one-half of the great organism that our combined crews had become. And then we were joined. Through what magic I cannot say, but the wide pane of crystal before me shifted and changed, and like an enchanted mirror from fairy tales, the glass reflected not my own visage, but Governor Smith's. The years had treated him gently. His mouse-brown hair was only touched by gray at the temple, his skin taut with the fat of rich feasts. His smile was the amiable one I had known once and allowed myself to count, however mistakenly, among my friends.

"Captain Lawton," the governor said, "I was hoping to find you home."

"Governor," I replied.

"Your captor's cause is lost. The criminal Carina Meer will be taken into custody by my allies, and her crimes will be answered. The only question remaining is how. I see that our guesses were correct. You and your men have been pressed into Captain Meer's service."

"I am no slaver," Carina Meer said. "It is the Ikkeans who take slaves and force others to their will."

"Be that as it may," the governor went on, "I have a proposition, Captain Lawton. My allies would prefer a clean transfer of the prisoner and her stolen goods. The ship itself is of no interest to them. If you and your men would be so good as to secure the person of Carina Meer and open your locks to our envoys, the *Serkeriah* will be yours by right of salvage."

"I cannot believe you are sincere," I said.

"On the contrary," the governor said. "I give you my word of honor, and as we both know, I never break my word."

It was true, Majesty. However devilishly he might construct his promises, however Mephistophelian his skills in breaking the spirit of a bargain, Governor Smith's word of honor had not been sullied, not even in the act of destroying mine. If he promised me the great ship that traveled between worlds in exchange for Carina Meer and her alloy, then the ship would be mine. I had no doubt.

Shall I say, then, that I hesitated? It is, after all, the action expected of a man of my repute. Shall I say that given the prospect of defeat on one hand and freedom and limitless power on the other, that my base nature swayed me? It did not. My reply to the governor was immediate, crude, heartfelt, and medically improbable.

The Ikkean boarding assault began at once.

To board a vessel in the abyss between the worlds is no easy thing. The attacking craft flew toward us, their infernal engines burning at the full. Cruel mouths pierced the ship's skin and spat out their warriors into the halls and domes of the *Serkeriah*. A great many, I believe, were lost in that first hour as my men and hers cut down the invaders even as they spilled forth. They were massive creatures, Majesty. But their vast arachnid bulk belied their terrible speed. From devices carried on the ends of their legs, they produced rays of purified light that could burn a man down in a few moments. And beside these devils from the pit were the colonial guard, in duty servants to the crown, but in truth the creatures of Governor Smith.

We fought them in the corridors and halls, the radium stores and the ship's vast eight-chambered heart. Doctor Koch drove them briefly back to their ships with a noxious gas he fashioned with the Manae engineer Octus Octathan. And Quohog, young Carter, and Mister Darrow contrived to salvage a cannon from the ruins of the *Dominic of Osma* that blew a dozen Ikkeans into yellow sludge and cracked bits of carapace. It is with great pride that I report my men, ruffians and blackguards all, fought like heroes of old. Their guns fired without pause, and their swords wove a flashing net of steel through which even the Ikkean horrors feared to pass. But such vigorous defense also left us terrible losses, and again and again we fell back. Near the end, I stood with Captain Meer, my own cutlass in one hand and a contrivance of glass and silver that burned with emerald light in the other, holding back the enemy. To this day, I can feel her back against my own as we stood our ground. For one moment, the stench of smoke and death parted and the scent of magnolia came to my nostrils. I hope when my time comes to die that will be the last memory my failing mind recalls.

Of course, we were overwhelmed. The cost to the enemy, I credit myself and my crew, was great, but at last the sheer force of numbers swamped us all. I was struck to the ground, then bound ankle and wrist, and roughly hauled to a prison chamber with the rest. There we lay, almost a hundred of our mixed crew. A quarter, perhaps, of my own men had perished, and their bodies were stacked against one wall with the bodies of Carina's people. These were men whose dreams I had come to know, whose fates had been bound to my own. Many of them were not good men, not kind or merciful or gentle, but they were mine and they were lost. Captain Meer lay bound beside me. A wide bruise covered her exposed shoulder and her lip had been cut by an enemy blow. I called out to Mister Kopler and Mister Darrow and was reassured to hear their voices.

"You should have accepted his offer," Carina Meer said.

Young Carter's voice said, *What offer was that?* but I ignored him.

"When you surrendered to me aboard the *Vargud,* I promised that you would come to no harm," I said. "I am fairly certain that Governor Smith would not have respected that. I had no choice."

She turned to me as best she could. Her eloquent smile carried sorrow and amusement, admiration and despair.

"And if you had made no such promise?" she asked. "If your somewhat tarnished sense of honor had not restrained you, would you then have betrayed me?"

I was silent for a time. I understood then only by my vague animal unease the dexterity with which the astonishing woman could unmake me as I knew myself and resurrect a different man in my place. Young Carter muttered: *Because if there was an offer, it might have been nice to hear what the terms were,* before Doctor Koch hushed him. I heaved a great sigh.

"I would not have," I confessed. "Though it would have saved my men their lives and me my own, I would not give anyone into the power of Governor Smith and his new allies."

"Consider, then, that though you have lost your honor, something must still constrain you," she said. "Honor is a burden that may be shifted or forgone. From goodness, I think, there is no escape."

What can I say, Majesty? I had that day suffered blows to my body and my soul. I had faced the charging mandibles of vast spider-beasts and said silent farewell to men as near to me as family. How strange, then, that the thing to destroy Alexander Lawton, Scourge of the Caribbean Sea, should be delivered so gently, so kindly. I lay in our crowded prison, my eyes to heaven, and confronted for the first time the proposition that the loss of my honor might not also be the loss of my soul. For so many years as a youth, I strove to protect and celebrate my honor, that in the end it became my weakness. My love for my good name was the vulnerability that Governor Smith had used to shatter me. My years upon the seas, my flaunting of law and decency, all of it became a pettiness. Would you expect the thought to bring joy? That the light of goodness might spill over me like some abstract and spiritual dawn? It did not. On the contrary, it stung. Like Achilles, I had gone to my tent to sulk, and with a gentle rebuke, Carina Meer suggested that the choice had been beneath me.

"Madam," I said, "your optimism is misplaced."

In my worst moments, Majesty, I can still see the surprise and the hurt in Carina Meer's expression at my gruffness. I think she might have gone on, pressed me to better explain myself, but I rolled my back to her and kept my own counsel instead. For a time I lay thus, pouting for my wounded masculine pride and regretting bitterly that I had ever come across the *Vargud van Haarlem*. Nor would I report this to you now had not this conversation had some bearing on the issue that has prompted me to deliver this account to you. Indeed, even so, I was sorely tempted to omit it. Whatever sins may remain marked against my soul, I can at least claim that a lack of candor is not among them.

"Captain Lawton, sir?" Mister Kopler said, his voice pulling me back to myself. I was astonished to find there were tears in my eyes. I coughed and wiped them away as best I could against my shoulder.

"Mister Kopler," I said. "You've freed your hands, then?"

"Yes, sir."

"You win this time," Mister Darrow said, grudgingly. "I got a cramp in one thumb, or I'd have beat him, sir."

"Let us hope there will be no call for a rematch in our immediate future," I said. "For now, make haste. We have a ship to recapture."

Boarding and taking a ship requires a very different logic than reclaiming one from within its own brig. In the first instance, all sides are armed, and all know the battle has begun. In the second, customarily speaking, only one side has the advantage of weapons and the other the knowledge that the struggle exists. Of the two, I much prefer the direct battle, not because I disdain stealth, but because weaponry is robust and surprise fragile. Once an alarm is raised, the usual balance is restored, and rarely to the benefit of the escaped prisoners. The first guards to come to us—an Ikkean spider-beast and two grenadiers in the governor's service—we overcame quickly and without incident, and with their weapons, we stole forth into the ship that had been our own. The brig in which we had been imprisoned lay far to the stern, a good distance from the bridge, but not from either the hold where the precious Incan alloy was stowed or from the vast engines that acted as mast, sail, and rudder to the *Serkeriah*. Time was short, and Captain Carina Meer took one force to the hold while I took the other to capture the engines. It might have seemed natural that each of us should take their own, but in practice, both groups were made from the crew of the *Dominic of Osma* and the *Serkeriah* in nearly equal proportion.

I wish I could say that the assault upon the engines went without fault, but the great, throbbing mechanisms—a dozen in number and each larger than a ship of the line—were encompassed by passages and cul-de-sacs so convoluted and complex that there could be no clean fight. Several times, I found myself cut off from my men, in desperate melee with the black grublike beings larger than a man that the Ikkeans used as slaves on their ships. I did not know for several months the origin of those repulsive half insects, and now that I have learned it, I wish I had not. Somewhere in the fury of battle, an alarm was raised, and our advantage evaporated.

When Carina Meer arrived with the alloy on a floating cart, the Ikkean soldiers were already on their way. The combined intelligence of Doctor Koch and Octus Octathan devised a temporary barricade by restricting the passageways leading to the engines down to the diameter of a coin, but by blocking the means of ingress, they had also stoppered our hope of escape. I saw no salvation, but I kept all despair from my demeanor. I walked the defenses, giving heart and cheer where I could. What few weapons we had reclaimed we trained upon the narrowed halls, and through the thin passages we heard the voices of men, the chittering of great spiders, and at last the slow, deep gnawing of a new passage being ground out.

When I returned to deliver the foul news to Carina Meer, she stood at another of the floating charts of light such as I had seen her use on the bridge. Only here, instead of the bright mark of the *Serkeriah* surrounded by the ruddy glow of the Ikkeans, the ship stood alone but spiked through with the enemy until she looked like nothing so much as the back of a cat covered in burrs. And curving below, the vast convex surface of Mars itself.

"We are trapped, and the enemy coming," I said.

"The Ikkean ships have all attached to the *Serkeriah*," she said.

"I am sorry to hear it," I said.

"It may yet work to our advantage," she replied, then reached into the play of light and volume to indicate a feature on the face of the world I had not noticed. It seemed hardly larger than a child's thumbnail, but it was gray amid the redness of the world. "This is the Palace of the Underworld, the fortress and gateway to the caves in which my people survive. This is where my brother waits now, and where I must deliver the alloy if there is to be any hope of freedom for my people."

"Carina," I said, for by now I had no hesitation in using her Christian name, "unless we are to carve a window in the flesh of the ship and drop it from here, I cannot see how this can be done."

I have never understood, not then and not now, how a woman's expression can be at once so very serene and utterly reckless.

"Directly," she said.

Mourn, Your Majesty, for the doomed *Serkeriah*. There was no nobler ship on sea or in sky than her, and we, her displaced and desperate crew, spiked her rudder. By the time the Ikkeans understood our dreadful intent, it was too late. The evil, parasitic ships tried to disengage, but the speed and violence of our descent confounded them. What few made the attempt were shattered in our fiery wake. The others clung tight and were smashed against the planet's rocky skin even as we reversed the shrieking engines and slowed from a fatal speed to one merely apocalyptic.

The *Serkeriah* died around us, the great crystalline plates shearing away as she bounced. One of the enormous engines came loose from its moorings and streaked off ahead of us before turning up toward the purple sky and detonating. The wind that beat against me smelled of overheated iron and tasted of blood. When the great ship lifted her head one last time toward the doubled moon, then came to rest, spent, destroyed, and noble as a bull defeated in the Spanish ring, Carina Meer's hand was in my own. Somewhere in the indigo shards and twisted metal, the wooden bones of the *Dominic of Osma* also lay. To the best of my knowledge, they remain there still, our two ships, nestled together in sacrifice and death like the knuckles of a husband and wife strewn in the same grave, and around them the bodies of their fallen enemies.

Unsteady after the wreck, I clambered out to the wide, red dunes of the planet. We had fallen not far from one of the great ruined cities. Its spires and towers reached toward the sky, lightning still playing about their outstretched tips. A great canal, wider than any river save the God-like Amazon, curved to the south, the waters low against its walls, black and sluggish. Carina Meer came to my side, her arm on my shoulder.

"One day," she said, "I will make all of this bloom. I swear it."

It was frantic work, preparing this last leg of our journey. Half of our remaining crew manned improvised barricades, keeping the Ikkean survivors of the wreck at bay with Martian ray pistols and their own good steel blades. The other half gathered the Incan alloy that had been scattered by the wreck and rigged the now crippled floating cart on which it had rested. One corner of the failing platform dragged a trail in the dust when they moved it. Doctor Koch tended to the wounded and La'an said words over the fallen. As the sun rose among the vast ruins of the Martian city, we affixed ropes to the listing cart, and, with the straining muscles of our bodies, we began to haul our cargo toward the horizon. How strange it felt to breathe air no man of Earth had ever breathed, to feel the dreamlike lightness of my flesh and dig my feet into the ruddy soil of another world. We had traveled farther than any subject of the empire had ever gone, farther even than the great general of Macedon whose name I bear could have dreamed, across the starry void, driven by powers too vast to contemplate. And still the fate of our mission rested on the effort of strong English backs and the willingness of men as unalike as a baboon from a bumblebee to make common cause. Our goal, the Palace of the Underworld, loomed in the distance, gray and massive and wreathed by ghostly flames of St. Elmo's fire.

There are no words to describe the desperation of those hours. The rope bit into my hands and the flesh of my shoulder as I pulled along with my men. Even the callused palms of a life at sea were unequal to the terrible task we performed. My body trembled with effort, my very ligaments creaking like the timbers of a ship. With every hour, new assaults were made upon us, and the great spiders moved with an alacrity on this, their native soil, that made them seem even more nightmarish and monstrous. Again and again, our mixed crew threw them back, blades dripping with yellowish ichor, our own wounds leaving matching trails across the sand. Until my dying breath, I will recall with pride the common will of my crew as we forged across the bloodied dunes.

The Palace of the Underworld had grown to almost twice its height when the enemy's flying scouts appeared.

Imagine if you will, Your Grace, the vast Martian sky, as purple as a lilac, with the same sun that shines on Westminster and London here taking on a wholly foreign aspect, with wide tendrils of rainbow snaking from its centrally glowing orb. See, if you will, the vast ruins that had once been the pride of seven races with their crystal hearts laid bare by storms and war; the massive, dying river, slow as an old man's blood; the bleeding and desperate crew hauling the hope of survival on a half-shattered cart that struggled and failed to rise from the ground like a wounded moth. The air was thin and held the scent of metal and spent gunpowder. The heat of the sun oppressed as powerfully as a tropical noontime. Now hear the familiar cry of Quohog—*awch loy*—smoke ahoy. Picture a storm of dragonflies, each as large as a man's arm. They rose in the east, thick as the billows of a vast conflagration, and spread out across the sky. I heard Carina Meer's cry when she caught sight of them and saw the blood drain from her tawny face.

"We must hurry," she said. "The central hive has discovered us. If we are not safely belowground when their fighting force arrives, there will be no hope."

"Must say," Mister Darrow said between gasping breaths. "I'm beginning to dislike these buggers."

Young Carter chuckled. "See what you did there? Bugs. Buggers. A bit funny, that."

"I do what I can in the service of levity," Mister Darrow intoned solemnly, and we drove our shoulders into the lines as if to break our backs. Time became a lost thing; only the strain, the agony, and the distant Palace of the Underworld remained in our collective and narrowed consciousness.

As we neared our object, the landscape shifted. The desert sands gave way to a low and purplish scrub brush, and small, insectlike lizards scuttled fearlessly about our feet. The vast and buzzing swarm of enemy scouts blotted the sun, and we labored in shadow. The landscape divided itself between labyrinths of cut-stone gullies and sand-swept plains. We knew not how soon the enemy forces might arrive, but only pressed forward with failing strength. What had once seemed wealth enough to please a king was a burden heavier than hope. The only advantage that I, in my weakened state, could perceive was that the harassment by Ikkeans had waned as we drew farther away from the *Serkeriah*, and those crewmen who had taken the role of protectors were able to relieve those of us who hauled the lines. I myself was permitted a few moments of rest and recuperation. Blood streaked my arms and breast, and sweat stung where my skin had rubbed raw. And yet, for all my discomfort, I saw that we were close to our aim. The Palace of the Underworld towered above us. Its vast stonework resembled nothing so much as a great cathedral, and the living energy that played madly along its surface appeared auroral and deep. Mister Kopler paced the long line of men, exhorting them to pull, to work, to crack their spines with their muscle's strength, and the tooth-baring effort in every countenance very nearly moved me to displace one of the more rested crewmen for the sheer joy of the toil. Sisyphus damned had no greater task than did we, only we had hope and determination and the love of our fellows, be they Carib or English, Sorid or Manae. So narrow as that is the difference between perdition and redemption.

Carina Meer appeared beside me. I can put it no other way, for in my flickering consciousness, there was no approach, only her sudden presence. Somewhere in our endeavors, she had suffered a cruel cut across her collar and a bright and painful-looking burn along the knuckles of her left hand, but she made no complaint.

"Captain Lawton," she said to me. "May I speak with you?"

"Of course," I replied, turning toward her. I knew even then what would be the subject of our conversation. We stepped a bit apart from our joint crew and stood under the blue shade of a vast outcropping of stone.

"We will not achieve our goal before the enemy finds us," she said. "Nor shall we be able to continue carrying this burden in the midst of a full attack."

"I had suspected as much."

"If you and your men will go ahead, then," she said. "Tell my brother that I am in need of reinforcements, and I will guard the gold against all comers as I did before."

Her smile would, I think, have convinced another man that her offer was what it seemed to be, but I had worked the figures in my own mind as well. The demise of the *Serkeriah* could not have gone unnoticed by our allies underground, nor would the activity of the Ikkeans who followed in our wake. That no relief had come could only be a sign that there was none to be had, and this, then, was Carina Meer's gambit to save my life and the lives of my men.

"There is another alternative," I said. "Allow me to call for parley. If Governor Smith is the guide to these creatures, they may well be swayed by him, and honor will not permit him to refuse."

"And what is it you would say to him or his masters?" she asked.

Now came my own turn to smile.

"Whatever comes to hand," I said. There was a moment's

distrust in her eyes. For the first time since I had collected her from the *Vargud van Haarlem*, I was asking that she put herself wholly within my control, and I take it as no insult that she hesitated.

Our preparations were not lengthy, and when they were complete, I used the rags of Doctor Koch's pale shirt and the branch of a strange and rubbery Martian tree to signal our intention.

It was something less than an hour before Governor Smith appeared upon the plain that I had chosen for our final confrontation. Carina Meer stood at my side, and our joint crew, reduced by half, sat or stood by the tarp-covered mass behind us, the blood-darkened hauling ropes trailing from it on the dusty soil.

They emerged from the gully to our east. Governor Smith and five Ikkean battle spiders. For the first time in a decade, I faced my nemesis in the flesh. His velvety black jacket was smeared with the dust of Mars and his disarranged hair stood at rough angles from the elongated egg of his skull. His expression was the same pleasant cipher I had known when I first had the misfortune to cross his path, but I venture to say this: There was something different in the set of his eyes. I recognize that I am not now nor was I then an impartial observer of the man, and still I ask that you believe me when I say there was in him something like madness.

"Good morning, Captain Lawton," he said. "Captain Meer. You have led me quite a merry chase. My congratulations on a game well played. I am pleased that we can end this like civilized men."

"That remains to be seen," I said. "We have not yet addressed the matter of terms."

"Terms? You are charming, Captain Lawton. The terms are that you and your allies will throw down weapons, or, by all that is holy, you shall not live to see another sunrise on any planet."

"All that is holy," I spat at him. "From a man who has joined himself to the devil."

"Say rather," he replied with his mocking smile, "that I have joined myself to the victors. An ambassador, if you will, though without the official title as yet. Someday soon the Ikkeans will rule both worlds, and their friends will rule with them."

Carina Meer's laugh was the platonic ideal of contempt.

"Unacceptable," I said. "You may have the advantage, but you have had that before only to see defeat. I insist upon guarantees of clemency."

The Ikkean at Governor Smith's side chattered, a horrible high-pitched sound with a thousand knives in it. I believe that Governor Smith flinched from it as much as did I.

"Captain Lawton, I made an offer to you before. Your aid in return for control of the *Serkeriah*."

I nodded. Behind me, young Carter said, *Oh, was that the offer then?*

"You are a clever man," the governor continued. "And I see that I was stingy in my price. Our situation is somewhat changed, and so is my proposal. Order your men to drop their lines and take into custody the rebel forces of Captain Meer. I will guarantee your safe return to our home world, and further, a full pardon. I will see to it that your good name is restored and your honor unquestioned in any corner of the British Empire. I will champion your cause personally."

I froze, Your Majesty. What a prospect it was! What vengeance it would be to use Governor Smith, of all men, as the agent of my social redemption. To be made right in the public eye. My honor restored. It was like the promise of love to the unrequited. For a moment, I was in the fine houses where once as a young man I supped. I recalled the delicate eyes of a young woman who loved me once, before my fall from grace. To see her again, to kiss those near-forgotten lips . . .

"It is not enough," I said. "I require a confession, written in your own hand and before witnesses to say it was not coerced. You will admit to all the subterfuge and deceit that brought me low.

That, and pardons for not only myself, but all of my men. Would you suffer that price, Governor?"

His eyes narrowed, and he let out a sound like the hiss of an annoyed serpent. I could feel the gaze of Carina Meer upon me and did not turn to her. My men and hers stood silent. A thin breeze stirred the dust about our ankles.

"Done," he said at last. "You have my word of honor, I will fulfill my part of the compact. For now, you will fulfill yours."

At that moment, as Providence had it, a change came upon the Palace of the Underworld, and a gout of green fire rose from it, up into the purple Martian sky. A cheer rose from the crew behind me and I saw Carina Meer settle a degree into herself.

"I will not," I said. "You sad, small-hearted pig of a man. Do you believe that you frighten me? I have ridden the most tempestuous waves in the seas. I have stood with naked steel in hand against men a thousand times your worth. Who are you to *pardon* me?"

"What is—"

"That fire you observed was the signal from those of my crew and Captain Meer's not present that they had arrived in safety at the Palace of the Underworld. All the time that you have wasted preparing for these negotiations and conducting them, our men have been taking the alloy beyond your reach."

When young Carter and Mister Darrow threw back the tarp to uncover the mound of rough Martian stone, the astonished gape of Governor Smith's mouth was a thing to behold. I could see where the dentist had removed one of his molars, so profound was his surprise.

"False parley!" he shouted, and pulled a pistol from his belt. Murder glowed in his eyes. "There is no shred of honor left in you, sir."

"You are a fool," Carina said. She lifted her chin, haughty as any queen. "Honor is a petty, meaningless thing if men such as you have it."

Governor Smith shifted his pistol, pointing it at her forehead, his finger trembling on the trigger. Carina narrowed her eyes in disdain but showed no sign of fear.

"Save your childish outrage," I said, stepping forward to draw his attention. "You haven't the will to fire. You're a coward and cheat, and every man here knows my words are as the gospel on it. I would no more accept pardon from you than drink your piss. If you have honor, then honor be damned. You are nothing, sir. You. Do. Not. *Signify*."

And then, Your Majesty, as was my hope and aim, the Honorable Governor Smith turned and shot me.

Was it a desperate ploy that brought the pistol's ball to my own belly rather than chance the death of the woman whom I admired above all others? Perhaps. But it was a successful one. The blow was not unlike being struck by a mule's hoof, though I am sure you have never had the ill fortune to experience such. I stumbled back and fell, unable to maintain my feet. I believe that Governor Smith had time enough to understand that his temper and impetuous violence had left him vulnerable, though God alone will have leisure to clarify this with him. Before he could call out to his demonic allies for aid, Carina Meer leapt forward and crushed the man's windpipe with a single strike of her right elbow. He stumbled back, my echo in this as in so many things.

The battle was immediately joined, and Carina Meer and what remained of our joined crew assaulted the Ikkean warriors. But we sat for a moment, he and I, our gazes locked. Blood spilled from my punctured gut. His face darkened as he struggled vainly to draw breath. And then his eyes rolled back and his body sagged to the Martian ground, and that, as they say, was that.

When the skirmish ended, Doctor Koch and Carina Meer were with me immediately. We had won the day, but only at peril to our lives. The massed Ikkean forces were descending upon us, and despite my entreaties, Carina and my men refused to leave my wounded body behind as the burden it was. Mister Darrow fashioned a rough litter from the legs of the defeated Ikkeans, and then . . .

Oh, Your Majesty, and then so much more. Shall I recount to you the battle at the edge of the Palace of the Underworld, and how young Carter saved us all by scaling the massive spider-ship as though it were rigging, his dagger in his teeth? Or the fateful meeting with Hermeton, brother to Carina Meer, and the fearful duplicity of his plan to defeat the Ikkeans? Shall I describe to you the great caverns below the Martian surface and detail the mystery and madness of the Elanin Chorus? The death dwarves of Inren-Kah? The hawk-men of Nis? The Plant-Queens of Venus? Like Scheherazade to her Caliph, I believe I could beguile you with these tales for countless nights. But to what end? I set forth here to explain my role in the death of Governor Smith, and I have done so.

Your Majesty, I did not slaughter the governor, but I was instrumental in his death. I broke the laws of custom and honor, rejected his offer of clemency, and drew his ire to myself in defense of a woman and of a world, both almost strangers to me but already of inestimable value. I did this knowing that I might die, and accepting that risk because there is a better and nobler thing than to be the servant of honor. I know this, for I have become it. And I was once an honorable man.

Yours,
Captain Alexander Augustus Lawton, Citizen of Mars

MELINDA M. SNODGRASS

A writer whose work crosses several mediums and genres, Melinda M. Snodgrass was story editor on *Star Trek: The Next Generation* and wrote the award-nominated "Measure of a Man," among other episodes. She worked on *Reasonable Doubts,* and was a writer/producer on *The Profiler.* She has written a number of SF novels, and was one of the cocreators of the long-running Wild Card series, for which she has also written and edited, and she has delivered a *Wild Card* movie to Universal Pictures. Her novels include *The Edge of Reason* and *The Edge of Ruin,* and she has just delivered the third book in that series. She also penned the Circuit trilogy, and *Queen's Gambit Declined.* Her most recent novels are *This Case Is Gonna Kill Me* and *Box Office Poison,* written under the pseudonym Phillipa Bornikova.

This story shows that, even on Mars, family can be a strength and a refuge, and it can also be a claustrophobic, smothering trap—or, sometimes, both at once.

Written in Dust

MELINDA M. SNODGRASS

The best memory is that which forgets nothing but injuries.
Write kindness in marble and write injuries in the dust.

—PERSIAN PROVERB

It was a festival day, and crowds strolled the jeweled streets.
Overhead, delicate glass spires echoed the colors of the pavements
below and scratched at the sky. The perfume of flowers both sharp
and sweet coiled about her.

A sticky-bun seller offered her one of his wares. The long face
like a horse's, but with faceted, insectoid eyes, nodded in
acknowledgment as she sang her thanks. She was small compared
with the crowds surrounding her. Tall, slim, swaying like dancing
reeds, every word a note, every conversation a symphony. The living
and the dead walking together.

The inhabitants' flowing attire seemed so much more
comfortable than the binding suit she wore. She entered a temple,
stood immersed in incense and the elegant curves of the abstract
figures painted on the walls.

The other worshippers turned to welcome her. For the first
time in a long time, she was happy. She reached up and removed
the bulky, confining helmet. Black hair tumbled onto her shoulders.

But my hair is brown.

Matilda Michaelson-McKenzie (Tilda to her friends and family)
awoke with a melody on her lips, but a melody that had little in common with any Earth tonal system, Western or otherwise.

She rose, sluiced off her face, and watched the water go swirling back into the recycling cisterns. This was the first time she'd had visions. *Was that really what the Martians had looked like?* Before, it had always just been sound without sight. And the memories seemed very human. Very explicable. Had she really been Miyako McKenzie?

Tilda was desperate to talk to someone about this latest development, but the only other person who heard the music was her father, Noel-Pa, and if they did talk, they would have to be careful. Tilda didn't want to bring down Grandpa Stephen's anger on her father—any more than it already was.

Noel-Pa had innocently mentioned the music the second morning after their arrival at the McKenzie farm hold, and received a barrage of abuse from his father-in-law. Daddy-Kane had shot his husband a pleading glance, and the slim, blond retired military man had pressed his lips together and hadn't responded, though Tilda knew that it had cost him. Since then, Stephen had never missed an opportunity to cut at his son's spouse.

And Daddy-Kane doesn't even try to defend him, Tilda thought bleakly. Thank God she would be leaving for Cambridge soon to start college, and out of the fraught situation where she currently found herself. But there was no escape for Noel—unless he left his husband, and that was beginning to seem likely, to their daughter's dismay.

Meantime, she was dreaming about a woman she'd never met, who'd walked into an alien city and committed suicide. Had Miyako been lured by the music? And what if it happened to *her*? Tilda felt panic fluttering in her throat. Now she *really* couldn't wait to get off Mars!

She thought back on how they had come to the red planet, the night their lives had changed. The call had come in from Mars, and Kane had gone into the study to visit with his father. Tilda floated in the sim cage playing a game, and Noel-Pa was kicked back in a recliner, reading one of his old dead-tree books.

When Daddy-Kane walked back into the living room, the expression on his face, and the etched lines around his mouth, had the footrest smashing down and Noel-Pa out of the chair with the lightning reflexes that marked him for a soldier.

"Your father?" Noel-Pa began, putting his arms around Kane.

Daddy-Kane shook his head. "No, he's fine. It's my stepmother . . . she's dead."

Tilda shut down the sim. Without needing words, they went into the kitchen and settled around the kitchen table. Outside, the fronds on the palms shook in an ocean breeze, rattling like living castanets.

"My God, they've only been married seven months! What happened?" Noel-Pa asked.

"She walked into the Martian city and took off her helmet."

"Good God! Why? What happened?"

"The Syndrome . . . I guess. Dad found her body two days later." His voice was low and heavy. There was a long pause. "He wants me . . . us, to come home," Daddy-Kane added.

Noel-Pa stood and busied himself pouring out iced teas for all of them. "This wasn't how we pictured life after my retirement."

Kane gazed down at his hands. "I know." To break the tension, Tilda darted up from the table and brought her father a cup of tea.

Noel leaned against the counter and gazed at his husband, while Kane studiously avoided that blue-eyed gaze. "He married Miyako to try and replace *you*," Noel said softly to himself.

"I know, but he needs me now. It'll only be for a while. Once he's gone, I'll sell the farm, and we'll come back to Earth."

"That could be a long time."

"He's seventy-seven. It won't be all that long."

Noel-Pa swirled his glass, the ice cubes chiming against the sides. "I suppose it's only fair. You've followed me from posting to posting—Luna, to Ceres, to Pinnacle Station, and around the world since."

So Noel-Pa mustered out of SpaceCom and they moved to Mars. To the McKenzie holding, five vast domes of red Martian soil under cultivation, and a sixth to house the homestead, bunkhouse, work-ers' houses, silos, warehouses, and garages. What Tilda hadn't an-ticipated was the delicate twisting spires of the ancient Martian city on the opposite shore of the old lake bed from the McKenzie farm.

Those gleaming glass towers in rainbow colors had almost rec-onciled her to the move, and she couldn't wait to explore the city. Except that Stephen had forbidden anyone to enter it after Miyako's death.

Tilda had surreptitiously done research after she started hearing the music some few days after her father. They called it Mars Reverie Syndrome, and, in its more extreme forms, people did enter the cit-ies and die. Usually people who were in poor health, or those who were deeply unhappy. Which said a lot about the May/December wedding of Stephen and Miyako. There was no indication that the twenty-seven-year-old Miyako had been ill. Which left only one ex-planation. An explanation that didn't redound to Stephen's credit.

It was the Syndrome, paired with the fact that most of the cities stood in places where the soil was rich, that had started the destruc-tion. Cities were leveled, and the Syndrome became an epidemic.

Hurriedly, the Union government put a ban on the destruction of the cities, but by the time the legislation made its way through parliament, only one city remained. The one across the lake. The cases of the Syndrome eased off, though it never completely van-ished, and now the Martians were singing in Tilda's head and she was walking in the head of a dead woman.

She shivered and realized that she had been standing, lost in thought, for far too long, and Noel-Pa could probably use her help with breakfast. She dressed in the colorful, imaginatively patterned envirosuit and pulled on the thigh-high boots that marked her as a Martian farm girl, and that her grandfather insisted that she wear.

Since most of SpaceCom's facilities on Earth were closer to the equator for ease of launch, she had spent her life in warm, exotic locations—Australia's Gold Coast, Hawaii, the Florida Keys, São

Paulo, where sandals and shorts or swimsuits were the unofficial uniform. Now she lived on an ancient, nearly airless world where a dome leak or a freak storm that crashed an ultralight could kill you. She supposed that there were things that could kill you on Earth too, she reflected as she fluffed out her hair, the curls dancing on her shoulders, but the home world didn't seem so actively *hostile*. God, she couldn't wait to get out of here!

She walked through the large living room, bootheels clicking on the stone floor. The McKenzie house had been hewn out of the red-rock cliffs that lined three sides of the ancient lake bed. It stood three stories tall, and two generations back it had held a boisterous clan, but now there were just the four of them, Grandpa Stephen, his son, Kane, Kane's husband, Noel, and their only child—Tilda.

Tilda checked her ScoopRing. There was a message from Ali Al-Jahani, one of the few people in the area close to her age. His family owned the farm to the west, and they had given him permission to play hooky from chores and say farewell to Mars before he headed off to Paris in a few weeks to begin his medical studies. Ali suggested a flight out toward Mons Olympus. She messaged back that she would join him.

Tilda had leisure time too, because while Noel-Pa had agreed to her learning to fly the long-winged ultralights that were the most common mode of fast transport on Mars, he'd resisted other Martian activities. Like Stephen's trying to put her to work in the sorting and packing sheds. Just like Ali, she was leaving for college soon. She didn't need to learn how to be a farmhand.

The yeasty scent of baking cinnamon rolls, cooking bacon, and the dark, sensual smell of coffee escorted her into the kitchen. Noel-Pa circled the big stone table, setting out plates and silverware.

On Earth, Daddy-Kane had kept "the home fires burning," as Noel-Pa had put it, but here at the McKenzie farm, Kane had skills that Noel lacked—how to run the big tractors, harvesters, threshers. Noel-Pa could have learned, but Daddy-Kane already had the knowledge, so they had switched roles. Tilda wasn't surprised that the former military officer proved to be as adept in the kitchen as he had been in combat.

He turned at her footsteps and dropped a kiss on the top of her head. She hugged him tight. "So, what can I do?"

"Beat the eggs for the frittata."

She beat three dozen eggs and helped Noel-Pa season them and pour the mix into an enormous iron skillet. The eggs joined the bacon in the oven.

"I dreamed about Miyako last night. I think I *was* Miyako. She was greeting the Martians and they were making her welcome, giving her food, and there was a temple," Tilda said softly to her father. He glanced at her, his expression tight and tense. "I'm not crazy!"

"I know."

"So, you've dreamed about her too?" Tilda asked.

Noel-Pa checked the watch set in the sleeve of his suit. Shook his head. "Not now. Not here," he said. Then he counted down. "And three . . . two . . . one."

There was the babble of voices and the rasp of boot soles being cleaned on the scraper just outside the back door. The unmarried field hands who lived in the dorm just down the road, Daddy-Kane, and Grandpa Stephen flowed into the kitchen.

Noel's thoughts were in complete turmoil as he pulled the frittata out of the oven. How could his father-in-law's dead spouse be invading both his and his child's dreams? His dreams had not been so pleasant. He had experienced all of Miyako's loneliness, sadness, and hatred. Resentment of her family for essentially selling her to Stephen. Hatred for her elderly husband. Or was he simply putting his own dislike of his father-in-law onto this phantom?

Noel sprinkled fresh parsley across the puffed-egg dish, and sliced it into individual servings. Tilda removed the bacon and the rolls, and everything was set on a long counter. Noel stepped back as the hungry workers lined up.

Stephen sat at the head of the table with Kane at the foot. No one left a seat open next to Kane, and Kane didn't object. Feeling absurdly hurt, Noel found room on a bench and sat down.

"What is this thing?" Stephen demanded.

"Frittata . . . sort of an Italian omelet," Noel replied.

"Well, why not just make a damn omelet?" the old man asked.

"A little hard to flip three dozen eggs, and this way I could time it for when you all came in," Noel said placidly. *Peace at any price,* he reminded himself.

The response from Stephen was a *harrumph.* Noel saw Tilda glance at Kane, but Kane kept his focus on his plate. In the first month after their arrival, Kane had constantly leaped in to shield Noel from his father's verbal attacks, but that had stopped. Initially, Noel had asked Kane to back off, thinking that Stephen would eventually come to accept him. But his charm offensive had failed, and lately, it felt like Kane was starting to agree with his irascible father's constant criticisms of Noel.

They had always had a vigorous and active sex life, but even that time of closeness was becoming less frequent due to plain physical exhaustion on Kane's part. At least that's what Noel told himself as he lay awake listening to Kane's snores and longing for his touch. Noel felt lonely and isolated.

As lonely and isolated as Miyako.

Noel studied his husband's familiar and beloved profile and wondered when it had become attached to a stranger. He tried to catch Kane's eye, and briefly succeeded before the younger man looked away. Noel knew that behavior. Knew what it meant. It meant something was up, something Kane didn't want to tell him. His appetite fled, and the food smelled almost nauseating. Noel pushed away his plate.

Stephen gave a loud snort. "Even you don't like this damn thing," he said.

Noel kept his expression pleasant but pulled his hands into his lap so that no one would see when they balled into fists. Once again the litany was running through his head—*have a stroke, have a stroke, have a stroke!*

He'd had very little interaction with his father-in-law prior to the move. Stephen and Catherine, Kane's mother, had attended the wedding on Earth. Catherine had been pleasant in a bluff, hearty kind of way. Stephen less so. It was clear that he hadn't wanted his son to marry a "mud crawler," even though Noel had had plenty of postings off-world in his career with SpaceCom. For Stephen, that didn't matter; you were either a Martian or you weren't, and Noel wasn't.

Stephen had been alone when he came for Matilda's christening, Catherine having died two years before from an aggressive cancer. At that time, the old man had tried to convince them to move back to Mars so that Tilda would be a *true McKenzie*. Kane had stayed firm and refused. Noel had just made commander, and admiral didn't seem outside the realm of possibility, and Noel knew that Kane liked the soft winds and warm sun of Earth. Liked walking at twilight hand in hand without the separation of an envirosuit. And that he never wanted to dig potatoes or thresh wheat again.

Noel knew that it had hurt Kane when Stephen had announced that he'd remarried, and the old bastard didn't mince words when he told his son why. Miyako was just a walking womb as far as the old man was concerned. A chance to start a new family, a farming family, a *Martian* family. A family that would understand history and continuity and never leave. Then came the tragedy of Miyako's death, and Kane had felt it was his duty to return—and if there was one thing Noel understood, it was duty.

Breakfast ended with Stephen and the hands trooping out to work. Noel was surprised when Kane stayed behind and helped him and Tilda clear the table and load the dishes into the big industrial-sized washer.

"What are you up to today?" Kane asked their daughter.

"Ali and I are taking our lights out toward Mons Olympus."

"Good. You have fun," Kane said, dropping a kiss onto her cheek.

"You checked the weather?" Noel asked, trying to keep his tone casual and not sound like an overly anxious parent.

"No dust storms predicted for the next two days," she answered brightly. Resting a hand on his shoulder, she stood on tiptoes and kissed his cheek. "Don't worry." Her blue eyes danced with mischief. They were the most obvious feature he had bestowed on their child. Her warm café au lait skin and curling brown hair were all Kane. His love for her manifested as a squeezing pressure in Noel's chest. The back door closed behind her, and it was suddenly very quiet in the kitchen.

He turned to his husband and smiled. "Hey, we have the house to ourselves," Noel said, giving a suggestive edge to the words. Kane's grim expression didn't lighten. In fact, it became even more pronounced. "What? What have I done now?" Noel asked.

"Let's talk in our room."

Noel shortened his stride so as not to outpace his smaller spouse. Their room was a perfect mix of both their personalities. Dead-tree books on a shelf, a few of Kane's abstract paintings that they had paid to ship from Earth. Kane had intended to paint once they got settled, but, like so many other plans, that had never materialized. Noel's battle armor stood in a corner like a warrior sculpture from some alien civilization.

"Okay, what's wrong?" Noel asked.

"Dad's enrolled Tilda at Lowell University in the agronomy department."

"Well, I hope he can get his money back," Noel said. "She's going to Cambridge, and she leaves in three weeks."

Kane looked away, then walked to the dresser and began rearranging items. "I canceled her booking to Earth, and called admissions."

"WHAT?" It was a tone and timbre Noel usually reserved for insubordinate recruits.

"She's the heir after me."

Noel forced himself not to shout. "What happened to *we sell it after he's gone?*" Kane paced to the other side of the room and didn't answer. "I take it that plan is no longer operative?"

"It's honest work, maybe noble. We feed Earth," Kane said defensively. "My great-great-grandfather built this house, broke the soil for the first time in who knows how many thousands of years. It's right that a McKenzie continue here."

"Tilda is also a Michaelson, and she has other plans. *I* had other plans."

"I thought your plan was to be with me," Kane said.

"It is, but . . . " Now it was Noel's turn to pace. "You didn't want this life. You said you never wanted to return."

"Things change."

"Obviously. But you and your horrible father don't have the right to make that decision for Tilda."

"So, now it comes out."

"Yeah, he's a bastard, and you know it. You used to *say* it. Tilda is going to Cambridge if I have to take her there myself."

"You can't. We'll stop you at the port. She's the daughter of a natural-born Martian, and underage. We can keep her here."

Noel ran agitated fingers through his hair. "I don't know who you are anymore. How could you do this to our daughter? To me?"

Kane crossed to him and gripped his shoulders. "Look, let him think he's had the win. When Tilda turns twenty-one, she can do whatever the hell she wants, but it gives me time to work on the old man . . . and . . . and . . . things can change."

"First, he doesn't change. He reminds us daily about how goddamn resolute he is," Noel said bitterly. "And second, I don't think you can count on him conveniently dying and saving you having to confront him. Finally, three and a half years will be too late for Tilda. How's studying agronomy at a shit college on Mars going to help her get into a quality university, especially after she backed out?"

Kane stiffened. "I graduated from Lowell."

"I didn't mean—"

"Yeah, you did. You think this is Hicksville."

"Don't change the subject. That's a distraction. You need to face up to what you're really doing. You're taking the coward's way out. Not defying your father, and letting Tilda and me suffer because of your lack of spine!" The moment the words were out, Noel wished he could recall them. Even with Kane's dark skin, Noel could see the blood rushing into Kane's face.

"And now I see what the famous SpaceCom officer thinks of me!" He whirled and stormed to the door.

"Kane, wait! I'm sorry, I—"

The heavy metal door whispered shut, but it felt like a slam.

Tilda pushed back the canopy and climbed into her garishly painted ultralight plane. Was it the unremitting red of Mars that made settlers so crazy for color? she wondered. Hers was painted silver, with blue stars and moons and streaks and swirls across the overly long wings and fuselage. She taxied down the runway, past the big crawlers that carried their goods to the spaceport in Lowell City. The long acceleration down the runway, and the extralong wings, caught enough of the thin Martian atmosphere, and she was in the air. In the distance, she saw Ali's black plane with silver lightning bolts also climbing into the ruddy sky.

She banked to come in next to him, and they flew wingtip to wingtip as they passed over the Martian city. She wondered what her dream Martians would make of it now. The jewel-tone towers were still the same, but now the avenues were washed with red dust and filled with the whine and moan of the incessant Martian wind instead of with songs.

The shadow of the ultralights' wings swept across the red sand and rock of the planet, and played tag with the swirling whirlwinds dancing across the craters and plateaus. The fragile light of the distant sun sparkled on the domes covering the farm fields of the settlers.

Through the front windshield, she watched the looming mass of Mons Olympus, the solar system's largest volcano, draw closer. The peak scraped at the red sky of Mars, and a few tattered clouds coiled about the shoulders of the mountain as if the massif were trying to wrap itself in a thin shawl.

Ali broke the silence. "I'm going to miss this."

"Have you been to Earth?" Tilda asked.

"No."

"You'll like it."

"My mom's afraid that I won't want to come back."

"What did you say to her?"

"I promised her I would." There was a hesitation. "But I lied. I don't know how I'm going to feel after college and med school, maybe a residency spent down the gravity well."

"Maybe it would have been better to be honest?" Tilda suggested.

"She cries all the time. Just think what she'd do if I'd said *that*."

They crossed over a canal, and on sudden impulse, Tilda said, "Let's land."

"Why?"

"I want to drop a rock into a canal. I haven't done that."

"You hoping something will crawl out?" Ali teased.

"No, of course not. I just . . . look, just go with it, okay?"

"Okay."

They found a level area not far from the sharp cut of the canal and landed. In Mars's low gravity they were able to take long, floating strides that quickly carried them to the edge of the canal. It was obvious that it wasn't natural. The edges were clean, as if cut by a laser, and the walls were impossibly straight. Tilda knew that early explorers had lowered probes into the canals but nothing had been found. Just sheer walls of fused glass. Why had the Martians made them? What purpose had they served?

Initially, the fear that something lived in those deep cuts had discouraged colonization, but years passed and nothing ever emerged from the canals, and necessity replaced fear. The home world, gripped in climate change and lacking enough cropland for her teeming billions, needed a new breadbasket. So the doomsayers had been overridden, and the settlers had arrived.

Tilda knelt on the edge of the canal and picked up a rock. Dropped it over the edge. Waited for what seemed like endless heartbeats. Predictably, nothing happened.

"It's so strange they left no written records," Ali said.

"I think O'Neill is right, and music is how they passed information," Tilda answered, referring to a theory formulated by Mars's most famous xenoarchaeologist.

"Seems supercumbersome. What if you were a Martian that couldn't sing? Would you be like a mute?"

Tilda laughed, happy to find herself able to laugh after so many weeks of tension. "That's a really interesting question."

"That's me, all interesting questions, and no answers," Ali said. He had a nice smile. "What do you want to do now?"

"I should probably get back," Tilda said halfheartedly.

"And I've got a pressure tent, and Mom put up a lunch for us. How about the Face? We can quote 'Ozymandias' to each other."

The flight took another hour. From the air, the Face was massive and easily discerned, the blank eyes frowning up at the red sky, mouth set in an uncompromising line. Once they landed, it appeared as just sheer red cliffs. Something that could be seen from space had to be too large to grasp from ground level.

"Wonder how they carved it?" Ali asked, as they set up the tent.

"Must have been aerial," Tilda said. "Lasers from above to cut away the rock."

"I'd hate to be the guy who missed the dotted line," Ali said as he hit the oxygen canister. Tilda set up a small heater, and, with a sigh of relief, removed her helmet.

Mrs. Al-Jahani was a wonderful cook, and she had packed baba ghanoush and curried chicken, both choices wrapped in tender pita bread. There was baklava dripping with honey for dessert. Fortunately, bees had taken well to the life in the Martian domes. Which was good, they had pretty much vanished on Earth.

Ali seemed nervous as he packed up the picnic basket. "I was thinking, I'm going to be in Paris. You'll be at Cambridge. Not that far apart. Maybe we can . . . get together."

"I'd like that," Tilda said, and suddenly the handsome, dark-haired Ali presented himself as potential boyfriend material. She'd have to think about that, but right now it gave her a warm, tingly glow.

They replaced their helmets, and broke down the tent, and stowed it back in Ali's ultralight. They then went to the side of the Face. Somewhere in the recent past, some human had carved steps into the side of the mammoth statue. Tilda felt guilty as she clambered up but ultimately shrugged and accepted it. She hadn't done it, and it was too late to undo it.

On top, they walked across the massive chin, across the cheek, and stood looking down into the notch of the left eye.

"I wonder who he was," Tilda said softly.

"And that's why they should have left written records," Ali said. He paused, then added, "Hey, you want to come back to our place for supper?"

Tilda thought about the morose silence that held court at the McKenzie table and nodded happily. "I'd like that, thanks. I'll radio home and let them know once we get in the air."

"Which we'd better do," Ali said, squinting at the distant, setting sun.

Noel-Pa gave her permission, but his voice sounded stretched and thin. She hoped that he and Daddy-Kane hadn't had another argument.

The sun, small and distant, sank below the horizon. The moons of Mars rose and passed each other as they raced in opposite directions across the sky. Without the cushion of deep atmosphere, the stars seemed fingertip close. As if by agreement, they flew in silence, soaking in the moment. Eventually, the farm domes came into view, glittering like captured stars on the horizon. The towers of the Martian city formed shadow fingers, stretching as if to capture the stars and moons.

Dinner at the Al-Jahani house was loud, delicious, slightly disorganized, and very fun. Mrs. Al-Jahani's face was like an exquisite cameo set in the frame of her headscarf. Mr. Al-Jahani held their youngest child, little Jasmine, on his knee. Ali's two younger brothers surreptitiously punched and pinched each other, and Siraj, his merry black eyes alight with mischief, kept up a singsong of "Ali's got a girlfriend." Which eventually earned him a punch from his elder brother.

It all reminded Tilda of the cheerful, cozy family dinners she'd enjoyed with her fathers before they had moved to Mars. Wistfully, she wondered what it would have been like if the men had crèched a little brother or sister for her, but she knew that such technology was expensive on a military officer's salary. Still, it might have made a difference now. Maybe one of these imaginary siblings would have wanted to be a farmer and mollified Grandpa Stephen.

After dinner, they played mahjong and Scrabble, much to the disgust of the younger boys, who had wanted to load up a SimGame and shoot aliens. When Jasmine fell asleep in her mother's arms, Tilda knew it was time to go. Ali walked her back out to her ultralight and briefly clasped her hand.

"This was fun. Thanks for spending the day with me," he said softly.

Tilda, studying the line of his cheek, and his mouth with its rather lush lower lip, thought how, on Earth, he would have leaned forward and kissed her now, but here they were separated by their helmets. She settled for giving his hand a tight squeeze.

"Thanks for inviting me. I had a wonderful time."

"We'll do it again before we leave." He got an arm around her and gave her a hug, which Tilda enthusiastically returned. She then climbed into the ultralight and made the short hop over the canal that separated the two farmsteads.

She was surprised to find both her fathers waiting for her in the cavernous living room. She noticed that Noel-Pa was paler than usual, holding his face so still that he seemed more like a marble statue than a living man. Daddy-Kane put an arm around her shoulders and guided her to the sofa, but she noticed that he never looked directly at her.

Then he began to talk, and with each word that Daddy-Kane spoke, Tilda felt herself dying. She wanted to scream, run, cry, batter at the stone walls that seemed to be drawing closer and closer. She hunched over, folding around the agony in her heart.

"But . . . but I don't want to study agronomy," she finally said. It was an effort to force out the words through a throat that ached with unshed tears. She mustered a smile. "I'm terrible with plants, Daddy, you know that. I killed a *ficus*, for heaven's sake!"

Always before, Daddy-Kane had responded to her teasing. This time, he remained stone-faced.

"You're a McKenzie. We grow things."

"And some of us kill things."

Tilda's eyes darted to her other father, and she was terrified by what she saw in Noel's face as he looked at his husband.

Kane's head jerked up and his eyes narrowed as he looked at Noel. "Well, that was certainly threatening."

"All I meant was that I was a soldier. Why aren't you pushing her to enlist? Why does it have to be *your* family tradition that she follows?"

"You said it yourself—you kill things." Kane's tone was nasty. "I want something different for her."

Tilda stood and laid a shaking hand on Kane's arm. "And I want something different for me too, but it should be what *I* want. I want to study philosophy and comparative religion. I want to understand the Martians, and the ice creatures on Europa. Please, Daddy." Her voice caught on the final words, and she feared she sounded like a five-year-old.

"The Martians are dead. The creatures on Europa may not even be intelligent, and all you'll be able to do with that degree is teach," Kane said.

"And what's so wrong with that?" Noel snapped.

"It's useless and pointless." Kane's breaths were ragged and harsh. Kane looked down at Tilda. "Until your majority, your grandfather and I pay the bills and set the rules. You're going to Lowell College. Classes start in five weeks."

It was the harsh tone more than the words that finally broke her control. Tilda gasped out a single sob and bolted from the room.

Blinded by tears, she ran for her bedroom; she heard Daddy-Kane say defensively, "She'll have a cry and be over it by tomorrow. Kids are resilient."

Noel answered harshly, "You've broken our daughter's heart! I don't think I can ever forgive you."

When Noel slipped into her bedroom, he discovered that she had fallen into an exhausted sleep. The soft shush of the door sliding didn't wake her, and he had to give her shoulder a gentle shake. She sat up, clawing the hair off her face. The skin around her eyes was swollen and red, and she winced as light hit her tear-burned eyes when Noel switched on her bedside lamp.

He sat on the edge of the bed, and she flung her arms around him. "Can they really keep me here until I'm twenty-one?"

"Yes. Martian law controls in this situation, and they've always been pretty old-fashioned."

"And you're going to tell me to be patient." The joy and youth had gone out of her voice. She sounded like an old woman.

"No. I'm not." He nervously pleated the edge of the sheet between his fingers. "There is a way around the age of majority. It's a case where Martian conservatism actually works for us."

She bounced up until she was kneeling on the bed, hope kindling in her eyes. "Okay. I'll do it. What is it?"

"Whoa. Wait. Hold on until I tell you. You might decide that Lowell College's school of agronomy is preferable." He paused, gathered a breath. "You enlist. You can enlist at seventeen with just the consent of one parent. Then you apply for the College Commissioning Program—Green to Gold. You'll serve a year enlisted, but with your test scores, discipline, and with the recommendations from flag officers who owe me favors, you'll get in. Cambridge is holding a slot for you already. You'll be attending university, and just have to meet the year-for-year commitment. And you'll be an officer."

She frowned, chewed at her lower lip. "Will I have to study what SpaceCom tells me to?"

"They don't care about the degree. Just about the process and achievement."

She sat with the idea for a few minutes. Noel wondered if she was picturing herself in one of the blue-and-gold uniforms. "You taught me to shoot."

"I did indeed."

"Is another war likely?" she asked.

"It's hard for me to answer that. I don't think so. Since the Belt Rebellion, the politicians on Earth seemed to realize that they need to talk to the settlers rather than bullying them. Hopefully, that will continue."

"And that's what you hate about this," Tilda said, gazing up at him. "You think we're being bullied?"

He hugged her tight. "Yes, I suppose I do."

"Okay, I'll—"

He placed a finger against her lips. "No, I want you to think about this carefully. Remember, there's no guarantee this will work. Plans can fall apart. Let me know in a few days. But whatever you do, don't let Stephen get a rise out of you. If he thinks you're rebellious or going to be mulish, it will make it harder for us to get away. If you should decide to enlist."

She took three days to consider. She watched war movies and documentaries about the Belter Rebellion on her ShowSim. Could she stand basic training? Probably. She was in good shape and liked to be active. Guns didn't scare her. Dying did. But how was that different from any other person currently living?

Tilda had followed her father's advice and not pitched a fit. Stephen read her silence for acquiescence and absolutely fawned over Tilda. Each time he hugged her, he threw a triumphant glance at Noel-Pa as if saying, *see, she's mine now.* Toward his son-in-law, Stephen became even more horrid.

On the third night, the three of them sat in the living room. Noel-Pa, seated on the sofa, mended one of Kane's shirts while Kane flipped through a seed catalogue that he'd brought up on his Scoop-Ring.

"With Tilda going off to school, I think I'd like to get out of the housework and join you in the fields," Noel-Pa said.

"I'd like that too, but maybe not right now. Dad likes working with me."

"Why can't he work with both of you?" Tilda asked, but it was more a challenge than a question.

Noel-Pa shot her a warning glance, and Kane looked bedeviled and irritated. "Look, this might not be the best moment. Let's all just stay . . . " His voice trailed away.

"*What?* Stay *what?*" Tilda demanded.

"I'm going to bed," Kane growled, and stomped off toward the bedrooms. Tilda noted how Noel's eyes followed him and how sorrow had etched lines into his face.

"Take a turn and look at the stars before bed?" she suggested.

Noel nodded and followed her out of the house. The dome softened the brilliance of the stars and gave an almost rainbow hue to Phoebus rushing overhead.

"I've decided. I want to enlist. And maybe once I've gone, Grandpa will have to accept you and stop looking to me."

He brushed her hand back with a gentle hand. "Don't worry about me. Let's get you onto a SpaceCom ship." He threaded her arm through his, and they walked out into a field, where they could see anyone coming and wouldn't be overheard. "Long-range forecasts show a hell of a dust storm coming day after tomorrow. It's heading toward Lowell City, and we can run before it."

"And Daddy and Stephen won't be able to follow, because by the time they've discovered we're gone, the storm will have grounded them, and the crawlers are too slow to catch us." The sense of secrets and plots was exciting.

"Exactly right. Go out with Ali tomorrow and pack what you want to take. Remember, pack light. SpaceCom footlockers don't hold much. Then just leave it in the cockpit of your plane."

Tilda almost quailed at the size of the storm. It was a monster, bulking on the southern horizon, the dust roiled into fantastic shapes by the force of the winds. At the moment, it was a low-level hum that set nerves on edge and had everyone snapping at one another, but when it arrived, the sound would be the howl of a thousand banshees.

Kane and Stephen were ordering the hands to check the various domes in advance of the storm's arrival.

"Tilda and I will check the ultralights," Noel-Pa called as they walked past the huddle.

"Wait!" Stephen began.

"Look, Dad, if there's one thing I know how to do, it's how to lash down a plane. I tied down enough fighters in my day." Noel-Pa didn't wait but took Tilda's arm, and they hustled to the airlock closest to the ultralights.

The wind hit them the moment they stepped through, and Tilda staggered. Noel-Pa grabbed her around the waist and steadied her. Hunching against the moaning gusts, they rushed to Tilda's ultralight. Noel-Pa wrestled with the canopy and got it open. He boosted her up, and she scrambled into the cockpit.

He pressed his helmet against hers and shouted, "I'll unlash you, and you get airborne."

"How will you—"

"I'll manage. Be ready."

He pulled the canopy forward and dropped to the ground. He then unlashed the ultralight. She felt it begin to sway. Once he was clear, she went taxiing down the runway with the wind buffeting the craft and setting the long wings to vibrating. She managed to get into the air, and circled, watching as her father ran to another ultralight and pulled back the canopy. He dropped back down and untethered one line.

The wind was getting worse and worse, and dust blotted out the sun, creating an unnatural twilight. Tilda fought the controls as her father ran to the next tether. A shaft of light spilled onto the red ground as the airlock cycled open.

A suited figure ran out and charged at Noel-Pa. Too short and broad to be Daddy-Kane. Tilda switched on her radio and heard her grandfather's voice raging in her headphones.

"Bastard! Son of a bitch. Like hell you're going to take her."

"Stephen." Noel-Pa's voice was loud but still placating. "This is—"

But he never got to finish. The older man barreled into him. Noel-Pa managed to keep his feet, but they were locked in anger's embrace. Stephen was raining blows onto Noel-Pa's body. The Space-Com officer was trying to hold him off and not strike back. The half-tethered ultralight was whipping back and forth like the tail of a frenzied scorpion.

Tilda forgot about the plan. She set her radio on emergency channel and screamed out, "Daddy! Daddy! Help!"

It was getting harder and harder to keep the wings level as the wind swirled and howled. Noel-Pa managed to push Stephen away, but he didn't see the tail of the plane swinging around, propelled by a vicious gust of wind. It smashed into his back and head, and he collapsed onto the sand.

"Papa!" Tilda screamed, and she turned the nose of her plane toward the runway.

She was trembling with fear, and that, coupled with the wind, made it a terrible landing. One wheel collapsed, and a wing dug deep into the sand and crumpled. She pushed back the canopy and scrambled down. She could barely keep her feet as she ran to her father. Stephen stood, hands hanging limply at his side, braced against the wind. He was staring down at Noel-Pa, an expression of both shock and fury on his lined face.

Tilda dropped to her knees next to her father's still form. "You monster! You hateful old bastard! You've killed him. I hate you! I hate you!" Her words seemed to drive Stephen back as much as the wind.

The airlock opened again, and another suited figure raced out. Daddy-Kane reached her side. He was gasping for breath.

"Noel. Oh God, Noel."

A gust of wind screamed past and sent Tilda's crashed ultralight tumbling across the sands.

"We've got to get inside!" Stephen screamed.

Daddy-Kane grunted with effort, but lifted his husband into his arms, and the foursome clung together and fought their way back to the airlock.

The storm raged on, blotting out the sun and setting everyone's nerves on edge as the wind screamed and moaned around the dome. Noel lay in bed and didn't regain consciousness. Henry, one of the hands who had some first-aid training, did what he could.

"He needs to be in the hospital in Lowell City," he said, but, of course, the storm made that impossible. Henry shook his head and slipped away, leaving Kane to sit next to the bed, holding his husband's limp hand.

Tilda sat with them. Hours passed and she felt limp with exhaustion. Once Stephen came to the bedroom door.

"Go away."

"Kane."

"I can't deal with you right now." Kane looked at Tilda. "Go to bed."

"I want to help. I want to be here," she said.

"Get some sleep. Then I'll have you take over and I'll rest. Okay?"

"You'll call me if . . . "

"Nothing's going to happen." She stood, came around to his side of the bed and kissed his cheek. He kissed her back, but never let go of Noel's hand, as if by sheer will he could hold Noel in life.

She undressed and crawled into bed. She hadn't thought she'd be able to sleep, but sometimes the body can trump the mind.

She was walking through the Martian city, and once again it was filled with Martians, tall and graceful. Among the aliens were two smaller figures. One was very slight with long black hair. The other Tilda instantly recognized. It was Noel-Pa. His arm was linked through the woman's.

Tilda ran forward. "Papa, Papa!" He released Miyako and took her in his arms. "What are you doing here?" But he didn't answer, just smiled down at her. "Come on," she urged. "We have to go home. Come with me."

She took his hand and tugged, but he resisted and slid his hand out of hers. He then linked arms with Miyako again, and they drifted away. Tilda ran after them, but she didn't seem to be making any progress, and they got farther and farther away. She looked around and saw a Martian standing at the top of the steps of what she called the temple. There was something familiar about that arrogant face and the set of the faceted eyes.

Ozymandias.

She ran up the steps and stood looking up at him. Unlike the other Martians, he looked down and seemed to see her.

"Where's my dad gone?"

The music crashed over her, filled with information that she couldn't process, and she awoke.

She returned to her fathers' bedroom, where a tense conference was under way. Henry had pulled back the eyelid on Noel's left eye. The pupil was so dilated that there was almost no blue left in the eye.

"His blood pressure is spiking," Henry said, "and his pulse is so slow I can barely find it."

"Meaning what?" Daddy-Kane demanded.

"There's probably a bleed inside his skull. If the pressure isn't relieved, he's going to die."

"So do it," Kane ordered.

Henry backed away, palms out as if pushing away Daddy-Kane's words. "No, no, not me. I don't have the skill or the training for something like that."

He fled the room before Kane could speak. Father and daughter stood staring at each other. "A storm this bad will jam the engine on a crawler," he said. "And it's a five-day trip to Lowell even in good conditions." His shoulders slumped, and she watched him accept the inevitable.

"That's why he's in the city," Tilda murmured almost to herself. "He's dying, and he's gone to the city."

"What are you talking about?" Daddy-Kane asked. Anger edged each word.

"I dreamed about Daddy and Miyako. They were in the city together. Ozymandias was trying to tell me something, but I couldn't understand." Her voice broke.

"That's crazy talk. And who's Ozymandias? And he's not going to die. I won't let him die!" He strode around the room as if he could outpace death.

Tilda's mind seemed to be fluttering in frantic circles. She kept trying to think of plans, solutions, alternatives, but all she saw was

Ali's warm brown eyes and soft smile. Then she realized that he was the solution. "Ali!" she shouted.

"What?"

"He was a scrub tech at the clinic in Bradbury. He's going off to medical school."

"They're on the other side of the canal, and we can't fly in this," Daddy-Kane said.

"Zip line. Across the canal."

Kane considered. "We won't have a lot of time. A storm this bad can overwhelm a suit too."

"Then we better do it fast," Tilda said, and went to call Ali.

It was a testament to the kindness of the Al-Jahanis that they didn't balk or hesitate. Grandpa Stephen declared the plan insane and ordered that none of the hands were to help.

Tilda felt her fingers curling into claws, and she was ready to launch herself at her grandfather. Any remnant of affection for the old man vanished at that moment, and she saw that something had happened with Kane too. He was chest to chest with his father, screaming into the old man's face.

"You son of a bitch! You *want* him to die. Someone will help me. Someone has to hate you as much as I do!"

Daddy-Kane's words hit like acid, and Stephen seemed to shrivel under the assault. And Kane was right. Several of the hands had come to like both Noel and Kane, and offered to help. Tilda wanted to go with them, but Kane didn't want her out in the storm.

"Stay with Noel," Daddy-Kane said, hugging her close. "Keep him with us." He started away, then looked back. There was a grey cast beneath his dark skin. "And don't let your grandfather into the room."

Eyes wide, Tilda just nodded. She locked the door and returned to Noel-Pa's side.

Forty minutes ticked past, with Tilda holding her father's hand, talking to him, reminding him of their life together. Eventually, the door opened, and Kane and Ali entered. The young man looked scared but determined.

Tilda leaped up and hugged him. "Thank you. Thank you." She brushed away the tears that sprang into her eyes.

"Don't thank me yet, but I think it's going to be okay. Neanderthals did trepannings, and I've got an uplink on my Ring to the Lowell Medical Center, and a neurosurgeon is going to walk me through it. So let's get started. We need to shave his head and disinfect the skull. And I need a drill."

The prep took longer than the actual procedure. Daddy-Kane steadied his husband's head while Tilda held a towel at the ready to mop up blood. Ali inserted the drill. The whine edged the teeth, and made the back of Tilda's eyes hurt. She tightened her sweat-limned hands on the towel as the drill bit slowly through the skin. A burning scent as it hit bone, then Ali was through and a geyser of blood hit him in the chest and face. Tilda jumped forward to block it with a towel, only to have the older, white-haired woman doctor in the ScoopRing holo say shrilly, "No, let it bleed. We want the pressure reduced."

The spurting blood slowed to a trickle, then stopped. Ali scrambled to his feet and held his ScoopRing over the hole in Noel's skull for the surgeon in Lowell City to inspect. Dr. Bush was leaning forward as if she could step across the hundreds of miles. Ali pulled out his earbud so that they could all hear the woman say, "Nice job, Ali. Looks good. Clean it, get a pad and a bandage on it, and he should awaken in a few hours."

Tilda hugged first her father, and then flung herself into Ali's arms. He bestowed an awkward kiss that pretty much missed her mouth, but it was still really nice.

Tilda went to her room to change into a clean shirt. Some of the spouting blood had hit her. She was rather proud of herself that she hadn't fainted or reacted to the gore. Maybe she could have been a soldier. Of course, she wasn't going to have a chance to find out now.

What was going to happen once Noel-Pa awakened? she wondered. But that line of thought was too fraught and filled with pain and dread. She returned to her fathers' bedroom.

Hours passed. The pupil in Noel's eye returned to normal. His blood pressure dropped, his pulse was normal. He didn't awaken. Ali called Dr. Bush back. She had him test muscle reflexes on the bottom of the soldier's foot. It all tested normal. But still he lay like an effigy, and with each passing hour, he seemed to fill out the sheet less and less, as if he were diminishing before their eyes. Kane's face sagged and went grey. Ali made hurried calls to Dr. Bush, but nothing she suggested helped.

The storm screamed itself out. Ali's father wanted to fly over and collect him, but Ali refused. "Not until my patient wakes up" was what he said, and Tilda wanted to kiss him again. Grandpa Stephen came by once and gazed with a bitter expression at the prone form of his son-in-law. Tilda was glad then that Ali had stayed; it kept all the hate and bile from being spoken aloud.

Tilda retreated to her bedroom and lay down. She was just going to rest her burning eyes for a few minutes—

Noel-Pa and Miyako were sitting on either side of Ozymandias on the top step of the temple. All three of them looked at Tilda as she walked down the long boulevard. The air around Tilda pulsed and—

She was suddenly elbow deep in a tea bush, carefully stripping off the tender leaves. Her hands were tiny, a child's hands, and the skin was pale almond. She glanced up at her father, who smiled over at her.

"This tea will be drunk in the White House and Buckingham Palace. It's as if we'll be there when they serve it," he said, and Miyako felt a shiver of excitement.

Her hands were larger now, gauntleted in armor, and they gripped a heavy rifle. There was a flash as a laser gouged a new crater on Ceres. Her faceplate darkened so that she wouldn't be blinded. She threw herself in a long dive into cover.

"Delia? Sam? Matt? Sound off. Talk to me, people." Her voice was a deep baritone.

Tilda had reached the foot of the steps, and she walked up to Ozymandias.

"Do you understand now?" he asked.

"The cities were the repository of memories," she said. "Somehow you all lived together—the living and the dead. Past and present in tandem. No wonder we couldn't understand. It was too much, so we interpreted it as music."

He nodded his long, thin head. "So many of us are lost. The voices of the ancestors, ground to dust by you rushing children."

"We didn't understand," Tilda said. "But Miyako became the bridge, didn't she?"

"And you and your father listened."

Tilda looked over at Noel-Pa. "But I'd like to take my father home now."

"Body and spirit are separated. And yours is not the call he will answer."

Tilda woke, scrambled out of bed, and ran to her father's room.

"That's crazy. You want to drag a sick man out into those ruins?" Daddy-Kane said.

"I'm sorry, I have to agree with your dad." Ali gestured at the bed. "He's getting weaker by the hour. The move might kill him."

"Right now he's dying by inches. Isn't he?" she demanded of Ali. He hesitated, then gave a slow nod. She turned back to Kane. "Please, Daddy. What have we got to lose? I'm telling you, he's gone to the city. Like Miyako. He doesn't think there's anything to come back to. *You* have to convince him, lead him home."

Kane chewed at his lower lip. Looked over at the bed. The sheet seemed to barely rise and fall over Noel's chest. He looked to Ali, who just shrugged helplessly.

"I don't think there's anything more I can do."

Kane slowly said, "My mom heard the music. She wanted to die in the Martian city, but Dad wouldn't hear of it. She begged me to

help her, but I took his side. He took her to Lowell City. To the hospital." It was a confession as raw as acid.

"Don't take his side this time," Tilda pleaded. "Noel-Pa doesn't
have to die. He just needs a reason to live. Please, Daddy."

For a breathless second, it hung in the balance, then Daddy-Kane
jumped up and grabbed Noel's envirosuit. With Tilda's and Ali's
help, they got him dressed. Kane lifted Noel into his arms.

"My dad's forbidden anyone to go into the city. You've got to cover
for us, okay?" Kane asked the young man.

"You got it."

Determining that Stephen was in the orchard dome, they hurried to the garage and the crawlers. As they rolled across the dry lake
bed, a dust plume rose like a phoenix's tail behind them. Then they
were at the city, and a wide boulevard stretched before them.

"Is there someplace in particular we're going?" Daddy-Kane
asked.

"Yes." Tilda was staring intently through the front windshield. "I
know the way."

The walls of the buildings gave back the echo of the crawler's big
engine, and the ever-present Martian wind sighed and whispered
through the streets. A flash of movement had Tilda's head jerking
around, but it was only a dust devil. Slowly, an overlay of the memory
city formed over the ruins. She could see the gaily dressed crowds,
the streamers and kites dancing in the wind, the rainbow hues of the
towers. The music was all around her.

"Jesus Christ!" Daddy-Kane muttered. "Is that . . . ? I hear it."

She guided them down now-familiar turns and streets, until the
temple stood before them. "Up there. We need to take him up there."

Ozymandias was on the top step. When Tilda climbed out of the
crawler, he gave her a slow nod and vanished.

Kane gathered Noel in his arms, and the trio climbed the steep,
high steps. Inside, the swirling patterns on the walls were faded and
broken in places, and sand gritted beneath their boots.

The music was like a river roaring past them, breaking like a prism into visions of alien lives and memories. Her father looked down at her, his face tense behind the helmet's faceplate. "I can barely think. I don't know what to do."

"Call him back. Tell him . . . you know what to tell him."

Kane nodded, knelt, and placed Noel on the floor of the temple. Then, taking Noel's gloved hand in his, he said softly, "Wake up, honey." Noel moaned and stirred slightly.

This is going to work, Tilda exalted.

Her ScoopRing chimed, a dissonant note in the Martian song. She wanted to ignore it, but its insistent clamor was starting to shatter the melody. She answered. It was Ali.

His face in the holo was tight and tense. "Tilda, it's your grandfather. He's freakin' the fuck out. Totally losing it. I tried to keep him out of the room, but he forced his way in. He knows where you've gone. He took off raving about how he was going to tear down the old city. How it's luring away his family. Your granddad's on his way to the city with a big earthmover."

"Oh Jesus," Tilda breathed. "Okay, thanks . . . I'll . . . I'll think of something." She cut the connection and looked toward her fathers.

Kane was huddled over his husband, talking intently. "I'm sorry, Noel. I lost my way for a while. I wasn't sure where my first loyalty lay. I know now. I love you. Come home."

There could be no help there. The connection between Kane and Noel was still too fragile, too tenuous. She couldn't pull Kane away at this critical juncture. Tilda slipped out of the temple, down the long stairs, and into the street. In the distance, she could hear the dragon's growl of heavy machinery, followed by a crash as a wall came down.

She broke into a run. She rounded a corner, and there was Stephen in the high glassed-in cab. Even through the layers of glass and his helmet, she could see how his face twisted in fury. He drove the giant earthmover into a building, battering at it with the front bucket.

Tilda ran forward, waving her arms over her head and shouting,

"Stop!" She got in front of the dozer. Her grandfather jammed to a stop only inches from her.

"Get out of my way!"

"No! You can't do this! You'll kill Noel-Pa. His soul is in the city."

"He's already dead. He gave in to these creatures. This *place*. I have to save Kane and you."

"You do this, and you'll lose us both," she screamed back.

He threw the massive machine into reverse, spun it around, and headed for another building. Desperation like bile filled her mouth. Tilda had no idea how to assault the behemoth and the man inside.

Miyako walked slowly and calmly out of the door of the building Stephen was approaching. The dozer ground to a stop, and Tilda realized that the torrent of memory had penetrated even Stephen's closed mind. Wind-driven sand swirled about her feet, and, suddenly, Tilda knew what to do. She ran forward, ripped off the fuel cap.

Miyako was talking. "You didn't love me. I was a means to an end. You never forgave me for being in Catherine's place." Tilda was frantically shoveling handfuls of sand into the gas tank. "All you talked about was the baby and how he would be better than Kane ever was. Even the baby was just a way to hurt Kane. It didn't matter. *I* didn't matter."

All through Miyako's speech, Stephen was muttering, "You're not real. You're a monster."

Oh God, she was pregnant, Tilda thought. *And it broke Granddad. Broke us all.* She shook her head, driving away the hopeless thought. *But not yet, damn it!*

Stephen threw the earthmover into gear and roared forward, trying to crush Miyako. Then the engine coughed and died. Screaming curses, the old man threw open the door of the cab and leaped to the ground. He was carrying a long, heavy spanner.

Tilda rushed up and paced at his side as he pursued Miyako, who drifted always just out of reach. "You can't kill her. You already did that. And you can't wipe out the memory of what you did to her. And if Noel-Pa dies, the memory of your cruelty to him will remain too. And I promise you I'll come here to die, so what you did to me won't ever be forgotten."

He stumbled over a curb, and his strides seemed less certain. Tilda pushed on, knowing that her words were cutting wounds in the old man's soul and not really caring.

"If you had let Catherine die in the city like she wanted to, her memories would be here. You wouldn't have lost her completely. Don't you understand? The more you grab at us, the more we fight to get free. And if your actions cause Noel-Pa to die, you'll lose your son too."

Stephen stumbled to a stop and leaned on the spanner like a cane. His shoulders were shaking. "God forgive me!" The words were broken, whispered, and Tilda barely caught them. "I'm so alone." He sank down to the ground.

Miyako's memory ghost walked up to him. Laid a hand on his shoulder. "We have a lot to talk about," she said simply.

Tilda left them there and ran back to the temple. To find Noel-Pa leaning against Kane, his helmeted head on his husband's shoulder. They opened their arms to her and she ran into their embrace.

A few weeks later, she and Ali walked together in the Martian city. It was a scene of frenzied activity as crews worked to clear away the sand and rubble, scientists pondered how the city recorded the life memories of the dying, and religious leaders prayed. The McKenzie farm had opened its doors to house the army of experts who had arrived.

"So, you don't regret staying?" Ali asked her.

"No. There's so much to do here. Noel-Pa and Stephen have the easiest access to Miyako, and I can talk to Ozymandias. I'm needed."

"Who was he?" Ali asked.

"The Martian who figured out how to keep memory alive."

"No wonder they built a monument to him." Ali paused and

surveyed the slender spires, now cleaned of the occluding dust. "It's sort of ironic the way your dad and granddad are working together now."

"Yeah, also kind of appropriate. And I'm still going to Cambridge. They're just letting me do it as a correspondence course." She smiled at him. "I'll miss you."

"It won't be forever."

"I thought you were staying on Earth."

Ali looked around. "I've got a lot of memories here. I'd hate to abandon them."

He gave her a hug, and she watched him walk back to his ultralight. She then headed home. Daddy-Kane and Noel-Pa were making breakfast, and, with so many people to feed, they could probably use some help.

MICHAEL MOORCOCK

One of the most prolific, popular, and controversial figures in modern letters, Michael Moorcock has been a major shaping force in the development of science fiction and fantasy, as both author and editor, for more than thirty years. As editor, Moorcock helped to usher in the "New Wave" revolution in SF in the middle 1960s by taking over the genteel but elderly and somewhat tired British SF magazine *New Worlds* and coaxing it into a bizarre new life. Moorcock transformed *New Worlds* into a fierce and daring outlaw publication that was at the very heart of the British New Wave movement, and Moorcock himself—for his role as chief creator of the either much admired or much loathed "Jerry Cornelius" stories, in addition to his roles as editor, polemicist, literary theorist, and mentor to most of the period's most prominent writers—became one of the most controversial figures of that turbulent era. *New Worlds* died in the early seventies, after having been ringingly denounced in the Houses of Parliament and banned from distribution by the huge British bookstore and newsstand chain W H Smith, but Moorcock himself has never been out of public view for long. His series of "Elric" novels—elegant and elegantly perverse "Sword & Sorcery" at its most distinctive, and far too numerous to individually list here—are wildly popular, and bestsellers on both sides of the Atlantic. At the same time, Moorcock's other work, both in and out of the genre, such as *Gloriana, Behold the Man, An Alien Heat, The End of All Songs,* and *Mother London,* have established him as one of the most respected and critically acclaimed writers of our day. He has won the Nebula Award, the World Fantasy Award, the John W. Campbell Memorial Award, and the Guardian Fiction Award. His other books include (among *many* others), the novels *The War Hound and the World's Pain, Byzantium Endures, The Laughter of Carthage, Jerusalem Commands, The Land Leviathan,* and *The Warlord of the Air,* as well as the collection *Lunching with the Antichrist,* an autobiographical study, *Letters from Hollywood,* and a critical study of fantasy literature, *Wizardry and*

Wild Romance. His most recent books include *London Peculiar and Other Nonfiction* and *The Whispering Swarm,* the first volume in the new Sanctuary of the White Friars series. After spending most of his life in London, Moorcock moved to a small town in Texas several years back, where he now lives and works.

Moorcock is no stranger to Mars, having visited there with a series of novels, written under the name of Edward P. Bradbury, that sent a swashbuckling Earthman to an ancient, habitable Mars: *Warriors of Mars, Blades of Mars,* and *Barbarians of Mars.* Now he takes us back to Mars in the company of a notorious outlaw on the run for his life, deadly pursuit hot on his heels, who blunders into a situation where he's forced to race against time to save the entire planet from being destroyed, with only a few short hours left on the clock . . .

The Lost Canal

MICHAEL MOORCOCK

1

Martian Manhunt

MAC STONE WAS IN TROUBLE. HE HEARD THE STEADY *SLAP-slap-slap* of the P140 auto-Bannings and knew they'd licked the atmosphere problem. That gadget could now find a man, stun him, or kill him according to whatever orders had come from Terra. If necessary, the bionic "wombots" it carried could follow him into space. The things worked by popping in and out of regular space the way you bunch up a piece of cloth and stick a needle through it to save time and energy. Human physiology couldn't stand those instant translations—in and out, in and out through the cosmic "folds"— but the wombot wasn't human; it moved swiftly and easily in that environment. Flying at cruising speed for regular space-time, the wombot could cross a million miles as if they were a hundred. The thing was a terrible weapon, outlawed on every solar colony, packing several features into one—surveillance, manhunter, ordnance. If Mac were unlucky, they'd just use it to stun him. So they could take their time with him back at RamRam City.

Why do they want me this bad? He was baffled.

They had him pinned down. In all directions lay the low, lichen-covered Martian hills: ochre, brown, and a thousand shades of yellow-grey almost as far as he could see. You couldn't hide in lichen. Not unless you could afford a mirror suit. Beyond the hills were the mountains, each taller than Everest, almost entirely unexplored.

That was where he was heading before a wombot scented heat from his monoflier and took it out in a second. Four days after that, they hit his camp with a hard flitterbug and almost finished him off. Nights got colder as the east wind blew. Rust-red dust swept in from the desert, threatening his lungs. It whispered against his day suit like the voices of the dead.

If they didn't kill him, autumn would.

Mac plucked his last thin jane from his lips and pinched off the lit end. He'd smoke it later. If there was any "later." The IMF had evidently gotten themselves some of the new bloodhound wombots, so compact and powerful they could carry a body to Phobos and back. Creepy little things, not much bigger than an adult salmon. They made him feel sick. He still hoped he might pick the site of his last fight. He had only had two full charges left in his reliable old Banning-6 pistol. After that, he had a knife in his boot and some knucks in his pocket. And then his bare hands and his teeth.

They had called Stone a wild animal back on Mercury, and they were right. The Callisto slave-masters had made him into one after they pulled him from a sinking lavasub. He'd been searching for the fabled energy crowns of the J'ja. The rebel royal priests had been planning to blast Spank City to fragments before the IMF found the secret of their fire-boats and quite literally stopped them cold, freezing them in their tracks, sending the survivors out to *Panic,* the asteroid that liked to call herself a ship. But the J'ja had hidden their crowns first.

So long ago. He'd been in some tough spots and survived, but this time it seemed like he'd run out of lives and luck.

You didn't get much cover in one of the old flume holes. They'd been dug when some crazy twenty-second-century Terran wildcat miners thought they could cut into the crust and tap the planet's plasma. They believed there were rivers of molten gold down there. They claimed that they heard them at night when they slept curled within the cones. Someone had fallen into a particularly deep one and sworn he had seen molten platinum running under his feet.

Poor devils. They'd spent too long trying to make sense of the star-crowded sky. Recently, he'd heard that the inverted cones were used by hibernating ock-crocs. Mac hoped he wasn't waking anything up down there. He doubted the theory and did his best not to think about it, to keep out of sight and to drop his body temperature as much as he dared, release a few dead fuel pods and hope that the big Banning bloodbees would mistake him for an old wreck and its dead pilot and pass him by.

"You only need fear the bees if you've broken the law." That familiar phrase was used to justify every encroachment on citizens' liberty. Almost all activities were semicriminal these days. Mars needed cheap human workers. Keep education as close as possible to zero. The prisons were their best resource. Industrial ecology created its own inevitable logic.

Sometimes you escaped the prisons and slipped back into Ram-Ram City, where you could live relatively well if you knew how to look after yourself. Sometimes they just let you stay there until they had a reason to bring you in or get rid of you.

And that's what they appeared to be doing now.

Slap-slap-slap.

Why were they spending so much money to catch him? He knew what those machines cost. Even captured, he wasn't worth a single wombot.

Wings fluttering, big teeth grinding, the flier was coming over the horizon, and, by the way it hovered and turned in the thin air, Mac's trick hadn't fooled it at all. Good handling. He admired the skill. Private. Not IMF at all. One guy piloting. One handling the ordnance. Or maybe one really *good* hunter doing both. He reached to slide off the pistol's safety. Looked like he was going down fighting. He wondered if he could hit the pilot first.

Stone was a Martian born in the shadow of Low-Canal's massive water tanks. The district had never really been a canal. It had been named by early explorers trying to make sense of the long, straight indentations, now believed to be the foundations of a Martian city.

But it was where most of AquaCorps's water was kept. Water was expensive and had to be shipped in from Venus. Sometimes there would be a leakage, and, with kids like him, he could collect almost a cup before the alarms went. His mother lived however she could in the district. His father had been a space ape on the wild Jupiter runs, carbon rods rotting and twisting as they pulled pure uranium from the Ki Sea. He'd probably died when the red spot erupted, taking twenty u-tankers with it.

When he was seven, his ma sold Mac to a mining company looking for kids small enough to fit into the midget tunnelers working larger asteroids and moons that were able to support a human being for a year or so before they died. His mother had known that "indentured" was another word for death sentence. She knew that he was doomed to breathe modified methane until his lungs and all his other organs and functions gave out.

Only Mac hadn't died. He'd stolen air and survived and risen, by virtue of his uninhibited savagery, in what passed for Ganymedan society. Kru miners made him a heroic legend. They betrothed him to their daughters.

Stone was back on Mars and planning to ship out for Terra when his mother sent word that she wanted to tell him something. He'd gone to Tank Town with the intention of killing her. When he saw her, the anger went out of him. She was a lonely old woman lacking status or family. He'd only be doing her a favor if he finished her off. So he let it go. And realized that she'd been holding her breath as he held his, and he turned and laughed that deep slow purr she knew from his father. This made her note his tobacco-colored skin, now seamed like well-used leather, and she wept to read in his face all the torments he had endured since she'd sold him. So he had let her die believing a lie, that they enjoyed a reconciliation. What he said or thought didn't mean much to the Lord she believed in.

After that, he'd started stealing jewels with a vengeance. Good ones. Big ones. He'd done very well. Hitting the mining trains. Fencing them back through Earth. Generous, like most thieves of his kind, and therefore much liked by the Low-Canal folk who protected him, he'd done well. He was one of their own, accepted as a Martian hero with stories told about him as V-dramas. Only two people had made it out of the Tanks to become famous on the V. Mac Stone was one, and Yily Chen, the little Martian girl he'd played hide-and-go-seek with as a kid, was the other. Yily now operated from Earth, mostly doing jobs the corps didn't want anyone to associate directly with them. Her likeness had never been published. He remembered her for her lithe brown body, her golden eyes. He'd loved her then. He couldn't really imagine what she looked like now. No doubt she'd become some hard-faced mother superior, pious and judgmental, like most tankers who grew up staying within the law, such as it was. She had put Tank Town behind her. He'd elected to stay. But he'd been sold out once again, this time to the Brothers of the Fiery Mount, whoever they were. They put him back to work on Ganymede with no idea he had family there.

Then some war broke out on Terra for a while. It couldn't have come at a better time. It destroyed the old cartels and opened the planet up to real trade. And everyone wanted to rearm, of course.

By the third month of Stone's return, his clan, riding a wave of similar revolutions through the colonies, had conquered a significant number of exec towers and looted a museum for a heliograph system they'd been able to copy. Communications. Codes. Bribes. Clever strategy. Guerrilla tactics. By the sixth month, as they prepared for the long tomorrow, they had won the moon and were doing business with four of the richest nations of Terra and New Japan.

Meanwhile, over at the freshly built Martian Scaling Station, the "black jump" was opening up the larger universe hidden in the folds of space-time through which the wombots traveled. They'd begun to realize that they were part of a denser, mostly invisible cosmos. Until recently, the "cosmic fog" had obscured so much from the astronomers. The discovery brought about new power shifts and unexpected alliances. With the right start, they said, some of those worlds could be reached in days! Now it didn't matter if Terra was dying. Was that really the prevailing logic?

Mac knew that he and the human race were at some sort of crossroads, poised at last on their way to the stars. They might find an unbeatable enemy out there. Or beatable enemies. Or they could learn to negotiate. The game Mac knew best wasn't necessarily the best game. For now, however, he needed capital to play with the big guys, and he was never going to get that kind of money in one piece. Not while he remained an outworld Martian wolfshead. He knew enough about those odds. He knew who the men were who owned the worlds. All of which was to his advantage. His equal share of the Ganymede profits wasn't large enough, and he didn't like his public profile getting bigger. He'd made his ex-brother-in-law boss and quietly returned to Mars and his old trade. He—or really the pseudonym he'd chosen—developed a serious reputation. He was credited with any number of unsolved cases. No one knew what to expect from him. Few knew his face or his real name. A fist diamond had paid to have every mug shot and most records wiped. He began to build his pile. The first thing he needed was a good ship of his own. He went into water brokerage. He had a half share in an atmosphere factory. He was earning that ship when he'd been, he assumed, betrayed. He wondered if that had anything to do with the sneaky little Venusian lep who had come to see him with a suspicious offer a week or two before his arrest.

To his surprise, because it was a special private prison, they took him straight to Tarpauling Hill. Or meant to. Escaping his escort had not been difficult. Escaping a planet was going to be harder.

This was his eighth Martian day on the run. There were no real maps of the hinterland. He knew the Interplanetary Military Force. They let their big robot Bannings loose if they thought that someone was hiding in an area. He could have stayed in RamRam City, hidden in the Tanks, but it would get expensive in terms of human lives. He'd had to lead them into wild, unpopulated country or they might have killed half Low-Canal's population. Out to the wide valleys and high mountains of the Monogreanimi, where, it was said, the old high queens of Mars still dreamed in the deep ice.

Mac was trying to find one of the legendary "blowholes," sunk by Mars's last race, who had been seeking air for the shelters in which they'd taken refuge from the Long Rain, the incessant meteor storms pulverizing the planet. The falling meteors had destroyed almost every sign of the dozen or so major civilizations that had once ruled a Mars almost as lush as Venus.

Mac hated Venus. He hated her fecundity as well as her unpredictable gas storms, which regularly wiped out hundreds. Terran Venusians went crazy just to survive the extremes. He hated native Venusians, the smelly little green people nicknamed leprechauns by Terrans. He hated Terrans, too. And he really hated Mercury. Mars, he could not help loving. He loved her vast, tranquil deserts, her hills and high, wild mountains where nothing breathed. Once he'd longed to make her self-sustaining again. He'd dreamed of bringing in enough water to make her bloom as she had in the days when the few surviving pictograms and engravings had been created. When she still had seas. There were other legends of how she had been, but these could all be traced back to myths created in the twentieth and twenty-first centuries.

All Mac wanted was the reality. To see the canals running again while sun and moons illuminated blue forests and small fields of brass-colored crops. To settle down on a few acres of land, growing enough to sell and sustain himself. Then maybe a family. To make a new Mars, a peaceful Mars where kids could grow. That's what he'd dreamed. That's what had kept him alive all these years. He let out a brief, not particularly bitter, laugh. Now the best he could hope for was a quick death.

He wondered if he could gain any time by giving himself up in the hope that he'd find another chance of escape. It would avoid what was probably an inevitable death out here. He had to take control of his own determined soul, which would rather fight and die than wait for another chance. But that was all he could do. He got hold of himself and, disgusted by his chosen action, he snarled and pulled a big white silk scarf out of a leg pouch in his leathers.

He was tying this to the barrel of his Banning when he felt something moist, cold, and scaly slip around his ankle and give it an experimental tug.

He yanked free. It took a tighter hold. It seemed patient. It knew he couldn't escape. He'd done his best to keep clear of the wombot's sensors, but his movement had already alerted the thing. It chickled out a challenge. Again, he tried to yank his leg away.

The wombot spit a bubble of death syrup all over the nearby rocks. They weren't going to waste valuable gas or darts on him unless they had to. At least he wasn't going to need a white flag. Now he knew that they wanted him dead rather than alive.

Below Mac, the ground powdered. The tentacle tugged harder and the area beneath him broke open, dragging him down a fissure, scraping every inch of his day suit. The suit's circuits wouldn't survive another attack. Suddenly, it was inky-dark. He heard the odd rattle and boom of the thing's heart-lung. He forgot the native name someone had guessed at, but it was without doubt an ock-croc.

Mac Stone prepared himself for death.

2

To Destroy the Future

HE WAS STILL TRYING TO POINT HIS PISTOL WHEN THE FISSURE became a tunnel, thick with something caked around its sides. The worst stink in creation. Croc dung! Threat of death really did sharpen the memory. That's what it coated its long burrow with. The Martian *wanal* or ock-croc was the only large predator left. These giant, tentacled reptilian insects drove deep burrows using old blowholes or wells; they weren't particular. They hibernated for years, woke up very hungry. The first hatchling typically ate all its siblings and sometimes its parent. Then it ate whoever was still hibernating. Although not radioactive themselves, they preferred areas still "buzzy" and lethal to humans. If the croc didn't eat Stone right away, the chances were he'd soon die painfully of radiation poisoning.

"Oh, damn!" He couldn't do anything with his holstered gun. The thing seemed to know precisely how to catch him so he did it the least damage. He had to be many meters down now, the Banning long since passed out of sight and no longer his main fear. A bionic wombot might follow him, but so far he felt relatively sanguine about that. The chances were the croc would also eat the wombot, built-in explosives and all. The thought gave Mac a brief moment of satisfaction.

The tunnel opened into a pit occupied by a huge pulsing head with six round eyes the size of portholes, which slowly retreated from him as a single tentacle—one of many—dragged him deeper.

Mac did all he could to slow his descent into the pit, where its own green-yellow luminescence revealed the croc's enormous carcass. A nightmare of snakelike waving arms with a long snout full of dagger-size needles for teeth, the wriggling body a black blob of scaly horror. More tentacles snared him so that he couldn't move any part of his body without making things worse. He was resigned to what must happen next.

He heard a double *click* as the thing disconnected its jaw, ready to swallow him. Then he thought he heard human speech. One tentacle released his right arm. If he could only get hold of his gun, he might not kill the croc but he'd give it the worst attack of indigestion it had known in all its long, quasi-reptilian life. He made one last lunge. His fingers clutched for the butt.

As his Banning came loose, something else fell out of the air and rattled on the rock. He looked down and saw a tiny blue flickering of flame. Voices seemed to jeer inside his head.

He felt horribly cold. At this rate, he'd freeze to death before the croc ate him. The questor had found him just as he was making camp. He'd had to move fast. When the Martian night caught him without his Hopkins blanket, it would be over anyway. The *wanal* only had to wait for him to lose a little more heat. They were famous for their cunning patience. Once, there had been a dozen varieties of the creature. Mac had seen pictures of them in the old hunting cubes of the Sindolu, the extinct nomads of the northern hemisphere, from whose encampments a few artifacts had been miraculously preserved. The *wanal* they had feared most had massive mandibles and ten tentacles. This was that kind of *wanal*.

It reached out for him again, giggling its nasty pleasure. Then it hesitated. Something red and dripping was thrown to it over the edge of the pit. Then a sharp command came from the darkness and it backed off, peering hungrily from him to the meat.

Snagging the hard case containing the flickering blue flame, Mac pocketed the thing and made haste to clamber as best he could up the other side of the rough pit. The slippery shale made climbing difficult, but he virtually levitated himself out of there. He took the case with the flickering flame out of his glove and put it on the palm of his hand. It made a small hiss. What in the nine inhabited worlds was it? He sensed danger, glanced to his right.

Mac glared in utter disbelief at a bulky "noman" staring down at him from illuminated eyes, hooked hands resting on its metal hips. A type of robot he'd never seen. It looked local. Like something he'd come across in the Terran Museum of Martian Artifacts. Only that one had been about a foot high and carved from pink teastone. The archaeologists thought it was a household god or a child's toy.

Just above the faceless noman, a pale green pillar fizzed like bad Galifrean beer. Then it coalesced into a figure that Stone was surprised to see was human. A bronzed man in the peak of physical condition, wearing less than was considered seemly even on Jambock Boulevard. Except for the little signs of regular wear and tear on his leather harness, the man looked like something out of a serial V-drama. At his right hip was a big, old-fashioned brass-and-steel pistol. Scabbarded on his left was some kind of long antique sword. For a wild moment, Stone wondered if he had been captured by those crazy reenactors who played out completely unlikely battles between invented Martian races. He'd seen groups of them in Sunday Field on vacation afternoons.

The guy in the green pillar fizzed again and broke up a few times before he stabilized long enough to say clearly: "You can't fight me. I'm not actually here. I'm a scientist. I'm from Earth like you. I came to Mars millennia ago, long before the meteor storms. I'm projecting this image into my future. It's interactive."

He smiled. "I'm Miguel Krane." Evidently, he expected Mac to know the name. He had an old-fashioned accent Mac associated with Terra. "We call this little device a chronowire. It sends images and sounds back and forth across time. It is the nearest we've been able to come to time travel. Living organisms get seriously damaged. We discovered to our cost that people and animals can't travel physically in time. The *wanal* won't bother you now. Her old responses are still reachable in her deep subconscious. In our time, we domesticate and use her ancestors to find lost travelers. Their natural instinct is to eat us, but thousands of years of training changed their brains. We found her down here with our explorer noman. We sent her for you. In case of any problems, we fed her some sleepy meat. I'm sorry about the crude robot, too. Believe it or not, he's code-activated! We have to work through remote control with what we can find. In this case, very remote! What do you want to know from me?"

Mac shuddered as he scraped gelatinous stuff from his battered day suit. He looked around. A man-made room. Two doors. A kind of stone box at his feet. He was surprised how warm it was. "You're not fooling me. Time travel? How the hell could you have gotten from Terra to Mars thousands of years ago? Before anyone had space travel?" He looked around at the cavern. Ingeniously reflected light. The walls were bright with luminous veins of phosphorescent ore and precious stones sparkling like stars. If he kept his knife, he might be able to dig out a few long diamonds and get away. Assuming he could dodge this madman.

The man in the projection shrugged. "Malfunctioning matter

transmitter. Lost control. I traveled backward to Mars. One way. You've probably heard of me. Captain Miguel Krane? Haven't you read my books? About my life on Mars? I'm surprised you don't know them. They didn't appear under my name, but I dictated them myself."

"I don't listen to books much."

The man in the green pillar seemed thrown by Mac's illiteracy. But Mac could read forty-seven interplanetary languages and write fluently in most of them. He had taught himself for purely practical reasons. He wasn't a scholar. He was a thief. He would have been insulted to be thought of as anything else.

For his own part, Mac was uneasy, still checking for his gun, reassured by the feel of a knife in his boot. Miguel Krane's voice was amused, but Mac didn't like to hear it in his head like that. Too creepy.

Yet Krane had been instrumental in saving his life. Somewhere over their heads, on the Martian surface, a wombot was still searching for him with the objective of covering him with jelly that could seep through his skin and eat his bones from the inside out. He was in no doubt about his preference. He'd take his chances here.

"Those chances aren't much better, Stone." Krane's voice was still amused. "Let's just say you'd be dying for a good cause."

Mac laughed. "When I hear words like that, I reach for my Banning. Where *is* my gun, by the way?"

"Look for yourself. I didn't take it. Neither did the noman. Want to know why I sent the *wanal* after you?"

"I guess." Mac looked down into the pit, where the nasty thing was finishing its bloody meal. He saw his gun some way up, where it had lodged on a shelf of rock.

"Do you recall a lep coming to see you a few weeks ago?"

"Yeah. Little green man about so high. One of those freaks from Venus. Had some sort of deal. I wouldn't go for it. I didn't like the smell of it. Thought he was lying. Too dangerous." He was on his belly, stretching for the Banning.

"So you told him."

"Was it him fingered me to the IMF?"

"Not exactly, but you didn't do yourself any favors turning him down before you listened."

"He was lying. I know leps. I didn't want to know what his pitch was. I used to get crazies like him all the time, offering to cut me in on some fantasy in their heads."

"The poor little guy was scared out of his wits. He'd found one of our time seeds and he thought we were magic. Ghosts of ancient Martians or something. Still, he did what I told him to do and he only once looked inside the bag. That nearly killed him. He almost dropped it and ran. The lep wasn't just bringing my message. He had a bag of indigo flame sapphires with him."

"A *bag*?" Stone laughed. The rarest jewel in the system, indigo flame sapphires couldn't be cut, polished, or broken up. They had extraordinary properties. There were three known existing sapphires. One was in the Conquest of Space Museum on Terra, one was in the hands of United System President Polonius Delph—he was the richest man in seven worlds, or had been until he'd paid cash for his jewel. The other had been stolen soon after its discovery. Maybe Delph had it. "There's no such thing."

"There is. And Delph wants them. He thinks you've got them on you. They tortured Gunz, the man I sent after the lep. He told them you had them."

"Oh, great! So I was set up by a Venusian leprechaun who was set up by a V-Image! That's why they've been willing to spend so much money hunting me down. They just want to know where those mythical jewels are. They don't care if they kill me. It's just as easy to interrogate a fresh corpse using a couple of ccs of dreme. You remind me of my mother!"

"I can only guess what strange patchwork of information comes through the time seeds. We scatter them into our future, more or less at random. Often they are destroyed or are recalled, damaged. Enough land unharmed to broadcast back. We aren't talking *linear* time as you imagine it, but *radiant* time. From what I understand of your world, Delph isn't the only one who wants the sapphires. He has rivals in the Plutocracy. Another mysterious collector? Or those rivals are competing for the presidency or they think they can ruin him. As you know, it's a vicious circle in politics. You can't get to be president unless you have the wealth, and you can't make really massive sums until you're president. It was much the same in my day."

"Your day?"

"That depends where you're counting from." The more he listened, the more Stone recognized the tone coming through the old accent. Miguel Krane spoke with the economical style of an army man. "Or which planet. So. Was this particular scenario set up by the IMF in order to trick you into giving up the jewels? No. The Interstellar Military Force has nothing to do with us. That was not an IMF ship pursuing you. Probably it's Delph's. I know you don't have the sapphires. The lep was too scared to keep them. He brought them back and left them with the noman."

In spite of this denial, Stone grew cautious again.

"Then who *are* you with?" he challenged. "And why are you so interested in me? Someone's spending a great deal of dough on hunting me down. A real pro, that's for sure. So—really—who are you?"

"My military experience was in Korea, in the middle of the twentieth century," said Krane. "I'm a scientist. Later, I worked on a matter transmitter for the Pentagon. I tested it on myself. It went wrong. I was dragged back to old Mars instead. The Karnala—the clan I fell in with—have access to ancient knowledge and technology left behind by an earlier intelligent race, the Sheev. This machine is some of it. We call it a 'memory catcher' in Karnalan. This is the most sophisticated type.

"What is it? It's an interactive device that can communicate across time. We've been studying them for years. We're not sure we're using the technology appropriately, but we've rigged it so it works for us, after a fashion. We have clear visuals and, when we get over language and other problems, can exchange information or even casual ideas! The Sheev scientists were masters of time. Many believe they abandoned Mars for past eras or the future of another planet, wherever conditions were ideal! Some think they had colonies on ancient Earth or in our future! But that is unlikely. This is about the best use we've found for their technology. And it's to ask of *you*, Mac Stone, something that I would do myself if I weren't merely an ethereal image in your world."

"So you want to make a deal. Isn't that usually the size of it? What can I do for you that you don't want to do yourself? Isn't that usually the deal?"

Krane's image smiled. There was a sense of rapport between the two men. "Usually."

"OK," said Stone. "What's the score? Oh, and don't forget to tell me more about those indigo flame sapphires. Presumably they come into your deal at some point. Let's hear it. I have plenty of time to listen."

Krane did not smile in reply. "Unfortunately," he said, "you haven't."

3

The Star Bomb

"THERE WAS A WAR," SAID THE BRONZED TERRAN. "WE WEREN'T ready for it. We thought we'd earned an era of peace. But we had enemies who hated all we stood for. A tribe that had hidden itself underground years earlier, after my people had defeated it. We have our own technology, but that earlier race—the Sheev—developed horrendous weapons. They never used most of them because everyone got scared at the same time. So the weapons, with many of the scientific instruments that helped make them, were locked away by common consent. We didn't know about one particular cache. Our enemy discovered it. An n-bomb probably powerful enough to destroy a whole planet. They planned to use the underground Ia canal to float it under our city, Varnal of the Green Mists, and blow us up. Meanwhile, our scientists found out about it. Thanks to many of the enemy's own people rebelling against their leaders, who were perceived as reckless, we defeated them. Only when we were discussing terms did we learn about the n-bomb and where it was. It would shortly be directly under Varnal, and would blow within hours.

"We got our best people down there. They could find no way of stopping the thing from detonating. All they could do was adjust the timer. Which they set about doing. By unlocking seven wards in sequence, the timer could be advanced but not neutralized. So the first thing our scientists did was to set the timer to detonate close to a million years into our future. The maximum the timer allowed. We figured that would be more than enough time to find a solution. I thought that Mars would no longer be highly populated by then. We would work on the problem until we had it licked. A million years—plenty of time! The second thing we did was to move the bomb away from the city. We did this by floating it farther on down the canal until it was under a barren, uninhabited part of the planet. Are you familiar with the Ia trans-Martian canal and its story?"

Stone jerked his thumb at the roof. "All the old canals have dried up. There's nothing left of them apart from traces of their beds. And no records, of course. Pretty much everything was lost during the great "four-millennia cannonade," when asteroids and meteors pounded Mars to dust, down to most of her farthest shelters. There are a few freak survivals. Nothing much. The canals were deep and wide once, designed to get the most from dwindling water supplies. The meteors leveled them. But this Ia canal? It was underground?"

"My clan's ancestors planned to build this great underground canal, protected from all foreseeable danger, completely encircling the planet, with branches serving other local systems. The canal was named for an ancient water goddess, Ia. Ia would connect to a series of hubs serving other canal systems. Its creators thought that it would, through the trade it would stimulate, bring peace to the entire planet. Ia would circle Mars from pole to pole, where the melting ice caps would continuously refill it. The project was abandoned long before my time."

"Abandoned? What happened?" In spite of his circumstances, Stone found the story engaging. "It sounds a great idea."

"During construction at the Pataphal cross-waterway intersection, after hundreds of miles of the Ia system had already been built, a terrible disaster struck. A whole section of the great Nokedu Cavern floor, which had been tested and found solid, fell away. Hundreds were killed. More of the cavern kept falling, until it formed a massive chasm, miles deep and far too wide to bridge. Black, unfathomable, the Nokedu Falls dropped deep into the planet's heart. The entire project was abandoned. It was considered folly to attempt another sub-Martian watercourse. No more would have been said had not an extraordinary phenomenon occurred maybe a month after the project was closed for good. A guard reported seeing the canal slowly filling with water!

"Some freak of natural condensation created a system that had the effect of filling the Ia canal with enough water to float a good-size barge. But of course, at Nokedu the water again rushed into the great chasm. Damming didn't work. It became pretty clear that the water had to circulate. Several expeditions had been made into the Nokedu Deep to find the cause of the phenomenon. The expeditions were lost or returned without success. The water supply remained continuous. Then, about five hundred years in your past, a quake dislodged the bomb."

Mac played dumb. "What—and sent it down the falls where it could explode harmlessly?"

"You don't seem to understand. The Sheev originally planned war against nearby planets, especially Terra. The bomb was too powerful. It was never meant to be detonated on *Mars*. Even in space, it had limited useful targets. It was a *star bomb*, intended to be launched at another planet and turn that world to cosmic dust!"

"And that's what's down there somewhere now?" Stone jerked

his thumb toward his feet. "Ticking away as we speak. When's it due to go off?"

"In just under seven hours," said Krane.

"Great! So you simply made your problem *our* problem?" Mac didn't try to disguise his disgust. Fear began to tie his insides together.

"Not deliberately. We only recently learned that Mars was still populated—or repopulated. This wasn't the first time we've tried to contact someone like you or to defuse it. This was the closest we could get to you on this time-line."

"If you know the future, you know what will happen."

"This is the *farthest* we can get in time. We get nothing back if we go farther . . ."

Mac was silent, thinking that over. He was familiar with Gridley's theories of radiant time. "So there might not be any future for us?"

The image shimmered as Krane picked up some kind of yellow gossamer scroll on which symbols sparkled. "Our best minds have worked on the problem ever since we knew about it. We have at last determined how to neutralize the n-bomb."

Mac still didn't speak. He just wanted to hear Krane's pitch.

"OK. So where do *I* come into it?"

"We need you to do the neutralizing."

"For what?"

"To save your planet. Research says you're a Martian, even more than I am. You're a survivor."

"Except that there are easier ways to live."

"That's why you'll get the sapphires."

"A *bag* of indigo flame sapphires?"

"What the lep tried to show you. What Delph heard about."

Mac grinned. "It's a sweet incentive. If you're right, I haven't a chance of getting out of this alive. I might as well take the lot of you—or them—with me. You're all as crooked as I am."

"Except that's not your style, Stone. You're a Martian. You were born on Mars. You don't want Mars to die like that. Not blown to bits."

"OK. Let's assume you're right. How would I get down to this canal and do what I need to do to the bomb?"

"It's not quite so simple," said Krane. "The bomb moved, as I told you. After the 'quake it actually floated down the canal. Until it hit white water. Happily the casing is very strong and relatively light. By luck, it eventually caught between some rocks above the falls. Water currents coming in from three sides actually held the thing steady. It's still there."

"Rapids? That's why your robot can't reach it?"

"One reason."

"Is it hard to dislodge?"

"That, unfortunately, *isn't* a problem. It should dislodge relatively easily."

"So? Where exactly is it?"

"It's pretty much on the brink of that chasm," said Krane. "Where the water of the Ia rushes over the broken canal floor and gushes down into we don't know what. Into the heart of the planet."

"On the brink of hell, in other words."

"Pretty much," said Krane. "But you'll have help. Look over to your left. At the noman's feet."

Stone saw a large steel-and-slate chest, about a meter square. It had some odd markings stenciled on the side.

"Look inside," said Krane. So Stone bent and lifted the catches, opening the lid, which eased up on its own. Inside was soft kalebite packing used for delicate scientific instruments. He picked this off carefully. The contents looked unexpectedly sturdy. He reached in both hands and took it out.

"It looks like a big helmet. Like one those old Terran firefighters had."

Krane said, "It's a Gollowatt'n battle hat. They once fought the Kolvini through the Martian catacombs and never once saw the light of day." Quickly, he described the helmet's intuitive features. "Modified for your use. It'll let you see in the dark for a start. Heat pictures. And there's a sensor that tunes to your own eyes so you can use them as supersensitive binoculars. There are extrapowerful lights for when you need to do fine work, such as on the bomb itself. There's a set of force-tools you can project and use. But it's a lot more than that. There are a million neurolinks so the helmet works intuitively according to the wearer's normal responses. We built a detector into it, too, if it survived the journey."

"Force-tools?"

"They're modified and mostly intuitive, tuned to your brain so you only have to visualize the problem, not the tool itself. Best make appropriate head movements."

"OK." Stone was dubious. "So what's the magic word?"

"There is none. The helmet was made for a Gollowat'n medic, believe it or not. That's why it was built with an empathy conceptor, so the medic could work on a wounded soldier or an injured civilian at the scene, usually in a battle situation. Empathy was a Gollowat'n middle name. The greatest doctors on seven worlds. They're porcine, of course, but close enough to humans for the helmet to work pretty well. It should be compatible with your suit. The noman will make any adjustments you need."

"It's no more than a couple of planets at stake." The helmet was light and felt unexpectedly organic. It shifted like flesh to his touch. It had a faint, pleasant smell, like brine. He lifted it over his head and brought it slowly down, fitting it like a hat. Then it seemed to flow over his skull and snuggle around his throat, his forehead. His suit suddenly buzzed recognition codes. Rounded blinkers fitted over his eyes, but he could see well. If anything, his eyes were sharper. For a moment, his cheekbones itched and he saw an uncomfortable series of cherry-colored flashes. Then a wash of dark red, almost like blood, gave way to enhanced clarity of vision.

The noman extended its arms, touching him gently here and there. His suit settled more comfortably on his body. He was surprised how healthy the thing made him feel. Maybe Gollowat'n medics had to be healthy in order to empathize with their patients. He had a sudden thought.

"This bomb? Is it sentient?"

"Not much," said Krane.

"So what do I have to do to turn the timer off?"

"You have to open a series of locks. Numbered right to left in what they call G-script. We coded them to a particular melody in a particular time signature. It's a tune, with each note representing a complex number. Do you know the old Earth tune 'Dixie'? Just whistle it to yourself. That number should cancel out the existing sequence and effectively baffle the bomb's key and register. The locks will snap off and it will probably simply go dead in your hand."

"And if it doesn't?"

"Well, it will still be live."

"And ready to blow."

"Yes. I'm assured there is very little chance of this going wrong, Mac Stone. Our people worked it out. Essentially, all you have to do is memorize that simple little tune. *Oh, I wish I was in the land of cotton*—"

"There is a problem." Stone was almost embarrassed.

"What's that?"

He flushed. "I'm tone-deaf," he said.

4

Dancing in the Dark

"THEN TRY TO REMEMBER THE INTERVALS." KRANE SEEMED bitterly amused, like a man who believes he's thought of everything only to be told of one obvious unconsidered fact. "The helmet should help you. We've entered the code and the helmet should translate it automatically."

Stone shrugged. "And if I succeed, I come back here and you give me the sapphires?"

"The whole bag. I promise."

Stone didn't have much choice now. He had to make a decision. Believe this strange Earthman or not? He laughed his long, low purr and tested the helmet's responses. He pulled the casque down a little more firmly, settling the bond with his suit. Somehow he knew what to do next. He blinked to make the lights come on. Then he lay down on the side of the pit, fishing up his gun. The *wanal* made an unpleasant noise but went on eating.

Stone wiped slime off the barrel of his Banning and shoved it back in its holster. "What now?"

"The helmet's programmed to help you find the bomb. If you leave this chamber, you'll be at the top of a flight of stairs leading to a wide walkway. It runs beside the canal. All the Sheev waterways were made like that and their successors copied them." There was a warm, Terran voice speaking to him now. Was this what Miguel Krane really sounded like? "There's a numbering system still based on Sheev. The Sheev system used predominantly eleven. One, two, eleven, eleven, twenty-two, and so on.

"The Ia was rediscovered by the last Martians. They followed us. They built cities where they could shelter from the meteors. Air enough and water. They cultivated plants that grew well in the hydroponic fields. They built the atmosphere factories. They traded up and down that stretch of the canal. They sustained their particular civilization for another thousand years or more. When the meteor storms had passed, as you know, the whole planet had been pulverized. Almost all trace of Martian life was wiped out, except for things that lived belowground. They never really came back to the surface."

Mac wondered what his own chances were. As he found the wide black steps that led downward, he thought of those ancient Martians who had built them back when the planet was still a world of gentle seas and green hills, of endless forests and big skies, before humans had evolved at all. And then came the Five Ages. The ages of the humanoid Martians. And then the meteors. The Martians would ultimately grow lonely as the remaining scraps of their culture were buried by the rusty Martian sands. They elected to find solitude below the surface and fade into death surrounded by the massive black stones of their eerie necropolis.

For all he was a loner, Stone found it hard to understand their mind-set. From the moment he burst out of his mother's womb, he'd had to fight to remain alive and had relished every second he won for himself, grateful for whatever air he could drag into his gasping lungs, for every sight and sound that told him that he still lived. Mac Stone had a human brain and he was proud of his Martian heritage. He didn't care whose lives he was saving or what reward he would receive. Mars was all he cared about. His battered flitboots echoed down wide steps of black pearl marble, as smooth and as stately and as beautiful in their subtle curvature as they had been on the day they were finished. He hardly noticed their grandeur. He thought of the big reflective tanks he had played among as a little boy and what so much water could do for the Low-Canal.

He breathed vanilla air, which reminded him of the shows he'd watched as a kid on the big public V-drome screens, sometimes as real as life, sometimes better, and he wondered if this was like that. Was this his life starting to replay at faster-than-real speed as his brain got ready to die? Was he already dead, remembering the high moments, the fine moments, of his wild life before he'd been sold? When he and Yily Chen would scamper like scorpions in and out of the blackness cast by the vast tanks and at night chase the flickering shadows cast by Phobos as she came sailing from the west, shreds of darkness skipping before her like familiars, spreading a trail of shades behind her . . . Oh, that raw intemperate beauty! Alive or dead, Mac swore he was never again going to leave Mars.

The noman had thoroughly repaired and recharged his day suit. Mac felt pleasantly warm as he reached the bottom of the stairs and stood on the edge of the great canal and looked out over it. He was stunned by the amount of water the planet was keeping secret! It could have been an ocean, with no far shore visible. To his left and right, the canal was endless. From what he could tell, much of it followed an old watercourse, but other parts were hollowed out by something that had sliced easily through the dark Martian granite and decorated it with deep, precise reliefs showing half-human creatures and unlikely beasts. Machinery of alien design and mysterious purpose. There were walkways cut into the canal walls, allowing animals or machines to drag boats beside them. Characters etched into the granite counted off *glems,* close to a meter, in what Stone knew as "Dawson," named for the script's first Terran translator.

He moved his head to his right. In the helmet's crisp illumination, he saw black water rippling, making its rapid way toward the falls, which had to be miles away and yet were already distinct. A distant roar. At a discreet sound from the helmet, Stone turned right, keeping the water on his left as the walkway widened, revealing the dark bulk of buildings, low houses, all abandoned. This had been a busy, thriving port. People had traded down here and been entertained, had families and lived complex lives. Mac wished that he had time to explore the town. Unlike the canal itself, the settlements along the bank were on a human scale and in different styles. This was where the last humanoid Martians had lived. The place had a bleak atmosphere. Mac saw no evidence for the legends he'd grown up hearing in the Low-Canal of enduring pockets of Martians still living down here.

They were not the last native Martians. Those were the *raïfs.* Never wholly visible, they flitted around the Low-Canal settlements— the so-called mourning Martians, whose songs sometimes drifted in from the depths of the dead sea-bottoms and whose pink-veined outlines were almost invisible by noon. They drifted like translucent rays, feeding on light. Their songs could be heartbreaking. Storytellers insisted that they were not a new race at all but the spirits of the last humanoid Martians, forever doomed to haunt the Low-Canal.

Stone had never felt quite so alone. The buildings were thinning out as he walked, and his helmet showed him an increasing number of great natural arches, of stalagmites and stalactites forming a massive stone forest beside the whispering waters of the Ia canal. Some had been carved by ancient artists into representations of long-since-extinct creatures. Every so often, he was startled by a triangular face with eldritch, almost Terran, features. Mac, used to so much strangeness, felt almost in awe of those petrified faces, which stared back at him with sardonic intelligence.

Nothing lived here, not even the savage crocs. Nothing flew or scampered or wriggled over the smooth marble, among the stone trunks of stone trees whose stone boughs bent back to the ground. The only noise came from the rushing water, and even that was muted.

He thought he heard a faint rustle from within the stone forest. He paused, and heard it again. A sound. Nothing more. He couldn't identify it. But he did know that he probably shouldn't be hearing that sound. Maybe some remnants of a civilization did still live down here after all?

He moved his jaw, his ears. As Krane had promised, the helmet responded intuitively and amplified some of the outside sounds while filters dampened others. All he heard was the steady flow of the canal waters. Had he imagined something? When it came again, he knew what it was. A biped in shoes was following him. Or keeping pace with him, out there in the endless caves. Louder. There it was. A light, steady footfall in step with his own. When he stopped, it stopped. It came from the seemingly endless stone archways on his right. His laugh was almost demonic. He reached to loosen his Banning in its holster and bent to feel for his knife, still in place. He recalled boyhood tales of fierce monsters down here, of horribly disfigured mutants who lived off human flesh. Until now, he'd believed none of them.

Another step. Stone blinked to turn off the helmet's lights. He crept as silently as he could into the nearest stone arch. The faintest scuttling sound came next. Carefully, he drew his blaster, dialing a swift instruction with his thumb. When he leveled the gun, it shot out a group of tiny light bursts, like so many brief, brilliant stars slowly arcing through that natural crypt, throwing a shadow against the curving stone pillars. A human. He *was* being followed. Some-body sent by Krane? Unlikely. The lep? Certainly not that noman. One of Varnal's ancient enemies? He now had a charge and three-quarters left in his Banning. Logically, there was only likely to be one other person in the catacombs—whoever had chased him down here in the first place. They would be very well armed!

He snarled into the blackness. "Listen, I don't know what you expect to get from me. If it's sapphires, not only do I not have them, I don't know where they are. And if you have any idea that I'm lying, I ought also to tell you that I'm on a mission. If I'm stopped, Mars will be blown to bits, and you with her. Now, I don't much care for what they've done to Mars, but I was born on this planet, and I'd like to spend a few more years here. So whatever you're after, Mister, maybe you should back off. Or show yourself. Or just come into the open and fight. I'll take whatever option you like."

No answer came out of that cold blackness, just the echo of the water whispering on its way to oblivion.

Keep moving.

Crunch!

A stunshell went off where he had been moments earlier. Only an amateur would have missed him. A suspicion became a thought in Stone's mind.

It had to be the same hunter who had been trailing him since RamRam City. He should know who it was by now. If it was a bluff, he'd been bluffed by a pro. Yes, there was no doubt. Someone was playing a game, maybe searching for his weaknesses.

With that, Stone snapped the helmet lights back on. There it was! A human shape fluttering among the stalagmites. He switched the light off, listening. Then, very quietly, he left the wide path. He passed among those great natural arches, seeking whoever hunted him. By the way they darted through the darkness, he couldn't help wondering how long they had lived on Mars. He recognized that same characteristic movement. A habit of approaching everywhere from the side or from behind. A habit of caution. The anticipation of attack. So this wasn't some Terran bounty hunter after his hide. This was a Martian.

Stone knew all the Martians likely to be offered the job and this wasn't their style, no matter how high a reward he had on his head. Except—

Again, he brought his lights into play, and this time he got more than a glimpse. A red-and-black night suit. Carrying extra air. Two Banning 22-40s. Every bounty hunter had a signature.

Could it be Yily Chen? Or someone working with Chen?

Crunch!

Now he knew that they didn't really want him dead. It had to be Chen. They had just been pretending up there before the croc got him. They had wanted him to think he was as good as dead. Or maybe they'd wanted to get him down here where they could take their time with him?

"If that's you, Yily, why are you after me? You're on Terra. I'm on Mars. We were never at odds."

Her voice hadn't changed as much as he'd expected. A sweet, light, lilting brogue came back out of the darkness. "Maybe the price was never high enough, Mac."

"I don't believe you."

"OK. Then you tell me why somebody wants you alive and doesn't want me to talk it over with you."

"You wouldn't torture me. I know it. Not me."

"Maybe. Circumstances change, Mac. Times change."

"Very true. But *you* don't. *I* don't. We're Martians. You're more Martian than I am. You don't have anyone they can get at you through. Same with me. We have identical reasons for keeping free of ties."

"We're different, Mac. Fundamentally. I'm a hunter. You're a thief. Sometimes hunters are commissioned to find thieves."

"So who gave you the job? Who wants you to bring me in?"

"Can't you guess?"

"Delph. And he has most of the money in the universe. But not enough to pay for me."

"Maybe so much money that I got curious. I wanted to know what he wanted that is worth such a lot. A bag I'm not supposed to look in. And which you don't have. I know you don't or you'd have used it as a decoy by now. I've hunted you for nearly a week, Mac. I've almost killed you half a dozen times. I've given you a chance to try all the angles. And you've tried them."

"What? You were testing me?"

"I guess."

She stepped out into the open, into the beam of light, a quick, boyish figure. Not at all what he'd imagined. She held her helmet in her left hand, one of her guns loose in the other. Her brown curly hair framed an impossibly beautiful triangular face with heavily slanted golden eyes. Her brows were thin and sloping, her lips red and bright as fresh blood. Few of those she hunted ever saw that face. Her clients rarely saw Yily Chen at all. She just delivered her "commissions," like packages. She'd been his sister. He'd played with her every day as a young child. For all he remembered her as smart and pretty, Mac could hardly believe how truly beautiful she had become.

"Hello, Yily. What are you really after?" He lifted his visor.

"Hi, Mac." She smiled and holstered her pistol. "You're a hard guy to fool. And hard not to kill, too. I guess I wanted to know what Delph needs so bad from you that he'd let me name my price."

Now he had a good idea what this was all about. He holstered his own Banning. She slipped her gun into its sheath and went back to drag something from the shadows. A bulky pack. She knelt to check the harness.

"And did you find out?"

Mac wondered why he remained so wary of her. The answer was probably simple. The strongest man, usually able to keep control of his emotions and stay cool, would find it hard to resist that beauty.

"Sure I did." She straightened her back. She moved toward him, half-smiling, looking up from under heavy lids, her voice husky. "But I couldn't trust him to pay."

Stone caught himself laughing. "I last saw you twenty years ago, stealing water from the tanks."

She grinned. He remembered that grin from when he had chased her through the bazaars of the Low-Canal and she had mocked him for his clumsiness. She boasted then that she had true Martian blood from a time when the great Broreern triremes had dominated the green seas swelling under a golden sun in the autumn of the planet's long history. Stone could easily believe her. Cynics said Yily's mother was a Terran whore and her father a Martian prison guard. But, with that glorious light brown skin, her beautifully muscled, boyish frame, that curly hair, her long legs, those firm, small breasts, her sardonic golden eyes, no one who saw her ever believed she was anything but a Mars woman reincarnated.

There were very few career possibilities on Mars for a girl of Yily's background and looks. She had chosen the least likely: first as Tex Merrihew's sidekick, learning the bounty hunter's trade, then as a fixer on her own account. Mac wondered if Yily Chen had other reasons for helping him. She was known to be clever and devious. Was her word as good as they said? "So what are you proposing, Yily?"

"A partnership, maybe."

"I didn't know you liked me that much."

"I don't like Delph at all. I don't like what he's done to Mars or what he *will* do if he gets what he wants. What *does* he want, Mac?"

"He believes I have a bunch of indigo flame sapphires."

"A *bunch*?"

"A bunch."

She was silent. He could almost hear her thinking.

"What was that about a bomb?" she said.

He saw no reason not to. So he told her all he knew.

When he had finished she said, "Then, I guess I'd better help you."

He asked why.

She grinned. "Because I'm a Martian, too." She bent and picked up her heavy pack. "And I'm not tone-deaf."

5
Whistling "Dixie"

THEY CAME TO THE FALLS, INCREASINGLY COMMUNICATING through their filtered helmet radios. The sound was deafening. An eerie pink light glared up from the chasm's depths.

"Some say that's Mars's core down there." She didn't elaborate.

"Have you been here before?"

"Once. Guy jumped bail on Terra. Thought he had immunity here. He did, but they framed him anyway because the judge in Ram owed the judge in Old London a favor. So I was in for double reward. A share of the bail money if I brought him in alive. Well, it turned out he had friends here. Archaeologists. Academics. They crack easily. They told me how they'd found evidence for what they called the lost canal. You know the story?"

He nodded. "Guy's out in the desert. He beds down for the night. Wakes up suddenly. He hears water. He listens more carefully. Running water. It's the ghost canal. A kind of mirage, leading travelers astray so they die of thirst convinced there's water all around them."

"They told him about a cave system. Legends said it was a way into another world. Some argued it came out on Terra, in Arizona somewhere. Some thought ancient Mars. Others linked it to the discoveries of the so-called hidden universe obscured from our astronomers by drifting clouds of cosmic fog." She shrugged. "You don't have to break many fingers before they put two and two together. I found the cave, found this place, found him, hauled him up, took him in, and took the money."

"Why didn't I ever hear of that entrance?"

"Because I destroyed it. Didn't want those archaeologists to be embarrassed again. My guy had two reasons not to talk. He might escape and hide out down here. And he knew what I'd do to him if news of the falls ever reached the surface. They sent him to Ceres. You don't live long there. As far as I know, he died with the secret."

The falls mesmerized them. They both found themselves walking too close to the edge, drawn by the vast, rearing walls of water spraying blue and gold, emerald and ruby, in that strange light. Old light, thought Mac without knowing why. Light that appeared to be pressed down by the cavern's impenetrable blackness. Mac saw all kinds of shapes in there. Faces from his past. People he had hated. Nobody he had loved. Men with weapons. Women wanting his money or contempt or both. Cruelty ran through interplanetary society like a fuel. Not his drug of choice. Peace. Why was he thinking like this as the pink flume blew into a million shapes and offered to hold him like a baby, safely, safely . . . ?

"Stone!"

Her strong hand grabbed his arm and yanked him back from the edge. "Damn! I thought you could look after yourself." Her anger was like a slap across his face. He swore. Those eyes, those glaring eyes! What had they held in that moment when she raged at him?

He shook his head. "Don't worry. I'm sorry. It won't happen again."

She was frowning now, peering through her distance glasses out across the raging falls and pointing. "What's that?"

A flash of electric lime green. An obviously unnatural color. Nothing like anything surrounding it. He switched over to the helmet's optics and brought it in sharply as instruments reported distance and size. She adjusted her own glasses to check it out.

About 1.5 meters square, the star bomb lay balanced between a rough circle of rocks. Almost peacefully, white water whirled around it. Contrary currents held it in suspension. Any one of the currents could alter course slightly and take the bomb over the brink, from where it would never be recovered. And would ultimately detonate, splitting the planet apart.

The falls bellowed, echoing through the vast cavern whose roof lay beyond sight in the glittering darkness. According to the helmet, its walls held deposits of gold, silver, diamonds, and many other metals now very rare on Terra. Stone could imagine what would become of the place once the likes of Delph found out about it. He scanned the falls as far as he could see, pointing out a possible pathway through to it, where a great slab of black granite formed a canopy on which tons of water fell by the second. The rocks beneath the canopy were given a little potential protection, at least for part of the way. Some of the rocks disappeared behind another great massing of fallen debris. They formed a blind spot. Neither Stone nor Chen could see what danger might be waiting for anyone who tried to cross beyond that point. There didn't seem to be a better route anywhere else.

"We'd best rope up." She lowered her heavy pack to the walkway. "We can't work on that thing out there. We're going to have to fetch it."

"I could try firing a grapnel from my Banning." He showed her the tonkinite hook on his belt. "It's attached to fifty meters of spider-wire. But even if it was a good idea, there's no way we could do it from here. We need to be sure we have the bomb securely held. We can't make mistakes. We need to switch over to gravity equalizers. They should hold off the worst of the force from the water. Does your suit have equalizers? Doesn't matter. We'll use mine. Both of us will probably have to go out there for at least as far as that route takes us."

They had little left to discuss. First, they tested the GE potential. This took the power of anything threatening them and, using the threat's own energy, converted it into a force field theoretically capable of equalizing any outside pressure. The idea behind the technology was brilliant, but there had been more than one infamous GE accident. You didn't get any second chances. They contacted Miguel Krane. He assured Stone that the helmet had been tested for all environments, particularly for the power of the falls. He was surprised to learn that Yily Chen was involved, but he saw no problem in both of them using the suit. "One or a dozen, it can theoretically protect against a considerably stronger power. Of course, we haven't allowed for human error. Just remember, it only takes one break in the circuitry and you'll both be swept over those falls in a blink." He suggested that they have her suit run on low power as a backup. "You'll have to decide between you if that would work." Krane sounded a little uncertain.

Soon they were ready. They roped up, using Mac's spiderwire. It was unwise to rely on their helmets' intercom. They would rely as much as they could on visual signals. Even with everything turned to minimum input they could still hear the heavy beating of the water against the rocks, the yelping gush of the canal as it spilled over into that bottomless gorge. Together, they inched out over the slippery causeway, hands, feet, elbows, and knees on full suction, allowing them to gain traction with every limb. The vast weight of water, even though not the full mass, smashed against their force converter, allowing them to move forward. They were tiny specks caught above those gigantic liquid walls. Able to see less than a meter ahead, they clung together, taking careful steps, often crawling on hands and knees, blinded by the screaming spray surrounding them. More than once, Stone lost his balance. She remained sure-footed and caught his cord before he followed his momentum down into the hungry core of the planet. He calculated that she'd saved his life at least seven times in as many minutes.

Above them, the wild spray boomed and shrieked. Their heads rang under the hammerblows of the surging current. Once, she was almost swept over the rim. He held on with hands and feet as he extended the field, hauling her back, kicking an impossible surge of power out of his equipment and falling backward as something caught his shoulder. Recovering, he saw that debris was also being carried down the falls, effectively doubling their danger. They watched for larger objects as much as possible, another eye on their chronometers, which were telling them roughly how much time still remained before the bomb was due to blow. Forty minutes. They reached a place where the water was suddenly quiet and even the sound seemed muted. For a moment or two they rested, gratefully recovering their strength in calm water forming little pools beneath the huge canopy of granite. They made up some of their lost time.

Once or twice, Stone looked back toward the bank, now invisible to him. Was all their effort worthless? Wouldn't it be better to accept the impossibility of their mission? He began to think Krane was mad. If there was a threat, then inevitably they would die. Death was the future of all people, all planets, all universes. Their struggle was symbolic of the futility of living creatures who fought against their own inevitable extinction. What were a few more years of existence compared to the longevity of a cosmos? In those terms, the whole history of their species lasted for less than a fraction of a second. And then, sheltering beside him under the protection of the energy equalizer, she looked up for a second, and, obscurely, he understood that the effort always would be worth it. Always had been worth it.

They emerged eventually from the overhang. They saw the gaudy lime-green box glittering on the far side of a rocky cleft. Stone could see no obvious way down to it. For a moment, it seemed that they had come this far only to fail. Then Yily nodded and signaled that if he held on to the spidercord, she might be able to swing down and snag the box. But it would mean switching over to her own untested equalizers. Whether her suit had enough capacity was uncertain. She shrugged and began tying herself on.

The falls coughed and grumbled, always treacherous.

Stone grew concerned that there wouldn't be enough spiderwire. He had trouble gauging the distance properly. He braced himself. He would have to switch off as soon as he could after she switched on, conserving power and maintaining stability for split seconds. He raised his hand and gave the signal. They knew a sickening few moments while the switch took place, then she was dropping out of sight before coming back into view, a far smaller figure than he had expected.

The blue and red of her suit was just visible, flashing on and off as she fell through a sickening weight of water. Her relative gravity, thanks to the converter, gave her extra resistance, and she stretched out her arms and clasped the n-bomb to her, swinging free over the rosy abyss. She cried out her triumph in a wild yell, her body curving back into the trajectory. He thumped the control and brought her up to where he perched, hanging on with everything but his nails and teeth. He was laughing like a fool as she swung to stand beside him, counting out with elated blows on his arm the measure to activate his helmet's converter so both were again protected. He could feel her elation as he hugged her tight.

They had the star bomb!

Now, somehow, they had to follow the steps back to the sheltering rock. Inch by inch, they crossed the exposed falls, feet feeling for holds as the minutes slipped by, and they dared not waste a moment trying to see how much time they had before the bomb did what it had been designed to do. The climb back to the walkway seemed to take longer than the whole rest of the mission. Increasingly, the strain on the equalizer became greater. Little bubbles of energy flinched and disappeared into the wavering field.

Stone was almost convinced that they had run out of time and strength. He gasped his surprise when, suddenly, his boots stood on the smooth granite and the bomb was on the ground before them. Manhandling it to the relative quiet of the stone arches, they were at last able to turn off the equalizers. The suit crackled and zipped, revealing flaws that moments later would have meant sudden death.

Stone triumphantly announced their success to Krane over the radio. The Earthman seemed less than overjoyed.

"You have twenty-seven minutes left," he said. "Do you think you can do it, Stone?"

Yily grinned and began to whistle.

"What's that?" Krane asked.

"It's not doing anything," she said. " 'Yankee Doodle,' right?"

But, even when the tune had been relayed back to them by Krane, only four of the eleven locks protecting the n-bomb snapped open. They needed seven in sequence. "The Yellow Rose of Texas" snapped open two more. "Moonlight on the Wabash" made two snap back. She tried different keys and speeds, new sequences. Two more. One more. But after that it was no good. She was embarrassed. "My grandma came to Mars in the Revival Follies. We used to sing them all before the dope took her."

"This is getting dangerous," Krane told them. "Something has jammed. Stop!" Oblivious of his growing concern, they kept trying and kept failing as the minutes and the seconds died. "You've got to stop!" Krane told them. "Unless every lock is undone in order, the bomb can't be neutralized. It took us years to work out those codes. We encrypted everything in easily remembered traditional tunes. We—we haven't time to work out the codes again! If anything, we've complicated the situation. We have eight minutes left."

Mac hovered over the bomb, trying different force-tools on the remaining locks. "This is hopeless. We could explode the thing at any moment." He watched the most recently tried force-tool fade from his glove.

"I guess neither of us is musical enough. Time for plan B." She reached with both hands into her pack and pulled out a large square metal container. Quickly, she dragged off the box's covering, revealing a compacted canister covered with government warnings, which, as she stroked it with her gloved fingers, began to expand, flopping and twitching like a living thing until it lay in her lap like a long khaki-colored barracuda. "I'd better set this now."

Stone recognized the unactivated B-9 wombot. He guessed her plan, but he said, "What are you going to do with that?" It was his idea too.

But she wouldn't stop. "I'm a lot lighter than you. Give me your big scarf," she said. "Hurry! And some of those tools might prove useful here. I'll tell you what to do. We need that spiderwire. Can you disconnect it from your suit?"

"I can try."

So he dragged out his long white scarf. She began to wind the thing around her waist. No clocks or numbers on the bomb told them how much time they had left. They had only their own chronometers. "Seven minutes."

He was still planning to do the thing himself. "Now," he said, "get those magnets situated. The scarf will be useful. It won't bear any serious strain, but it'll keep the bomb in position while we spiderwire it to the wombot. Leave those ends free. Screw drill might help."

The thing grew firm in her hands as she helped give the cables a few more turns. "OK," he said. "More magnetic clamps. As many as we have between us." The bomb was settled on the ground, the wombot beside it. At his count, they seized the bomb, rolled it, and bound it with the wire while they fixed the eight magnetic manacles she normally used for heavy-gravity truants. They held the wombot squarely on the bomb. Six minutes. He took a deep breath.

Then, while he was still thinking about it, she had straddled the whole contraption, binding herself to it with the scarf and the remaining spiderwire, leaving her limbs free. There wasn't time to argue. Stone grew more and more unhappy. He realized that he couldn't take over. Too late to start arguing.

Soon she had the whole contraption firmly beneath her, the wombot now fighting like a fish to be free. He gripped it as hard as he could with his numbed hands. Then she began powering up her suit.

He couldn't find any more words. He felt sick. He had an unusual set to his jaw as he watched her first switch her own equalizer to run, then eased the bomb but not the wombot outside her suit's circle of power. She tapped in codes on her arm. Wouldn't she need a helmet? There was a faint flash and she winced. Not a suicide mission! Don't say it was that! The sound of the falls still drowned any noise they made without using the radio. The powerful bionic drone jumped in her hands and lifted over Stone's head with Yily still clinging to it. It bucked and pirouetted and bucked again. He yelled for her to let go, that he would catch her.

"I have to test it first," she said. "There isn't much time."

"Maybe we should say good-bye." Suddenly calm, though scarcely reconciled, he stepped back.

"Maybe." And then she released the wombot.

It leapt into the air, looped once, with her hanging on for dear life, her e-suit flickering and flashing. The wire secured the bomb. She was held only by a few magnetic clamps, spiderwire, and her own strength. But Stone could have sworn he saw her grinning.

The contraption began to move in a straight line. Out over the Nokedu Falls—out through the distant spray, gold and silver in the pink light—and, to Stone's utter horror, *down!*

Down flew Yily Chen. Down she flew! Out of sight as she was dragged by the wombot into that vast rosy chasm and those wild, dancing, deadly waters. Stone had never known so much fear before. Never so much fear than when he saw her vanish. "Oh, God!" He tried to get his radio back on, but there was no reception. "Oh, Yily!" He felt ill. He scanned the gold-flecked air with his enhanced eyes. Nothing.

The Nokedu Falls shouted its beautiful, monstrous laughter.

Then, triumphantly, the wombot leapt like a salmon up the falls, into the air above the canal, and seemed to hover for a moment with Yily flying behind it, going through some weird contortions, maybe to gain altitude. Up she came, then back, hurtling almost directly toward him. He dove clear of the thing as it seemed to home in on him. Was he the nearest heat? Had he really been the target all along? Then here she came, just in time, jumping clear of the flying bomb, down onto the walkway as the wombot performed a perfect turn and flew like a radium ray straight and true back along the way they had first come—then vanished from normal space-time. Now it would push through the folds of unseen space, seeking maximum heat, blinking up to the surface through the rock until it hit thin air, still skewering through the folds of space-time, on its way to Sol.

He rolled over as she switched off her suit and fell, laughing, into his arms.

Then Stone did what unconsciously he had wanted to do since he'd first chased the tousled, brown-skinned Martian girl playing hide-and-go-seek in and out of the deep shadows of the tanks. He took her in his arms, tossed away his helmet, and kissed her full on her blood-red lips. She kissed him back with a passion, biting his tongue and grinning as he responded.

Up in RamRam City, a scummer lying on his back, high on jojo juice, saw a quick blossom of brightness appear in Sol's NW quadrant, a crimson flower against dull orange, and had no notion how lucky he was to be alive or what that brief moment had earned.

Soon Stone and Yily followed the long walkway of polished black granite beside the wide canal and up the great staircase to the chamber where he had first met Krane. The Earthman was gone, but on a hook extending from the deactivated noman's right arm was a soft grey ratskin bag, and when Stone poured the contents into her open palm Yily gasped.

Stone lit the last three inches of his jane, drew deep, smiled, contentedly watching her as she laid them out, side by side on the bag: seven perfect flame sapphires, pulsing with constantly shifting shades of indigo. Each was a different world. Each was utterly fascinating, ready to reflect and amplify your secret dreams. Should you wish, you could live in one forever.

"Yeah," said Stone happily. "Quite a sight."

EPILOG

THEY KNEW WHAT WOULD HAPPEN, OF COURSE, WHEN THE mining companies and the archaeologists discovered a plentiful supply of water. That water would still be contaminated by centuries of leakage from an alien superbomb and would have to be filtered, probably not very thoroughly. That wouldn't be much of a problem, especially with expendable prison labor working down there. Stone guessed what the exploiters would do with the great calm waterway perpetually pouring into a bottomless canyon to be captured and recycled, by some mysterious process, back into the canal again. Power.

"It'll all go," said Yily Chen. "It'll be sensationalized and sanitized. People will run boat tours to the safe parts. There'll be elevators directly down to the falls. Tourist money will bring a demand for comfortable fiction. Guides will play up invented legends and histories. Art critics will explain the grandeur of her design, the beauty of her reliefs, the ingenuity of her architects and engineers. She'll give birth to a thousand academic theories. Crazy theories. Cults. Religions. And that won't be the worst of it when people like Delph start tearing out the metals and the precious jewels . . ."

"No," he said. "It doesn't have to happen. We can keep it to ourselves. Just for a while."

It was what Yily wanted too. She smiled that sweet, sardonic Martian smile. "I guess I was planning to retire," she said.

So they bought Mars. She only cost them two indigo flame sapphires, sold to a consortium of Terran plutocrats. For the pair, Stone and Chen got the mining companies, a couple of ships, RamRam City and other settlements, the various rights of exploration and exploitation, and the private prisons Stone had known so well and subsequently liberated so promptly.

Later, it might be possible to create on Mars a paradise of justice and reason, a golden age to last a thousand years where their Martian descendants could grow up and flourish. But meanwhile, for a few good months, maybe more, they had the lost canal to themselves.

PHYLLIS EISENSTEIN

Phyllis Eisenstein's short fiction has appeared in *The Magazine of Fantasy & Science Fiction, Asimov's, Analog, Amazing,* and elsewhere. She's probably best-known for her series of fantasy stories about the adventures of Alaric the Minstrel, born with the strange ability to teleport, which were later melded into two novels, *Born to Exile* and *In the Red Lord's Reach.* Her other books include the two novels in the Book of Elementals series, *Sorcerer's Son* and *The Crystal Palace,* as well as stand-alone novels *Shadow of Earth* and *In the Hands of Glory.* Some of her short fiction, including stories written with husband Alex Eisenstein, has been collected in *Nightlives: Nine Stories of the Dark Fantastic.* Holding a degree in anthropology from the University of Chicago, for twenty years she was a member of the faculty of Columbia College, where she taught creative writing, also editing two volumes of *Spec-Lit,* a softcover anthology showcasing SF by her students. She now works as a copy editor in a major ad agency, and still lives, with her husband, in her birthplace, Chicago.

Here she spins a tale that denies the truth of the old saying that you can't go home again. You *can* go home again, but you may have to look for it in the strangest places, and go a very long way to reach it.

The Sunstone

PHYLLIS EISENSTEIN

HE HAD EXPECTED HIS FATHER TO MEET HIM AT THE MERIDI-
ani spaceport. But when he disembarked after the monthlong flight
from Earth, duffel bag over his shoulder, the only people waiting for
the passengers were strangers. After two Martian years away, with a
brand-new Ph.D. in archaeology under his belt, Dave Miller had
thought that the man who had scrimped and saved to ensure that his
son got the best graduate-school education in the solar system would
be there to welcome him home.

The other passengers, whom he had gotten to know on the journey, collected their luggage and their local contacts—family, friends,
hosts—and dispersed. Some were Marsmen like him, some were
new settlers, still filled with enthusiasm for the open land that had
been so effectively advertised to them, and a few were wealthy tourists. Dave had made sure the latter had his contact information:
"Tour the ruins of the lost Martian civilization with the men who
discovered them," said his card. It was not quite a lie in his own case
because, as a teenager, he had found a cluster of foundations and a
few lengths of sand-scoured wall no higher than his knee near one
of the lesser canals that splayed out from Niliacus Lacus, and Rekari,
his father's Martian business partner, had pronounced them seven
or eight thousand Martian years abandoned. His father, the famous
Dr. Benjamin Miller, to whom the card really referred, had decided
they were not worth adding to the tourist round. But that hadn't
made them any less a discovery.

When there seemed no point in waiting any longer, Dave went
into the terminal and found a phone. He'd bought a personal com-
municator back on Earth, but on Mars, where dust storms so often

interfered with wireless communications, landlines were more reliable. The terminal clerk told him the local phone would probably work—it had yesterday—but when he tried his father's number, there was no answer, not even with a recording.

He chewed on his lip for a few seconds, then gave in and tapped his sister's number. He hoped her husband didn't answer; his sister had always been hard enough to deal with.

The child's voice on the other end did not know who Uncle Dave was, but was finally persuaded to pass the call to his or her mother.

"David." It wasn't a friendly voice, but it was his sister's. In two years, she had not answered one of his letters.

"Yes, I'm back," he said. "How have you been? How's the family?" He didn't even know how many kids she had now.

"Don't pretend you care, David," she said. "What do you want?"

"It's been two years, Bev. That's not much of a welcome."

He could hear the snort at her end. "I honestly didn't think you'd come back. Was Earth that big a disappointment?"

"Earth was fine," he said, "but staying there was never the plan."

"Oh yes," said his sister. "You were always going to come back here and help Dad dig more things up. Maybe find one of those lost cities he was always looking for. He hasn't come home in months, you know."

"Months?" said Dave. "How many months?" His father had always spent long stretches of time in the field, but . . . months?

"I don't know. Four? Five? It's not like I see him very often when he's not out there."

"Have you talked to Rekari?"

There was a pause at her end. "I never understood what Dad saw in that piece of Martian scum."

"But have you . . . ?"

"No, I haven't talked to him. And he hasn't talked to me, either."

"Beverly—"

"Dad always liked him better than his own family. And you did, too. Don't try to tell me anything different."

Dave didn't answer that. Rekari had always been a good companion for a growing boy. "Did he go out with Dad?"

"How should I know?"

"He didn't answer the phone."

"Does he even know how to use a phone?"

Dave took a deep breath. On Earth, he had learned not to respond to people who said nasty things about Martians and the humans who lived on Mars, though it had taken more than a few fistfights to make those lessons stick. "I'll be at Dad's if you want me," he said.

"Fine," she said, and she broke the connection.

It was the longest conversation they'd had in a decade, and it made Dave worry. Months? He let the phone go and walked back to the clerk to arrange for transport to Charlestown. There was none, of course, but the clerk was willing to sell his own scooter to a fellow Marsman. And he was happy enough to take Earth creds, which usually came from tourists and the people who dealt with them; Dave had acquired a pretty decent supply from part-time jobs during school. He slung his duffel on the back, checked the charge gauge, and closed the canopy to head north. The scooter had a mapper, but he didn't need it; he had a good sense of direction, it wasn't all that far, and you couldn't get lost following the Hiddekel canal. The sky was dark when he started out, but the scooter's headlight was bright and the road was in good shape, well cleared of the water-seeking nettles that perpetually encroached on the canal. He made it to Charlestown by dawn.

Charlestown had never been much of a town, even though it was on the route to the confluence of two canals, but then, even the major cities on Mars were nothing compared to the ones on Earth. But Dave had had enough of the crowds and bustle of Earth, and Charlestown looked very good to him, its single main street lined on both sides with ramshackle houses that doubled as stores and bars, with lanes of smaller homes spreading outward on the side away from the canal. North of the town was the boat dock, with half a dozen barges and three small sailboats moored there, and beyond that, the arc of Martian cottages where Rekari and his extended family lived. As Dave expected, only a few people were on the main street that early, and he recognized them all. One even called his name as he passed, and he raised an arm in greeting though he didn't stop.

His father's place, close to the north end of town, was both office and home, with a sign above the door that announced, in faded lettering, "Ben Miller and Sons, Tourism. See the Ancient Ruins." His father had been optimistic while his mother was alive, but there had never been more than one son; and the son-in-law who might have worked with him but worked for the regional utility instead was unimpressed by the grants his father-in-law had gotten from Syrtis University and the remains of the six ancient villages he had discovered over the last thirty years; archaeology on Mars, Bev's husband said, wasn't worth much beyond entertaining a few tourists.

Dave closed the scooter into the side shed and tried the office door. It wasn't locked. Nothing in Charlestown was ever locked, although a key hung from the handle in case anyone wanted to use it. Inside, he found the tiny front room that served as an office dark, its windows too grimy to admit more than a hint of morning sunlight, and the light switch dead under his hand. He left the door open, and the splash of light showed undisturbed dust everywhere. He flicked on the battery-powered flash every Marsman carried and went to the door separating the business from the living quarters. In his father's bedroom, the bed was rumpled, but the bureau drawers were closed, the clothing in them neatly folded, and the jacket he always wore in the field was missing from its hook. Farther on, Dave's own bedroom was just as he had left it, with a couple of school trophies on the bureau and a pair of old shoes under the bed.

"You don't have to come back," his father had said. But Dave had always known he would. Ben Miller and Sons. Home.

The first few months away had been hard. There had been homesickness, of course, but he had pushed that aside with exercise, first on the ship and even more on Earth itself, until the feeling of wearing a backpack that weighed twice as much as he did eased. By then, graduate school and all the sights and experiences of the exotic mother planet had absorbed him, and thinking about home no longer bothered him. Except perhaps when he woke up on a clear morning and saw that piercingly bright sunlight—the light that was never so strong on Mars—between the curtains.

He dropped the duffel on the bed and opened his own bureau drawers one by one, trying to remember what else he had left behind. Not much. There were a couple of T-shirts in the bottom drawer. And underneath them was a small notebook.

He'd always carried a notebook when he went out exploring, but his had gone with him to Earth and were in his duffel now. This was one of his father's. Only the first page had anything written on it. There was a date at the top, nearly five Martian months ago, and below that were a few lines in his father's familiar hand, about likely ruins where the Alcronius canal emerged from the northern ice cap. It was a good lead, his father's notes said, because it came from the oldest Martian he had ever met, who had once helped him by translating some barely legible inscriptions. A good lead, but a long trip, and he was sure he and Rekari would be gone for quite a while, checking it out. At the bottom were the coordinates of the place.

As of the date of the entry, the northern ice cap had been as melted as it ever would be, and the canal current had ebbed. You could easily take a boat north then. Rekari had a boat. Dave had seen it at the dock.

He was tired after the long ride, but he was even more hungry. The cabinets in the tiny kitchen were empty; his father had probably taken their contents on the trip north. So Dave went out to see if one of the local restaurants had anything interesting, which on Mars meant anything at all. Jacky's, just down the street, had peanut butter and flatbread for breakfast, and Dave was glad enough for that. As a student on Earth, he hadn't eaten much better.

"I don't know that your dad thought you'd come back," said Jacky. She was tall and thin, with cheeks weathered by the Martian winds, but she had a smile for him, and a treat of homemade blackberry jam. Jacky had always been a better big sister than Bev, and Dave had often wondered why his father hadn't married her and made her a real part of the family.

"He's been gone quite a while, hasn't he? My sister said months."

Jacky looked at her watch. "One hundred and thirty-three days."

Dave leaned an elbow on the table, gathered up a few crumbs of the flatbread, and tossed them into his mouth. "I saw Rekari's boat at the dock. Did he go along?"

Jacky nodded. "But he came back, a month or so ago. He said somebody had to look after the business. Not that there's been any lately. I haven't seen a tourist since last year."

Dave paid the check in Earth creds, and Jacky tucked them into her shirt. "It's good to see you back, kid. Maybe there'll be something better for dinner. I hear the Warners have an extra chicken. I might be able to talk them out of it."

"I'd like that," said Dave.

"Check back at five."

He went outside and headed for the Martian quarter.

The main street was busier now, with people doing their morning shopping before heading out to the scrubby fields of genetically modified peanuts, potatoes, and barley that stretched eastward from Hiddekel. On the west side of the canal, someone seemed to be trying to raise wheat again—that happened every decade or so, according to his father, when new settlers arrived from Earth. It never worked very well, but it usually produced enough spindly stalks to feed a few goats. Dave had eaten plenty of wheat bread on Earth, and he didn't think it was anything special. Chicken, though, was something else.

Several people stopped to say hello to him, to ask about his experience on Earth, to tell him how good he looked, and it was much more than a ten-minute walk before he finally reached Rekari's compound. The arc of cottages there, with its open side to Hiddekel, which the Martians called Moreyah, had stood, Rekari once said, for a thousand years, which wasn't all that long by Martian standards. The cottages themselves were made of a local soft red stone, with roofs of woven plant fiber coated with hardened clay. The Martians grew the plants for their seeds, which humans considered inedible, and fed the seeds not just to themselves but to small lizards living in burrows in the canal walls. The lizards were their primary source of protein, and humans also considered them inedible. Dave had tried lizard stew once, and only courtesy kept him from spitting out his first and only mouthful. He had always thought it was a good thing that Rekari's people felt much the same about human food—that meant there was little competition for those kinds of resources between Martians and Marsmen. Although his father had insisted that in an emergency, Martian food would not kill him. Fortunately, Dave had never needed to test that claim.

Rekari's son Burmari was in the center of the arc, working on a boat that was obviously new and nearly finished, only the mast and sail missing. When he saw Dave, he made the Martian sign for welcome, then walked over to clap him on the shoulder in a human greeting. Like all Martians, Burmari was thin and wiry, with ruddy skin and large, pale eyes, and he was more than a head taller than any Marsman. Dave smiled and reached up to return his greeting. They had known each other all of Dave's life.

"School treated you well," said Burmari. "You look healthy and strong."

He spoke in the local Martian language, but Dave had no trouble understanding him; since childhood, he had been as fluent in it as in English.

"Extra gravity will do that," said Dave. "But I'm happy to be back where there is less of it. Where is your father?"

But before his son could respond, Rekari came out of the cottage at the far end of the arc, and he made the sign of greeting, then held his arms out for a very human-style embrace.

After that, there was a gathering of the rest of Rekari's family from every point on the arc, his wife, his younger brother and his wife, and their two children. A table and stools were brought out, and cups of an herbal drink that both humans and Martians liked, mint-flavored and faintly alcoholic. Dave could see the curiosity on the faces that surrounded him, but only the nephew, who had been little more than a knee-high nuisance when Dave left, was impolite enough to ask about Earth. Settling himself with a cup, Dave talked about the cities, the crowds, the school, and his teachers, trying to give an overview of the experience, and they seemed willing to listen as long as he wanted to go on. Eventually, though, Rekari called a halt, saying that Dave was too tired to keep talking. Adult Martians were generally good at reading humans—much better than humans were at reading them—but Dave actually felt less tired than before his meal. But he knew that if anyone had answers to his own questions, it was his father's Martian business partner.

"I think we should speak in the office," Rekari said, raising a hand in a gesture that meant to wait a moment. He ducked inside one of the cottages and came back with a green Martian lamp. There wasn't much left of the old civilization, but the sun-loving lichen that the ancients had either discovered or created were still around, and they could be persuaded to give a little light back for a few hours every day if you knew exactly how to treat them. Rekari had tried to teach Dave the trick, but he had always ended up overfeeding them, which stifled their light.

"I have a flash," Dave said, patting one of his jacket pockets.

"I'm sure you do," said Rekari, but he took the lamp anyway.

In the office, Rekari closed the front door and set the light on the long table that served as a desk and a display surface for maps. He brushed the dust from his usual chair and sat down. Dave took his father's chair and waited. He knew that Rekari would eventually get around to telling him what he wanted to know, and there was no use trying to rush him. Martians always took their time.

Rekari folded his long fingers on his knee. "Did you find school on Earth to be useful?" he asked.

Dave had spent his undergraduate years at Syrtis University, where his teachers were all his father's former students, and he had been satisfied at the prospect of earning his doctorate there. But his father had insisted that the Earth experience would make him a better archaeologist, even though on Earth he would be working at digs that had already been thoroughly explored by several generations of Ph.D. candidates. In the end, he realized that his father had been right. The range of knowledge of his teachers on Earth was astonishing, and they were more than willing to mentor the son of Dr. Benjamin Miller.

"Yes," Dave said. "Extremely useful."

Rekari's hands moved in the Martian sign of approval. "Your father was pleased that you went. One of his old friends there wrote to him and said you were doing well."

Dave waited.

Rekari seemed to be studying him. At last, he said, "Your father was ill."

Dave felt a chill run up his back. It was bad news, then. "What do you mean?"

"His heart was not functioning properly."

"He seemed fine when I left."

Rekari made the Martian negative sign. "There were pills to help, even before you left."

Dave frowned at him. "You should have told me."

"The doctor said there was nothing to be done beyond the medication. A procedure on Earth might have helped, but the doctor was not certain your father would survive the journey. And your father did not wish to waste the ticket on himself."

"I would have given it to him, gladly."

"He knew that."

Dave sighed heavily. His father had always been so stubborn. "You really should have told me."

Rekari's voice was low. "That may be, but he did not wish it."

Dave understood, but it was so frustratingly Martian. They had immense respect for their own elders, and that spilled over to the humans they knew best. You just didn't cross an elder if you were a Martian. That was why Rekari had gone along on so many expeditions even when he didn't believe they would result in anything.

Rekari had been his father's business partner for more years than Dave had been alive, helping his father guide rich Earth tourists through the best-preserved Martian ruins, offering lore that was traditional if not always accurate—as he admitted privately—and translating ancient inscriptions in colorful ways. In the long periods between tourist visits, the two of them searched for more ruins as well as for any interesting minerals that the long-depleted Martian landscape had to offer. The ancient civilization had used up most of the planet's easily accessible resources, leaving a legacy of rust thinly scattered over the surface, but his father had once found a narrow vein of opal in a cliff exposed by the melting of the northern ice cap. Now there were rings and pendants of that opal among the more affluent residents of Syrtis City, although the gold for the settings had been brought from Earth in the luggage of the city's only jeweler. The opal money had helped to finance several expeditions to sites that seemed to have exceptional archaeological potential. Nothing significant came of any of them, though. The old Martian cities had been lost for a very long time. But his father had never given up.

"I found his notebook," said Dave. "It says he had some promising coordinates."

The Martian lifted one hand in his version of a shrug. "Your father heard a story. You know, he was always hearing stories."

Dave nodded.

"He thought he had some coordinates. So we took the boat and went, and we spent weeks searching at the edge of the northern ice. To my eyes, there was nothing, but in one area, your father saw . . . perhaps . . . some traces of what once might have been. We had brought the excavator along, of course, and he used it to strip off the top layer of soil, as always. Then he went down on his hands and knees with a trowel and began to scrape at some markings he said appeared to be the remains of wooden footings. He had done the same so often before, I did not think it would harm him. I knelt beside him and tried to help, but he pushed me away. It was delicate work, he said. Leave it to the expert, he said. I had used my trowel before, many times, but your father did have a surer hand."

Dave wasn't certain that was true, but he didn't say so. Elders—and they were both his elders, after all—were not to be contradicted.

"I could see he was in great pain," said Rekari. "His hands were shaking so much that he could not open the pill bottle. I took it from him and opened it and gave him a pill, but it was no help. The doctor had said a second pill, if necessary, but that, too . . ." He made a sign that Dave had never seen before, and his thin shoulders sagged as if he was immensely tired. "I buried him in the north and came back here. When anyone asked, I said that he and I had decided that one of us had to return to the business, and he preferred to stay in the field." He made the new sign again, an emphasis by repetition that Martians rarely resorted to. At Dave's inquiring gesture, he said, "It is sorrow, David. It is not a sign that the young should use."

Dave took a deep breath and made it anyway. "I would like to visit his grave."

"He would not wish it," said Rekari.

"That doesn't matter. I wish it."

Rekari reached into his jacket pocket and pulled out a wad of cloth the size of his fist. "This is what he wished, David. To give this to you." He unrolled the cloth to expose a pale, teardrop-shaped pebble, smoothly polished, pierced at one end and threaded with a silver chain. Its surface glimmered faintly, like the ghost of an opal, and Dave knew immediately what it was. Its Martian name translated as "sunstone," and it was traditionally worn by the heads of Martian families and passed down from parent to child, generation after generation. Rekari, who had been head of his family since the death of his father nine years before, wore one, usually tucked inside his shirt. The humans on Mars did not consider sunstones especially attractive, though Dave had always thought Rekari's was pleasant-looking.

He hadn't known his father owned one.

Rekari held the stone out to Dave, the chain dangling from his long fingers.

Dave took it and held it close to the lamp. "Where did this come from?"

"Many years ago," said Rekari, "before you were born, before I became your father's associate, a child was lost from a Martian town some forty kilometers to the south. Your father had already explored considerably in the area, looking for ruins, and so, knowing the landscape, he volunteered to help in the search. He was, in fact, the only man of Earth who did. And he found the child. But the season was winter, and he was too late. The child had died of the cold. Still, the family was grateful, and the child's grandfather, who was head of the family, never forgot. For the sake of that child, who had been their only hope of a future, he helped your father over the years, translating inscriptions, telling stories passed down from ancient times, even drawing maps of places that once were but are no more. And some months ago, in the last days of his life, when his family was coming to an end, he called your father to his side and, for the sake of that child, gave him this sunstone so that the family might be carried on, even if by a man of Earth. And it was he who told your father of the place that might have been a city in the old times, because he knew how much your father wanted to find such a city. One more story, of many that your father heard in his years on Mars.

"We went," said Rekari. "How could we not go? We always went. But this time, all we found was your father's death. And now you are the head of your family."

Dave let the stone rest in his cupped palm, thinking about how his father must have worn it, about the old Martian whom he had never met, and about that lost child. He was feeling a bit lost himself. Ben Miller and Sons. He wished he could have shaken his father's hand one last time, embraced him one last time. He didn't feel like the head of anything. "Well, there's Bev," he said.

"She has joined herself to another family," said Rekari. "And your father did not mean for her to have the stone. I know you under-stand that."

Dave made the sign for agreement. He slipped the chain over his head, then, because it seemed so strange to be a human and wearing a sunstone, and because Rekari wore it that way, he tucked it inside his shirt where no one would see it. "I assume his grave is near the site," he said. "I wish to visit both." Cool at first, the stone warmed quickly against his chest, and he could not help feeling oddly com-forted by it, as if some tiny part of his father were with him.

Rekari made the sign for sorrow one more time. Then he mur-mured, "When the new boat is finished, I will take you there. It is a long journey."

Dave thought about the boat, fresh and sleek-looking, a beautiful pleasure craft, but not for the impatient, and he found that he was very impatient. He calculated how many Earth creds he had left.

More than enough. "I'll buy a motor for the boat," he said finally. "Not so long a journey as with a sail."

Rekari gave him a surprised look. "Have you come home rich?"

"There was money to be earned on Earth, and I spent less than I was paid. I have enough to use for important things."

Rekari stood. "Then the decision is made. We will go north, you and I. Buy the motor, and I will ready the boat to receive it." He went to the door, where he turned back for just a moment to make the sign of temporary farewell before walking out into the midday light.

Dave slumped in his father's chair. He felt drained by their con-versation and suddenly overwhelmed by the day's events. He slid the sunstone from beneath his shirt and curled his hand around it. "You should have told me, Dad," he whispered, and he shut his eyes hard against the tears that he had not allowed Rekari to see. Going on without his father was something he could barely imagine. They were going to be a team. For two Martian years he had thought about how he would change that sign. "Ben Miller and Son, Archaeology. Tour the Ancient Ruins." The bold truth. He had planned on paint-ing the new one himself. Ben and Dave Miller were going to find one of those lost cities and revolutionize the human view of the ancient Martian civilization. Oh, he had such plans, with his new-minted Ph.D. He shook the sunstone, as if through it he could shake his father. "Why didn't you tell me?" And then the real question, "Why did you have to die?"

When the tears finally eased, he wiped his eyes on the shoulder of his shirt. Dragging himself out of the chair, he pushed the front door shut. Rekari had left the lamp, and somehow its greenish glow was comforting, reminding him of his childhood and evenings spent in Rekari's own home. But he didn't need its light to find his way around. He left it where it was and staggered into the living quarters and his own bedroom, where he eased himself onto the bed. He turned the thin pillow over and put his head down.

The next thing he knew, someone was ringing the office doorbell, which was hand-operated by twisting a knob and did not rely on the nonexistent utility power. He blinked the sleep from his eyes and sat up. The windows were even darker than before—night had fallen. He lurched off the bed and stumbled to the office, where the lamp had faded almost to nothing. Pulling the flash out of his pocket, he went to the door and pulled it open.

It was Jacky, with her own flash held beside her hip. Behind her, a few soft lights in the buildings across the street were the only other illumination. "Still interested in chicken?" she said.

He blinked a few more times and realized he was very hungry. He nodded.

"Come on over," she said. "I've got beans and tomatoes, too."

It sounded great. "I'll be there right away."

Three other people were gathered for the meal. Dave knew them all—old-timers, friends of his father. He didn't know if he should tell them his father was dead. He decided he couldn't face that conversation yet, so instead, they traded some small talk, including some about Earth, then Dave excused himself and paid his bill.

"Going out to help your dad, are you?" Jacky said as she took his creds.

"Where'd you hear that?"

"Rekari's boy stepped the mast today. That means a launch. Pretty convenient."

"Well, maybe I'll go for a sail," said Dave. "Just to see how things have changed in two years."

Jacky laughed. "Nothing ever changes here."

Dave pointed over his shoulder in the general direction of the canal. "There's the wheat."

"It's like the cycle of the seasons," said Jacky. "It gets a little warmer, the water rises, it gets a little colder and it falls back. There won't be any wheat."

Dave shrugged. "Wheat means new settlers, new homes. There'll be things to see."

"And lost cities to hunt." She winked at him and turned to another customer.

He was still tired after eating, so he decided to go back to bed, and when he finally woke, just before dawn, he felt better. The shower was unusable due to the lack of power, but there was a bucket in the side shed, and he was able to scoop up water from the canal, dissolve a disinfecting tablet in it, and sluice himself off. He changed to some reasonably fresh clothes from the duffel and tucked the sunstone under his shirt. By then, Jacky's place was open for breakfast, and her flatbread and peanut butter tasted very good. Dave went out feeling ready for just about anything.

About a hundred meters down the street was Mike's Power Shop. He had a few motors in stock, adaptable to boats for people who thought sails were too slow—there were always a few, especially newcomers. Newcomers were more likely to have money, of course, while those who had been on Mars awhile had a tendency either to tap their relatives for help or to offer barter. Mike was more than happy to sell his best for Earth creds and to throw in a full charge. He loaned Dave a cart to take it down to the Martian quarter.

Burmari was waiting for him. The boat was already on the slide that would carry it into the canal, the sail was mounted but still tightly furled, and the brackets for the motor had been installed.

"It will tolerate a motor," said Burmari, "but it will not move as beautifully with one." Martians did not care for motors; they weren't using any when the first Earthman arrived, though most archaeologists believed that their ancient ancestors must have had them. How could they have achieved such a high civilization, they argued, without that kind of power? But Dave always remembered that the ancient civilizations of Earth had used the power of human and animal labor and nothing else. And the pyramids still stood—he had seen them with his own eyes.

"It won't move as beautifully," he agreed, slipping the motor into the brackets and closing the latches. The screw rested just below the surface of the water. "But sometimes it's all right to sacrifice beauty for speed."

Burmari's polite expression did not betray how little a Martian would believe that.

Rekari emerged from the house at the far end of the arc. "Did you sleep well, David?"

"Very well," said Dave.

"And when do you wish to begin the journey? As you see, the boat is quite ready."

"We have to lay in supplies."

"The work of a morning for me," said Rekari. "Is that possible for you as well?"

"I'll find out."

"If so, we can leave after the midday meal."

It didn't take Dave long to gather supplies from a local shop—mainly peanut butter, barley flatbread, and dried beans that could be reconstituted with boiled canal water. He stowed it all under the gunwale on one side of the boat while Rekari put his own supplies under the other. They checked the motor's mapper, and it seemed accurate, showing their destination on a standard grid-style projection of the planet. His father's excavator, a lightweight miniature bulldozer whose larger cousins Dave had used on Earth and which Rekari had stored for him, fit snugly in the stern beside Dave's personal bundle of tools. Rekari's wife and Jacky collaborated on a send-off lunch of grilled lizard, goat cheese, and potatoes—something for everyone—and just before noon, Dave and Rekari pulled away from the dock to the sound of the softly churning screw. Rekari estimated the trip at two weeks.

For the first few days, they followed Hiddekel north through an area Dave had visited with his father, where there were human settlements and Martian ones, ruins that Earth tourists had paid well to view and others that were barely visible to an untrained eye. But eventually they shifted into an eastward-tending canal and entered territory unknown to him. By day, Dave and Rekari alternated at the tiller. At night, they dropped anchor, heated their meals in a unit that plugged into the motor, and slept in the boat on inflatable pads. And Dave thought, not for the first time, how much more beautiful the stars were without that big, bright Earth satellite to spoil them; the Martian moons were far more modest, with Phobos a fraction of the size and brightness of Earth's moon and Deimos just another pinpoint in the great darkness.

Beginning on the second night, after their meal, with Rekari's lamp glowing at the boat's prow, the Martian talked about his travels with Dave's father, about their discoveries in the Syrtis, Sabaeus, and Tharsis areas. They had not been familiar with the farther north. No ruins had been found there—too much ice during the winter and too much flooding during the melt, Rekari said; the old Martians had probably chosen not to establish any major population centers in such a volatile area.

"Of course, your father did not believe that. He had perhaps an exaggerated idea of the ancients. As most of you do. They weren't very different from us. They loved their boats, as we do. The old stories say they had great fleets of boats, with sails patterned like the leaves of the alaria tree." He leaned back against the mast, the bottom of its furled sail brushing his shoulder. "There aren't many alarias left. Like so many other things. There were shallow seas in those days, and there would be boats sailing on them on summer afternoons, as far as the eye could see. It was very beautiful."

"I wish I could have seen that," Dave said.

Rekari looked out into the darkness. "Yes, it must have been a great sight." He was silent for a moment, then he said, "There were more of them, back then, than we are now. We don't have very many children now." He glanced at Dave. "I am more fortunate than most in that."

On the sixth day, just after they had shifted into an easterly-tending canal that would link to one that continued north toward their coordinates, Dave noticed that they were being followed. He hadn't thought so when he saw the boat for the first time, its mast and furled sail faintly visible against the sky. He had assumed it was a Martian trader, though when it kept up with them, he knew it had to be motorized, which was unusual for a Martian boat. Perhaps it was some Marsman's pleasure craft. Or it could have been two or three different boats that he was conflating. When it made the turn into the new canal, though, he knew—Martian or Marsman—it was following them.

When he woke at dawn on the eighth day, it was only a dozen meters away. Sometime during the night, its crew had taken the sail down completely to make better speed, and the cloth was rolled up and tied along one gunwale, the mast standing oddly naked in the center of the boat. In the bow, three Martians, strangers to Dave, were lowering the anchor over the side, and he waited till they were finished to signal a greeting. They returned the greeting, but there was something hesitant about their gestures, as if they were not comfortable using their signs with Marsmen. When they shifted their gazes to his left, he realized that Rekari had risen from his sleeping pad and was standing beside him.

Dave murmured, "Do you know these men?"

"It is possible," said Rekari.

Dave called out to the men in the Martian language. "Is there some way in which we can help you?"

They seemed startled, and Dave guessed they hadn't had much contact with Marsmen who spoke their language. One of them gestured the Martian imperative at him, a sign normally used by parents toward young children, mildly discourteous to an adult, and he accompanied it with English words. "You wear a sunstone that does not belong to you."

Dave laid a hand over the sunstone that was hidden beneath his shirt. "It belonged to my father," he said. "He gave it to me."

"It belonged to our cousin," said the Martian. "We are his nearest relations, and it should come to us."

Rekari stepped forward. "Venori continued his family through this one's father. I was witness to it."

The men in the boat all signed the negative. "It is not proper that a man of Earth should wear the stone," said the one who had spoken, and the others made multiple gestures of agreement.

"His elders judged it proper," said Rekari.

The strangers put their heads together and whispered among themselves. They seemed to be having a very quiet argument. Finally, one of them hoisted in the anchor, but instead of turning around and starting south, the three pulled short paddles from the bottom of the boat and sculled closer to Rekari's craft, so close that their spokesman could leap the gap between the two.

"It is ours," he said, and before Dave could do more than take a single step back, the Martian's long-fingered hand had darted out and caught at the sunstone's chain where it showed at the collar of his shirt.

Dave felt the chain bite at his neck, and he grabbed the Martian's wrist to keep him from pulling harder. *"Letann!"* he shouted.

The Martian froze for a moment, and then his fingers opened and the chain dropped free. Wrenching his wrist out of Dave's grip, he lurched backward, and his right leg slammed the gunwale, knocking him off balance. Before he could stop himself, he was falling over the side and into the canal.

Letann? As soon as the word left his mouth, Dave knew it was an ancient one, a command subsuming "No" and "Stop" and "How dare you?"—the deepest possible level of indignation. Where had he learned that word? In his childhood? He couldn't remember. He knew he had never used it before.

The wet Martian's companions helped him back into their boat, and the three had another whispered conversation, accompanied by quite a few glances in Dave's direction. Finally, without any word or gesture, they hoisted in their anchor and started south.

Dave rubbed his neck where the chain had scraped the skin and watched the other boat pull away. When it was well beyond shouting distance, he said, "Do they really have a claim to it?"

Rekari made the negative sign. "Their family and Venori's have been separated for more than forty generations. They have their own stone. One of them may inherit it, in time."

"But if they're his closest relatives . . ."

"You are his closest relative, David. Of that, I am certain."

Dave signaled a child's acknowledgment of his elder, but Rekari gestured a negative, though a mild one.

"You are not a child, David. Not with a sunstone on your neck." His hand hovered over the part of Dave's shirt that covered the stone. "This is a responsibility. Your father knew that when he told me to give it to you."

"I understand," said Dave. He didn't have much of his father beyond it, just a shabby house and a few pieces of furniture. Some copies of the papers his father had written on Martian antiquities. And his father's reputation, of course, intangible as that was. The sunstone represented all of that.

Dave sat at the tiller, and Rekari handed him a piece of flatbread and a container of peanut butter. Then he pulled up the anchor, and they began moving again, and the other boat quickly dwindled behind them.

After a time, Dave asked, "Why did they give up?"

Rekari chewed on his own meal of dried lizard meat. "Because they knew," he said, and he would not say more.

On the fourteenth day, Dave stood in the prow of the boat. "We're almost there." He looked at the mapper. "Not more than another kilometer." The banks of the canal had risen steadily over the last couple of days, and now, every few hundred meters, there were rough steps cut into them, unmistakably artificial. Above the banks, low hills were visible, silhouetted against the eastern sky.

Rekari sat by the mast. He made no attempt to look ahead. Instead, he looked back at the way they had come. "Your father was right. There was a city here once," he said. "Long ago, when there was less ice all through the year. It was a beautiful city, with graceful spires where flying creatures sometimes made their nests and theaters open to the sky for actors in masks with fanciful fronds sprouting from the living wood. Gorgeous masks. And the alaria trees lined every avenue and perfumed the air and shed their white blossoms on the water like so many miniature boats." He made that sign of sorrow again. "It has all been gone so long. How do they bear it?"

"How does who bear it?" Dave asked.

Rekari laid his hand on his chest. Then he slid his fingers into the opening of his shirt and pulled out his own sunstone and held it for a moment, looking at it, and it glimmered in the afternoon light. Then he tucked it away again. "The elders," he said, and he reached back with one hand and cut the motor. "I believe we have arrived." He swung the tiller over.

The boat bumped the canal bank at a set of steps, and while Rekari saw to the anchor, Dave climbed them. At the top, he was surprised to see a broad, open space. So far from the settled areas of Mars, and so close to a canal, it should have been covered by nettles, but a half circle some fifty meters in diameter was bare of them, though beyond it, starting just past a clump of huge boulders, they grew thickly in every direction, all the way to the distant low hills. His father had always said that big nettle fields implied underground water and marked the oases in the vast deserts of Mars—good places to hunt for lost cities. They had certainly helped him find some of the ruins now on the tourist round. He must have cleared these away himself, probably with the traditional herbicide the Martians used. Which meant he really thought something significant was here.

Rekari came up the steps to join him. "I buried your father over there," he said, pointing to the north.

Martians marked their gravesites with an outline of rocks pressed hard into the soil—whatever rocks happened to be around—and if there were no rocks nearby, they just used a raised rim of soil, which meant that their graves tended to disappear over time, rocks scattered or covered by windblown dust, shallow earthworks worn away. It didn't seem to bother them; they weren't in the habit of visiting their dead later on. His father's grave was still visible, not far from the canal, its rocks lined up neatly, though some dust had gathered on them. Dave knelt and brushed them clean with his hands. He wished he could have been there to help dig the grave and to stand with Rekari in the brief Martian ritual that marked the end of life. He had witnessed the ritual once, with his father. Now he could only kneel beside the grave and remember the last time he saw the famous Dr. Benjamin Miller, at the Meridiani spaceport, waving and shouting good-bye. He could almost hear his father's voice now, calling his name. And then, for a moment, he thought he really could hear that voice, and he looked up automatically, but of course no one was there but Rekari. He shook his head and got to his feet and looked out over the nettle-free space that stretched north and east from the grave. A city, Rekari had said. Was that reality or just myth? It was hard to tell with Martians, with a civilization so much older than any on Earth.

He began to walk, charting a mental grid over the barren ground. It didn't take him long to find the area his father had stripped of its surface soil and, within it, a smaller space where he had focused his efforts—the trowel marks were unmistakable. What had he seen here? Dave wasn't sure he could make out anything that hinted at ancient structures. He went back to the boat for a large flask, which he filled with canal water, and for the spray nozzle that fit it, and he used them to begin dampening the area, a standard archaeological technique to bring out markings that had faded away due to the dryness of the soil. Rekari helped him, making a dozen trips for more water and even scattering some of it by hand, and between the two of them, they left the ground moist but not muddy. The sky was beginning to darken when they spread the sail over their efforts, weighting its edges with rocks, to let the dampness work overnight. Then they ate their evening meals and slept on land for the first time in two weeks.

The next morning, after a quick breakfast, Dave gathered up his other tools—the folding shovel, the stiff-bristled brush, and the sharp trowel he had brought from Earth that fit into a scabbard at his belt. Then he went to the sail, took a deep breath, and pulled the fabric aside. As expected, the dampness had spread under the protective cloth, and after some minutes on his hands and knees, Dave thought he could see variations in its absorption—the faint shadows of wooden footings, long since rotted away, forming a vanished entrance that framed a rectangular space of long-ago disturbed soil. The differences were subtle, but something in him said yes, they really were there. The idea that the entrance had been made of alaria wood popped into his mind, though he assumed that was because Rekari had mentioned alarias.

He pulled out the trowel and scraped at the damp soil with its finely honed edge. When the top layer came up fairly easily, he decided to use the excavator, and Rekari helped him maneuver it out of the boat and roll it into place. He flipped the switch, and the small machine came to life and began to scuff at the surface and toss the soil aside. He ran it over the suspicious area, and at each pass, it dug deeper, a centimeter at a time.

Fifty centimeters below the surface, it exposed a polished stone surface. He jumped down into the shallow pit and went to work with trowel and brush to clean it off and find its edges.

Fully exposed, the smooth stone measured a little less than one meter by two, oriented with the longer side running almost precisely north and south. The western edge merged with rougher stone that extended toward the canal. The eastern edge ended sharply, and when he dug a narrow trench downward there, he found a smooth vertical face about fifteen centimeters in depth, with another horizontal surface at the bottom. He lengthened his trench eastward, found another edge after about forty centimeters, another vertical face, and another horizontal surface below that. It looked like the beginning of a stairway. He started the excavator again, set the depth control to maximum, and spent the rest of the afternoon clearing the three steps. Not long before sunset he had a hole two meters by three, almost a meter deep, and three steps that led . . . to what?

Rekari had been sitting at the edge of the hole for most of the excavation. Now Dave climbed up and sat beside him in the waning sunlight. "There has to be something down there," he said. "Nobody builds stairs to nowhere."

Rekari signed his agreement.

"If this were Earth, I'd say maybe a sunken amphitheater. There's room for a pretty broad arc before you reach those boulders." He gestured toward them.

"An interesting thought," said Rekari.

"Maybe there's a polygon of steps." He looked left and right, measuring the area with his eyes. "That would be a major excavation. I'd have to ask for a grant from Syrtis University and a crew of grad students to help. It could be very exciting."

"It's only three steps," said Rekari.

Dave signed agreement. "I'll need more evidence before I can write that grant proposal." He swiveled his legs out of the hole and stood up. "Well, more digging tomorrow." He smiled at Rekari. "It begins to seem like Dad had a really good lead."

Rekari looked down at the steps, now in deep shadow. "Your father taught me a great deal in the years of our partnership," he said. "He might have wondered if the ground level was lower thousands of years ago, and if these steps might not have led upward from there to something that no longer exists."

Dave crossed his arms over his chest and looked into the hole, too. "Well, that's possible," he said. "And a lot less exciting. But I have to find out. I could use some peanut butter now, and a good night's sleep."

The next day, he found more steps leading downward. And more. Periodically, he pulled the excavator back to the surface and lengthened the opening, two meters at a time, so that the forward wall would not collapse from being undercut. In the pit, the excavator was soon beyond its ability to loft soil the entire distance to the surface, and so he and Rekari alternated using the shovel to finish clearing away what the machine tossed to the higher steps. By midafternoon, the hole was more than five meters long, and there were ten steps leading down. By midafternoon two days later, it was ten meters long, with twenty steps.

That was when they hit the door.

It was an elliptical panel, vertical, about two meters tall and a meter and a third wide. As he brushed the packed soil away and examined it with his flash, Dave saw that it was set flush into a smooth stone wall, but the panel itself was made of metal, and he was amazed at its condition—the corrosion was minimal, as if the door had been left there a hundred years ago instead of thousands.

"Look at this," he whispered, as if Rekari, standing behind him, needed to be told that something was there.

Rekari stretched out a hand and touched the door almost reverently.

There was no handle, no lock that might admit a key or a tool, no obvious way to open it. But it was wider than the step in front of it was deep, which meant it had to open away from the stairway. Dave set both of his hands against its right side and pushed tentatively, then with increasing effort. The door did not move. He tried the other side, with the same results. "I didn't think I'd need to bring a crowbar," he muttered. Holding the flash close, he peered at the metal, going over it centimeter by centimeter, but all he could find were two hairline joins, one the length of the vertical axis, the other at the horizontal, both too tight to admit even the sharp edge of his trowel.

He leaned his forehead against the cold metal. Most archaeologists considered chisels too destructive, but he was beginning to wish he had brought one along. He took a deep breath. Patience, he reminded himself, was the essence of archaeology. *Dad,* he thought, *I know this is what you were looking for.* He leaned his whole body against the door from his cheek to his knees and pushed with every muscle he had. He could feel the sunstone under his shirt biting into his chest from the pressure.

The panel shivered.

He kept pushing.

Suddenly the door parted along those hairline joins, each quarter drawing back into the stone frame, leaving the ellipse open.

Beyond, illuminated by a dozen green lamps set on as many tripods, stood two Martian men. They stared at Dave.

He stared back. *What the hell . . . ?*

Rekari had caught his arms to keep him from falling through the opening. Now he let go slowly, and in Martian, he said, "This is the son of my friend."

The two men did not sign a greeting in response to the introduction. They just kept staring.

Dave stepped over the curving threshold and looked around. The room inside the door was perhaps five meters square, and its walls were as smoothly polished as the steps had been, and empty of any decoration. At the far end of the room was another downward stairway, this one lit by green lamps hanging on its walls; he could see them descending. He signed a greeting to the two men, and when they did not answer it, he went to the stairway and started down. They did not try to stop him, but he could hear them following and speaking to Rekari in Martian.

"He cannot wear the stone," one of them said. "He is a stranger."

Dave guessed that Rekari signed the negative, because he said, "I cradled this child in my arms the day he was born. He is not a stranger."

"He is of Earth," said one of the men.

"He went to Earth for his education," said Rekari. "He did not stay."

Dave didn't look back to see what else they might have been signing at each other. He was more interested in finding out what lay at the bottom of the steps. The door alone was an archaeological treasure; what else could be hidden below, where rain and wind and dust couldn't touch it? He could feel so many things drawing him downward—curiosity, fascination, regret that his father couldn't be here with him. Especially regret. And yet, he felt he was fulfilling his father's goals by descending those stairs.

It was a long, long way down, but finally the steps opened up into a huge room that seemed originally to have been a natural cavern, with walls rippled by deposits left behind by water. Green lamps lit the space, standing on tripods ranged in concentric arcs all around. In the center of the room was a pair of large tables shaped like two half circles with an arm's-length gap between them. There were no chairs.

The two men moved to either side of him then. "We are the caretakers," they said in English. "Now you will give us the sunstone."

Dave looked at Rekari. "You said it was mine."

"They cannot take it from you," said Rekari, and he seemed to be speaking to them as much as to him. "The elders won't allow it. We saw that with Venori's cousins."

"You must leave it here," said one of the men.

Dave signed the negative. "My father gave it to me," he said in Martian. "I will not give it up."

"You will," said the man. Gesturing for Dave to follow him, he walked over to the tables and stood at one end of the gap between them. There, he traced a symbol on one table with his left hand and on the other with his right, and a panel of dark wood rose up between them, almost filling the space.

It was crowded with sunstones, row upon row of them, hanging on hooks shaped like miniature fingers.

"You will leave the sunstone here," said the Martian, "with all of the others whose families have ended."

Dave stared at the stones. There were so many of them. So very many families gone. He could almost feel them calling to him from the dust of ages, and without thinking, he eased past the caretaker and slid two steps into the gap. He reached out with both hands and spread his fingers, so much shorter than Martian fingers, across as many stones as he could.

A sudden kaleidoscope of images sprang up around him, blotting out the array of stones, the table, the cavern. He found himself surrounded by strange tall trees with multicolored leaves, by boats with sails as colorful as the leaves, gliding across a glassy sea, by sprawling buildings topped with spires like blades pointing to the pale sky, by crowds of Martian men, women, and children, walking, running, gesticulating, all of those myriad images overlaid upon each other in a riot of color and motion. It was day, it was night, it was rain, snow, and sunshine. And the noise was deafening, a thousand thousand voices laughing, weeping, calling out, a chattering cacophony, with snatches of music rising above it all, like the singing of birds and the creaking of hinges in need of oil. The stones were speaking to him, speaking through his own stone, and inundating him with Mars as it was and would never be again.

And then, in his vision, someone reached out to him, took his shoulders with immaterial hands, and steadied the dizzying rush.

All motion halted, all sound receded, and in front of everything a form coalesced.

Dr. Benjamin Miller.

"Hello, son," he said.

Dave felt his mouth open, but no words came out. He didn't know what to say or do first. He wanted to throw his arms around his father, but when he reached out to him, there was nothing to touch but air. Finally, hoarsely, he said, "Dad!"

His father smiled. "It's good to see you, son. I'm sorry I couldn't be at Meridiani to meet you."

"Dad . . ."

"I wanted us to go out into the field together one more time. But the old pump didn't make it." He shook his head and sighed. "I remember lying on the ground and hearing Rekari call my name, then the pain was just too much. The next thing I knew, I was here."

"Here in the cavern?" said Dave.

His father made the Martian sign of negation. "In the sunstone I'd been wearing, that you're wearing now."

Dave's fingers went to the stone. "In it?"

"In it," said his father, "with Venori and all of his elders. Sunstones turn out to be much more than symbols, son. Everyone who wears a stone carries his elders in it—every elder who ever wore it, their memories, their knowledge, their personalities. I still haven't finished sorting it all out, even with Venori's help. I think it must be easier for the Martians since they expect it. He and I will both help you."

Dave swallowed hard. "So I'm dead, too?"

His father made the negative sign again. "You've just had the full experience for the first time. Venori says it was triggered by all these stones being so close to you. But it's been growing. I know you noticed it."

Dave thought back to all the feelings he'd had, all the intuitions, all the impulses. "I guess I have."

"And now that you've seen this place, you have to decide whether you want to make your reputation from it, or whether you want to search for something else. It's a great find, son. The kind an archaeologist spends a lifetime hoping for."

Dave looked past his father to the frozen multitudes, and he thought again about all those sunstones and the lives they represented—the parents, the children, the long history that archaeologists only guessed at. And he said, "What do they think?"

His father shook his head. "They're in the past, son. As I'm in the past. The future has to make that decision. But first, you have to get out of here. And to do that, you have to open your eyes."

"What?"

"Open your eyes. Open your eyes now."

His father's voice faded away, and his form wavered, became translucent, and beyond him all the frozen figures began to move and talk, faster and faster, until they closed in on him and he couldn't be told apart from the multilayered blur of the rest. Dave felt surrounded by that dizzying motion again, and he pressed his hands to his eyes and took deep breaths and tried to push it all away. He felt himself crumple, felt the pain of hip and knee and elbow slamming against an unyielding surface, felt himself curl into fetal position, then black silence overwhelmed him.

Some time later—he didn't know how long—he opened his eyes behind his hands, and when he pulled his hands away from his face, it didn't make any difference. He was lying on a cold stone floor in darkness. He rolled to his knees, wincing at the pain of his bruises. He pushed up to his feet. "Rekari?" he said. There was no answer. In the Martian language, he called out, "Is anyone nearby?" Again, there was no answer.

He patted his pockets, found the flash, and snapped it on. They hadn't taken it. Of course, they couldn't. He wore a sunstone, and they didn't dare touch him without his permission. He understood that now. It had taken every iota of courage Venori's forty-generations-removed cousin had been able to summon simply to touch the chain, and Dave shouting in ancient Martian had been too much for him. Patting his chest, Dave verified that his sunstone was there.

He played the flash around. He was still in the cavern, though the panel of sunstones had slid back down between the tables. The green lamps had all been covered; he pulled the shields off several to make a softly lit path to the stairway. He ran up the steps, exposing lights as he went. At the top, the elliptical door was closed, and it would not open for him, even when he touched it with the sunstone. Someone had locked it.

The caretakers, of course. They couldn't take his stone, but they could lock the stranger into the cavern and let him die there. He wondered what they had said to Rekari to make him cooperate.

He went back down to the cavern.

He stalked through the room, taking the shields off all the lights. Then he hitched himself up on one of the tables and looked around. The elliptical door had been buried. It was obviously an ancient entrance to this cavern, no longer used. But the caretakers had to get in and out somehow, if only to replenish the lamps. He made a circuit of the room, but it seemed to be completely sealed. He licked a finger and held it up, searching for a breeze, but there was nothing noticeable.

All right, he thought. It was time to stop being stupid.

He curled his hand around the sunstone and spoke in his most formal and respectful Martian. "Venori," he said, "my elder who chose my father to be his son, tell his son how to leave this place."

He thought he could hear a faint whisper, like a broom sweeping a wooden floor. And then his own vision turned dark again, except for one small spot on his right, and when he turned toward it, he felt as if he was looking down a long, narrow tunnel that ended at a circle low on the cavern wall. He slid off the table and walked toward the circle, stumbling once because he couldn't see the floor beneath his feet, and though the spot remained as bright as Phobos, it shrank before him until, at the wall, it was no larger than the sunstone that hung about his neck. It stood at knee height, and when he bent close to it, he saw nothing special to mark it. He touched it with one finger, and when nothing happened, he pressed the sunstone to it.

The darkness in his vision cleared away as the wall opened into an ellipse, its stone quarters withdrawing into the walls just as the metal segments of the ellipse at the top of the stairs had done. Beyond was a stairway upward, lit by more green lamps. Dave climbed. At the top was another stone wall, and his vision shrank again, for just a moment, to show him where to press the sunstone to it. When that wall opened, late-afternoon daylight invaded the stairwell.

Dave stepped out. He found himself in the clump of boulders that stood at the far end of the nettle-free area; two of them had slid aside to allow him to pass, and as he emerged, they closed up behind him.

Outside, Rekari and the two caretakers sat atop one of the other boulders. Rekari jumped down to embrace Dave. "I knew you could do it."

"So it was a test," said Dave.

Rekari made the sign of agreement, twice.

"And what if I had failed?"

Rekari held him at arm's length and looked into his face. "If two days had passed and you had not found the way, I would have gone back and brought you out. But I knew you would not fail. I knew when you opened the first door that the elders had accepted you."

Dave turned back to the place where the boulders had parted to let him out. There was no way to tell that anything had happened there, but he knew he could open it again at any time. "My father has suggested that I could become famous by revealing the cavern to the people of Earth. On Earth, many such places have been visited by scholars and tourists. Caves at Altamira and Lascaux. Graves in Greece. The pyramids of Egypt. Sacred places. I visited a few of them myself when I was in school there."

The caretakers glanced at each other. "And will you do this?" said one of them.

Dave fingered the sunstone at his neck. He looked at Rekari. "The people who made those places on Earth are long gone. The people who made this place on Mars are still here. What would the elders say if I stole it from them?" He made the sign of the negative. "The elders will help me find the ruins of cities where no one has lived for twenty thousand years. That is the proper work of archaeologists, not helping to despoil what has not been abandoned. There will be enough other places to make my reputation."

Rekari gripped Dave's arm. "Your father will be pleased. I know it."

He thought about his father then—he could feel his presence in the stone. They would go out in the field again together after all, just not quite in the way either of them had hoped. And Dave would break the news of his death to Jacky, who would care, and to Beverly, who would perhaps realize that she also cared, because that was what one did for one's elders. He knew that neither of them would believe that his father lived on in the stone. He didn't think he would even try to tell them. It was, after all, a private thing between him and his elders.

"Will you work with me?" he said to Rekari.

"That would please me greatly," said Rekari.

They walked back toward the hole they had dug.

"We should fill that in," said Dave. "We don't need it anymore."

They had left the excavator on the third step from the bottom. Now they dragged it up to the surface, and Dave leaned against it for a moment, looking down the stairway. "You could have shown him lost cities, couldn't you?" he said. "You and your elders know where they are. Why didn't you?"

"That was his desire," said Rekari. "Not mine."

"But it didn't matter in the long run. I'm going to do what he would have done."

"It matters a great deal," said Rekari, "because as much as I liked and respected your father, he was not a Martian. And you are."

"Am I?" said Dave. But he didn't need Rekari to answer that. He already knew, and so did all of the elders in his sunstone.

"Perhaps we can paint a new sign," said Rekari. "For the new proprietor of the Miller family business."

Yes, thought Dave. *We'll do that.*

Dave Miller, Archaeology. Tour the Ancient Ruins.

Home.

Prolific Texas writer Joe R. Lansdale has won the Edgar Award, the British Fantasy Award, the American Horror Award, the American Mystery Award, the International Crime Writer's Award, and nine Bram Stoker Awards. Although perhaps best known for horror/thrillers such as *The Nightrunners, Bubba Ho-Tep, The Bottoms, The God of the Razor,* and *The Drive-In,* he also writes the popular Hap Collins and Leonard Pine mystery series—*Savage Season, Mucho Mojo, The Two-Bear Mambo, Bad Chili, Rumble Tumble, Captains Outrageous*—as well as Western novels such as *The Magic Wagon,* and totally unclassifiable cross-genre novels such as *Zeppelins West, The Drive-In,* and *The Drive-In 2: Not Just One of Them Sequels.* His other novels include *Dead in the West, The Big Blow, Sunset and Sawdust, Acts of Love, Freezer Burn, Waltz of Shadows,* and *Leather Maiden.* He has also contributed novels to series such as Batman and Tarzan. His many short stories have been collected in *By Bizarre Hands; Sanctified and Chicken Fried; The Best of Joe R. Lansdale; The Shadows Kith and Kin; The Long Ones; Stories by Mama Lansdale's Youngest Boy; Bestsellers Guaranteed; On the Far Side of the Cadillac Desert with the Dead Folks; Electric Gumbo; Writer of the Purple Rage; Fist Full of Stories; Bumper Crop; The Good, the Bad, and the Indifferent; Selected Stories by Joe R. Lansdale; For a Few Stories More; Mad Dog Summer: And Other Stories; The King and Other Stories; Deadman's Road; High Cotton: The Collected Stories of Joe R. Lansdale;* and an omnibus, *Flaming Zeppelins: The Adventures of Ned the Seal.* As editor, he has produced the anthologies *The Best of the West, Retro Pulp Tales, Son of Retro Pulp Tales* (with Keith Lansdale), *Razored Saddles* (with Pat LoBrutto), *Dark at Heart: All New Tales of Dark Suspense* (with wife Karen Lansdale), *The Horror Hall of Fame: The Stoker Winners,* and the Robert E. Howard tribute anthology, *Cross Plains Universe* (with Scott A. Cupp). An anthology in tribute to Lansdale's work is *Lords of the Razor.* His most recent books are two new Hap and Leonard novels, *Vanilla Ride* and *Devil Red,* as well as the short novels *Hyenas* and *Dead Aim,* the novels *Edge of Dark Water* and *The Thicket,* two new anthologies—*The Urban Fantasy Anthology* (edited with Peter S. Beagle), and *Crucified Dreams*—and three new collections, *Shadows West* (with John L. Lansdale), *Trapped in the Sunday Matinee,* and *Bleeding Shadows.* He lives with his family in Nacogdoches, Texas.

Here he tells the suspenseful story of a young girl who sets off on a rescue mission with many lives at stake, realizing quite well that it's dangerous—but perhaps not realizing quite *how* dangerous it's going to become.

King of the Cheap Romance

JOE R. LANSDALE

(In memory of Ardath Mayhar)

I GLANCED AT THE BODY AND TREMBLED. I LOOKED AT THE blue ice directly in front of me, and beyond that at the vast polar regions of Mars, stretched out flat, and way beyond that was a mountain rise. Past that rise was where I needed to go. I felt cold and miserable and sad, and for one long moment I wanted to quit. Then I told myself, that's not what Dad would have wanted. That's not what he would have wanted his daughter to do.

We Kings, we weren't quitters. It had been drummed into my head since birth. I looked down at Dad's corpse, all that was left of my family, wrapped in silver bedding, lying on the sled, and it was as if I could hear him now. "Angela, put your ears back and your nose forward, and keep going. That's how we do. Just like an old mule. That's how we Kings are. We keep on going when everyone else has already quit."

That made me feel strong for a moment or two, then I was thinking back on how I had ended up where I was, and that took the zip out of me again. I couldn't get hold of being here on the ice, after only moments before being high in the air. It felt as if it was all some kind of dream, some astral visitation of someone else's life who looked like me and had a dead dad. But the real me was somewhere else, and at any moment I'd snap awake and find myself back in the silver airship, cruising high above the Martian ice.

I didn't, though.

It was really me. Angela King. Out on the ice, breathing out air puffy and white as clouds, the body of my father lying on a sled at my feet.

I took a deep breath of chilly air and determined then that I had to get over my feelings of defeat. I was a King. I couldn't quit. Something might quit me, but I wouldn't quit. Not until I was as dead as Dad.

What happened was this.

The fever hit the Far Side, as we called the city long beyond the mountains. The Martian fever is a nasty beast. It comes on sudden and hot and burns the mind right out of a person, turns them red, mounds up pus-filled lesions quick-time, makes a person quiver, scream and rave, go completely off their nut. No one really knew how it gets started, but it happened now and then, comes out of nowhere like rain from a clear, sunny sky. It was thought to have something to do with certain kinds of Martian water, melted snow that flowed down out of the mountains and joined up in streams and creeks that got into the water supply. Mars was mostly hot, dry desert, but up around the ice caps it was rich in water, cold and savage.

Though the fever was brutal, there was a cure, and it was mighty effective, if not readily available. That's what my father and I were trying to do, make it available. It was considered a routine trip, though any trip on Mars can blow out and go bad in quick-time. Just when you thought things were good and the land was tamed, Mars would throw a trick at you.

The ship we had was quick and light. It held us and a couple of sleds, which we didn't think we'd need, an emergency stash of supplies, and a small, padded leather bag of vaccine. That's all it took, a small bag containing a few vials. A bit of it went a long way. In fact, Dad said a drop would fix the fever and keep you from having it again, which meant it didn't take much at all to cure an entire Martian city, and on Mars a city was about two to three thousand. Dad said on Earth you'd call that kind of gathering a town, maybe even a community. But on Mars it was a city. I didn't remember Earth too well, and had yet to go back, the return trip being so expensive and me not really wanting to go. I liked it on the Red Planet, out in the area where it wasn't red at all, but blue and white with freezing ice.

Anyway, Dad said a drop of vaccine would do, and he ought to know. He was a doctor before he died out there on the ice.

Dad had not wanted me to come. He always said, "On Mars, things can and do go wrong, regular as clockwork, and irregularly too."

But since my mom was dead and I would have had to stay with people I didn't know well, I whined my way into the glider, and up we went, powered by sunlight, carried by whining turbines, darting fast through the thin-aired Martian sky. When we started out, both moons were up and shiny as silver. Dad said he could never quite get used to two moons. I didn't remember much about Earth, but I did remember it had one moon in the sky. That seemed pretty deficient after living on Mars with one moon fast and one moon slow, both bright in the sky and looking not so far, as if you could stand on a ladder and touch them.

We sailed along under the moonlight. The night air sucked into the turbines and fed them and charged them along with solar and whatever those pellets were that Dad put in the sliding tray that slid in and out of the instrument panel.

I sat in the copilot chair, having learned a thing or two about navigation, and we cruised through the last of the dying night; and then the light rose up and the world below went from shiny black to blue-and-white ice. What I think about is how if we'd have left a few seconds earlier, or a few seconds later, none of it might have happened. But there we were with first light on the windshield, then the shield turned dark, and there was a whomp, a sound like some kind of machine tearing metal. It wasn't metal though, It wasn't the ship. It was the scream of the Martian Bat. The damn things are huge, and, unlike Earth bats, which Dad says travel by night, Martian Bats travel day and night but are blind, their eyes huge and white as snow.

They are guided by some kind of in-built radar. That radar helps them find prey, and I guess the bat thought we were one of the great blue birds that fly over the ice, for it came at us and let out with its horrid scream that sounded like metal ripping. The craft twisted and swirled, but held to the sky all right, at least until the Bat bit us and clawed us and we started to come apart.

The craft killed the bat due to the collision of its wings or part of the beast's being sucked into a turbine. Whatever did it, we both went down. I remember seeing out the windshield a glimpse of bat's wings, a near subliminal glimpse of those white eyes and that toothy mouth. The front end of the ship bent up, and down we went. Had the bat not had hold of us, had what was left of its massive wings not held and glided, we would have dropped faster than a stone and with the sudden impact of ripe fruit being slammed on rocks.

Still, when we hit, I was knocked unconscious.

Coming to, I discovered I was lying on the ice. I had on my insulated suit. Dad had insisted I wear it, even in the craft, and I was glad then I had. I didn't have the hood pulled up, though, and when I sat up on the ice, stiff and sore, I pulled it over my head and lifted up the goggles and the chin cover that had been lying on my chest, suspended there by a dangling strap.

I tried to get up, but it was like I was wrestling someone invisible. I just couldn't do it, at least not at first. It was as if whatever kept me balanced had been knocked off its gyro. I finally got my feet under me, which took me so long I thought maybe a Martian year had passed. When I did get to my feet, I looked around for Dad but couldn't find him. Over the hill, I saw the Martian buzzards gathering, their red-tipped wings catching the rays of the sun. I stumbled over a little mound of snow, and there was the ship. Or what was left of it. It was so wadded up with the bat, which was about the same size, that it looked as if a great leathery black animal had mated with a silver bird and fallen to earth in blind passion.

Moving that way, I soon saw Dad, lying out on the ice. When I trudged to where he lay, I saw the snow around him had blossomed red and frozen, like a strawberry ice drink. I got down on my knees and tried to help him. He put out a hand.

"Don't touch me," he said. "It hurts too much."

"Oh, Dad," I said.

"There's nothing for it," he said. "Not a thing. I'm bleeding out."

"I know how to sew you up," I said. "You taught me."

He shook his head. "Won't do any good. I'm all torn up inside. I can feel how stuff has moved around, and I'm not getting any stronger here. Prop me up."

There was a seat cushion, and I got that. I took it back to Dad, gently lifted him up, and rested his head on it.

He said, "When the sun gets to the middle there, I won't be with you."

"Don't say that," I said.

"I'm not trying to scare you," he said. "I'm telling you how things are, and I'm about to tell you how things have to be, before I'm too weak to do it. I'm going to die, and you should leave me here and take the medicine, if it survived, if you can find it, and you got to take one of the sleds and go across the ice, into the mountains, and make your way over to Far Side."

"That's miles and miles," I said.

"It is, but you can do it. I have faith. Those people have to have the cure."

"What about you?" I said.

"I told you how that's going to turn out. I love you. I did my best. You have to do the same."

"Jesus," I said.

"He didn't have anything to do with it. Alive or dead, he never shows up. You got to do it on your own, and the thing that's got to carry you is knowing that you're a King. Think of it like an adventure, like those cheap romance novels I used to read to you."

He meant adventure novels. They were old stories, like *Ivanhoe*, and he said they were called romances, but they were primarily stories of high adventure. Right then, I didn't feel too terribly adventurous. I wanted to lie down beside him and die right along with him. When I was dead, I didn't care what happened to us. Frozen in ice, or eaten by snow runners, or those buzzards with red-tipped wings. It was all the same to me.

"You got to see yourself as a hero," Dad said. "You got to see yourself as a savior. I know that sounds prideful, but you got to see yourself that way. You got to find that bag, and you got to put it and you on a sled and start out. The supplies may have survived too. You'll need them. There are plenty of things out there on the Martian ice, so you got to stay alert. You'll be able to make it. Go quick as you can. But watch for the ice, and what's under the ice, and what flies above it, and what lives on it."

I nodded.

Dad grinned then. "I'm not making it sound easy."

"No," I said. "You're not."

"Well, it isn't easy. But you're a King. You can do it."

And I swear right then, no sooner had he said those words, he closed his eyes and was as long gone as the day before.

The smart thing to do was to leave him, but I couldn't. Not to be eaten by Martian birds, and whatever else might come along. I strapped him onto one of the sleds that I found in the wreckage. There were two. The other had been crunched up and was nearly in a ball. The one I used had some bends and gaps in the metal, but it was serviceable. I searched around for the medicine and supplies. They were easy to find. I put them on the sled.

The supplies had food and water and lighting, first aid, flares, blankets, tubes of this and that, and even a pair of snowshoes, all tightened up in a little bundle; but with a touch of a finger they would spread out and form to any foot.

I went then and got Dad and dragged him over to the sled. Being so confused, I didn't have enough sense to take the sled to him. I pulled one of the five weather blankets from the supply packet and wrapped him in it. It fastened up easy on the sides, and over his feet and head. I managed him into the sled, up near the front. I put the supplies and the medicine in there with him.

I took my place in the seat and pulled the clear lid over me and sat there and thought a moment. Looking out in front of me, seeing Dad's body shaped in the blanket, I started to cry. That went on for a while. I won't lie to you. It was a tough moment, and right then, once again, I thought maybe the Kings *did* quit; at least this one might.

Finally, I got myself together and turned the switch and hit the throttle. The sled jumped forward and I steered. As I went, I popped one of the compass pills. I didn't feel anything at first, but then there was a subtle twist in my brain, like a hot worm trying to find a place to rest, and I knew. I knew how to go. The pills were like that. One could get you set in the direction you needed. They were made from a Martian worm, which is why I said I felt like a worm was in my head. It was that kind of sensation. Something in the worm's DNA allowed it to travel from one end of Mars to another; consuming one, you got the same ability. You knew what the worm knew, and all it knew was direction. You didn't have to wait as long for it to kick in. It was nearly an instant sensation.

The sled hummed and the rig beneath it split the snow and slid across the ice. It had some lift about it too. I needed it, the machine could float up to ten or twelve feet, and I could float on water, and it was airtight enough to act for a short time like a minisubmarine. It sure beat snowshoes.

All this world, and all the worlds there are, and all the stars, and all that is our universe, are connected. That's what Dad used to tell me. I, however, felt anything but connected. I felt like a particle to which nothing could be fastened.

I sled-bumped a few spots where the snow had drifted across the ice, then there were no drifts, just this long expanse of blue and white like a sheet stretched tight, and far away a thin line of mountains on the horizon that seemed to recede, not come closer.

After some time, I stopped and popped the lid on the sled and got out. Inside the sled, it was comfortable because there was a heater and I had wrapped my legs in one of the thermal blankets, the same sort Dad's body was wrapped in. Outside, the air cut like a frozen knife. I found a spot to relieve myself that looked like all the other spots available. I dropped my pants and squatted to pee. It was cold on my butt. Anyway, I did my business, and while I was doing it, I saw it coming.

At first, I thought it was an illusion, mirage. But no, it was real. A black fin had broken the ice, and it had broken it violently enough that I heard it crack, though I figure I was a quarter mile from that fin. I didn't know what it was from experience, but I had read about it and recognized it that way.

It was an ice shark, big as killer whales on Earth, but sleeker, with a black fin and tentacles that exploded from its head like confetti strands but were considerably more dangerous. It could travel on the surface or underneath, and could even crawl on land for a long time. Its fin was harder than any known metal and could crack the ice without effort. The ice shark had a tremendous sense of smell, a bit of radar, not as highly developed as the bat, but effective enough. It could squeeze into tight places, like oatmeal sliding through a colander. It had most likely smelled my urine and had come for lunch.

I yanked up my pants and made a quick-step trip back to the sled, slid into place, and closed the lid and gave it the juice. Too much juice. It jumped, came back down with a smack. For a horrid moment, I thought maybe I had done myself in, destroyed my transportation and shelter, but then, away it went.

I pulled the view screen over and took a look through the backview cameras. It was still coming, and it looked closer, and I knew those cameras were not entirely accurate; the shark was considerably closer than it appeared.

The sled had more juice to be given, but I saved it because the more you used, the more sunlight you needed to keep it charged, and now, to make matters worse, the light was dropping down over the moving mountains. When nightfall came I would have power, but it sometimes faltered then, if the sled was given full throttle. Still, if I slowed too much, the shark would catch me. Crunch the craft in its great teeth, snapping it apart, getting to the gooey, tasty center inside, meaning, of course, me and my dad.

That shark couldn't have known I would be more vulnerable come night, but it sure seemed to. It came fast behind me but was never able to catch me, even though I had only pushed the throttle a little more than before. Yet, it was like it knew I had limitations. That if all it did was wait, I would have to slow down and it would have me.

It was growing dark, but I could still see the line of mountains and the vast expanse of nothing around me, then all of a sudden the light washed out and the moons rose up. I turned on the lights.

And then it happened.

Even inside the sled, I could hear the ice crack, and then I could see them. I had never actually seen them for real, just vids, but there they were, cracking up through the ice and rising up and sliding along—the Climbing Bergs. They were rises of solid ice that came down from the depths where it was cold and wet and where the old, old Mars was. They would break open the surface and slide along and suck in the air. They were mounds of ice full of living organisms that owned them. Living organisms that came up for air and pulled it in and renewed themselves like Southern Earth ladies with hand-shaking fans on a hot day in church. Sometimes they were empty ice—clear ice you could see all the way through. And sometimes the ice held the ancient Mars inside of it. I had heard of that, extinct animals, and even Martians themselves, though there had only been fragments of that discovered, and most stories about them were legends, as the ice soon sank back down into the depths, taking their ancient treasures and information with them.

The ice cracked loud as doom and rose up and the moons flashed on the clean, clear ice, and the moonlight shone through it. It covered my entire path, and inside of the ice I could see something: a dark shadow. The shadow was in the center of the ice, and it was a shadow that covered acres and rose up high. Then I was close enough that I could see better what the shadow was. It almost took my breath away, almost made me forget about what was behind me. It was a slanting slide of ice that went directly up against the icy wall of the berg, and inside the berg was a huge set of stone stairs that rose up to a stone pyramid, and the stairs went inside and dipped into the dark. The ice between the outside and the pyramid looked thin, as if it might be hollow inside the berg.

I knew this much. I couldn't keep outrunning the shark. In time the sunlight would wear, and the sled would slow. I had a sudden wild thought, but it was the only one I had. Besides, going around the berg might take hours; it was that big.

I glanced in the mirror and saw the shark's fin, poking high, and I could see its shape shimmering beneath the ice. A huge shape, and I could see that it was, as I said, a monster that in spite of its name was really nothing like a shark. It was a dark form that was formless; it moved like gelatin, except for the fin, which stayed steady, sawing through the ice effortlessly.

Aiming the sled for the natural slide of ice, I gave the machine full throttle. I knew I was sacrificing some of my juice, but it was as good a plan as any I could think of.

I slid up the ice and came hard against the cold, clear wall of the berg, and killed the engine. I flipped the top and got out, leaned over and tore the supply bag open. Jerking out three of the thermal sticks, better known as flares, I gave them a twist and tossed them against the ice. They blossomed with flame. The flames rose up high and the heat singed my hair and made a kind of hissing sound as it melted a big hole in the ice. It was as I had hoped, a thin wall of ice, and inside, it was open; it was as if the ice were a glass cake cover of unusual shape and design, dipped over a pyramidal cake.

I looked back. The shark tore its whole body through the ice. It shifted and twisted and wadded, and finally it roared. It was a roar so loud I felt the ice beneath me shake. The roar and the wind carried its horrid breath to me. It was so foul I thought I might throw up. Its shape changed, became less flat and more solid, tentacles flashed out from its head, and I could see flippers on its belly, between those dipped little legs with bony hooks for feet. It was slithering and clawing its way across the cold space between me and it.

Back in the sled with the lid pulled down, I gunned forward and drove in and bounced up the steps, and then I was inside the pyramid. The lights on the sled showed me the way. I went along a large hallway, if something that large could be called a hall. On either side were strange statues of tall, thin creatures that resembled men. I zoomed by them and came to two wide-open doors made of something I couldn't identify. They were wide enough for me to sled through, leaving several feet on either side.

Once I was inside, I grabbed a light from the supply bag, got out and tried to push one of the doors, but it was too heavy. Then I had an idea. I got back in the sled and circled it back against one of the doors and pushed, and it moved, slammed shut. I did the same with the other. I got out to make sure, flashed the light around. I could see there was a lock on the doors. It was too large for me to handle. I saw on one side of the door a rectangular gap. Running over there, I poked the light inside. There was a switch in there. I grabbed hold of it and tugged. It creaked and made a noise like a begging child, then I heard the lock slam into place. I had taken a guess, and I had been lucky. I had pulled the right switch, and the amazing thing still worked. It had most likely not moved since before the beginnings of civilization on Earth, and yet, there was no rust, no decay. It worked. A little squeaky, but otherwise, fully serviceable. If I hadn't been in such a tight spot, I might have marveled even more at this turn of events.

It wasn't really damp inside the pyramid. Inside its icy den it was clean and clear and there was air. If I remembered what I had read about the microscopic things in the ice, they would rise every now and then—maybe centuries passed before they rose—and they would suck at the air, and they would give off air as well, they would fill the void around them with it. Before, this had merely been speculation, but I was breathing that air and I could verify it. In fact, the atmosphere inside the pyramid was so rich it made me feel a little light-headed.

Then I heard the shark hit the door. It had come out of the ice and onto the steps. It struck the door hard. The door shook, but held. I crawled back inside the sled, and with the lights guiding my path, I drove it deeper into the structure's interior.

I finally came to a large room, and, even more amazing, it was lighted. The lights were like huge blisters on the walls, and there were plenty of them. They gave off an orange glow. They were not strong lights, but they were more than adequate to see by. I killed the sled's beams and engine, got out and looked around. At first, I couldn't understand how the lights could exist, but then I thought about the old Martian technology that had been uncovered over the years. Things that had existed and survived and not decayed for millennia, such as that door lock. They had been so far ahead of us in many ways that it was impossible to comprehend. Add to that this strange iceberg, this thing made of ice and creatures that sealed off this world from water and decay, provided oxygen, then sunk back to the bottom of the sea, and it was enough to make my head spin.

There were sheets of ice where one wall of the pyramid had actually been destroyed by what looked like an explosion. That part of the wall had a large bubble of ice that swelled out from it, and there was a sheet of ice on the outside of the pyramid, and, inside the enclosed bubble, there were beings. I blinked. They were sitting in great stone chairs, and they were frozen solid. They were easily eight feet high and golden-skinned, with smooth heads and closed eyes. Their noses were flat against their faces and their mouths were slightly open, and I could see yellow teeth that looked hard and like little carved stones. They had long fingers and, leaning against the seats or thrones on which they rested, weapons. Things that might have been guns, long and lean of barrel, without any real stock, but with apparatus on both sides that looked like sights and triggers. There were harpoons, twelve feet long, at least, with long blue-black blades. They looked heavy.

Whatever had broken the outside wall, it had caused these beings to be frozen, instantly. I could only imagine a war in ages past, an explosive that opened them to the outside air, which must have been freezing. But the truth is, I can't really explain it. All I can say is there they were and I have seen them.

I walked about the huge palace room, for that was what I concluded it was. That was only a guess, of course, but it was the one I decided on. Now that my eyes had adjusted, I could see that there were thumb-sized red worms on the floor, and my feet were crunching them as I walked. There were worms in the walls, at least where the stones had separated, and when I looked up I could see movement on the high ceiling. I flashed my light up there, to help brighten the orange glow of the room. I saw that it was the worms. They skittered over the ceiling on caterpillar legs, fell to the floor now and again like bloody rain.

In the distance, I could hear a booming sound. I realized that it was the ice shark, slamming itself against the great doors of the pyramid. My idea was to find a back way out. Use a couple of the thermal flares to cut the ice cover loose and flee, maybe without the monster knowing I was gone. But all I found was a gap in the wall and a split of six tall and wide corridors that fled into darkness.

Hurrying back to the sled, I closed the lid and fired it up, moving across the floor with the sled's lights sweeping before me. I came to the divided corridors and hesitated. I had no idea which one I should take, or if any of them led to an exit. I sat there and thought about it, finally decided to take the middle one. I reached out, gently touched Dad's wrapped body for luck, then I throttled off into the middle corridor.

In the lights, the red worms seemed to leak from the stones. As I went, behind me I heard a loud shattering sound. The doors. The ice shark had broken them down. That had to be it. I couldn't believe it. The damn thing was not a quitter. Like a King, it stayed on track.

All I could do was concentrate on what was in front of me. Along I went and it was deep dark in there. My sled lights had begun to flicker and waver. I had probably used more of its energy than I thought while fleeing the ice shark. I didn't know what to do other than to keep going forward, so I did. When I felt I would go on forever, there was a glow, and I was out of the tunnel, which emptied out onto an icy ridge. It was the moons that gave the glow, and in front of the ridge was a great long, sleek ship of shiny metal, a seagoing ship with massive, paper-thin metal sails. It took a moment before I realized that it too was inside the icy bubble. The bubble had broken in spots, and new barriers of ice had developed, and there were sheets that dipped down from above and onto the ship, like ice-fairy slides. The stern of the ship was open, and there was a drop door that lay on what had once been the dock. I directed the sled that way and drove inside.

I drove along the open path, and it was wide and tall, for it had been made for the golden Martians. That made it so that I could use it like a road. I drove into the depths of the ship and along a corridor. Finally, I stopped and got out, pulled open a partially open door, and looked inside. It was a great room. The sled, though powerful when completely charged, is light as a feather. I pushed it inside the room effortlessly, came out, and closed the door. I thought I would leave it there for safekeeping while I looked about for a way out on foot. I wanted to preserve what power it had left. If I could get out on the ice, and if I could manage to keep it moving until daylight, it would start soaking up the rays of the sun again, and the more sun it got, the faster it would go.

Moving along quickly, I came to a vast opening, with great portholes on either side. In front of me, I saw an immense chair in front of a wide stretch of viewing shield.

I eased in that direction and saw a long, massive leg poking out. When I went around and looked, there was one of the Martians. Golden and huge. Bigger than the others. His hands lay on a large wheel, and at his right, and on his left, were gears and buttons and all manner of devices, and beneath them were squiggle shapes that I figured were some kind of long-lost language.

I examined his face. His eyes were open, and he still had eyes. They had not rotted. They were frosted over, like icing on doughnuts. Part of his skin had fallen away in a few spots, and I determined this wasn't from decay. It was from wounds that had been inflicted. He had been attacked while he sat in this chair. Perhaps trying to direct the ship to sea. On the wall to the far right was a row of harpoons like those I had seen earlier. They were on racks and I figured they were for show, maybe old, ceremonial weapons more than ones they might have used when their world went from top to bottom, from air to ice, but those blades looked mighty sharp and dangerous nonetheless.

It took some work, but I climbed on the control panel and looked out through the great view glass in front of the Martian and his chair. The moons were bright and there was a thin see-through icy barrier in front of the ship, and beyond it, more flat ice, and way, way off, the dark pattern of the mountains. It looked so far away, right then I felt sick to my stomach.

Then came a wheezing sound, a cracking of things, and I knew instinctively that the ice shark had followed me here.

———

I'll be honest. I thought the ice shark would quit. They can survive off the ice and out of the sea, but I didn't know they could stay out so long—but sure enough, it was the shark; I could smell it. I couldn't see it, but that odor it had was of things long dead in water, of all its recent meals come up in gassy bubbles from its stomach (stomachs, I'm told), and it had all oozed out in an aroma so bitter I felt as if my eyebrows were curling.

I went and stood on a counter in front of the rack that held the weapons and picked the smallest harpoon there. This one would have been really small in the hands of that seated Martian, a light throwing spear for him, but for me it was heavy yet manageable. I pulled the harpoon down, jumped to the floor and moved swiftly to the opening that led out, then I heard it coming down the hall. It was wheezing and slipping and sliding over that ship's ancient floor, and it sounded near.

Back in the control room, I climbed up on the counter again. It ran along the wall and past the portholes. I hustled to one of the portholes and used the tip of the harpoon to pry at it. I worked hard, but it didn't move. I could hear the ice shark coming, and its smell was overwhelming. Just when I thought that the thing was in the room with me, the porthole snapped beneath my prodding, popped completely out, and went shattering onto the deck below. I tossed the harpoon out, then lowered myself out of the hole and dropped about eight feet to the deck. I picked up the harpoon and hustled along the deck, trying to find my way to the room where I had left the sled and my poor dad's body.

When I glanced back, that monstrous thing was easing out of the porthole like it was made of grease. When its dark head poked through, it ballooned wide again and the rows of teeth reassembled and tentacles popped from its head. Its bright white china-plate eyes turned toward me on a thin neck, which was swelling large as it eased out of the porthole. I knew then that it would never give up. I remembered my dad said: "The ice shark is a big booger, but it's got a brain about the size of an apple. A small apple. It rests right between the bad thing's eyes. That's what makes it dangerous. That small brain. It doesn't consider alternatives. It's a lot like a lot of people in that respect. It makes a decision and sticks to it, whether it makes any sense or not. It finds its prey and it doesn't give up until it eats it or it gets away."

The shark's head hit the deck with a plop, and it began to slither. As the rest of it came out of the porthole, it swelled, and tentacles popped from the rest of its gooey form and those little legs sprang out. What was coming out of the porthole was at least twenty times bigger than me.

For too long a moment, I was welded to that spot by fear; and then the spell broke. I think it was the stink that did it, struck me like a fist. I turned and ran along the deck. Behind me, the ice shark wailed so loud that my ears ached. I grabbed at a door that led inside. Locked. I tried another. More of the same.

I finally found one that was not locked, but it wasn't coming open easy. I put my whole 140 pounds and six feet against it (I'm a big girl), but it still didn't move. Along came the shark, slithering and making that unpleasant screeching noise. I gathered up all the strength I had, and some I borrowed from somewhere I didn't know existed, and shoved and shoved at that door with all my might. The door moved. It made a crack wide enough for me to slip inside. On the floor by the door was the corpse of one of the Martians. It had fallen there some ages ago in combat, perhaps against invaders that had killed it and the others and went away with heaps of spoils. Its head was almost lopped off its body, and a dark goo had run from it and dried to the floor and turned solid as stone.

I jumped over the body and scrambled down the hall just as the shark broke through. I turned my head to see both of its eyes looking at me in the near dark. They glowed like white fire. Then it dipped its head and took to that long-dead Martian's body, began gobbling it up with a sound like a turkey choking to death on too much corn. I wondered if it had done the same to the Martian in the chair, gobbled it up, but I must admit, neither of those long-dead creatures was a big concern. What I was worrying about was if I was going to get away.

Doors were closed in the hall, and the only light was the dual moonlight slanting through portholes on my right side. And then the hall came to an end. It emptied at a wide-open door that was not an exit, but was in fact a row of shelves, and the shelves had dividers, like a bee's honeycomb. There was nowhere for me to go now.

I was trapped.

There's no true description of how I felt. You can't put that kind of desperate emptiness into real words. I can say it was like a pit opened up and I dropped through, but that can't be right because that's at least someplace to go. I could say everything fell in on me, but that would have either killed me outright or given me something to hide behind. No. I was out there. Naked in state of mind. The ice shark was coming. I could hear it slurping along the floor, wailing so loud the ship's walls shook. My heart beat so hard against my chest that I thought it was going to spring out of me. It was as the old Earth saying went: It was die dog or eat the hatchet time.

The shelves were large and easy to climb, so I took that route. It was a route to nowhere, but I took it anyway. I pushed the harpoon into one, then climbed up on it, pushed the harpoon into the higher shelf, and climbed into that one. When I got to the top, the shark entered the room. I turned just in time, clutched my harpoon, and put my back against the wall of my cubbyhole, pushed the haft of the harpoon under my arm so that it was braced against the wall too, and waited for it, knowing full well it wouldn't have any problem entering that little space where I waited, not with what its body could do.

Let me tell you how it came.

Like the proverbial bullet, that's how. There was the space before me, empty, then there was the stink; and then—

—it was there.

It thrust forward hard against the opening of the shelf with a flash of teeth, a glow of white eyes, like head beams, and it hit the harpoon point and let out with a scream like an old woman on fire. It writhed and slammed against the walls of the shelf hard enough that I heard them crack, then its head flexed rapidly, and it became smaller, and it tried to dart into the shelf with me. I shifted the harpoon, remembering what Dad had said about that small brain, that little apple between its eyes, and I poked at that, and I poked at that. It popped back and away, throwing those tentacles that were sometimes concealed in its head out wide. They flexed and flashed in the air like Medusa's snakes. It came again, and I screamed with fear and anger, lunged, stuck it deep with that harpoon. I kept lunging, and ichor like a stomped caterpillar sputtered out of it and splashed my face. It felt like pus from exploded pimples. I kept jabbing, and it kept shrieking, then—

—it went away.

Or rather moved out of my sight.

I sat there trembling with fear, my body covered in its innards, or brains, or whatever that mess was.

Had I killed it? Walking on my knees I made my way to the edge of the shelf, poked my head out—

—it rose up like a serpent and stuck with a screech.

It was reflex. I screamed almost as loud as it was screeching, poked out with the harpoon, not at any target mind you, just poking at it, poking in fear. The harpoon went in deep, and the shark jerked back, and that yanked the harpoon from my grasp. I thought: Okay, Angela, this is it, you might as well hang your head between your legs and kiss your ass good-bye, because in the next few moments it will have you, and the last thing you'll hear is a crunch as it bites through you, then for you it's ice-shark digestion and a bowel release of your remains beneath the icy sea.

It slammed against me then, cracking the shelf. The haft of the harpoon, which had been jerked from me, hit me between the eyes. Stars gathered up and filled my head. The shelf cracked more, then I fell and the stars dropped backward into the blackness.

When I awoke, I was *on* the shark, and it had gone flat, like a dishrag. I got up slowly and looked about. Only its head was a mound, and I could see the harpoon sticking out of it like a unicorn horn.

The thing had spread out so much it filled the long hall and trailed all the way down it. I got up slowly and fell back against the wall by a porthole. I had, by accident, not by design, hit that apple between its eyes. I had tried repeatedly to do that without success; and then, due to fear, desperation, and happy accident, I had managed it.

I laughed. I don't know why. But I laughed way loud.

Gathering myself—and let me tell you, at that point there was a lot to gather—I started looking for my sled. I went down the corridor, walking on the ice shark for a long way, and finally I came to another corridor, and that led to another. I realized I was getting more confused, so I backtracked the way I had come, and finally I came to where the Martian body had lain by the door but was now gone, consumed by the dead ice shark. I went out that door and along the deck of the ship, looked up at the porthole I had dropped out of. It was too high up to climb. And as if that wasn't bad enough, I felt the ship shift. Then shift again.

I assumed for a moment that the berg was merely moving, but when I looked past the bubble of ice that contained the ship, I saw that the frozen surface over the sea was cracking. The berg was about to settle again, way down in the deeps like an enormous stone. And I was trapped.

I couldn't leave Dad, not here in this icy grave, so I rushed along the deck and followed it around. Eventually, I came to the stern of the ship. There was a staircase there. I took it. I went down and found where the ship was open at the rear, where I had driven in with the sled, and I ran back inside, the way I had come earlier. Finally, I arrived at the room where I had left the sled and Dad's body. Pulling the sled out, I opened its top and slipped in behind the controls and started it up and let the lights sweep before me. I drove back the way I had come, through the long corridor, to where those incredible red worms climbed the walls. I drove on, and as I did, I could hear ice cracking and there was starting to be water on the floor of the pyramid.

By the time I came to the mouth of the pyramid, the water was rushing in; and then it covered the sled as the iceberg sank, taking me down with it, pushing me back with the might of the sea.

As I said, the sled had submergible abilities. The lid was fastened tight. The lights cut at the dark water, but the problem was that I was still inside the mammoth berg, it was going down hurriedly, and the sea was darker down there. Ice was crashing all about and bits of it were sliding in through the gap I had made with the flares, banging against the sled like mermaids tapping to get in.

I levered it forward and bounced against the sides of the pyramid, fighting the power of the water with all the juice there was in my little machine. I saw a bit of light, the moons piercing the water, making a glow like spoiled milk poured on top of cracked glass. And then that light began to disappear.

I pushed on, and though I had some idea where the gap in the ice was, I had a hard time finding it. I couldn't figure it. Then I realized that it had begun to ice over already; the creatures in the ice, they were sealing it up. I went for where I thought the gap had been, hit it hard with the nose of the sled. The sled bounced back. I went at it again, and this time I heard a cracking sound. I thought at first that it was the sled coming to pieces. But the lights showed me that it was the ice shattering. It was just a glimpse, a spiderweb of lines against the cold barrier. I hit it again. The sled broke through and the ice went all around me in slivers. Up and out I went. And then the lights began to blink.

The sled slowed. It drifted momentarily, started going back down into the jet black, following the descending pyramid and ship. I tugged back on the throttle and the engine caught again, and up I went, like an earthly porpoise. The sled shot up through a hole in the ice, clattered on the surface of the frozen water. The lights blinked, but they kept shining.

Tooling the sled out wide and turning, I headed in the direction of the dark bumps that were the Martian mountains.

For a moment, I felt invigorated, but then I began to feel weak. I thought it was food, and I was about to dig in the bag of goods, when I realized that wasn't the problem at all. My shoulder was wet, but not with cold water, but with warm blood. The ice shark had hit me with one of its teeth, more than one. It had torn a gap in my shoulder that my adrenaline had not allowed me to notice until then.

I thought I might pass out, something I had been doing a lot of lately. I aimed the sled the way my head said go, the way the worm pill in my body said go. I dug in the bag and got out a first-aid kit, tore it open, found some bandages. I pushed them against the wound. They grew wet, through and through. I pulled them off and put on some more. Same thing. I let them stay, sticking damp to my flesh. I dug in the bag and found a container of water, something to eat in hard, chewy bar form. It tasted like sawdust. The water hit my throat and tasted better than any water I had ever drunk, cool and refreshing.

The sled was heading straight toward the mountains. Depending on how long the charge lasted, I should be there in about eighteen hours. I knew that as easy as I knew my name was Angela King. I knew that because Dad had taught me to judge distance. Beyond the mountains, on the Far Side, I had no idea how much more I would have to go. I was living what my dad had called a cheap romance. I had found a lost world of dead Martians encased by ice and busy microbes; I had fought a Martian ice shark with a harpoon and won. I had gone down in an iceberg, down into a deep, dark, cold sea; and now I was gliding along the ice, bleeding out. I knew I'd never make it as far as the mountains; I damn sure wouldn't make it to the other side. If I didn't die first, the engine on the sled would go, out of sun-juice. By the time morning came and the sun rose up hot and slowly charged the engine, I'd be a corpse, same as my dad. That was all right. I had done my best and I hadn't quit. Not on purpose. I looked out once more at the moonlit ice and the rolling mountains. I laughed. I can't tell you why, but I did. I lifted my head and laughed. My eyes closed then. I didn't close them. They were hot and heavy and I couldn't keep them open.

I reached out with the toe of my foot and touched Dad's covered head, then I passed out. That was starting to be a habit, but I figured this would be the last time.

If you die on Mars, do you go to Martian Heaven? Did the old gold Martians have a heaven? I know I didn't believe in one, but I was thinking about it because I seemed to be going there. Only I was starting to feel warm, and I thought, uh-oh, that's the other end of the bargain, the hot part, Hell. I was going right on quick to Martian Hell, for whatever reason. I was going there to dance with big tall Martians carrying harpoons, dancing down below with the ice sharks and the other beasts that lived at the bottom of it all, dancing in lava pits of scalding fire. That wouldn't be so bad. Being warm. I was so tired of being cold. Martian Hell, I welcome you.

Then I awoke. The sled was no longer moving. I was warm now and comfortable, and not long before I had been cold. It took me a moment, but finally I knew what had happened. The sled had quit going, and the heater inside had quit, and it had grown cold, and I had dreamed, but here I was alive, and the sun was up, and the sled had been pulling in the rays for a few hours now, heating up the solar cells, and it was roaring to warm, vigorous life. The throttle was still in forward-thrust position, and the sled began to move again without me touching a thing.

I couldn't believe it. I wasn't dead. Glancing out at the ice, I saw the mountains, but I knew by the worm in my head that I had drifted off course a bit, though I had gone farther than I expected. Placing my hand on the throttle made my whole body hurt. My shoulder had stopped bleeding and the bandage I had made was nothing now but a wet mess. But it had done the job. I was careful not to move too much, not to tear too much.

Over the ice the sled fled, and I adjusted its navigation, kept it pointed in the right direction.

When I came to the mountains it was late afternoon. I began to look for a trail through them. My body was hot and I felt strange, but I kept at it, and finally I came to a little path that split through the mountains, and I took it. I went along smoothly and thought it would break up eventually, or suddenly a high wall of rock would appear in front of me, but it didn't. The path wasn't straight, but it was true, and it split through the mountains like a knife through butter.

It was nightfall again when I came to a larger split of land, and below me, where it dipped, was a valley lit bright with lights. Far Side.

Plunging down the slope, away I went, driving fast. It all seemed to be coming together, working out. I was going to make it just fine. And then in the head beams, a rock jumped up. I hit the throttle in such a way that the sled rose as high as it could go. For a moment, I thought I was going to clear the rock, but it caught the bottom of the sled and tore it, and the sled went crashing, spinning, the see-through cover breaking around me, throwing me out where the valley sloped off on a hill of wet winter grass. I went sliding, then something bumped up against me.

It was my father's body. I grabbed at it, and the two of us were going down that hill, me clinging to him, climbing on him, riding his torso down at rocket speed.

Down.

Down.

Down we went, Dad and I, making really good time.

Until we hit the outside wall of a house. Hit it hard.

There's not much to tell after that. Making it to my feet, I staggered along the side of the house and beat on a door. I was taken inside by an old couple, then the whole town was awake. People were sent up the hill to find the sled, to look for the vaccine, and my father's body next to the wall. The sled was ruined, the vaccine was found, and my dad was still dead. People came in and looked at me as if I was a rare animal freshly brought into captivity. I don't remember who was who or what anyone looked like, just that they came and stared and went away and new people took their place.

After the curious had gone, I sat in a chair in the old couple's house, and they fed me soup. The doctor came in and fixed my wound as best he could, said it was infected, that I had a concussion, maybe several, and I shouldn't sleep, that it was best not to lie down.

So, I didn't.

I took some kind of medicine from him, sat in that chair till morning climbed up over the mountain as if it was fatigued and would rather have stayed down in the dark; and then I couldn't sit anymore. I slid out of the chair and sat on my butt a long while, then lay on the floor and didn't care if I died because I had no idea if I was dying or getting well; I just plain had no idea about anything at all.

Someone got me in a bed, because when I awoke that's where I was. I was bandaged up tight and was wearing a nightgown, the old woman's I figured. The bed felt good. I didn't want to get out of it. I was surprised when the old woman told me that I had been there three days.

I guess what happens in those cheap romances Dad talked about is that they end in a hot moment of glory, with all guns blazing and fists flying, but my romance, if you can truly call it that, ended with a funeral.

They kept Dad's body in an open barn, so the cold air would keep him chilled, protect him from growing too ripe. But in time, even that couldn't hold him, and down he had to go, so they came and got me ready in some clothes that almost fit, and helped me along. The entire town showed up for the burying. Me and Dad were considered heroes for bringing the vaccine. Good words were said about us, and I appreciated them. Pretty much overnight, the whole place was cured because of that vaccine.

Hours after Dad was buried, I got the goddamn Martian fever and had to have the vaccine myself and stay in bed for another two or three days, having been already weak and made even more poorly by it. It was ironic when you think about it. I had brought the vaccine but had never thought to immunize myself, and neither had Dad, and he was a doctor.

I won't lie. I cried a lot. Then I tucked Dad's memory in the back of my mind in a place where I could get to it when I wanted, crawled out of bed, and got over it.

That's what we Kings do.

CHRIS ROBERSON

Chris Roberson has appeared in *Asimov's, Interzone, Postscripts, Subterranean,* and elsewhere. He's probably best known for his alternate history Celestial Empire series, which, in addition to a large number of short pieces, consists of the novels *The Dragon's Nine Sons, Iron Jaw and Hummingbird, The Voyage of Night Shining White,* and *Three Unbroken.* His other novels include *Here, There & Everywhere; Paragaea: A Planetary Romance; Set the Seas on Fire; Book of Secrets;* and *End of the Century.* Recently, he's been writing graphic novels, including *Elric: The Balance Lost* featuring Michael Moorcock's characters, and two *New York Times* best-selling *Cinderella* miniseries spinning off Bill Willingham's *Fables.* His most recent book is a new novel, *Further: Beyond the Threshold.* In addition to his writing, Roberson was one of the publishers of the small press MonkeyBrain Books, which has recently launched a digital comics imprint, Monkeybrain Comics. He lives with his family in Portland, Oregon.

Here's a robust and exciting sea story, complete with pirates and swordfights, except that the seas our swashbuckling adventurers are sailing are not the seas of Earth but the endless sand seas of Mars . . .

Mariner

CHRIS ROBERSON

THE SHIP SPED ALONG AT FULL SAIL, WITH NOTHING BUT RED sands as far as the eye could see in all directions. It had been days since they last caught sight of water.

Jason Carmody stood in the prow of the *Argo*, scanning the horizon with his handmade telescope, searching for easy prey. From time to time, the leatherwing that perched on the railing beside him would flap its wings and squawk petulantly, and Jason would quiet it with a strip of dried meat from the pouch that hung at his belt. If he waited too long to satiate his pet's appetite, the leatherwing would nip at Jason's hands with its jagged snout, to motivate him.

"'Ware, captain, lest the beast take a digit away in its maw," a voice from behind Jason said.

Without turning around, Jason dropped another morsel into his pet's waiting mouth. "Bandit prefers the dried meat, actually. But I'm sure he'd settle for one of my fingers in a pinch."

He turned, smiling at the approach of his first officer.

"Perhaps if the beast were to eat enough of them," the first officer said, "you'd finally have the proper number." He waggled the three digits at the end of one arm in Jason's face.

"Where *I* come from, Tyr," Jason said, "it's considered the height of pirate fashion to lose whole body parts. The best pirate captains have a wooden leg, or a hook for a hand, or a patch over a missing eye."

The first officer grew serious and tapped the small stone pendant that hung from the breather that encircled his neck, covering his gills. "I am sure that, when they go to their final reward, their missing appendages are there waiting for them. As scripture tells us, the Suffocated God makes all things whole in the seas of the dead."

Jason took in the first officer's weathered flesh, the green of his skin marred everywhere by old wounds and scars that mapped the long years of duels, battles, and beatings Tyr had survived.

"It's nice to think so," Jason said thoughtfully, then grinned. "To be honest, though, I'd settle for a decent burger."

Tyr clacked his mandibles, the Martian equivalent of laughter. "With our luck, we'd likely find nothing but the thin gruel our former jailers fed us instead." Remembering himself, he stilled his mandibles, his forehead flushing yellow with shame, and fondled the stone pendant in repentance. "The Suffocated God forgive my blasphemy."

When Jason had first met him, in a Praxian jail half a lifetime before, Tyr had been a priest of the Suffocated God, imprisoned for speaking out against the Hegemony that had risen to power in the southern network of Praxis. Jason had only recently arrived on the red planet when he was captured by the Praxians himself, and he and the priest had shared a cell while they waited for their turn on the executioner's stone. They had been wary of each other at first, but gallows humor and close quarters bred first familiarity, then friendship. When, weeks later, the two had escaped imprisonment together and fled out onto the sand seas in a makeshift raft, they had become as close as brothers.

"Tyr, did you ever think that we'd one day have a command of our own, and sail—"

"Captain!" a shout from above interrupted. "Ship ahead, due east!"

Jason raised the makeshift telescope to his eye and trained it in the direction the lookout indicated. There, just cresting the horizon, was a mercantile galleon, riding fat and low on the sands.

"Breaktime is over, folks," Jason called out to the rest of the crew. "We have *work* to do!"

Jason Carmody had grown up dreaming about sailing around one world but ended up sailing around another instead.

In his more sardonic moments, he blamed *National Geographic*. When Jason was still in grade school, he read a series of articles about a teenager who had set out to sail around the globe by himself, and done so. All through middle school, Jason studied globes and maps of the Earth, devoured books on navigation and seamanship, watched any movie or television show he could find that had anything to do with the oceans, or sailing, or exploration. In high school, while his classmates fretted about their SAT scores and agonized over which colleges to attend, Jason spent every available moment of his free time sailing small one-man boats on nearby lakes and rivers, and spent his holidays out on the Gulf of Mexico, daring himself to sail beyond sight of land and navigate back using only a compass and his wits.

The week after he graduated from high school, and after tearful farewells with his friends and family, Jason set off from Galveston, Texas, in a twenty-four-foot cutter, intending to continue sailing until he came back to port from the other direction.

But he'd not even managed to complete the first leg of his journey. He was still in the Caribbean when, under the light of a full moon, he came upon a strange vortex in the dark waters. A swirling whirlpool, it grew from nothing in a matter of moments, too quickly for Jason to change course to avoid it. One instant Jason was sailing along under a starry sky, and the next his boat hit the vortex and everything changed.

Jason had squinted his eyes, bracing for impact, and when he opened them again, he looked out onto another world.

He was on Mars, he would later learn. Not the Mars he'd seen in pictures sent back by NASA probes, though. Had he been transported to the distant past of the red planet, or its future? Or perhaps into some analogue of the fourth planet that existed in another dimension? Jason had never learned for certain. He tried to see what the Earth looked like, to give him some sense of context, but the best telescopes he had managed to construct showed him only a blurry image of a blue-green planet in the sky, and his knowledge of constellations did not extend to calculating how those same stars would appear on another world and at another time.

But those were facts that Jason would only discover later. On that first day, at that first instant, he knew only that he was somewhere he'd never seen before.

The cutter lay half-buried in fine sands, under a brilliant blue sky, across which two moons sailed in their stately orbits toward each other. Jason had stepped off the deck of his boat onto the sands, in a daze, and immediately sunk up to his waist. The grains of sand were so small, so fine, that the ground behaved more like a liquid than a solid, almost like quicksand. And as he floundered in the sands, barely able to keep afloat, he noticed the menacing silhouette of a bony ridge knifing through the red sands toward him.

Jason's first day on his new world would have been his last, his journeys ended in the belly of a sand-shark, had a passing Praxian naval ship not hauled him on board. The crew had never seen a human before and returned to the Praxis canals in the south with Jason as much an object of curiosity as he was their captive. Despite the language barrier that separated them, when they reached port, Jason managed to communicate to his captors that he needed air to breathe. Had he taken much longer to get his message across, he would have drowned, as they began to force him down into their underwater community with them.

In the days that followed, Jason learned just enough of the common tongue in Praxis to offend the sensibilities of the Praxian Hegemony, who refused to entertain the notion that life might exist anywhere else in the universe but the red planet, despite any and all evidence to the contrary. He was convicted of heresy and confined to a cell, where he would await execution. It was there that Jason met the first Martian whom he would call "friend," and the course of his life was forever changed.

But through it all, Jason cursed the editors of *National Geographic*. Had it not been for them, he might just have gone to college or gotten a job like any other regular person.

It was near midday by the time the *Argo* closed the distance to the galleon. A vicious sandstorm had kicked up, limiting visibility severely, but through squinting eyes they were able to make out the colors of the Vendish mercantile fleet flying from the galleon's masts.

But while Jason Carmody and his crew had been approaching from the west, another vessel had evidently been approaching from the south. And though the *Argo* still had ground to cover before they could even parley with the crew of the galleon, much less begin an attack, the other vessel was already alongside her.

"It's a Praxian naval corvette," Jason said, lowering his telescope and squinting against the bright midday glare.

"Does Praxis war with Vend?" a crewman wondered aloud.

"If so, this will be the first we hear of it," Tyr answered.

"Well, they're certainly not *friends*." Jason pointed to the galleon, whose three masts had already been splintered and split. As if to underscore his point, at that moment a sound like thunder rolled across the sands as the Praxian corvette fired from its forward launchers upon the merchant vessel.

A sudden shower of rocks rained down upon the galleon, further damaging her masts and hull, and making bloody green messes of several of the crewmen who could be seen on her deck.

"They look to make short work of her." Tyr scratched a spot on his shoulder where his skin had grown rough and scaly in the dry air. "Your orders, captain?"

Under normal circumstances, the *Argo* would steer clear of any confrontation with a naval vessel if at all possible, either the Praxians in the south or the ships of the Vendish fleet in the north. But these were clearly not normal circumstances.

Jason scowled. "If we return to Freehaven without a hold full of plunder, we'll catch hell from Rac and the other captains. We've been sailing light for a little too long, I think." He looked from the naval vessel to the galleon and back again. "And that galleon must be hauling *something* of value if the Praxians want her so badly."

"So the Hegemony turns to piracy, then?" Tyr mused.

"Or the crew of this corvette has, maybe." Jason rubbed his lower lip. The naval vessel had launched grappling hooks over the deck of the galleon, and was pulling the two ships closer together, preparing to board. "They don't appear to have noticed us."

"With the wind at our backs," Tyr answered, "we have the sandstorm blowing before us. And their attention is on their present prey, in any event."

A slow smile tugged the corners of Jason's mouth. "Once the Praxians board the galleon, their corvette won't have much more than a skeleton crew left on board."

"And if we hang back and let the sandstorm shield us from their notice . . ." Tyr clacked his mandibles together softly, chuckling.

Jason turned to the rest of the crew who were gathered on the deck of the *Argo*, awaiting orders. They huddled against the drying sands that buffeted them in the high winds, little puffs of steam erupting here and there from the breathers that kept their gills wet and supplied with oxygenated water.

"To your stations!" Jason drew the curved sword that hung at his waist, raising it high overhead. "Run out the catapults! Prepare to engage!"

The first inkling that the sailors aboard the Praxian corvette had of the approaching *Argo* was the fusillade of rocks and debris that pelted down upon them, fired from the pirates' catapults. So intent had the Praxian sailors been on taking the galleon, though, that their first instinct was that the mercantile vessel had somehow managed to return fire. It was only when Jason Carmody and the other pirates of the *Argo* swung onto the corvette's deck, the captain shouting a war cry and the others hissing menacingly through their mandibles, that the sailors realized that they were under attack by a third party.

"Pirates!" one of the sailors shouted, fumbling for the long knife sheathed at his waist. "Warn the—"

Jason silenced the rest of the sailor's call for alarm, driving the point of his sword through the breather around the sailor's neck and into the fleshy throat beneath. There had been a time when Jason had balked at the use of lethal force, back when he and Tyr had first been taken on board by a pirate ship and invited to join the crew. Jason had tried to carry out his duties with a minimal use of force, incapacitating if possible, killing and maiming only if absolutely necessary. But that had been half a lifetime ago, and in the years since, he had seen firsthand what the Praxian Hegemony and its faithful servants did to any who defied their laws. Jason had seen too many broken and mutilated victims of Praxian "justice" to spare any mercy now for those Praxians who meted it out.

Jason yanked his sword free of the sailor's neck, and before the body had hit the deck, Tyr was at his side, an electrified whip coiled in one hand.

"The Suffocated God guide your passage," the first officer muttered over the fallen sailor. Though technically he hadn't been a priest since before Jason knew him, and there was little chance that the sailor had shared his faith, old habits died hard.

"On your right!" Jason barked, stepping alongside Tyr. A trio of sailors charged toward them, clubs and knives in hand.

Jason skewered through the belly the first sailor to reach him, halting his advance, and lashed out with a high kick that knocked loose a second sailor's breather. As the first dropped to his knees, trying unsuccessfully to keep his black innards from spooling out through the wound, the second gasped in the dry, dusty air for breath, his eyes wide with panic.

Tyr lashed out with his whip, catching the third sailor around the neck. As the sailor grabbed hold of the whip and yanked back, clearly hoping to pull Tyr off his balance, Tyr simply thumbed a stud on the whip's handle, and sent a bristling charge of electricity coursing down the length of the whip. The sailor jerked and thrashed, eyes rolling back in his head, and Jason caught a scent that reminded him of seafood grilling over an open flame back home.

As Tyr shook his whip loose from the sailor's neck, Jason took stock of the situation. A half dozen of his crewmen had boarded the corvette along with him and the first officer, and a quick accounting showed that all of them were still standing, having at worst suffered only minor wounds. All of the Praxian sailors in evidence were fallen at their feet.

"It would seem that the ship is ours," Tyr said, coiling his whip.

"Take a few men belowdecks," Jason instructed, "and make sure there aren't more of the ship's crew down there that we'll need to worry about before we move on to the galleon. We'll have enough trouble dealing with the sailors who boarded the—"

"Captain!" one of the pirates shouted.

Jason turned quickly in that direction. Through the sand that gusted all around them, he could see across to the galleon, lashed by grappling hooks to the side of the corvette.

An entire detachment of Praxian sailors were surging over the railing from the galleon, murder in their eyes.

"Never mind." Jason flashed Tyr a quick smile. "You get the idea."

There had been a time when the mere sight of a pink-skinned figure breathing *air* had been enough to give Jason's opponents a moment's pause, usually just enough for him to gain a tactical advantage against them. But enough stories had circulated in the years since of the so-called human who sailed the sand seas aboard a pirate vessel, that Jason had largely lost the element of surprise. That he'd grown older in the interim, and no doubt needed that moment's advantage now more than ever, was a cruel irony that was not lost on him.

So it was with a labored sigh that Jason met the sailors' charge. Not one of them even *blinked* when they saw his skin, his hair, or his lack of gills.

He felt like a once-popular TV star, now reduced to offering autographs to uninterested passersby at a boat show . . .

If taking the corvette had been comparatively easy, at the cost only of a few minor injuries, defending it from the returning sailors would clearly come at a higher price. The corvette's crew outnumbered the pirates three to one, and though Jason had always boasted that each of his crewmen was worth any three other fighters combined, proving that boast was more difficult in practice than it had been in theory.

While Tyr and two other pirates dealt with the sailors who had been belowdecks manning the launchers, the rest contended with those who had returned from taking the galleon. And Jason himself faced the master of the corvette, who bore the rank insignia of a commodore in the Praxian navy tattooed on his forehead. At the end of one arm, the commodore carried a sword, and, in the other, a burning torch.

Jason was surprised to see the open flame. The natives of the red planet typically used fire only for manufacturing purposes, most often in foundries on rocky atolls far from their aquatic homes in the canal networks. It was not entirely unknown for fire to be used as a weapon, but it was far from common.

"You are either brave, mad, or a fool," the commodore said in a heavy Praxian accent. "But whichever it is, you will die!" To punctuate his words, he lunged forward with his sword, aiming it squarely at Jason's chest.

"Everything dies, commodore." Jason parried the Praxian's lunge and flashed a smile. "So I'm certain I'll die *eventually*." Jason riposted, thrusting his own sword at the commodore. "But not *today*!"

The commodore hissed menacingly as he sidestepped Jason's sword, barely avoiding the thrust.

"You, a pirate, would *protect* these . . . these *heretics*?" The commodore's anger was almost palpable. "But *why*?"

Heretics? Jason scarcely had time to think, as the commodore swung the torch he bore at Jason's head.

Jason danced back out of the way, feeling the warmth of the torch on his face. Had he been a native Martian, the heat itself would have been enough to dry his eyes for an instant, forcing opaque nictitating membranes to slam shut, momentarily obscuring his vision. No doubt that was the reason the commodore took the risk of fighting while carrying an open flame. But Jason's eyes simply stung and watered, and though his lids squinted against the heat and smoke, he never lost sight of his opponent's position.

But he allowed the commodore to *think* that he had.

Eyes half-lidded, one hand groping erratically through the air in front of him, Jason feinted with his sword, aiming well clear of the commodore's body. He could hear the soft clacking of mandibles as the commodore chuckled to himself, sure now of an easy victory.

As the commodore lunged forward, aiming his sword at Jason's midsection in a killing thrust, Jason handily sidestepped at the last moment. Natives were always surprised by how quickly Jason could move in the lower gravity of the red planet and how much stronger he was than he appeared, facts that he had long since learned to use to his advantage. Before the startled commodore could react, Jason brought his sword slamming down on the commodore's breather, slashing the back of the commodore's head in the process.

The commodore pitched forward, gasping for breath, dropping both sword and torch as he groped for the back of his head, where dark green blood was already welling freely.

Jason reached for the still-burning torch as it clattered away across the deck, but before he could grab it, another of the Praxian sailors, following close on the commodore's heels, rushed at him, swinging a heavy club. For every one of the precious few moments it took Jason to fend off the sailor, he worried over where the torch would end up. Like most of the ships that plied the red planet's sand seas, the corvette was primarily composed of a kind of lightweight concrete, sturdy enough to be a considerable weight but with enough pockets of air throughout that it was not too heavy to glide across the sands. More important, although the concrete itself was largely impervious to flame, the planks were mortared with a tarlike substance that *wasn't*. Careless fire management would leave a ship as little more than a charred pile of planks and spars, its crews left stranded on the sands at the tender mercy of scavengers like the leatherwings and the sand-sharks.

So it was with a weary sigh that, as soon as he dispatched the club-wielding sailor, Jason turned to see that the commodore's torch had come to rest atop the seam between two planks in the deck, and that traceries of flame already raced in either direction, following the mortar's path.

"Captain!" Tyr shouted, having just returned from belowdecks, a freshly bleeding cut across his left shoulder. "Fire!"

"I see it!" Jason glanced about the deck of the corvette. He had lost two of his men in the skirmish, and including Tyr, three more were wounded, but the last of the Praxian sailors appeared to have been seen to. But already the flames had reached both fore and aft, and had leapt to the corvette's sails, which were slowly transforming to smoke and ash.

"The *Argo* is out beyond the range of the Praxian launchers," Tyr shouted. "She'll never reach us in time!"

Jason scowled. The order for the *Argo* to retreat after he and the others boarded the corvette had been his. He had no one to blame but himself if it meant his death now.

"Cut the grappling lines!" Jason shouted, as he leapt over the flames, heading for the railing. "If we're lucky, we can get the galleon clear before *it* catches fire, too!"

Tyr and the other surviving pirates needed no further instruction, but scrambled over the side of the corvette and onto the galleon's deck, severing the heavy lines that held the two vessels together as they went.

Jason was the last one to leave the corvette, as the deck planks began to fall apart beneath him. Tyr and the others had already begun to shove the merchant ship away from the corvette, using long sections of the galleon's shattered masts to push against the hull of the other ship. But as Jason thudded onto the deck of the galleon, twisting one knee badly in the process, bits of burning sail and ash rained down around him.

"We need to *move* this tub!" Jason shouted as he clutched his knee in agony, sprawled on the deck. "And somebody put out these flames before they *spread!*"

A pair of Jason's crewmen scrambled around the deck of the galleon, stomping out the burning bits of sail, while Tyr directed the others in using the longest pieces of the broken mast to push the two vessels as far apart as possible. Black smoke intermingled with the sands that the heavy winds were blowing across from the corvette, but just when it appeared that all hope was lost, the winds shifted, blowing back over the Praxian ship, sending smoke, ash, and licking flames out over the sands instead.

Tyr helped Jason to his feet as they watched the burning pyre of a ship drift away from them across the sands. It had taken all the strength the pirates could muster to get the corvette to move, but now that it was in motion, its inertia would continue to carry it away from them. Not far, but far enough.

"Well," Jason said, "let's go belowdecks and see what she's carrying."

"Whatever it is," Tyr answered as he helped Jason limp across the deck, "the Praxians very much wished to possess it."

Jason was thinking back to what the commodore had said, puzzling over it, when Tyr lifted up the hatch in the deck that led down to the galleon's hold.

As the two stared down into the hold, Jason's mouth hung open in surprise, and Tyr tapped the drystone amulet at his breast.

"Or perhaps it is something they did not wish to *possess*," Tyr muttered, "but to *destroy*."

Down in the gloom of the galleon's hold, dozens of frightened eyes glinted up at them.

They spoke a dialect that Jason had trouble following, and it was clear they had difficulty understanding his accent, but Tyr was able to act as interpreter. They were mothers and fathers, children, grandparents, all crowded together in the cramped confines of the galleon's hold. Rather than wearing personal breathers, as Jason's crewmen and the Praxian sailors did, they huddled around portable dispensers that sprayed brief jets of lukewarm water from short hoses, keeping their skin as damp and their gills as oxygenated as they could manage. But all of them had taken on the greyish brown tint to their skins that suggested they were close to the point of complete dehydration and suffocation.

The drystone amulets that each of them clutched marked them as worshippers of the Suffocated God. There was some irony in the fact that they might emulate their martyred god not only in the way that he had lived but also in his manner of dying.

"They are Praxian refugees," Tyr explained, "fleeing oppression."

Jason could see that Tyr was having difficulty controlling his temper but seemed mollified whenever the refugees addressed him with the word that Jason recognized as meaning "Reverend." It had been many years since Tyr had been a priest, but it was clear that it was a role that still held great meaning for him.

"They say that things have gotten even worse in Praxis," Tyr continued. "The Hegemony continues to chip away at the freedoms of those they rule. Once, one was censured for speaking out against the

Hegemony's tenets or questioning their right to govern. Now, it seems, simply harboring private beliefs that are not sanctioned by the Hegemony is grounds for punishment."

Jason noted the scars that many of the older refugees bore, signs of flogging, torture, and worse. Some were even missing digits at the ends of their arms or had empty sockets where eyes had once been. And all of them, from the oldest to the youngest, had the kind of haunted expression on their faces that made it clear that they had seen things that scarred their minds and souls in ways that could never fully heal.

"They made a deal with a Vendish merchant, the master of this galleon, to ferry them north across the sands to Vend," Tyr said, his tone bitter. "They hoped to find a new home there, where they would enjoy the freedom to practice their beliefs in peace."

Jason sneered. The mention of "freedom" in such close proximity to "Vend" was a bitter irony.

"How much money do they have?" Jason asked, acid in his tone.

Tyr repeated the question to the refugees, who answered him with confused expressions and bewilderment.

"They don't understand," Tyr said. "None of them have ever held or used currency before."

In Praxis, all things were held in common, apportioned by the ruling Hegemony to each according to his needs. At least, that was the theory. In practice, most of the population lived in crushing poverty, assuming that it was simply their lot in life.

"Ask them what they have of *value*," Jason clarified. "They must have traded *something* precious to this merchant in exchange for passage—jewelry, heirlooms, goods. How much of that is left?"

Tyr relayed the question. The refugees looked from one to another, then answered.

"They gave everything they had of value to the Vendish merchant," Tyr translated. "They have nothing left."

Jason slammed a fist into the open palm of the other hand,

seething with frustrated rage. He was angry at the Vendish merchant who had agreed to ferry the refugees and angry with the refugees themselves for clearly being duped.

"This ship wasn't sailing them to *freedom* in Vend!" Jason shouted. "They were heading toward *slavery!*"

Tyr answered in a low voice, speaking for himself, not for the refugees. "Captain . . . Jason . . . they've been through so *much* already . . ."

"No," Jason shot back, "they should *know. You* know what I'm talking about. Tell *them!*"

Tyr's mandibles quivered, the native equivalent of a sigh. And then he turned back to the refugees, and in patient tones explained to them the reality of the situation.

Jason could follow little of what Tyr was saying, but it hardly mattered since he could guess. It was well-known on the sand seas that it was against the law in Vend to be a vagrant. And anyone who set foot in the waters of Vend was considered a vagrant if they could not establish proof of residency. Anyone who was apprehended on charges of vagrancy could buy their way out if they had sufficient funds to secure lodging. But if not, they would be arrested on the spot, declared guilty without a trial, and sold into indentured servitude. In theory, an indentured servant could eventually earn their way to freedom; in practice, it never happened.

It was easy to see what the master of this galleon had intended. The few trinkets and baubles he'd taken from the refugees might have had some minor value, but the real prize would come when they reached Vend. It was a common practice for the portmasters of Vend to make deals with ship captains to "arrange" for an unwanted or problematic crewman to be arrested for vagrancy, with the portmaster sharing the proceeds from the sale into indentured service with the captain who had supplied them. Some pirate captains even engaged in the practice, taking prisoners from among the crews of ships that they defeated and transporting them north to be sold into service. It effectively amounted to a kind of slave trade, but one that was entirely legal under the laws of Vend.

So the refugees had sailed away from one form of oppression, and had been heading right toward another.

From the howls of despair that they began to make, Jason could tell that Tyr had managed to get that point across.

"So what shall we do with them, then?" one of the pirates asked, once Jason and Tyr were back above deck.

The *Argo* had sailed up alongside the galleon, as the winds that had whipped up the sandstorm gradually died away, and now the entire crew had been made aware of the nature of their "plunder." It simply remained to decide what they would do about it.

"What is to decide?" another pirate asked. "They are none of our lookout. The wind and the sand-sharks will see to them soon enough."

Jason had to admit that the crewman was right about one thing, at least. From the deck of the ruined galleon, he could see the signs of sand-sharks skimming through the fine grains of desert sands, searching for prey. If the refugees were foolish enough to try to travel across—or rather *through*—the sands, they would not last long. Even assuming that their portable dispensers had enough water within them to keep the refugees from suffocating and desiccating in short order, the sand-sharks would make a meal of them soon enough.

But while that crewman, at least, seemed perfectly content to leave the Praxian refugees to their own devices, it was clear that others among the pirates were not as sanguine about the possibility. And his first officer in particular.

Tyr clutched the drystone pendant that hung from his breather, a haunted look on his face. Jason imagined that he must be remembering his own family and friends whom he had been forced to leave behind when the two of them escaped from a Praxian prison half a lifetime ago, and thinking about what horrors they might have endured because of their faith in the years since. In the faces of the despairing refugees, Tyr no doubt saw all of those people reflected.

"We could return them whence they came," another said.

"Back into the oppression they narrowly escaped?" Tyr scoffed. "We would be condemning them to agony and death. Perhaps instead we could ferry them on to Vend. At least *there* they would have a chance at life."

Another crewman made a gesture that carried much the same nuance as a human spitting on the ground in disgust. "At least the Praxians believe they serve a greater good. Those Vendish devils serve nothing but their own *profits*."

"It would be a mercy to kill them ourselves and be done with it," another pirate put in.

A ripple of nods among the other crewmen showed this would be an acceptable solution to the ethical dilemma for many of them.

Life on the red planet was hard and had produced cultures that tended to make hard decisions. But life on the sand seas was harder still.

"No," Jason announced. "They're coming with us."

The crewmen all turned to him, some with confused looks, some with expressions of defensiveness.

"Come with us to *where*?" Tyr asked. "You don't mean to return them to Praxis, do you? Or ferry them to Vend? Either way you'll be consigning them to oppression, death, or *worse*."

Jason crossed his arms over his chest and shook his head.

"No, they're coming back with us to Freehaven."

The angry muttering from some of the crewmen made it clear this was *not* a solution they would have preferred. Jason hoped that it wouldn't come to a vote.

Every member of the *Argo*'s crew had signed the Articles of Freehaven, the list of rules and regulations that governed the life of pirates on the red planet, both aboard their ships and at home in Freehaven. The Articles outlined, among other things, how plunder was to be spread among all the members of the crew, with a portion being set aside to contribute to Freehaven's community coffers, to be doled out to residents in times of need. But perhaps more important, the Articles also specified who would lead, both ship and community, and when.

Jason was the captain of the *Argo* because he had been elected to the position by the crew, though they were technically the crew of the *Sand-shark's Tooth* before Jason became her master and gave the ship a new name. Likewise, the headman of Freehaven was the captain who had been elected by the community at large to govern them.

But simply because Jason had been elected once did not mean that he held the post for life. Just as he had challenged the authority of his ship's previous captain, so too might his crew challenge his. One method would be for enough of the crew to be dissatisfied with his command that they mustered the quorum necessary to call for a vote and simply elected a new captain. That was how Jason had come to command.

The other method, a holdover from the pirates' less egalitarian days, would be for one of the crew to challenge Jason to single combat, with the winner of the duel being the one who had proven himself fit for command. This latter method had seldom been used in recent generations, and never during Jason's time as a pirate, in large part because the rules required that the combat must be to the death; but it was kept in the Articles as a tribute to the early pioneers who had risen up out of the waters and sought the freedom of the high sands, proving their worth not by persuasive argument but by the strength of their sword arms. It was the last vestige of a time before Freehaven had truly earned its name.

When Jason could see the ruins of the buried city from the deck of the *Argo*, it meant that they were almost home.

"Where is that beast of yours?"

Jason turned to see Tyr approaching. He had spent much of his time in recent days belowdecks tending to the needs of the Praxian refugees, leading them in recitations of scripture, sharing memories of happier days, and so on.

"You mean Bandit? I'm sure he'll turn up sooner or later," Jason answered. "He always does." His leatherwing pet had flown off before their fight with the Praxian corvette, and Jason hadn't seen him since. But it was hardly unusual. His "pet" was only one step removed from a wild animal and clearly valued its independence.

Tyr joined Jason at the railing and looked out over the buried city as it drifted slowly by. They could hear the muttering of some of the other crewmen, who still rankled at the presence of the Praxian "rabble" belowdecks.

"We were a better people once," Tyr said to Jason in a low voice, glancing sidelong at the disaffected crewmen. "A *great* people. But the drought that dried our world, I fear, dried out the wellsprings of compassion in too many of us."

When he had first arrived on Mars, Jason had been surprised to discover that the dominant life-form of a desert world was aquatic. But he had soon learned that, when life had first evolved on the red planet, Mars had been entirely shrouded in deep oceans. Complex civilizations had flourished in the ancient waters of Mars, vast city-states woven in a complex web of trade and cultural exchange.

But just a few thousand years before Jason's arrival, that had all changed. The oceans had begun to recede, slowly at first, then more quickly with each passing year. Skeptics among the populace had argued that what they were experiencing was a natural cycle and that the waters had ebbed and flowed many times before. But the more forward-looking had seen what lay ahead if the seas continued to shrink. And they had a solution.

By the time that places like the buried city before them had been lost to dry land, a complex system of canals had been constructed, linking points of extremely low elevation where, it was hoped, the waters would be retained even if they disappeared from the rest of the globe. The populace relocated to these new sanctuaries, leaving their old homes behind but retaining as much of their former cultures as possible as they continued to exchange goods and ideas along the narrow canals that connected their new homes.

And for a few generations, it appeared that the worst was behind them. The oceans had receded drastically, but there were still waters in the canals and in the low-elevation sanctuaries. Life continued much as it always had, albeit under considerable strain.

But the drought that had dried their world had only slowed, not stopped, and in time some of the canals became shallower and shallower, until in the end they were no longer navigable by the aquatic residents of the sanctuaries. What had been a globe-spanning system that connected every living person on Mars became fragmented networks, isolated from one another, separated by the unforgiving sands.

Now all that remained of the once-proud globe-spanning culture were ruins like this buried city, where crumbling statuary, the spires of the highest roofs, and the tallest columns were all that rose above the sands, like an orchard of tombstones.

Jason looked from the ruins to Tyr, a solemn expression on his face.

"Your people can be great again, you know. If enough of you *want* it."

The *Argo* had reached the anchorage outside of Freehaven, and while the crew prepared to leave the ship, Tyr led the refugees down the gangplank onto the stone docks, and from there down into the waters of the oasis. There were nearly a dozen other sand ships at anchor, nearly all of those who called Freehaven home, some of them in the process of unloading their most recent plunder, others preparing to sail out onto the sands again.

When the engineers of several millennia past had constructed the network of canals that connected the areas of lowest elevation, there were a handful of likely spots that were too far distant from the others to be included. One such was the lake the first pirates had named "Freehaven." It was several days' sail across the high sands from the nearest point in any of the canal systems, its location a closely guarded secret. Shielded from view by the ruins of the buried city to the east and by a mountain range that ran from southwest to northeast, it could be approached only from the south, and even then captains had to be careful to navigate clear of the many hidden baffles and traps that had been set by the inhabitants just beneath the sands. Any who tried to approach Freehaven without knowing the circuitous route to take would find themselves stranded out on the sands, their hulls shattered to splinters, at the mercy of the pirates' defenses.

Jason was on deck, in the process of strapping on the complex breathing apparatus that allowed him to move through the streets of Freehaven without drowning. The building he called home was pressurized with breathable air within and air locks in place of doors, but with enough standing water in indoor fountains and pools that his native friends could visit him without running the risk of drying out or suffocating. But in order to reach his home, he had to pass for a considerable distance beneath the waters, as he did when he wanted to join in with the daily life of the Freehaven community.

So it was that Tyr already had the refugees over the docks and down into the waters by the time that Jason was able to join them, his ditty bag slung over his shoulder, a transparent globe-shaped helmet completely enclosing his head. The knee he had injured aboard the galleon was better but had not healed entirely, and so he was thankful to get underwater and take his weight off it.

Tyr had already removed his encumbering breather, and the refugees were glorying in the sensation of breathing freely for the first time since they boarded the Vendish galleon some weeks before.

"Finally!" A voice echoed through the material of Jason's helmet, loud enough to carry through the waters. "You bring us something of *value*, pink-skin!"

Jason cupped one hand palm forward and the other palm back, and waved his arms to spin himself around in place. It was sometimes difficult for him to discern one Martian voice from another underwater, but he knew exactly who had spoken this time.

"Rac," he said. Inside the helmet, the name sounded like a curse in Jason's own ears. But his words were being picked up by a microphone beneath his chin and amplified through speakers incorporated into the outer shell of his breathing apparatus, at a volume that the natives could perceive, and he wasn't sure if the venom in his voice was lost in the process. "How *nice* to see you."

"That's *Captain* Rac, I remind you." The water before Rac's face rippled with waves, the visual cue that his mandibles were clacking with laughter. He stood with his crew, who were in the process of preparing to put out to the high sands.

It was custom when at home in Freehaven for all residents to be treated as equals, their ranks and titles only evoked when they were aboard their ships. But one major exception was the captain who was selected by the others to govern Freehaven itself, who was regarded as the commander of the entire community.

Rac approached, giving the refugees gathered nearby an appraising look. "And here I thought you always disapproved of selling prisoners to the Vendish. This is a sorry rabble you've netted, but still will their sale swell the coffers of Freehaven."

Jason bristled, and from the corner of his eye, he saw Tyr take a defensive posture. They had first come to blows with Rac on the pirate ship that had taken them on board after their escape from Praxis, on which Rac had served as a junior crewman. He had resented the fact that the pink-skinned outlander and the defrocked priest had been welcomed as members of the crew and not sold into slavery, and tensions between them had only been prevented from erupting into a duel to the death by the intercession of the Articles, which forbade crewmen from doing harm to one another.

In the years since, Rac had gone on to get command of his own ship, as Jason had his, but the enmity between them had only faded, never truly vanished. They argued frequently, especially since Rac had been elected by the others as the head captain of Freehaven, and never more so than when the subject of selling prisoners into indentured servitude was discussed.

"These are not *prisoners,*" Jason sneered, fighting the urge to draw his sword. "They are our *guests.*"

The waters in front of Rac's face swirled and ebbed as his mandibles vibrated with laughter. "Very funny, pink-skin! Like that beast you call a pet, I imagine?" He laughed even harder, the waters practically becoming a whirlpool.

Jason took a step forward. "No, Rac. I'm *serious.* You're *not* touching them."

The water rippled in a brief chuckle. Then Rac grew serious. "Have they signed the Articles?"

Jason shook his head inside the bubble helmet. "No, of course not. *Look* at them. They couldn't handle the life of a pirate."

"If they have not signed the *Articles* of Freehaven, then they are not *residents* of Freehaven." Rac pushed up off the ground and drifted through the waters closer to Jason until he was within arm's reach of the refugees. "And if they are not *residents,* then they must be classified as *plunder.* And no one man can keep a ship's plunder all to himself. It must be divided among the crew and among the other residents."

"They are free individuals!" Jason shouted. "You can't just treat them like property!"

Rac scoffed. "Freehaven is the only home of the *truly* free. All others are slaves of one kind or another, whether to wealth or to ideology."

"Freedom should be everyone's birthright!" Jason countered.

The crews of the other ships that were loading and unloading at the dock had taken note of the exchange, and many of them had lingered, waiting to see what transpired, including many of their captains.

"Watch yourself, pink-skin," Rac said. "You come close to violating the Articles with that kind of talk."

Jason looked around at the faces of the assembled residents, seeking out the other captains. He could see that more than a few of them were clearly sympathetic to his position but that others were decidedly not.

"And as Captain of Freehaven," Rac went on, addressing himself to the assembled crowd, "I claim Freehaven's portion of the *Argo*'s plunder *now*." He grabbed the arm of the nearest refugee, a woman just entering the age of maturity, and motioned for his crewmen standing nearby to approach. "And since your contributions to the coffers have been inadequate for some time now, leaving the *Argo* in arrears under the terms of the Articles, Freehaven's portion will include *all* of this rabble."

As Rac's crewmen rounded up the confused refugees, preparing to escort them onto Rac's ship in preparation for transporting them north to Vend, Tyr came alongside Jason, bristling with barely restrained rage.

"You must *do* something," Tyr said in a quiet voice.

Jason had gone completely still and quiet, trying not to let his emotions overcome his judgment, trying to work out a solution.

"Captain," Tyr urged again. Even at home, he was ever the first officer, never entirely comfortable treating his captain as an equal.

Jason realized that his hand gripped the handle of the sword at his side so tightly that his palm ached.

Tyr grabbed Jason's shoulder. "You know what will become of them in the north."

He could try to convince enough of the other captains to form a quorum, Jason knew, and call for an election in the hopes of ousting Rac as the head of Freehaven. But that would take time, and Rac would have long since sailed away before he had time to speak to enough captains to make a difference. And there was no guarantee that the next captain elected to succeed Rac wouldn't feel the same way about the slave trade.

Tyr tightened his grip on Jason's shoulder.

"Captain Rac!" Jason called out, pulling away from Tyr and stepping forward, drawing his sword. "I challenge you, by the First Article, for the right to lead Freehaven."

All eyes swung first in Jason's direction, then to Rac, who stood with his arms folded over his chest, the water before his face swirling with mirthless laughter.

Jason stood atop the shoulders of a headless statue that was buried to the waist in the sands. A short distance off, just outside of arm's reach, Rac crouched on top of a broken column that rose like a tree leaning in a high wind.

Tradition demanded that, as the challenged, Rac had the choice of venue for the single combat. It was hardly surprising that he would choose the drystone dueling sands of the buried city.

"Your freak muscles won't do you much good *here*, pink-skin," Rac scoffed. "Jump as high and far as you like, and chances are *they* will be there waiting when you come down." He pointed at the sands that surrounded them, where the threaded traces of sand-sharks passing by rippled all around.

Jason's right knee still ached from the injury he'd taken aboard the galleon days before. From a way off, he could hear the sound of Rac's partisans laughing at his barb. Some half dozen sand ships drifted at anchor all around them, their decks crowded with nearly the entire population of Freehaven. Aboard Rac's own ship, the Praxian refugees were herded together, shackled in chains, gasping for breath as they passed their portable breathing dispensers from one to another.

Tyr and the rest of Jason's crewmen were on the deck of the *Argo*, their expressions solemn and tense. If Jason's challenge to defeat Rac failed, the *Argo* would be electing a new captain. Either Jason would prevail, or he would die. There was no third option.

Jason could see that Tyr was praying, arms raised overhead. It was upon a drystone just like the one Jason stood atop that Tyr's god had been martyred. And it was for much the same reason that the inhabitants of Freehaven had selected the buried city as one of their principal dueling grounds in generations past. There was no escape for a Martian from this place, nowhere to hide. The sun bore down mercilessly from above, and the sands held dangers of their own. Once a Martian's breather ran out, he would die of suffocation and dehydration in short order.

But the weapons that the combatants carried ensured that neither of them would have to wait quite that long.

"Rac, there's still time for me to withdraw the challenge," Jason called out. "We don't have to do this. Just let those people go, and we can . . ."

The rest of his words were drowned out by the high-pitched pop of a whip snapping only inches from his face, the dry air crackling with the electrical discharge from its tip.

"I've heard enough of your talk for one lifetime," Rac shouted. "Shut up and *die*."

As the challenged party, Rac had been given the choice of weapons, as well. So naturally he had chosen one that least suited Jason's talents.

"All right," Jason snarled. He flicked the whip he held in his right hand, allowing it to uncoil and hang down past his feet. "Enough talking."

Jason raised his arm overhead in a slow swing, the whip trailing through the air, then pulled back with a jerk after making a complete circle, sending the tail of the whip racing ahead, only to snap back just as it reached the column atop which Rac stood.

Rac's mandibles quivered with laughter as he leapt nimbly from the column to a rooftop that rose above the sands, just in time to avoid Jason's lash.

"You never could get the hang of it, could you, pink-skin?"

Since arriving on the red planet, Jason had made full use of the increased speed and strength that he enjoyed relative to the natives of the low-gravity world. But tasks that called for finesse and a light touch, requiring him to rein in his strength, were actually more difficult for him. The whips, which the natives were able to manipulate like sinewy snakes beneath the water and like lightning in the air above, had always presented Jason with difficulty.

But he wasn't about to give up yet.

Rac's own whip shot through the air again, and as it whistled toward him, Jason managed to step to one side, almost—but not quite—managing to avoid it. The whip's tip grazed his bare shoulder, sending a shock of pain across his chest, accompanied by the acrid tang of cauterized flesh. It was almost enough to make him lose his grip on his own weapon. But even a full charge wouldn't have been fatal, assuming it had struck him in the same spot. A shock to a limb he could survive, but one to his trunk might well stop his heart from beating, and one to his head could fry his brain.

While Jason recovered his balance and lashed out with his own whip, Rac had already alighted on another roof, and by the time Jason's whip cracked in empty space, Rac had leapt to the top of another ruined statue. The sand-sharks below circled hungrily, tracking their movements, and, overhead, a flock of leatherwing scavengers wheeled silently, patiently.

Rac's whip swept forward again, and Jason jumped off the top of the column with as little force as he could manage, aiming to come down on top of a temple roof that jutted out of the sands at an angle. But he misjudged the distance, overcompensating for the strength of his jumps, and failing to take into account the diminished strength of his injured knee, and almost fell short. His arms pinwheeling on either side, as if he might somehow swim through the thin air, he just managed to grab hold of the roof's edge with his free hand and dangled for an instant off the precipice, almost losing hold of his whip in the process.

As Jason scrambled to pull himself up onto the canted roof, he heard a whistle and crack, followed by a riot of pain in his left leg. He lost his grip on his whip, which went tumbling down to the sands below, where it was instantly swallowed whole by one of the sandsharks. Jason collapsed forward onto the roof, his leg spasming and twitching violently, having received almost a full charge from Rac's whip.

He managed to roll over onto his back, just as Rac's whip whistled and popped above him once more. A second slower, and it would have caught him square in the face.

Jason was struggling into a sitting position as Rac landed lightly on the other side of the temple roof, some fifteen feet away. Rac's whip snaked in his grip as he swung his arm back and forth, building up speed, slowly stalking toward the place where Jason lay.

"I should have killed you the first moment I laid eyes on you," Rac said, swinging his whip in a wide arc overhead, slowly at first but faster with every rotation. "You've been nothing but a pain in my side ever since."

Jason couldn't stand, his left leg still rendered useless and twitching by the shock. His arms and hands still worked, but without a weapon in them, he was unable to strike back. Rac could keep his distance and hit Jason with his whip as many times as it took to kill him, or drive him off the roof, whichever came first. Of course, if Rac managed to hit Jason's head, it would only require one shot.

Unless Jason managed to even the odds a bit.

"Good-bye, pink-skin," Rac said, mandibles clattering with vicious laughter. "You won't be missed!"

Rac swung his arm forward, then back, sending the tip of his whip snapping straight toward Jason's head. Just at the last instant, as the whip whistled toward his face, Jason reached up with blinding speed and grabbed hold of the whip with both hands, gripping as tightly as he could manage.

Jason's arms shuddered and twitched with the charge, but he kept hold of the whip. His mind reeled with the pain, but he held on.

"Fool," Rac cursed, and yanked back on the whip with all of his strength.

Jason chose that moment to pull the whip toward *him*, and, in a test of brute strength, even in spite of the pain he was enduring, he came out on top. Rac swore angrily as the handle of the whip was pulled out of his grip.

Using the last of the strength and control in his now almost-entirely-numbed limbs, Jason swung the heavy handle of the whip back over his head, letting go when it was at the top of its arc. Rac's whip sailed out over the ground, landing on the sands just long enough to draw the attention of a pair of sand-sharks, who each took hold of one end and devoured it down to the center in mere moments.

Jason flopped back onto the warm, dry surface of the temple roof, his arms shuddering uncontrollably on either side. He was having difficulty breathing, but somehow held on to consciousness.

A shadow fell across Jason's face as Rac loomed over him.

"Pity we can never reach whatever world you come from, pink-skin." Rac leaned closer. "If it is filled with the likes of you, we could conquer the lot in no time."

Rac reached down, and his fingers closed on Jason's shoulders. Rac lifted him partially off the surface of the roof, and began to drag him bodily toward the edge.

"Whatever afterlife awaits creatures like you," Rac said, "I hope it is a disappointment to you."

Rac leaned as he struggled with the weight of Jason's body, but just as he approached the edge of the roof, Jason used the only limb still under his control. He kicked out, snapping one of Rac's legs at the joint. As Rac howled in pain, Jason hooked his leg around Rac's other leg, and *pulled*.

Still howling in pain and rage, Rac went plummeting over the edge. Jason collapsed back onto the roof, eyes closed, unable to move another muscle. But when Rac's screams ended with a soft thud, quickly followed by the sound of gnashing teeth, Jason allowed himself a bitter smile.

Another shadow flitted across his face, and he felt sharp claws digging into his abdomen.

"Oh, come *on*," he said. Surviving single combat with a devious enemy, only to be a meal for a scavenging leatherwing? Where was the justice?

But instead of feeling the pain of the leatherwing's snout biting into his soft tissue, eating him alive, Jason felt a tug at his belt, as the leatherwing tried to get at a pouch that hung there.

He opened his eyes and managed a weary smile.

"You know, Bandit, if you'd shown up just a few minutes ago you might have *helped* me . . ."

The sun was just beginning to pink the sky in the east as the *Argo* caught sight of water, dead ahead.

"Are you certain about this course of action, captain?" Tyr asked, warily eyeing the leatherwing that perched on Jason's shoulder.

"You can be a great people again," Jason answered with a smile. "You just need a few obstacles moved out of your way."

Tyr's mandibles clacked with a dry chuckle. "I'll signal the rest of the fleet."

As his first officer went to relay his orders to the dozen ships that sailed in their wake, Jason looked across the sands at the network of canals just now coming into view.

It hadn't been easy, but once he'd become head of Freehaven, he'd been able to convince enough of the other captains to back his plans. Now, months later, they were finally being put into motion. Praxis would be first. They would cut off the Hegemony from any outside trade, then launch strike teams in amphibious assault, arming Praxian dissidents while dismantling the Hegemony's ability to suppress dissent.

It would not be easy, and it would not be quick, but in time the Hegemony would fall.

And once the people of Praxis knew the meaning of "freedom," they would turn their attentions north, to Vend. And once the choke hold the Vendish wealthy had on the rest of the population was broken, Jason would continue sailing, routing out oppression wherever he went. He would sail clear across the world if he had to. But Jason wasn't worried. He'd sailed around the world before.

IAN MCDONALD

British author Ian McDonald is an ambitious and daring writer with a wide range and an impressive amount of talent. His first story was published in 1982, and since then he has appeared with some frequency in *Interzone, Asimov's Science Fiction,* and elsewhere. In 1989 he won the *Locus* "Best First Novel" Award for his novel *Desolation Road.* He won the Philip K. Dick Award in 1991 for his novel *King of Morning, Queen of Day.* His other books include the novels *Out on Blue Six* and *Hearts, Hands and Voices; Terminal Café; Sacrifice of Fools; Evolution's Shore; Kirinya; Ares Express;* and *Brasyl,* as well as three collections of his short fiction, *Empire Dreams, Speaking in Tongues,* and *Cyberabad Days.* His novel *River of Gods* was a finalist for both the Hugo Award and the Arthur C. Clarke Award in 2005, and a novella drawn from it, "The Little Goddess," was a finalist for the Hugo and the Nebula. He won a Hugo Award in 2007 for his novelette "The Djinn's Wife," won the Theodore Sturgeon Award for his story "Tendeléo's Story," and in 2011 won the John W. Campbell Memorial Award for his novel *The Dervish House.* His most recent books are *The Dervish House,* the starting volume of a YA series, *Planesrunner,* and another new novel, *Be My Enemy.* Born in Manchester, England, in 1960, McDonald has spent most of his life in Northern Ireland, and now lives and works in Belfast. He has a website at http://www.lysator.liu. se/~unicorn/mcdonald/.

In most recent wars, entertainers have visited the frontline troops, often putting themselves in considerable danger. None have ever visited a battlefield as strange, though, or performed for an audience as bizarre and inhuman, or put themselves in as much imminent danger, as do the hapless entertainers in the brilliant and slyly funny story that follows . . .

The Queen of the Night's Aria

IAN MCDONALD

"GOD. STILL ON BLOODY MARS."

Count Jack Fitzgerald, Virtuoso, Maestro, Sopratutto, stood at the window of the Grand Valley Hotel's Heaven's Tower Suite in just his shirt. Before his feet, the Sculpted City of Unshaina tumbled away in shelves and tiers, towers and tenements. Cable cars skirled along swooping lines between the carved pinnacles of the Royal Rookeries. Many-bodied stone gods roosted atop mile-high pillars; above them, the skymasters of the Ninth Fleet hung in the red sky. Higher still were the rim rocks of the Grand Valley, carved into fretwork battlements and machicolations, and highest of all, on the edge of the atmosphere, twilight shadows festooned with riding lights, were the ships of Spacefleet. A lift-chair borne by a squadron of Twav bobbed past the picture window, dipping to the wing beats of the carriers. The chair bore a human in the long duster coat of a civil servant of the Expeditionary Force. One hand clutched a diplomatic valise, the other the guylines of the lift-harness. The mouth beneath the dust goggles was open in fear.

"Oh God, look at that! I feel nauseous. You hideous government drone, how dare you make me feel nauseous first thing in the morning! You'll never get me in one of those things, Faisal, never. They *shit* on you; it's true. I've seen it. Bottom of the valley's five hundred feet deep in Mars-bat guano."

I come from a light-footed, subtle family, but for all my discretion, I could never catch Count Jack unawares. Tenors have good ears.

"Maestro, the Commanderie has issued guidelines. Mars-bats is not acceptable. The official expression is the Twav Civilization."

"What nonsense. Mars-bats is what they look like, Mars-bats is what they are. No civilization was ever built on the basis of aerial defecation. Where's my tea? I require tea."

I handed the Maestro his morning cup. He took a long, slurping sip—want of etiquette was part of his professional persona. The Country Count from Kildare: he insisted it appear on all his billings. Despite the titles and honorifics, Count Jack Fitzgerald had passed the summit of his career, if not his self-mythologizing. The aristocratic title was a Papal honor bestowed upon his grandfather, a dully devout shopkeeper who nonetheless was regarded as little less than a saint in Athy. The pious greengrocer's apples would have browned at his grandson's flagrant disregard for religion and its moralizing. The Heaven's Tower Suite's Emperor-sized bed was mercifully undisturbed by another body. Count James Fitzgerald drained his cup, drew himself to his full six and a half feet, sucked in his generous belly, clicked out cricks and stiffnesses in his joints.

"Oh bless you, dear boy. None of the others can make tea worth a tinker's piss."

For the past six months, long before this tour of Mars, I had been slipping a little stiffener into the morning tea.

"And did they love us? Did strong men weep like infants and women ovulate?"

"The Joint Chiefs were enchanted."

"Well, the enchantment didn't reach as far as their bloody pockets. A little consideration wouldn't have gone amiss. Philistines."

A gratis performance at the Commanderie for the Generals and Admirals and Sky-marshals was more or less mandatory for all Earth entertainers playing the Martian front. The Army and Navy shows usually featured exotic dancers and strippers. From the piano, you notice many things, like the well-decorated Sky-lord nodding off during the Maestro's Medley of Ould Irish Songs, but the news had reported that he had just returned from a hard-fought campaign against the Syrtian Hives.

"Ferid Bey wishes to see you."

"That odious little Ottoman. What does he want? More money, I'll warrant. I shan't see him. He spoils my day. I abjure him."

"Eleven o'clock, Maestro. At the Canal Court."

Count Jack puffed out his cheeks in resignation.

"What, he can't afford the Grand Valley? With the percentage he skims? Not that they'd let him in; they should have a sign: no dogs, uniforms, or agents."

We couldn't afford the Grand Valley either, but such truths are best entrusted to the discretion of an accompanist. I have talked our way out of hotel bills before.

"I'll book transport."

"If you must." His attention was once again turned to the canyonscape of the great city of the Twav. The sun had risen over the canyon edge and sent the shadows of Unshaina's spires and stacks and towers carved from raw rock chasing down the Great Valley. Summoned by the light, flocks of Twav poured from the slots of their roost-cotes. "Any chance of another wee drop of your particular tea?"

I took the cup and saucer from his outstretched hand.

"Of course, Maestro."

"Thank you, dear boy. I would, of course, be lost without you. Quite quite lost."

A hand waved me away from his presence.

"Thank you. And Maestro?"

He turned from the window.

"Trousers."

For a big man, Count James Fitzgerald threw up most discreetly. He leaned out of the sky-chair, one quick convulsion, and it fell in a single sheet between the sculpted pinnacles of Unshaina. He wiped his lips with a large very white handkerchief and that was it, done. He would blame me, blame the sky-chair bearers, blame the entire Twav Civilization, but never the three cups of special tea he had taken while I packed for him, nor the bottle that was his perennial companion in the bedside cabinet.

Checkout had been challenging this time. I would never say so to Count Jack, but it had been a long time since I could parlay the Country Count from Kildare by name recognition alone.

"You are leaving the bags," the manager said. He was Armenian. He had never heard of Ireland, let alone County Kildare.

"We will be returning, yes," I said.

"But you are leaving the bags."

"Christ on crutches," Count Jack had exclaimed as the two sky-chairs set down onto the Grand Valley's landing apron. "What are you trying to do, kill me, you poncing infidel? My heart is tender, tender I tell you, bruised by decades of professional envy and poison-ous notices."

"It is the quickest and most direct way."

"Swung hither and yon in a bloody Bat-cab and no money at the end of it, as like," Count Jack muttered as he strapped in and the Twavs took the strain and lifted. He gave a faint cry as the sky-chair swung out over the mile-deep drop to the needles of the Lower Rook-eries, like an enfilade of pikes driven into the red rock of the Grand Valley. He clung white-knuckled to the guylines, moaning a little, as the Twav carriers swayed him between the scurrying cableway gon-dolas and around the many-windowed stone towers of the roosts.

I rather enjoyed the ride. My life has been low in excitements—I took the post of accompanist to the Maestro as an escape from filing his recording royalties, which was the highest entry position in the industry I could attain with my level of degree in music. Glamorous it was, exciting, no. Glamour is just another work environment. One recovers from being star-struck rather quickly. My last great excite-ment had been the night before we left for Mars. Ships! Space travel! Why, I could hardly sleep the night before launch. I soon discovered that space travel is very much like an ocean cruise, without the promenade decks and the excursions, and far, far fewer people. And much, much worse food. However tedious and braying the company for me, I derived some pleasure from the fact that for them it was three months locked in with Count Jack.

I have a personal interest in this war. My grandfather was one of the martyrs who died in the opening minutes of the Horsell Common invasion. He was the first generation of my family to be born in England. He had been at prayer in the Woking Mosque and was consumed by the heat ray from the Uliri War Tripod. Many thousands died that day, and though it has taken us two generations to master the Uliri technology to keep our skies safe, and to prepare a fleet to launch Operation Enduring Justice, the cry is ever fresh: remember Shah Jehan! I stood among the crowds on that same Horsell Common around the crater, as people gathered by the other craters of the invasion, or on hilltops, on beaches, riverbanks, rooftops, holy places, anywhere with a view of open sky, to watch the night light up with the drives of our expeditionary fleet. The words on my lips, and the lips of everyone else on that cold November night, were Justice, Justice, but in my heart, it was Remember Shah Jehan!

Rejoice! Rejoice! our Prime Minister told us when our drop-troopers captured Unshaina, conquered the Twav Civilization, and turned the Grand Valley into our Martian headquarters and munitions factory. It's harder to maintain your patriotic fervor when those spaceships are months away on the far side of the sun, and no one really believes the propaganda that the Twav were the devious military hive-masterminds of the Uliri war machine. Nor, when that story failed, did we swallow the second serving of propaganda: that the Twav were the enslaved mind-thralls of the Uliri, whom we had liberated for freedom and democracy. A species that achieves a special kind of sentience when it roosts and flocks together seems to me to embody the very nature of the demos. The many-bodied gods atop the flute-thin spires of Unshaina represent the truth that our best, our most creative, our most brilliant, may be all the divinity we need.

It has been a long time since I was at prayer.

Count Jack gave a small moan as his sky-chair dipped down

abruptly between the close-packed stone quills of Alabaster Needles. The chair-boss whistled instructions to her crew—the lowest register of their language lay at the upper edge of our hearing—and they skillfully brought us spirally down past hives and through arches and under buttresses to the terraces of the Great Western Dock on the Grand Canal. Here humans had built cheap spray-stone lading houses and transit lodges among the sinuously carved stone. The Canal Court Hotel was cheap, but that was not its main allure; Ferid Bey had appetites best served by low rents and proximity to docks.

While Count Jack swooned and whimpered and swore that he would never regain his land legs, never, I tipped the chair-boss a generous handful of saucers and she clasped her lower hands in a gesture of respect.

"We're broke," Ferid Bey said. We sat drinking coffee on the terrace of the Canal Court watching Twav stevedores lift and lade pallets from the open hatches of cargo barges. I say coffee; it was Expeditionary Force ersatz, vile and weak and with a disturbing spritz of excremental. Ferid Bey, who as a citizen of the great Ottoman Empire, appreciated coffee, grimaced at every sip. I say terrace; spaced beside the garbage bins, it was a cranny for two tables, which caught the wind and lifted the dust in a perpetual eddy. Ferid Bey wore his dust goggles, kept his scarf wrapped around his head, and sipped his execrable coffee.

"What do you mean, broke?" Count Jack thundered in his loudest Sopratutto voice. Startled Twavs flew up from their cargoes, twittering on the edge of audibility. "You've been at the bum-boys again, haven't you?" Ferid Bey's weakness for the rough was well-known, particularly the kind who would go through his wallet the next morning. He sniffed loudly.

"Actually, Jack, this time it's you."

I often wondered if the slow decline of Count Jack's career was partly attributable to the fact that, after years of daily contact, agent had started to sound like client. The Count's eyes bulged. His blood pressure was bad. I'd seen the report from the prelaunch medical.

"It's bums on seats, Jack, bums on seats, and we're not getting them."

"I strew my pearls before buffoons in braid and their braying brides, and they throw them back in my face!" Count Jack bellowed. "I played La Scala, you know. La Scala! And the Pope. I'd be better off playing to the space-bats. At least they appreciate a high C. No Ferid, no no: you get me better audiences."

"Any audiences would be good," Ferid Bey muttered, then said aloud, "I've got you a tour."

Count Jack grew inches taller.

"How many nights?"

"Five."

"There are that many concert halls on this arse-wipe of a world?"

"Not so much concert halls." Ferid Bey tried to hide as much of his face as possible behind scarf, goggles, and coffee cup. "More concert *parties*."

"The Army?" Count Jack's face was pale now, his voice quiet. I had heard this precursor to a rage the size of Olympus Mons many times. Thankfully, I had never been its target. "Bloody shit-stupid squaddies who have to be told which end of a blaster to point at the enemy?"

"Yes, Jack."

"Would this be . . . upcountry?"

"It would."

"Would this be . . . close to the front?"

"I've extended your cover."

"Well, it's nice to know my ex-wives and agent are well provided for."

"I've negotiated a fee commensurate with the risk."

"What is the risk?"

"It's a war zone, Jack."

"What is the fee?"

"One thousand five hundred saucers. Per show."

"Tell me we don't need to do this, dear boy," Count Jack said to me.

"The manager of the Grand Valley is holding your luggage to ransom," I said. "We need to do it."

"You're coming with me." Count Jack's accusing finger hovered one inch from the bridge of his agent's nose. Ferid Bey spread his hands in resignation.

"I would if I could, Jack. Truly. Honestly. Deeply. But I've got a lead on a possible concert recording here in Unshaina, and there are talent bookers from the big Venus casinos in town, so I'm told."

"Venus?" The Cloud Cities, forever drifting in the Storm Zone, were the glittering jewels on the interplanetary circuit. The legendary residences were a long, comfortable, well-paid descent from the pinnacle of career.

"Five nights?"

"Five nights only. Then out."

"Usual contract riders?"

"Of course."

Count Jack laughed his great, canyon-deep laugh. "We'll do it. Our brave legionnaires need steel in their steps and spunk in their spines. When do we leave?"

"I've booked you on the *Empress of Mars* from the Round 'O' Dock. Eight o'clock. Sharp."

Count Jack pouted.

"I am prone to seasickness."

"This is a canal. Anyway, the Commanderie has requisitioned all the air transport. It seems there's a big push on."

"I shall endure it."

"You're doing the right thing, Jack," Ferid Bey said. "One, and another thing; Faisal, you couldn't pick up for the coffee, could you?" I suspected there was a reason Ferid Bey had brought us out to this tatty bargee hostel. "And while you're at it, could you take care of my hotel?"

Already, Count Jack was hearing the distant applause of the au-

dience, scenting like a rare moth the faint but unmistakable phero-
mone of *celebrity*.

"And am I . . . top of the bill?"

"Always, Jack," said Ferid Bey. "Always."

From our table on the promenade deck of the *Empress of Mars,* we
watched the skymasters pass overhead. They were high and their
hulls caught the evening light that had faded from the canal. I lost
count after thirty; the sound of their many engines merged into a
high thunder. The vibration sent ripples across the wine in our
glasses on the little railed-off table at the stern of the barge. One
glass for me, always untouched—I did not drink, but I liked to keep
Count Jack company. He was a man who craved the attention of
others—without it, he grew translucent and insubstantial. His hopes
for another involuntary audience of passengers to charm and intim-
idate and cow with his relentless showbiz tales were disappointed.
The *Empress of Mars* was a cargo tug pushing a twelve-barge tow
with space for eight passengers, of which we were the sole two. I was
his company. I had been so enough times to know his anecdotes as
thoroughly as I knew the music for his set. But I listened, and I
laughed, because it is not the story that matters but the telling.

"Headed east," Count Jack said. I did not correct him—he had
never understood that on Mars, west was east and east was west.
Sunrise, east; sunset, west, dear boy, he declared. We watched the fleet,
a vast, sky-filling arrowhead, drive toward the sunset hills on the
close horizon. The Grand Valley had opened out into a trench so
wide we could see the canyon walls, a terrain with its own inner terrain. "Godspeed that fleet." He had been uncharacteristically quiet
and ruminative this trip. It was not the absence of a captive audience. The fleet, the heavy canal traffic—I had counted eight tows
headed up-channel from the front to Unshaina since we began this
first bottle of what Count Jack called his "Evening Restorational"—
had brought home to him that he was headed to war. Not pictures of

war, news reports of war, rumors of war, but war itself. For the first time, he might be questioning the tour.

"Does it make your joints ache, Faisal?"

"Maestro?"

"The gravity. Or rather, the want of gravity. Wrists, ankles, fingers, all the flexing joints. Hurt like buggery. Thumbs are the worst. I'd have thought it would have been the opposite, with its being so light here. Not a bit of it. It's all I can do to lift this glass to my lips."

To my eyes, he navigated the glass from table to lips quite successfully. Count Jack poured another Evening Restorational and sank deep in his chair. The dark green waters of the canal slipped beneath our hull. Martian twilights were swift and deep. War had devastated this once populous and fertile land, left scars of black glass across the bottomlands, where heat rays had scored the regolith. The rising evening wind, the *Tharseen,* which reversed direction depending on which end of the Grand Valley was in night, called melancholy flute sonatas from the shattered roost pillars.

"It's a ghastly world," Count Jack said after a second glass.

"I find it rather peaceful. It has a particular beauty. Melancholic."

"No, not Mars. Everywhere. Everywhere's bloody ghastly and getting ghastlier. Ever since the war. War makes everything brutal. Brutal and ugly. War wants everything to be like it. It's horrible, Faisal."

"Yes. I think we've gone too far. We're laying waste to entire civilizations. Unshaina, it's older than any city on Earth. This has gone beyond righteous justice. We're fighting because we love it."

"Not the war, Faisal. I've moved on from the bloody war. Do keep up. Getting old. That's what's truly horrible. Old old old and I can't do a thing about it. I feel it in my joints, Faisal. This bloody planet makes me feel old. A long, slow decline into incompetence, imbecility, and incontinence. What have I got? A decent set of pipes. That's all. And they won't last forever. No investments, no property, and bugger-all recording royalties. Bloody Revenue cleaned me out. Rat up a drainpipe. Gone. And the bastards still have their hands out.

They've threatened me, you know. Arrest. What is this, the bloody Marshalsea Gaol? I'm a Papal Knight, you know. I wield the sword of the Holy Father himself."

"All they want is their money," I said. Count Jack had always resented paying lawyers and accountants, with the result that he had signed disastrous recording contracts and only filed tax returns when the bailiffs were at the door. This entire Martian tour would barely meet his years of outstanding tax, plus interest. "Then they'll leave you alone."

"No, they won't. They won't ever let me alone. They know Count Jack is a soft touch. They'll be back, the damnable dunners. Once they've got the taste of your blood, they won't ever let their hooks out of you. Parasites. I am infested with fiscal parasites. Tax, war, and old age. They make everything gross and coarse and pointless."

Beams of white light flickered along the twilight horizon. I could not tell whether they were from sky to ground or ground to sky. The fleet had gone. The heat rays danced along the edge of the world, flickered out. New beams took their place. Flashes beyond the close horizon threw the hills into momentary relief. I cried out as the edge of the world became a flickering palisade of heat rays. Count Jack was on his feet. The flashes lit his face. Seconds later, the first soft rumble of distant explosions reached us. The Twav deckhands fluttered on their perches. I could make out the lower register of their consternation as a treble shrill. The edge of the world was a carnival of beams and flashes. I saw an arc of fire descend from the sky to terminate in a white flash beneath the horizon. I did not doubt that I had seen a skymaster and all her crew perish, but it was beautiful. The sky blazed with the most glorious fireworks. Count Jack's eyes were wide with wonder. He threw his hand up to shield his eyes as a huge midair explosion turned the night white. Stark shadows lunged across the deck; the Twav rose up in a clatter of wings.

"Oh, the dear boys, the dear boys," Count Jack whispered. The sound of the explosion hit us. It rattled the windows on the pilot deck, rattled the bottle and glasses on the table. I felt it shake the core of my being, shake me belly and bowel deep. The beams winked out. The horizon went dark.

We had seen a great and terrible battle, but who had fought, who had won, who had lost, whether there had been winners or losers, what its goals had been—we knew none of these. We had witnessed something terrible and beautiful and incomprehensible. I lifted the untouched glass of wine and took a sip.

"Good God," Count Jack said, still standing. "I always thought you didn't drink. Religious reasons and all that."

"No, I don't drink for musical reasons. It makes my joints hurt."

I drank the wine. It might have been vinegar, it might have been the finest wine available to humanity, I did not know. I drained the glass.

"Dear boy." Count Jack poured me another, one for himself, and together we watched the edge of the world glow with distant fires.

We played Camp Avenger on a stage rigged on empty beer barrels to a half-full audience that dwindled over the course of the concert to just six rows. A Brigadier who had been drinking steadily all through the concert tried to get his troopers up on stage to dance to the Medley of Ould Irish Songs. They sensibly declined. He tripped over his own feet trying to inveigle Count Jack to dance to "Walls of Limerick" with him and went straight off the stage. He split his head open on the rim of a beer keg.

At Syrtia Regional Command, the audience was less ambiguous. We were bottled off. The first one came looping in even as Count Jack came on, arms spread wide, to his theme song, "I'll Take You Home Again, Kathleen." He stuck it through "Blaze Away," "Nessun dorma," and "Il mio tesoro" before an accurately hurled Mars Export Pale Ale bottle deposited its load of warm urine down the front of his dickey. He finished "The Garden Where the Praties Grow," bowed, and went straight off. I followed him as the first of the barrage of folding army chairs hit the stage. Without a word or a look, he went straight to his tent and stripped naked.

"I've had worse in Glasgow Empire," he said. His voice was stiff with pride. I never admired him as much. "Can you do something with these, dear boy?" He held out the wet, reeking dress suit. "And run me a bath."

We took the money, in full and in cash, and went on, ever up the ever-branching labyrinth of canals, ever closer to the battlefront.

The boat was an Expeditionary Force fast-patrol craft, one heat ray turret fore, one mounted in a blister next to the captain's position. It was barely big enough for the piano, let alone us and the sullen four-man crew. They smoked constantly and tried to outrage Count Jack with their vile space trooper's language. He could outswear any of them. But he kept silence and dignity and our little boat threaded through the incomprehensible maze of Nyx's canals; soft green waters of Mars overhung by the purple fronds of crosier trees, dropping the golden coins of their seed cases into the water, where they sprouted corkscrew propellers and swam away. This was the land of the Oont, and their tall, heronlike figures, perched in the rear of their living punts, were our constant companions. On occasion, down the wider channels and basins, we glimpsed their legendary organic paddle wheelers, or their pale blue ceramic stilt towns. The crew treated the Oont with undisguised contempt and idly trained the boat's weapons on them. The Oont had accepted the mandate of the Commanderie without a fight, and their cities and ships and secretive, solitary way of life went unchanged. Our captain thought them a species of innate cowards and traitors. Only a species tamed by the touch of the heat ray could be trusted.

For five hundred miles, up the Grand Canal and through the maze of Nyx, Twav stevedores had lifted and laid my piano with precision and delicacy. It took the Terrene army to drop it. From the foot of the gangplank, I heard the jangling crash, and turned to see the cargo net on the jetty and troopers grinning. At once, I wanted to strip away the packing and see if anything remained. It was not my piano—I would never have risked my Bosendorfer on the vagaries of space travel—but it was a passable upright from a company that specialized in interplanetary hire. I had grown fond of it. One does with pianos. They are like dogs. I walked on. That much I had learned from Count Jack. Dignity, always dignity.

Oudeman was a repair base for Third Skyfleet. We walked in the shadow of hovering skymasters. Engineers in repair rigs swarmed over hulls, lowered engines on hoists, opened hull sections, deflated gas cells. It was clear to me that the fleet had suffered grievously in recent and grim battle. Skins were gashed open to the very bones; holes stabbed through the rounded hulls from side to side. Engine pylons terminated in melted drips. Entire crew gondolas and gun turrets had been torn away. Some had been so terribly mauled they were air-going skeletons, a few lift cells wrapped around naked ship spine.

Of the crews who had fought through such ruin, there was no sign.

The base commander, Yuzbashi Osman, greeted us personally. He was a great fan, a great fan. A dedicated lifelong fan. He had seen the Maestro in his every Istanbul concert. He always sat in the same seat. He had all the Maestro's recordings. He played them daily and had tried to educate his junior officers over mess dinners, but the rising generation were ignorant, low men—technically competent but little better than the Devshirmey conscripts. A clap of his hands summoned batmen to carry our luggage. I did not speak his language, but from the reactions of the engineers who had dropped my piano, I understood that further disrespect would not be tolerated. He cleared the camp steam bath for our exclusive use. Sweated, steamed, and scraped clean, a glowing Count Jack bowled into the mess tent as if he were striding onto the stage of La Scala. He was funny, he was witty, he was charming, he was glorious. Most of the junior Onbashis and Mulazims at the dinner in his honor could not speak English, but his charisma transcended all language. They smiled and laughed readily.

"Would you look at that?" Count Jack said in the backstage tent that was our dressing room. He held up a bottle of champagne, dripping from the ice bucket. "Krug. They got me my Krug. Oh the dear, lovely boys."

At the dinner, I had noted the paucity of some of the offerings and marveled at the effort it must have taken, what personal dedication by the Yuzbashi, to fulfill a rider that was only there to check the contract had been read. Count Jack slid the bottle back into the melting ice. "I shall return to you later, beautiful thing, with my heart full of song and my feet light on the applause of my audience. I am a star, Faisal. I am a true star. Leave me, dear boy."

Count Jack required time and space alone to prepare his entrance. This was the time he changed from Count James Fitzgerald to the Country Count from Kildare. It was a deeply private transformation and one I knew I would never be permitted to watch. The stage was a temporary rig bolted together from skymaster spares. The hovering ships lit the stage with their searchlights. A follow spot tracked me to the piano. I bowed, acknowledged the applause of the audience, flicked out the tails of my evening coat, and sat down. That is all an accompanist need do.

I played a few glissandi to check that the piano was still functioning after its disrespectful handling by the dock crew. Passable, to the tin ears of Skyfleet engineers. Then I played the short overture to create that all-important sense of expectation in the audience and went straight into the music for Count Jack's entrance. The spotlight picked him up as he swept onto the stage, "I'll Take You Home Again, Kathleen" bursting from his broad chest. He was radiant. He commanded every eye. The silence in the deep Martian night was the most profound I think I have ever heard. He strode to the front of the stage. The spotlight adored him. He luxuriated in the applause as if it were the end of the concert, not the first number. He was a shameless showman. I lifted my hands to the keyboard to introduce "*Torna a Surriento.*"

And the night exploded into towering blossoms of flame. For an instant, the audience sat transfixed, as if Count Jack had somehow summoned the most astonishing of operatic effects. Then the alarms blared out all across the camp. Count Jack and I both saw clearly the spider-shapes of War Tripods, tall as trees, wading through the flames. Heat rays flashed out, white swords, as the audience scattered to take up posts and weapons. Still, Count Jack held the spotlight, until an Onbashi leaped up, tackled him, and knocked him out of the line of fire just as a heat ray cut a ten-thousand-degree arc across the stage. He had no English, he needed no English. We ran. I glanced back once. I knew what I would see, but I had to see it: my piano, that same cheap, sturdy hire upright piano that I had shipped across 100 million miles of space, through the concert halls and grand opera houses, on dusty roads and railways, down calm green canals, my piano, exploding in a fountain of blazing hammers and whipping, melting wires. A War Tripod strode over us, its heat-ray arms swiveling, seeking new targets. I looked up into the weaving thicket of tentacles beneath the hull, then the raised steel hoof passed over me and came down squarely and finally on our dressing-room tent.

"My Krug!" Count Jack cried out.

A heat ray cut a glowing arc of lava across the ground before me. I was lucky—you cannot dodge these things or see them coming, or hear their ricochets. They are light itself. All you can be is moving in the right direction, have the right momentum: be lucky. Our Onbashi was not lucky. He ran into the heat ray and vanished into a puff of ash. A death so fast, so total that it became something more than death. It was annihilation.

"Maestro! With me!"

Count Jack had been standing, staring, transfixed. I took his hand, his palm still damp with concert sweat, and skirted around the end of the still-smoking scar. We ducked, we ran at a crouch, we zigzagged in our tails and dickey bows. There was no good reason for it. We had seen it in war movies. The Uliri war machines strode across the camp, slashing glowing lava tracks across it with their heat rays, their weapon-arms seeking out fresh targets. But our soldiers had reached their defensive positions and were fighting back, turning the Uliri's own weapon against them and bolstering it with a veritable hail of ordnance. The troopers who had manned our spotlights now turned to the heat rays. Skymasters were casting off, their turret gunners seeking out the many-eyed heads of the Uliri Tripods. The war machine that had so hideously killed the brave Onbashi stood in the river, eye blisters turning this way, that way, seeking targets. A weapon-arm fixed on us. The aperture of the heat ray opened. Hesitated. Pulled away. Grasping cables uncoiled from between the legs. We scuttled for cover behind a stack of barrels— not that they would have saved us. Then a missile cut a streak of red across the night. The war machine's front left knee joint exploded. The machine wavered for balance on two, then a skymaster cut low across the canal bank and severed the front right off at the thigh with a searing slash of a heat ray. The monster wavered, toppled, came down in a blast and crash and wave of spray, right on top of the boat that would have carried us to safety. Smashed to flinders. Escape hatches opened; pale shapes wriggled free, squirmed down the hull toward land. I pushed Count Jack to the ground as the skymaster opened up. Bullets screamed around us. Count Jack's eyes were wide with fear, and something else, something I had not imagined in the man: excitement. War might be brutal and ghastly and ugly, as he had declaimed on the *Empress of Mars,* but there was a terrible, primal power in it. I saw the same thrill, the same joy, the same power that had commanded audiences from Tipperary to Timbuktu. I saw it and I knew that, if we ever returned to Earth and England, I would ever be the accompanist, the amanuensis, the dear boy; and that even if he sang to an empty hall, Count John Fitzgerald would always be the Maestro, Sopratutto. All there was in me was fear, solid fear. Perhaps that is why I was brave. The guns fell silent. I looked over the top of the barrels. Silvery Uliri bodies were strewn across the dock. I saw the canal run with purple blood like paint in water.

The skymaster turned and came in over the canal to a low hover. A boarding ramp lowered and touched the ground. A skyman crouched at the top of the ramp, beckoning urgently.

"Run, Maestro, run!" I shouted, and dragged Count Jack to his feet. We ran. Around us heat rays danced and stabbed like some dark tango. A blazing war machine stumbled blindly past, crushing tents, bivouacs, repair sheds beneath its feet, shedding sheets of flame. Ten steps from the foot of the ramp, I heard a noise that turned me to ice: a great ululating cry from the hills behind the camp, ringing from horizon to horizon, back and forth, wash and backwash, a breaking wave of sound. I had never heard it, but I had heard of it, the war song of the Uliri padva infantry. A hand seized mine: the skyman dragged me and Count Jack like a human chain into the troop hold. As the ramp closed, I saw the skyline bubble and flow, like a silver sheen of oil, down the hillside toward us. Padvas. Thousands of them. As the skymaster lifted and the hull sealed, the last, the very last sight I had was of Yuzbashi Osman looking up at us. He raised a hand in salute. Then he turned, drew his sword, and, with a cry that pierced even the engine drone of the skymaster, every janissary of Oudeman Camp drew his blade. Sword points glittered, then they charged. The skymaster spun in the air, I saw no more.

"Did you see that?" Count Jack said to me. He gripped my shoulders. His face was pale with shock, but there was a mad strength in his fingers. "Did you? How horrible, how horrible horrible. And yet, how wonderful! Oh, the mystery, Faisal, the mystery!" Tears ran down his ash-smudged face.

We fled through the labyrinth of the night. We had no doubt that we were being pursued through those narrow, twining canyons. The skycaptain's pinger picked up fleeting, suggestive contacts, of what we had all heard: terrible cries, echoes of echoes in the stone re-doubts of Noctis, far away but always, always, always keeping pace with us. The main hold of the skymaster was windowless, and though the skycaptain spoke no English, he had made it most clear to us that we were to keep away from his crew, whether they were in engineering, the gun blisters, or the bridge and navigation pods. So we sat on the hard steel mesh of the dimly lit cargo hold, ostensibly telling old musician stories we had told many times before, pausing every time our indiscriminate ears brought us some report of the war outside. Hearing is a much more primal sense than vision. To see is to understand. To hear is to apprehend. Eyes can be closed. Ears are ever open. Maestro broke off the oft-told story of singing for the Pope, and how thin the towels were, and what cheap bastards the Holy See had turned out to be. His ears, as I have said, were almost supernaturally keen. His eyes went wide. The Twav battledores on their perches in the skymarine roosts riffled their scales, shining like oil on water, and shifted their grips on their weaponry. A split second later, I heard the cries. Stuttering and rhythmic, they rose over three octaves from a bass drone to a soprano, nerve-shredding yammer. Two behind us, striking chords and harmonics from each other like some experimental piece of serialist music. Another an-swered, ahead of us. And another, far away, muted by the wind-sculpted rock labyrinth. A fifth, close, to our right. Back and forth, call and response. I clapped my hands over my ears, not from the pain of the shrill upper registers, but at the hideous musicality of these unseen voices. They sang scales and harmonies alien to me, but their music called the musician in me.

And they were gone. Every nerve on the skymaster, human and Twav, was afire. The silence was immense. My Turkic is functional but necessary—enough to know what Ferid Bey is actually saying—and I recalled the few words of the skycaptain I had overheard as he relayed communications to the crew. The assault on Camp Oude-man had been part of a surprise offensive by the Tharsian War-queens. Massive assaults had broken out along a five-hundred-mile front from Arsai to Urania. War machines, shock troops—there had even been an assault on Spacefleet: squadron after squadron of rockets launched to draw the staggering firepower of our orbital battleships from the assault below. And up from out of the soil, things like nothing that anyone had ever seen before. Things that put whole battalions to flight, that smashed apart trench lines and crumbled redoubts to sand. As I tried to imagine the red earth parting and something from beyond nightmares rising up, I could not elude the dark thought: might there not be similar terrible novelties in the sky? This part of my eavesdropping I kept to myself. It was most simple: I had been routinely lying to Count Jack since the first day I set up my music on the piano.

"I could murder a drink," Count Jack said. "If there were such a thing on this barquadero. Even a waft of a Jameson cork under my nose."

The champagne on the deck of the *Empress of Mars* must have corrupted me, because at that moment I would gladly have joined the Maestro. More than joined, I would have beaten him by a furlong to the bottom of the bottle of Jameson.

Up on the bridge, a glass finger projecting from the skymaster's lifting body, the skycaptain called orders from his post at the steering yoke. Crew moved around us. The battledores shifted the hue of their plumage from blue to violent yellow. I felt the decking shift beneath me—how disorienting, how unpleasant, this sense of everything sound and trustworthy moving, nothing to hold on to. The engines were loud; the captain must be putting on speed, navigating between the wind-polished stone. We were flying through a monstrous stone pipe organ. I glanced up along the companionway to the bridge. Pink suffused the world beyond the glass. We had run all night through the Labyrinth of Night, that chartless maze of canyons and ravines and rock arches that humans suspected was not entirely natural. I saw rock walls above me. We were low, hugging the silty channels and canals. The rising sun sent planes of light down the sheer, fluted, stone walls. There is nothing on Earth to compare with the loveliness of dawn on Mars, but how I wish I were there and not in this dreadful place.

"Faisal."

"Maestro."

"When we get back, remind me to fire that greased turd, Ferid."

I smiled, and Count Jack Fitzgerald began to sing. "Galway Bay," the most hackneyed and sentimental of faux-Irish paddywhackery ("Have you ever been to Galway Bay? Incest and Gaelic games. All they know, all they like"), but I had never heard him sing it like this. Had he not been seated on the deck before me, leaning up against a bulkhead, I would have doubted that it was his voice. It was small but resonant, perfect like porcelain, sweet as a rose and filled with a high, light innocence. This was the voice of childhood, the boy singing back the tunes his grandmother taught him. This was the Country Count from Kildare. Every soul on the skymaster, Terrene and Martian, listened, but he did not sing for them. He needed no audience, no accompanist: this was a command performance for one.

The skymaster shook to a sustained impact. The spell was broken. Voices called out in Turkic and Twav flute-speech. The skymaster rocked, as if shaken in a God-like grip. Then, with a shriek of rending metal and ship skin, the gun-blister directly above us was torn away—gunner, gun, and a two-meter shard of hull. A face looked in at us. A face that more than filled the gash in the hull, a nightmare of six eyes arranged around a trifurcate beak. The beak opened. Rows of grinding teeth moved within. A cry blasted us with alien stench: ululating over three octaves, ending in a shriek. It drove the breath from our lungs and the will from our hearts. Another answered it, from all around us. Then the face was gone. A moment of shock—a moment, that was all—and the skycaptain shouted orders. The Twav rose from their perches, wings clattering, and streamed through the hole in the hull. I heard the whine of ray rifles warming up, then the louder crackle and sizzle of our own defensive heat rays.

I thought that I would never hear a worse thing than the cry through the violated hull. The shriek, out there, unseen, was like the cry I might make if my spine were torn from my living body. I could only guess: one of those things had met a heat ray.

We never saw any of the battledores again.

Again, the skymaster shook to an impact. Count Jack lunged forward as claws stabbed through the hull and tore three rips the entire length of the bulkhead. The skymaster lurched to one side; we slid across the decking in our tailcoats and smoke-smudged dickey shirts. An impact jolted the rear of the airship, I glimpsed blackness, then the entire tail turret was gone and the rear of the Skymaster was open to the air. Through the open space I saw a four-winged flying thing stroke away from us, up through the pink stone arches of this endless labyrinth. It was enormous. I am no judge of comparative dimensions—I am an auditory man, not a visual one—but it was on a par with our own limping skymaster. The creature part furled its wings to clear the arch, then turned high against the red sky, and I saw glitters of silver at the nape of its neck and between its legs. Mechanisms, devices, Uliri crew.

While I gaped at the sheer impossible horror of what I beheld, the skymaster was struck again, an impact so hard it flung us from one side of the hold to the other. I saw steel-shod claws the size of scimitars pierce the glass finger of the bridge like the skin of a ripe orange. The winged Martian horror ripped bridge from hull, and, with a flick of its foot—it held the bridge as lightly and easily as a pencil—hurled it spinning through the air. I saw one figure fall from it and closed my eyes. I did hear Count Jack mumble the incantations of his faith.

Robbed of control, the skymaster yawed wildly. Engineering crew rushed around us, shouting tersely to one another, fighting to regain control, to bring us down in some survivable landing. There was no hope of escape now. What were those things? Those nightmare hunters of the Labyrinth of Night? Skin shredded, struts shrieked and buckled as the skymaster grazed a rock chimney. We listed and started to spin.

"We've lost port-side engines!" I shouted, translating the engineers' increasingly cold and desperate exchanges. We were going down, but it was too fast . . . too fast. The chief engineer yelled an order that translated as "Brace for impact" in any language. I wrapped cargo strapping around my arms and gripped for all my worth. Pianists have strong fingers.

"Patrick and Mary!" Count Jack cried, and we hit. The impact was so huge, so hard, that it drove all breath and intelligence and thought from me, everything except that death was certain and that the last, the very last, thing I would ever see would be a drop of fear drool on the plump bottom lip of Count Jack Fitzgerald, and that I had never noticed how full, how kissable, those lips were. Death is such a sweet surrender.

We did not die. We bounced. We hit harder. The skymaster's skeleton groaned and snapped. Sparking wires fell around us. Still we did not stop, or die. I remember thinking, *don't tumble, if we tumble, we are dead, all of us,* and so I knew we would survive. Shaken, smashed, stunned, but surviving. The corpse of the skymaster slid to a crunching stop hard against the house-sized boulders at the foot of the canyon wall. I could see daylight in five places through the skymaster's violated hull. It was beautiful beyond words. The sky horrors might still be circling, but I had to get out of the airship.

"Jack! Jack!" I cried. His eyes were wide, his face pale with shock. "Maestro!" He looked and saw me. I took him by the hand and together we ran from the smoking ruin of the skymaster. The crew, military-trained, had been more expeditious in their escape. Already they were running from the wreck. I felt a shadow pass over me. I looked up. Diving out of the tiny atom of the sun—how horrible, oh how horrible! I saw for the first time, whole and entire, one of the things that had been hunting us and my heart quailed. It swooped with ghastly speed and agility on its four wings and snatched the running men up into the air, each impaled on a scimitar-claw. It hovered in the air above us and I caught the foul heat and stench of the wind from its wings and beak. This, this is the death for which I had been reserved. Nothing so simple as an air crash. The sky horror looked at me, looked at Count Jack with its six eyes, major and minor. Then with a terrible, scrannel cry, like the souls of the dead engineers impaled on its claws, and with a gust of wing-driven wind, it rose up and swept away.

We had been marked for life.

Irony is the currency of time. We were marked for life, but three times I entertained killing Count Jack Fitzgerald. Pick up a rock and beat him to death with it, strangle him with his bow tie, just walk away from him and leave him in the dry gulches for the bone-picking things.

I reasoned, by dint of a ready water supply and a scrap of paper thrown in, that showed a sluggish but definite flow, that we should follow the canal. I had little knowledge of the twisted areography of the Labyrinth of Night—no one did, I suspect—but I was certain that all waters flowed to the Grand Canal and that was the spine and nervous system of Operation Enduring Justice. I advised us to drink—Count Jack ordered me to look away as he knelt and supped up the oddly metallic Martian water. We set off to the sound of unholy cries high and far among the pinnacles of the canyon walls.

The sun had not crossed two fingers of narrow canyonland sky before Count Jack gave an enormous theatrical sigh and sat down on a canal-side barge bollard.

"Dear boy, I simply cannot take another step without some material sustenance."

I indicated the alien expanse of ruck, dust, water, red sky, hinted at its barrenness.

"I see bushes," Count Jack said. "I see fruit on those bushes."

"They could be deadly poison, Maestro."

"What's fit for Martians cannot faze the robust Terrene digestive tract," Count Jack proclaimed. "Anyway, better a quick death than lingering starvation, dear God."

Argument was futile. Count Jack harvested a single egg-shaped, purple fruit and took a small, delicate bite. We waited. The sun moved across its slot of sky.

"I remain obdurately alive," said Count Jack, and ate the rest of the fruit. "The texture of a slightly underripe banana and a flavor of mild aniseed. Tolerable. But the belly is replete."

Within half an hour of setting off again, Count Jack had called a halt.

"The gut, Faisal, the gut." He ducked behind a rock. I heard groans and oaths and other, more liquid noises. He emerged pale and sweating.

"How do you feel?"

"Lighter, dear boy. Lighter."

That was the first time that I considered killing him.

The fruit had opened more than his bowels. The silence of the canyons must have haunted him, for he talked. Dear God, he talked. I was treated to Count Jack Fitzgerald's opinion on everything from the way I should have been ironing his dress shirts (apparently I required a secondary miniature ironing board specially designed for collar and cuffs) to the conduct of the war between the worlds.

I tried to shut him up by singing, trusting—knowing—that he could not resist an offer to show off and shine. I cracked out "Blaze Away" in my passable baritone, then "The Soldier's Dream," anything with a good marching beat. My voice rang boldly from the rim rocks.

Count Jack touched me lightly on the arm.

"Dear boy, dear dear boy. No. You only make the intolerable unendurable."

And that was the second time that I was close to physically killing him. But we realized that if we were to survive—and though we could not entertain the notion that we might not, because it would surely have broken our hearts and killed us—we understood that to have any hope of making it back to occupied territory, we would have to proceed as more than Maestro and accompanist. So, in the end, we talked, one man with another man. I told him of my childhood in middle-class, leafy Woking, and at the Royal Academy of Music, and the realization, quiet, devastating, and quite quite irrefutable, that I would never be a concert great. I would never play the Albert Hall, the Marinsky, Carnegie Hall. I saw a Count Jack I had never seen before, sincere behind the bluster, humane and compassionate. I saw beyond an artiste. I saw an *artist*. He confided his fears to me: that the days of Palladiums and Pontiffs had blinded him. He realized too late that one night the lights would move to another and he would face the long, dark walk from the stage. But he had plans; yes, he had plans. A long walk in a hard terrain concentrated the mind wonderfully. He would pay the Revenue their due and retain Ferid Bey only long enough to secure the residency on Venus. And when his journey through the worlds was done and he had enough space dust under his nails, he would return to Ireland, to County Kildare, buy some land, and set himself up as a tweedy, be-waistcoated, red-faced Bog Boy. He would sing only for the Church, at special Masses and holy days of obligation and parish glees and tombolas; he could see a time when he might fall in love with religion again, not from any personal faith but for the comfort and security of familiarity.

"Have you thought of marrying?" I asked. Count Jack had never any shortage of female admirers, even if they no longer threw underwear onto the stage as they had back in the days when his hair and mustache were glossy and black—and he would mop his face with them and throw them back to shrieks of approval from the crowd. "Not a dry seat in the house, dear boy." But I had never seen anything that hinted at a more lasting relationship than bed and champagne breakfast.

"Never seen the need, dear boy. Not the marrying type. And you, Faisal?"

"Not the marrying type either."

"I know. I've always known. But that's what this bloody world needs. Really needs. Women, Faisal. Women. Leave men together and they soon agree to make a wasteland. Women are a civilizing force."

We rounded an abrupt turn in the canal and came upon a scene that silenced even Count Jack. A battle had been fought here, a war of total commitment and destruction. But who had won, who had lost? We could not tell. Uliri War Tripods lay draped over ledges and arches like desiccated spiders. The wrecks of skymasters were impaled on stone spires, wedged into rock clefts and groins. Shards of armor, human and Uliri, littered the canyon floor. Helmets and cuirasses were empty, long since picked clean by whatever scavengers hid from the light of the distant sun to gnaw and rend in the night. We stood in a landscape of hull plates, braces, struts, smashed tanks, and tangles of wiring and machinery we could not begin to identify. Highest, most terrible of all, the hulk of a spaceship, melted with the fires of reentry, smashed like soft fruit, lay across the canyon, rim to rim. Holes big enough to fly a skymaster through had been punched through the hull, side to side.

Count Jack raised his eyes to the fallen spaceship, then his hands.

"Dear God. I may never play the Hammersmith Palais again."

Chimes answered him, a tintinnabulation of metal ringing on metal. This was the final madness. This was when I understood that we were dead—that we had died in the skymaster crash—and that war was Hell. Then I felt the ground tremble beneath the soles of my good black concert shoes and I understood. Metal rang on metal, wreckage on wreckage. The earth shook, dust rose. The spoilage of war started to stir and move. The ground shook, my feet were unsteady, there was nothing to hold on to, no surety except Count Jack. We held each other as the dust rose before us and the scrap started to slide and roll. Higher the ground rose, and higher, and that was the third time I almost killed him, for I still did not fully understand what was happening and imagined that if I stopped Jack, I would stop the madness. This was *his* doing; he had somehow summoned some old Martian evil from the ground. Then a shining conical drill head emerged from the soil, and the dust and rocks tumbled as the mole-machine emerged from the ground. It rose twenty, thirty feet above us, a gimlet-nosed cylinder of soil-scabbed metal. Then it put out metal feet from hatches along its belly, fell forward, and came to rest a stone's throw from us. Hatches sprang open behind the still-spinning drill head, fanned out like flower petals. I glimpsed silver writhing in the interior darkness. Uliri padvas streamed out, their tentacles carrying them dexterously over the violated metal and rock. Their cranial cases were helmeted, their breathing mantles armored in delicately worked cuirasses, and their palps held ray rifles. We threw our hands up. They swarmed around us, and, without a sound, herded us into the dark maw of the Martian mole-machine.

The spider-car deposited us at a platform of heat-ray-polished sandstone before the onyx gates. The steel tentacle tips of our guards clacked on the mirror rock. The gates stood five times human height—they must have been overpowering to the shorter Uliri—and were divided in three according to Uliri architecture, and decorated with beautiful patterns of woven tentacles in high relief, as complex as Celtic knotwork. A dot of light appeared at the center of the gates and split into three lines, a bright Y. They swung slowly outward and upward. There was no other possibility than to enter.

How blind we humans had been, how sure that our mastery of sky and space gave us mastery of this world. The Uliri had not been driven back by our space bombardments and massed skymaster strikes, they had been driven *deep*. Even as the great Hives of Syrtia and Tempe stood shattered and burning, Uliri proles had been delving deeper even than the roots of their geothermal cores, down toward the still-warm lifeblood of their world, tapping into its mineral and energy resources. Downward and outward; hive to nest to manufactory, underground redoubt to subterranean fortress, a network of tunnels and delvings and underground vacuum tubes that reached so far, so wide, so deep, that Tharsia was like a sponge. Down there, in the magma-warmed dark, they built a society far beyond the reach of our space bombs. Biding their time, drawing their plans together, sending their tendrils under our camps and command centers and bases, gathering their volcano-forged forces against us.

I remembered little of the journey in the mole-machine except that it was generally downward, interminably long, and smelled strongly of acetic acid. Count Jack, with his sensitivities, discreetly covered his nose and mouth with his handkerchief. I could not understand his reticence: the Uliri had thousands better reasons to have turned us to ash than affront at their personal perfume.

Our captors were neither harsh nor kind. Those are both human emotions. The lesson that we were slow to learn after the Horsell Common attack was that Martian emotions are Martian. They do not have love, anger, despair, the desire for revenge, jealousy. They did not attack us from hate, or defend themselves from love. They have their own needs and motivations and emotions. So they only seemed to gently usher us from the open hatches of the mole-machine (one among hundreds, lined up in silos, aimed at the upper world) into a vast underground dock warm with heart-rock, and along a pier to a station, where a spider-shaped glass car hung by many arms from a monorail. The spider-car accelerated with jolting force. We plunged into a lightless tunnel, then we were in the middle of an underground city, tier upon tier of lighted windows and roadways tumbling down to a red-lit mist. Through underwater waterfalls, through vast cylindrical farms bright with the light of the lost sun. Over marshaling yards and parade grounds as dense with padvas as the shore is with sand grains. Factories, breeding vats, engineering plants sparkling with welding arcs and molten steel. I saw pits miles deep, braced with buttresses and arches and spires, down and down and down, like a cathedral turned inside out. Those slender stone vaults and spires were festooned with winged horrors—those same four-winged monsters that had plucked us out of the sky and so casually, so easily, dismembered our crew. And allowed us to live.

I had no doubt that we had been chosen. And I had no doubt why we were chosen.

Over another jarring switchover, through another terrifying, roaring tunnel, then out into a behemoth gallery of launch silos: hundreds of them, side by side, each loaded with fat rocket ships stiff with gun turrets and missile racks. I feared for our vaunted Space-fleet, and, realizing that, feared more for myself. Not even the alien values of the Uliri would show us so much if there were even the remotest possibility we could return the information to the Commanderie.

Count Jack realized it in the same instant.

"Christ on crutches, Faisal," he whispered.

On and on, through the riddled, maggoty, mined and tunneled and bored and reamed Under-Mars. And now the onyx gates stood wide and the padvas fell into a guard around us and prodded us through them. The polished sandstone now formed a long catwalk. On each side rose seats, tier upon tier of obsidian egg cups. Each held an Uliri—proles, gestates, padvas, panjas—arranged by mantle color and rank. From the detail of the etchings on their helmets and carapace covers, I guessed them to be of the greatest importance. A parliament, a conclave, a cabinet. But the true power was at the end of the long walk: the Queen of Noctis herself. No image had even been captured, no corpse or prisoner recovered, of an Uliri Queen. They were creatures of legend. The reality in every way transcended our mythmaking imaginations. She was immense. She filled the chamber like a sunrise. Her skin was golden; her mantle patterned with soft diamond-shaped scales like fairy armor. Relays of insemi-nators carried eggs from her tattooed multiple ovipositors, slathering them in luminous milt. Rings of rank and honor had been pierced through her eyelids and at the base of her tentacles. Her cuirass and helmet glowed with jewels and finest filigree. She was a thing of might, majesty, and incontestable beauty. Our dress heels click-clacked on the gleaming stone.

"With me, Faisal," whispered Count Jack. "Quick smart." The guard stopped, but Count Jack strode forward. He snapped to attention. Every royal eye fixed on him. He clicked his heels and gave a small, formal bow. I was a heartbeat behind him. "It's all small beer after the Pope."

A tentacle snaked toward us. I resisted the urge to step back, even when the skin of the palp retraced and there, there was a human head. And not any human head: the head of Yuzbashi Osman, the music lover of Camp Oudeman, whom we had last seen leading a bold and stirring—and ultimately futile—charge against the padva hordes. Now the horror was complete. The Yuzbashi opened his eyes and let out a gasping sigh. The head looked me up and down, then gave Count Jack a deeper scrutiny.

"Count Jack Fitzgerald of Kildare-upon-Ireland. Welcome. I am Nehenner Repooltu Sevenniggog Dethprip; by right, battle, and acclaim the uncontested Queen of Noctis. And I am your number one fan."

One finger of rum in Count Jack's particular tea. And then, for luck, for war, for insanity, I slipped in another one. I knocked, waited for his call, and entered his dressing room. We might be somewhere in the warren of chambers beneath the Hall of the Martian Queen, miles beneath the sands of Mars, but the forms must be observed. The forms were all we had.

"Dear boy!" Uliri architecture did not accommodate human proportions. Proles had been at work—the prickly tang of scorched stone was strong—but I still had to duck to get through the door. Count Jack sat before a mirror of heat-ray-polished obsidian. He adjusted the sit of his white bow tie. He filled the tiny cubbyhole, but he still took the tea with an operatic flourish and took a long, County Kildare slurp.

"Ah! Grand! Grand. My resolve is stiffened to the sticking point. By God, I shall have need of it today. Did you slip a little extra in, you sly boy?"

"I did, Maestro."

"Surprisingly good rum. And the tea is acceptable. I wonder where they got it from?"

"Ignorance is bliss, Maestro."

"You're right there." He drained the cup. "And how is the piano?"

"Like the rum. Only I think they made it themselves."

"They're good at delicate work, the worker-drone thingies. Those tentacle tips are fine and dexterous. Natural master craftsmen. I wonder if they would make good pianists? Faisal? Dear God, listen to me listen to me! Here we are, like a windup musical box, set up to amuse and titivate. A song, a tune, dance or two. Us, the last vestige of beauty on this benighted planet, dead and buried in some vile subterranean cephalopod vice pit. Does anyone even know we're alive? Help us for God's sake help us! Ferid Bey, he'll do something. He must. At the very least, he'll start looking for us when the money doesn't materialize."

"I expect Ferid Bey has already collected the insurance." I took the cup and saucer. Our predicament was so desperate, so monstrous that we dared not look it full in the face. The Queen of Noctis had left us in no doubt that we were to entertain her indefinitely, singing birds in a cage. Never meet the fans. That was one of Count Jack's first homilies to me. Fans think they own you.

"Bastard!" Count Jack thundered. "Bastarding bastard! He shall die, he shall die. When I get back . . ." Then he realized that we would never get back, that we might never feel the wan warmth of the small, distant sun, that these low tunnels might be our home for the rest of our lives—and each other the only human face we would ever see. He wept, bellowing like a bullock. "Can this be the swan song of Count Jack Fitzgerald? Prostituting myself for some superovulating Martian squid queen? Oh the horror, the horror! Leave me, Faisal. Leave me. I must prepare."

The vinegar smell of the Uliri almost made me gag as I stepped onto the stage. I have always had a peculiar horror of vinegar. Lights dazzled me, but my nose told me that there must be thousands of Uliri on the concert hall's many tiers. Uliri language is as much touch and mantle color as it is spoken sounds, and the auditorium fistled with the dry-leaf rustling of tentacle on tentacle. I flipped out my tails, seated myself at the piano, ran a few practice scales. It was a very fine piano indeed. The tuning was perfect, the weight and responsiveness of the keys extraordinary. I saw a huge golden glow suffuse the rear of the vast hall. The Queen had arrived on her floating grav-throne. My hands shook with futile rage. Who had given her the right to be Count Jack's number one fan? She had explained, in her private chamber—a pit filled with sweet and fragrant oil in which she basked, her monstrous weight supported—how she had first heard the music of Count Jack Fitzgerald. Rather, the head of poor Osman explained. When she had been a tiny fry in the Royal Hatchery—before the terrible internecine wars of the queens, in which only one could survive—she had become intrigued with Earth after the defeat of the Third Uliri Host at the Battle of Orbital Fort Tokugawa. She had listened to Terrene radio and become entranced by light opera—the thrill of the coloraturas, the sensuous power of the tenor, the stirring gravitas of the basso profundo. In particular, she fell in love—or the Uliri equivalent of love—with the charm and blarney of one Count Jack Fitzgerald. She became fascinated with Ireland—an Emerald Isle, made of a single vast gemstone, a green land of green people—how extraordinary, how marvelous, how magical! She had even had her proles build a life-size model Athy in one of the unused undercrofts of the Royal Nest. Opera and the stirring voice of the operatic tenor became her passion, and she vowed, if she survived the Sororicide, that she would build an incomparable opera house on Mars, in the heart of the Labyrinth of Night, and attract the greatest singers and musicians of Earth to show the Uliri what she considered the highest human art. She survived, and had consumed all her sisters and taken their experiences and memories, and built her opera house, the grandest in the solar system, but war had intervened. Earth had attacked, and the ancient and beautiful Uliri Hives of Enetria and Issidy were shattered like infertile eggs. She had fled underground, to her empty, virginal concert hall, but in the midst of the delvings and the buildings and forgings, she had heard that Count Jack Fitzgerald had come to Mars to entertain the troops at the same time that the United Queens were mounting a sustained offensive, and she seized her opportunity.

The thought of that little replica Athy, far from the sun, greener than green, waiting, gave me screaming nightmares.

Warm-up complete. I straightened myself at the piano. A flex of the fingers, and into the opening of "I'll Take You Home Again, Kathleen." And on strode Count Jack Fitzgerald, arms wide, handkerchief in one hand, beaming, the words pealing from his lips. Professional, consummate, marvelous. I never loved him more dearly than striding into the spotlights. The auditorium lit up with soft flashes of color: Uliri lighting up their bioluminescent mantles, their equivalent of applause.

Count Jack stopped in midline. I lifted my hands from the keys as if the ivory were poisoned. The silence was sudden and immense. Every light froze on, then softly faded to black.

"No," he said softly. "This will not do."

He held up his hands, showed each of them in turn to the audience. Then he brought them together in a single clap that rang out into the black vastness. Clap one, two, three. He waited. Then I heard the sound of a single pair of tentacles slapping together. It was not a clap, never a clap, but it was applause. Another joined it, another and another, until waves of slow tentacle claps washed around the auditorium. Count Jack raised his hands: enough. The silence was instant. Then he gave himself a round of applause, and me a round of applause, and I him. The Uliri caught the idea at once. Applause rang from every tier and level and joist of the Martian Queen's concert hall.

"Now, let's try that again," Count Jack said, and without warning, strode off the stage. I saw him in the wings, indicating for me to milk it. I counted a good minute before I struck up the introduction to "I'll Take You Home Again, Kathleen." On he strode, arms wide, handkerchief in hand, beaming. And the concert hall erupted. Applause: wholehearted, loud-ringing, mighty applause, breaking like an ocean from one side of the concert hall to the other, wave upon wave upon wave, on and on and on.

Count Jack winked to me as he swept past into the brilliance of the lights to take the greatest applause of his life.

"What a house, Faisal! What a house!"

About the Editors

George R. R. Martin is the #1 *New York Times* bestselling author of many novels, including the acclaimed series A Song of Ice and Fire—*A Game of Thrones, A Clash of Kings, A Storm of Swords, A Feast for Crows,* and *A Dance with Dragons.* He won both the Hugo and Nebula awards for his novelette "Sandkings," and, in 2012, he was given the Lifetime Achievement Award by the World Fantasy Convention. As a writer-producer, he has worked on *The Twilight Zone, Beauty and the Beast,* and various feature films and pilots that were never made. He lives with the lovely Parris in Santa Fe, New Mexico.

Gardner Dozois has won fifteen Hugo Awards and thirty-seven Locus Awards for his editing work, plus two Nebula Awards for his own writing. He was the editor of *Asimov's Science Fiction* for twenty years, and is the author or editor of over a hundred books, including *The Year's Best Science Fiction.* In 2011 Dozois was inducted into the Science Fiction Hall of Fame.

About the Type

This book was set in Scala, a typeface designed by Martin Majoor in 1991. It was originally designed for a music company in the Netherlands and then was published by the international type house FSI FontShop. Its distinctive extended serifs add to the articulation of the letter forms to make it a very readable typeface.